ABOUT HE

Are You Ready For A Comedy Like No Other...?

Christina Matteo had a humiliating prank pulled on her in high school by rich, party boy Bill Havenwood. It changed her whole life and she never forgot it—or him.

Older, wiser and tougher, she meets him again years later and decides to get even! She wants revenge and comes up with a perfect plan. But things don't go her way when she stupidly crashes her car into his expensive sportscar while tailing him one day.

Not recognizing her, Bill blackmails the cash-poor Christina into helping him stay in his billionaire father's good graces by pretending to be his fiancée for one month. Christina decides to go along with his ruse. After all, who knows what dirt she can find out about the jerk from the inside?

But as Christina scams Bill and Bill scams his father—his father scams the both of them. William Havenwood Sr. knows all about their phony engagement and begins to push the couple to marry for real in order to get them to crack under pressure.

And then Christina's little revenge plan begins to spiral out of control when she finds herself actually falling in love with her avowed enemy, Bill. It's enough to make a girl sick to her stomach! But can she really continue to go through with her plans to make him pay when she's so attracted to the creep? Christina is just stubborn enough to find out!

HER PERFECT REVENGE is a funny, romantic comedy story where its three strong and smart main characters—Christina, Bill and his father, William—find themselves engaged in a clever battle of wits where games, lies, secrets and deceptions rule the day. Who will win? And will Christina risk everything to get her payback?

HER PERFECT REVENGE

BY

ANNA MARA

"I have always found that mercy bears richer fruits than strict justice."

-Abraham Lincoln

CHAPTER 1

16 Years Earlier…

WAS IT HER imagination or was everyone staring at her? No, everyone was staring at her—and they were laughing too!

Putting her head down, fourteen-year-old Christina Matteo walked quickly down the school hall, trying to avoid catching anyone's eye. Clutching her books to her chest, she increased her speed but as she went by a gaggle of girls lurking at their lockers, the girls suddenly burst out laughing.

Ignoring them, Christina continued her brisk pace down the hall towards her locker. It was probably just her imagination. This was only her third week of her freshman year at Cloverdale Public High School. She didn't know anybody here—and they didn't know her.

Super shy and self-conscious, Christina had kept to herself since school had started. Except for her girlfriend Jenny, she hadn't socialized with anyone. Not that anyone would want to anyway. After all, short, dumpy girls who wore glasses and railroad tracks on their teeth weren't exactly on everyone's party list.

"Hey, baby."

Christina swiveled her head to her right. Tall, skinny Gary Porter, a senior at the school, was in a corner with his friend, Barry Mahoney.

"Why don't we party tonight and you can do me?" Gary puckered his lips and made a slurping, sucking sound at Christina. Barry burst out laughing.

Mortified, Christina swung away and kept walking. What the

hell was happening? Reaching her locker, Christina fumbled with the combination lock. She just wanted to get her stuff and get the hell out of the hallway.

"Chrissy?"

Nervous and tense, Christina jumped. She turned to find a very out-of-breath Jenny beside her.

Jenny rambled on. "I ran all the way here. I thought I was late again and…" Suddenly, she stopped her speech as she noticed Christina's pale face. "Chrissy, what's wrong?"

"Nothing." Embarrassed, Christina kept fumbling with her lock.

Jenny studied her friend. Her street smarts were telling her something was wrong. Even though they were the same age, Jenny was taller and more developed than Christina. She was also more confident and tougher, but still not a member of the A clique, or the B, or C—not even the D, but she didn't care. Jenny was lower class and knew how to fight dirty.

The two girls had been best friends since grade school. Christina had begged her parents to send her to Cloverdale High when she'd found out Jenny was going. Although her parents had wanted her to go to St. Joseph's, an all-girl, private boarding school outside Philadelphia, they'd relented after an entire summer of pleading from their daughter.

Not rich by any means, Nunzio and Gabriella Matteo had scrimped and saved, and had wanted the very best for their little girl. That meant a private, convent school. But their resolve had melted with Christina's tears and they allowed her to stay at home in Bensonhurst, New York, and attend public school.

Jenny continued to study Christina's bent head. "Chrissy, what's happened?"

"Nothing," Christina mumbled, as her lock finally released.

As she swung open her locker door, an envelope fluttered out. Jenny bent down to pick it up. It was an envelope addressed to 'Chrissy Matteo'. She handed it to her friend. Perplexed, Christina quickly tore it open. Whomever it was from had wedged it between the door and upper frame of her locker.

It was a letter from the Anderson Family Planning Clinic—and—shocked, Christina looked up at her friend.

Jenny snatched it from her shaking hands and began reading it out loud.

"Dear Miss Matteo… We regret to inform you that a sexual partner of yours, who has requested to remain anonymous, has contracted gonorrhea and is currently being treated at our clinic. We are writing to urge you to seek medical attention as soon as possible to determine whether you have also been infected… holy crap! Is this…?" Jenny looked up at Christina with new eyes.

"No, it's not true! Jenny, how can I get that… that disease when I've never even kissed a guy?" Christina hissed.

"Well, you don't get it from kissing."

"Jenny!"

"Okay, okay. But why is this addressed to you? And in your locker?"

"I don't know." Panic coursed through Christina's system and she felt weak.

Jenny was studying the letter again. "You know what this is? It's a joke."

"What?"

"Chrissy, official letters from medical clinics don't get stuffed into student lockers. And look." She held up the envelope. "There's no stamp on it. These kinds of letters get mailed to you or they try to contact you on the phone."

"But who would do that? We don't know anybody here."

"I don't know but we're going to find out." Jenny's face set with determination.

"Jenny, no!" Christina shouted, as the first bell rang warning everyone to get to class. "If my parents find out, they'll ship me off to convent school and you know how much I had to beg to stay here." Christina snatched the letter from Jenny's hands and stuffed it into her sweater pocket. "Promise me you won't say anything to anybody." Jenny stubbornly remained silent. "Jenny?"

"Okay, I won't."

Inside their English 101 classroom, Christina and Jenny took their seats along with the other freshmen. The final bell hadn't rung yet and their teacher, Mrs. Lauder still hadn't arrived.

Jenny leaned over to Christina and whispered, "Maybe it's Ashford over there." She nodded toward Stevie Ashford, a big, bulky kid who excelled in sports but not in school. "I think he likes you."

Christina gave Stevie a sideways look before turning back to Jenny. She kept her voice low. "If he likes me, why would he do that? It doesn't make sense."

"Maybe you're right. I'll bet he can't even spell gonorrhea."

"Jenny, shut up. Somebody's gonna hear you."

"Maybe it's…"

"Hey, you're Chrissy, right?"

Christina looked up to see Billy Havenwood, class leader and super hunk, sidle up to her desk and place his elbows on it. He leaned forward into her face and the room went deathly quiet.

"Y…Yes," she replied.

Christina was wary. Billy Havenwood had never spoken to her. The school term had only begun three weeks ago and everyone had already been pigeonholed into his or her clichéd roles—class clown, nerd, jock, wannabe. Billy was none of those. He and his best friend, Jake Monroe, were the superstars. Popular, brash, arrogant and gorgeous, they knew what they had and what they could command.

Rumor had it that Billy came from a wealthy family. His mom, a liberal, hippy-type, had insisted her son attend public school in order to learn how 'normal' people lived. His businessman father had sternly objected but then finally relented.

And Billy? Well, he didn't care where he went as long as he could party. His drinking exploits in his first few weeks of school had already made him a semi-legend. Even the seniors were impressed.

Christina was not—although she did have a secret crush on him. All the girls did. But why was he talking to her now with that wild, glazed look in his eyes?

"I've got some advice for you." He slurred his words slightly.

Repulsed by the smell of beer on his breath, Christina leaned back. "W…What?"

A slow smirk spread across Billy's face. "Next time you wanna hump, use one of these." He threw a wrapped condom at her. As if on cue, the entire class burst out laughing. Then Billy yelled, "Now." And, suddenly, the other students pelted Christina with condoms.

Christina sat there in shock as a hot fire of humiliation spread from the top of her head to the tips of her toes.

Looking around at the sea of laughing faces, her breathing stopped. Billy stumbled back to his seat and gave his friend Jake a high five.

Aghast, Jenny jumped up and started yelling around the room. "Stop it! Stop it!"

No one paid any attention. They just kept laughing.

Suddenly, both Christina and Jenny spotted a photocopy of Christina's family planning clinic letter tacked onto the bulletin board. Everyone had seen it!

Christina's bottom lip quivered. She had never been so embarrassed in all her life. What was going on? And why?

Summoning all her courage, she finally spoke up.

"It's… it's a lie. It's not t…true." She spoke louder. "It's not true."

Jenny made a beeline for the letter and tore it off the board. "All of you, shut up," she ordered.

As if on cue, the other classmates pulled out their own copies and held them high. Everyone had one. Christina finally broke down. With tears streaming down her cheeks, she grabbed her books and turned to her peers.

"W… why are you all being so m…mean to me? I never did anything to any of you!" She sobbed and screamed.

The laughter died down and Christina looked into their faces.

This couldn't be happening to her—her of all people. She'd always done everything right. She'd been nice to everyone, always blended into the wallpaper, and never made waves. Why this? Why now? Why her?

With a final cry of anguish, she clutched her books and ran from the room in tears.

CHAPTER 2

JENNY FOUND CHRISTINA sitting inside a stall in the first floor girl's washroom sobbing her heart out. She bent down. Yup—those were Chrissy's shoes, all right. She knocked on the door.

"It's me, Chrissy."

Slowly, Christina opened the door and came out. Her eyes were red and swollen.

"Is everyone still laughing?" Christina tentatively asked.

"No, they all shut up pretty fast when Mrs. Lauder came in."

"How can I ever go back there again after what happened?" Fresh tears started flowing down Christina's cheeks.

"You can and you will." Jenny was angry for her friend. "Now listen, I found out who's responsible."

"Who?" Christina stopped crying.

"Billy Havenwood and Jake Monroe."

"But why? They don't know me."

"I was told they had to pull a prank on the…" Jenny looked at her friend apprehensively.

"On the what?" Christina demanded.

"On—the class nerd."

"And that's me?" Christina began to feel the first stirrings of anger. "Who said?"

"Mindy Mackenzie. She said Billy picked you out as the class nerd."

"Why?"

"Because you're smart and shy and you wear glasses, I guess. I don't know."

"That creep!" Christina was seeing red. This wasn't fair. She didn't deserve this treatment. Not from them. Not from anyone.

Jenny continued. "Mindy said Billy and Jake had to come up with a really clever stunt on you if they wanted to get in good with some of the seniors. Kinda like an initiation. Word would spread around the school and they'd be cool."

"And I would be the laughing stock?" Christina was getting madder. "What about his buddy Jake?"

"You know that story. Jake goes along with whatever Billy says."

"Yeah."

"Jake stole some official stationery from the Anderson Family Planning Clinic and they wrote you that letter. Then they made copies for everybody and Billy bought all the condoms. After you left, he picked them all up saying it was his supply for the week." Disgusted, Jenny rolled her eyes. "Then he and Jake split before Mrs. Lauder came in."

"They skipped?"

"Yeah; Mindy said she overheard them talking about going drinking under the bleachers."

"Oh really…" Christina quickly gathered her books. She was all fired up and like a volcano, about to blow. She needed to release this anger and direct it at the one who had caused it—Billy Havenwood—that big jerk! Determined, she stalked to the door.

"Where are you going?" Jenny asked.

"To tell Mr. 'Popularity, I-Can-Do-Whatever-I-Want' Havenwood off. You comin'?"

"I told old Lauder I was just going to the bathroom, but you go get him girl." Jenny smiled and gave her friend a thumbs up sign.

Christina was now on the warpath and operating on pure adrenaline.

CHAPTER 3

CHRISTINA COULD BARELY make out the shape of two people crouching low in a back corner underneath the school bleachers outside by the track—but they were there. She knew it.

The schoolyard was empty and no one had seen her. Coming closer, she could hear laughing and snickering—probably at her expense, those jerks. Creeping to the open side of the bleachers, Christina scooted underneath. She could see them now—Billy Havenwood and Jake Monroe. They were half-sitting, half-lying down in the dirt and both were drinking from beer cans.

Christina slowly made her way towards them, clutching her books against her chest for protection. Suddenly, in his inebriated haze, Billy Havenwood finally noticed her.

"Who the hell are you?" he slurred his words.

He squinted his bloodshot eyes trying to focus on her face. Jake just sat there and burped.

"I... I..."

And that's when it happened. Christina lost her last remaining nerve and froze. What was she doing? She couldn't go through with this. It was one thing to talk about what you were going to do when you were safe in the girl's washroom, but it was another when you were actually facing them. She was feeling weak again and her knees started to shake. Any moment now, she would faint—right in front of these bozos and be embarrassed all over again.

Billy suddenly stood up. With beer can in hand and wobbling a little, he came towards Christina.

"I know you. You're that class nerd." He burst out laughing, as did Jake. Jake, still on the ground, didn't know what was going on but if Billy laughed, he laughed.

Mortified, Christina turned to run. This had been a bad idea and she needed to get away as fast as possible. She took a few quick steps, but in her haste her foot landed in a hole in the dirt and she fell onto her hands and knees.

And there she was—on all fours—with her bum stuck in the air—right in front of them. Billy laughed harder.

"Hey, is that an invite?" he asked, as he slugged back more beer. "Because if it is, I don't do charity."

At that moment, something in Christina snapped and she could feel anger roiling through her system again. Who the hell did this jerk think he was? Slowly she stood up, brushed the dirt from her clothes and picked up her books. She turned to face Billy Havenwood and defiantly raised her chin up.

"Go fuck yourself." There. She'd said it. What a relief!

Jake drunkenly laughed in the background. "Whoa…no chick's ever said that to you before," he cackled.

Billy's eyes dangerously narrowed on Christina and his spine straightened. "What? What did you just say to me?" he demanded.

"You heard me. And I may be the class nerd, but it's better than being the class drunk like you," Christina accused forcefully.

No one had ever spoken to Billy like that before, except maybe his father. This was new territory and he didn't like it one bit. Who the hell was this little nobody telling him off anyway? Throwing his empty beer can to the side, he took a few predatory steps towards Christina. She instinctively took a few steps back.

Suddenly, Christina realized that this was not a very good place to be—alone with two drunken guys, hidden under the bleachers with no one else around. What if they…? Nobody would hear her screams or cries for help. Her courage deserted her and she took a couple more frightened steps back.

"Stay a…away from me," she stammered.

And in that instant, Billy Havenwood read her mind. So this chick thought he might force himself on her, was that it?

He laughed to himself. Why not play along and teach this little bitch a lesson? He wouldn't do anything, of course, but she didn't know that. And this might be fun. She deserved to be taught a lesson after what she'd just said to him.

He smirked at her then. "What do ya think I'm gonna do?" He asked menacingly, taking more steps towards her. "Have a little fun?"

Christina backed away even more. "I... I... said... stay away. Don't come any clo... closer." Her words came out breathy, as fear coursed through her system.

"Is that why you came to find me, for a little mid-morning action? Because baby, if you wanna fuck, I'm ready." He was leering at her now with those glazed drunken eyes of his, as he brazenly looked her up and down. "You know, for a class nerd, I gotta say you've got great tits." He slurred his last few words as the five beers he'd already had that morning took their toll on his body.

Shocked at his dirty language and frightened to the very pink-polished tips of her toes, Christina suddenly turned and ran out from under the bleachers. She could hear Billy Havenwood laughing and laughing as she kept running at full speed across the track, through the parking lot, and into the school building. She didn't stop until she reached the first floor girl's washroom.

Panting hard, Christina splashed cool water on her face. This had not been a good day but things were about to get worse.

CHAPTER 4

CHRISTINA GOT HOME at 4:05 p.m. that day. After secretly slinking out of the washroom, she'd left the school and spent the day at the mall. She had skipped school for the first time in her entire life, but she just couldn't go back today and face all those people who had laughed at her.

Throwing her sweater and books on the kitchen table, she shuffled to her room, threw herself on the bed and reached behind her nightstand to pull out her secret diary and began to write about the day's events. Journaling was something that Christina had discovered the previous year. It was as if by putting her feelings down on paper, she didn't have to carry them around in her heart and mind anymore.

Putting down her pen, she let her mind wander over the day's events. She wondered if the story had already made the rounds. Did her peers know it had all been a joke? In which case, it would make her a dweeb. Or did they believe the letter and think she was a slut? Would she now have a reputation? Would everybody forget about this in a week's time and move on to somebody else?

Suddenly, Billy Havenwood's handsome face floated into her mind. What a disgusting creep! Christina remembered the way he'd been smirking at her with those arrogant, drunken lips of his and a tremor ran down her spine. And his laughter! She could still hear it playing over and over again in her head. He'd been enjoying himself at her expense. She'd never been a joke before.

Christina put her hands over her eyes, trying to blot out the images, but to no avail. She then remembered his eyes—his gorgeous, green eyes—and the way they had leered at her. And what about those dirty things he'd said to her? Was he really going to try something? A shiver of fear ran down her back.

"Christina?"

Great, her mother was calling her. What did she want?

"Christina?" This time her mother yelled her name.

"Coming!"

Christina hid her diary behind her nightstand, got up from the bed, and trudged to the kitchen where she suddenly stopped short. Her mother was clutching 'the letter' in her hand and was staring at her in shock.

"This fell out of your sweater when I was hanging it up." Gabriella whispered.

Petite and attractive but with an aura of strength, Gabriella Matteo was the glue that held her family together. At thirty-eight, the Italian-American housewife was a great mother, but she had a penchant for the dramatic. And she didn't appreciate nonsense of any kind in others, especially from her husband, whom she blamed for everything.

Speechless, Christina could only gawk at her. Her mother always seemed to make any situation worse than it actually was. There were no such things as 'discussions' in this family. Everything that happened happened at high decibel and over-the-top, and this scene was promising to be a showstopper.

"I… I," Christina stammered, not knowing what to say.

"Oh my God! How could you? You're only fourteen." Gabriella's voice started to rise. "Who's the boy?" she yelled.

"It's not true. It's a joke," Christina defensively pleaded. "There is no boy."

But Gabriella wasn't listening as she continued. "And what's your father gonna say? I knew we should never have allowed you to go to that public school. And this boy… who is he? Tell me! Oh, I'm gonna be sick. I feel faint." She gripped the edge of the table. "Get me some water. Quick!"

Christina ran to the sink and let the water run. She was on the verge of tears herself. "Mommy, it's not true. This guy at school…" She quickly brought her mother the glass of water as Gabriella collapsed into a chair.

"What guy? The guy in the letter?"

"No. There is no guy in the letter. It's a lie!" Christina was now yelling loud enough to match her mother's voice.

"Oh Holy Mother of Jesus, what if you have this disease? I'm making an appointment with Dr. Marchese right away."

"No! It's not true," Christina began to cry. "Some kids at school played a joke on me and…"

"What? You mean other people know about this? Oh, saints in heaven." Gabriella put her fingers in the glass of water and started splashing the droplets onto her face.

At that moment, the back door opened and in walked Nunzio Matteo, dressed in grubby clothes and with lunch pail in hand. He'd just finished his shift at the construction site and was looking forward to a good meal and some TV. But as he had approached the house through the garage entrance, he'd heard the shouting.

"What's goin' on here?" he inquired.

Gabriella got up and shoved the letter at her husband. "Read this. I knew we should have sent her to St. Joseph's. This is all your fault."

Nunzio quickly began to read the letter. Christina stopped crying and held her breath as she waited for her father's explosive reaction.

Nunzio looked up at his daughter. "Is this true?" he asked quietly.

Caught off guard by his softly spoken words, she quickly regained her wits. "No, it isn't. Some kids at school were playing a joke and they thought it was funny and they sent me this letter but it's not true and…"

Nunzio held up his hand and Christina stopped speaking. He looked at her for a few hard seconds. "I believe you."

"You do?" Christina was shocked.

"I know my daughter and I know you'd never get involved in this sort of garbage." Nunzio waved the letter in the air.

For the first time that day, Christina smiled and let out a sigh of relief, but unfortunately her father kept talking.

"But tomorrow…," he dictated, "…you're packing your things and going to that convent school in Philadelphia."

"Noooo… I don't want to," Christina wailed. Tears spurted in her eyes and she stamped her foot in frustration.

But Nunzio was firm and there was no dissuading him. "My daughter is not going back to a school with these types of people who would treat her like this and that's final." He looked at his wife and she nodded her approval.

"It's not fair," Christina sobbed, as she ran from the kitchen and into her room, slamming her door shut.

Throwing herself on the bed, she let out all the anger and trauma of the day. Tears flowed as she punched her pillow. Billy Havenwood and Jake Monroe had done this to her. It was all their faults—those jerks, those creeps, those bastards!

And within a week, Christina was shipped off to boarding school for the next four years.

CHAPTER 5

16 Years Later…

PRESENT DAY

Click. Click. Click.

Christina kept snapping pictures of the eight protesters outside the Fido Dog Food Company head office building as they chanted and waved huge placards in the air. "Say No To Fido," screamed the rowdy bunch. They called themselves 'The Guardians of Mother Earth' or 'GME' for short.

A scruffy-looking, sixties throwback named Teddy, who was carrying a large sign that read 'Fido Owns Samco Oil, Samco Oil Pollutes Our Planet, Boycott Fido', ran over to Christina who was crouching down trying to get a better shot with her camera.

"Hey man, you from Streetwise Magazine?" he asked.

"That's me." She straightened up and gave him a dazzling smile.

Teddy's eyes widened with admiration. At thirty, Christina was a beauty with long brown hair framing her pretty features. The railroad tracks on her teeth had long come off her pearly whites and her thick glasses had been replaced by contacts.

At fourteen she may have been short and dumpy, but by fifteen she'd shot up to 5'6". By sixteen, she'd taken up competitive swimming and lost over 30 pounds, giving her a sleek frame. And by seventeen, she'd discovered makeup.

Teddy was clearly impressed. "You're one hot chick for a reporter."

Christina laughed. "I'm a photographer, not a reporter."

"Well, you're pretty hot for that too."

"Not as hot as your cause, from what I hear."

"Yeah," Teddy grinned. "We've been getting a lot of publicity and we're really stickin' it to them." He inclined his head towards the Fido building as Christina took pictures of the entrance.

"How long have you been out here?" she asked.

"Two weeks and we're gonna stay here until those corporate vermin clean up their mess, man."

Christina put her camera down. "So tell me about what you're trying to do here. The Magazine didn't say much."

Streetwise Magazine was an under-financed, New York City, free street paper—the kind available at record shops and clubs. Christina had been freelancing for them for about eighteen months. The money was lousy and the hours terrible but she was doing anything she could to become a professional photojournalist. She'd gotten the position through her best friend Jenny, who worked there as a receptionist.

After Christina had been sent away to boarding school, the girls had written to each other for a while. But six months into the school year, Jenny's father had been transferred to a new job in Chicago, her family had moved and they'd lost touch with each other. Three years ago, a newly divorced Jenny with her little girl Taylor, moved back to New York and had looked Christina up. Their friendship resumed and it was as if the years apart had never happened.

But they had, and they had changed both girls. Christina had became stronger and more self-assured as she'd learned to be independent at boarding school, and then later at Georgetown University where she'd majored in political science. Confident, tougher and a little bit more cynical, she'd had to grow up very fast on her own.

Jenny, on the other hand, had lost her brash, adolescent confidence and wasn't as tough as she used to be. She'd never made it to college and had married young. She'd had a baby and lived for years in an unhappy marriage until she'd mustered what courage she could to move on.

"Hey man, you listening?"

"Sorry." Christina focused on Teddy again.

"I was saying how Samco Oil, which is owned by Fido Dog Food, is pumping crude oil through old, leaking pipelines in the Russian Arctic. They're destroying the environment, man, and they don't give a shit."

"So why hasn't somebody done something about it?"

"Because it's happening in the Russian Arctic, man. Who cares about that? We just got word that the pipeline is leaking in at least twenty places… twenty damn places… and the oil is beginning to seep up through the ground. It's spreading and forming its own lakes. Can you picture that? Lakes of black crude oil." Teddy shook his head in disgust. "Mother Earth is weeping. We're killing her!"

"How long has GME been at this?" Christina asked, as she took a few more pictures of the protesters.

"Two months. We tried letters, we wrote to the papers, everything. You know, this is ten times worse than the Exxon Valdez and it's been virtually ignored by the media. This is our last resort."

"But doesn't Samco or Fido or whoever lose money if their oil is leaking out?" Christina was confused.

Teddy shook his head. "No way. They get paid for the oil they put into that pipeline, not what comes out the other end."

"But don't they care?"

"Look. The only thing these pricks care about is their precious bottom line. Gotta keep Wall Street and the shareholders happy. So what if all the fish in the Kulva River have been wiped out, it doesn't affect them."

One of the protesters called out to Teddy. "Hey, Teddy? You with us or what?"

"Yeah, I'm coming." He turned back to Christina. "Take as

many pictures as you can. We appreciate anything you can do for us." He turned to walk back to the others.

Christina readjusted her lens and resumed taking her pictures. When the little guy took on big business, it always made for a riveting photo spread.

Crossing the street, she angled her camera into position to get the protestors and the dog food company in the same frame.

Click. Click. Click.

Suddenly, out of the corner of her eye, she saw something red flash by. It was a bright red Ferrari pulling into the parking lot. Who was that, she wondered? Maybe one of the bigwigs showing up for work? Who else could afford a $300,000 car?

Christina took several pictures of the car and its occupant. Mr. Bigshot, she reasoned, would have to cross the picketers and a confrontation would probably ensue—with tension, heated words—maybe even a fistfight if she was lucky. Wouldn't that be fantastic!

Click. Click. Click.

Through her zoom lens, she could see Mr. Bigshot finally getting out of the Ferrari. Tall, dark brown hair, good build, slick suit… he turned then and Christina got a great shot of his face.

About thirty, handsome, strong jawline, gorgeous green eyes, movie star looks—holy crap! Suddenly, Christina gasped and drew in a deep breath as she recognized the face. It couldn't be. It just couldn't be him!

She took a few more pictures as he walked confidently towards the protestors. Oh God, it was him. After all these years, it was him—her nightmare from high school—Billy Havenwood! How many hellish dreams had she had of that face, that horrible, smug, arrogant face? Hundreds, thousands, even.

She may have physically changed since those first few weeks in high school, but he hadn't. Oh sure, he'd gotten bigger, taller and better looking, but it was those green eyes, those hypnotic, gorgeous, green eyes of his—she'd recognize them anywhere.

And that smirk, that confident, 'I-can-do-whatever-I-want-and-get-away-with-it' smirk!

Christina's fingers were shaking, but she forced herself to continue taking pictures. She watched through her camera lens as Billy Havenwood strode through the protestors as if he hadn't a care in this world—or a care 'about' this world.

"Globalists! Rapists! You're destroying the planet!" The picketers were shouting at him. His only response was to calmly give them the finger before entering the building.

He didn't even look back.

Christina finally lowered her camera and felt sick to her stomach. Here she was, an adult who was confident, strong, making it on her own—and felled by a childhood memory in one second flat. Only, he wasn't a memory, was he? He was flesh and blood real.

"Hey man, did ya get those pictures of Havenwood?" Teddy had come running across the street to where Christina was stationed.

"Y... yes."

"Alright." Teddy was obviously thrilled. He gave his fellow protesters a thumbs up sign and they started cheering.

"Y... you said his name was Haven... Haven..." She couldn't even say his name.

Teddy helped her out. "Havenwood, Bill Havenwood. His daddy owns the company."

"What?" Christina couldn't hide her shock.

"Yeah, William Havenwood Sr. owns the whole show and Billy Jr. is his only kid. Gonna get everything when the old man kicks off."

"So they're the...?"

"Yeah, the pricks who are polluting our planet."

It was all getting to be too much for Christina's brain. She was on overload and needed to get away. What if he came back, saw her and recognized her? She turned back to Teddy and covered her nervousness with a smile.

"Well, thanks for the photos and I'll see about getting you some write-ups in Streetwise." Absentmindedly, Christina gave him a polite smile before turning to walk away.

"Thanks, and the name's Teddy, man," he called after her.

Christina nonchalantly waved back as she raced to her car. She had to get back to her apartment and download the pictures as soon as possible. She just had to see that face again. She didn't want to but she just had to.

Like picking at a scab—you just can't help yourself.

CHAPTER 6

CHRISTINA ENTERED HER one bedroom, fifth floor walkup apartment. As apartments went, it wasn't much—a small kitchenette to the left of a tiny living room and an even tinier bedroom. She raced to her laptop computer sitting on her desk and quickly began to download the photos.

An hour later, Christina was staring at 8" X 10" glossies of 'him'. 'Him' getting out of his Ferrari. 'Him' walking through the protestors. ' Him' giving them the finger. 'Him' smirking.

Especially 'him' smirking.

That bastard.

Look at him, she thought to herself. He had everything—money, position, looks—and a cold heart. He probably didn't even remember her, she'd bet on it. He'd destroyed her life in one day and he'd forgotten about it, except maybe to have a good laugh at her expense. Jenny had told her that after Christina had been sent away to boarding school, her name had never been mentioned again by anyone at Cloverdale High. She'd been discarded like used toilet paper.

But Christina had never forgotten her one-day fiasco. It had been imprinted into that part of the brain that stored childhood traumas and it had stayed with her all these years.

Just seeing Billy again this afternoon had reduced her to a jumble of nerves. She'd actually been shaking, for God's sake—she, who was tough and strong and not that shy, insecure schoolgirl anymore, had been shaking like jelly.

Christina studied the photos and suddenly her legs turned to mush again. Why was she feeling like this? What was wrong with her?

Billy Havenwood—that's what was wrong with her. She stared at his handsome, arrogant face.

"No, Billy Havenwood, you're not doing this to me again. I won't let you!" she intoned aloud.

Forcing herself to take a couple of deep breaths, she began to calm down. Why should she be the one to feel like this? Why shouldn't it be him? It should be him!

Suddenly, Christina smiled, as she made an instantaneous decision. Yup, she was going to 'get' him. She didn't know how, she didn't know when, and she didn't know where, but somehow she was going to make him feel what it was like to have your whole life ripped out from under you and turned upside down. This was going to be payback, and she owed him one—a big one.

Reaching for her black journaling book, Christina began to write her thoughts and feelings into it and immediately felt better.

Putting her pen down, she reached for one of the pictures of smug Billy Havenwood getting out of his ultra-expensive sports car.

"Look at you, Mr. Havenwood," she whispered, "You've probably never had a crushing, humiliating, soul-destroying moment in all of your privileged, rich boy life. Well, get ready because you're about to have one." A feeling of calm and strength coursed through Christina's system and her decision was made.

*

Jenny Lewis was sitting across from Christina at Sal's Sandwich Shop next door to the Streetwise Magazine office in Greenwich Village. As Christina attacked her sandwich, Jenny stared at the pictures of Billy Havenwood.

She shook her head in disbelief. "I can't believe it."

"Believe it. It's him, all right."

"You're sure he didn't see you? I mean, this one here." Jenny pointed to one where it appeared that Billy was facing the camera. "He's looking right at you."

"No, I was across the street with the zoom." Christina took a quick sip of water before resuming her lunch.

"Incredible. Billy Havenwood," Jenny mumbled. "And he still looks…" She stopped and quickly looked up at Christina.

"Say it."

Jenny let out her words in a rush. "Really, really, really hot." Christina frowned and Jenny quickly added, "For a low-life, scumbag, of course."

Her friend smiled. "His father owns the Fido Dog Food conglomerate."

"So that's where his money came from—dog food." Jenny paused, "Was Jake Monroe anywhere around?"

"No, I only saw him."

Jenny studied Christina's face. "Why aren't you more upset? Here you are, calmly eating your lunch and discussing Billy Havenwood with as much emotion as you discuss the weather. What gives?" She, of all people, knew how deeply her friend had been hurt all those years ago.

"Jenny, I'm getting even," Christina gleefully announced. "I'm going to make him pay for what he did to me."

"What? How?"

"I'm going to get some dirt on him. I'm gonna find the skeletons rattling in his closet and expose all his little secrets. You know his type always has them."

Jenny was flabbergasted. "And then what?"

"Then I'm going to turn his life upside down like he did to mine. When I'm through with him, his Achilles heel will need a podiatrist."

Jenny didn't like this at all. "And how are you going to dig up all this wonderful information? You're broke. You can't afford a private investigator."

"That's why I'm going to be my own private investigator."

"But Chrissy, you know nothing about that."

"What's there to know? All you need are the three c's—a car, a camera and a computer. By using my computer access at the Magazine, I found out where he lives. Now all I have to do is use my car and my camera and tail him. You know, find out where he goes, what he does and with whom. He'll lead me to what I need to know, I'm sure of it."

Jenny was shocked. *"You're gonna stalk him?"*

"No, I'm not," Christina defensively shouted back. "Stalking is an ugly word. Only weirdoes and psychos do that. I'm going to 'research' him, just like when I'm on assignment for the Magazine."

She chomped down on her sandwich again and smiled at her friend. Ever since she'd come up with this plan and had written all the details in her journal, she'd felt her strength return. It was time someone taught that creep, Billy Havenwood a life lesson and she was just the girl to do it.

But Jenny was worried. Christina was her friend and she feared she'd be hurt all over again. Guys like Havenwood always had the upper hand. Their money and position ensured that.

"Chrissy, forget this idea. It's crazy."

"No."

"Yes. Listen to me. Revenge isn't the answer. When Derek left me for that other woman I wanted to hurt them both, but I realized that the best thing was to let go of all those negative feelings and move on."

"You had Taylor to think about."

"That's not the point."

"Then what is the point?"

"Don't you see? The reason you saw him again today is you're being given the chance to forgive him and move on, not to go after him for justice."

"Thanks for the new age sermon, Jenny, but I thought you of all people would understand." Christina was miffed. This was not the reaction she expected to get from her best friend.

"I do understand," Jenny sighed. "I just don't want to see you get hurt again, that's all."

Christina smiled. "Don't worry. I'm smarter than he is."

But Jenny wasn't convinced. She had an awful feeling that disaster was on the way.

CHAPTER 7

THERE IT WAS. 14025 Wickingham Drive.

Christina parked her beat-up old car under a canopy of trees down the street from the gates of the impressive thirty-room French chateau house owned by William Havenwood Sr., Bill's father. The mansion, located in Locust Valley, New York on Long Island's North Shore, was an imposing 2-1/2-story brick façade surrounded by shrubbery and tall trees. It sat on a very exclusive and very expensive 5-acre parcel of land. The entire house and grounds reeked of wealth, position and prestige.

By using the computer research facilities at Streetwise Magazine, Christina had learned that her little Billy lived here with his dad, William Sr. who was the owner and founder of the hugely successful Fido Dog Food empire. The company not only manufactured pet food but also owned other corporations, including Samco Oil. William Havenwood, a British immigrant, had started his business with nothing and had built up Fido Dog Food into one of the largest companies in the country today. It had been a true self-made-man, rags-to-riches story.

There were many business articles written about him.

There was very little written about Bill. All Christina found on the son was that he worked at Fido, was the heir apparent and his mom had divorced old William about five years ago.

Well hidden by the foliage, Christina rolled down her window and began taking pictures of the estate. It must be worth what, she thought? Ten, fifteen, twenty million? She'd read in one of the articles that the entire Fido empire had been conservatively estimated at $1 billion dollars with the Havenwoods owning enough shares to control it. It was probably worth more.

She readjusted her camera and began to take more pictures. Suddenly, a red Ferrari came barreling from around the house. It was him! Christina could see Billy in the driver's seat. She quickly snapped more photos and her heart began to pound. Within seconds, the red car raced up the long drive and stopped at the closed gates. The gates opened magically and Havenwood sped off down the street.

This was it, time to tail the creep. Christina dropped her camera into the passenger seat and turned the key in the ignition. But nothing happened; the car wouldn't start. She tried again. The engine was trying to turn over but—again, nothing. And, oh no, he was getting away! She could see the Ferrari becoming a small, red speck in the distance. She frantically tried the key again but the car was dead.

Damn it! Christina punched the steering wheel with her fist. You know who was to blame for this? Billy Havenwood, that's who. That man was a jinx, just plain bad luck.

Disappointed and angry, Christina reached into her purse and pulled out her cell phone to call for help.

And that's how Christina spent the first day of her 'research project'. Waiting for a tow truck, underneath the blistering, hot sun, stranded on billionaire's row.

CHAPTER 8

Day Two.

STAKEOUT AT 14025 Wickingham Drive. High noon.

Christina was again inconspicuously parked outside the gates of Bill Havenwood's home, waiting for her prey to emerge. She'd seen William Sr. leave in his limo at 7:30 a.m. that morning, probably on his way to the office. A tall, very distinguished and handsome gentleman of about sixty with gray hair pulled into a small ponytail at the back, Christina had recognized him immediately from a picture in Business Review. Admiring his classic features, she smiled to herself.

She could certainly see where Junior got his good looks.

As for Junior? No sign of him yet. Probably sleeping in—or should she say, sleeping 'it' off? That drunk! But what if he wasn't home? Maybe he'd spent the night elsewhere?

Christina hadn't thought of that before. She checked her watch. It read 12:03 p.m. "Give it time, Christina, give it time," she admonished herself. After all, he'd left the estate around noon yesterday, hadn't he?

Yesterday—what a disaster that had been! She'd spent the rest of the day at the garage having her car fixed and maxing out her credit card on a new alternator and battery.

Thankfully, her car was running again and she'd be able to tail him today with no problems. If only he'd show up and—wait—there he was!

The Ferrari came barreling down the drive and through the gates. Christina felt a surge of adrenaline kick start her nervous system. This was it. She said a small prayer and turned the ignition. The car started. Letting out a huge sigh of relief, Christina put the gearshift into drive and she was on her way.

*

Christina followed the Ferrari into the city. Staying a safe distance behind, she managed to keep the car in sight without being spotted—or so she hoped.

Havenwood had finally stopped outside Carbiri's, a chic, Italian restaurant on the Upper West Side. Dressed impeccably in a dark navy designer suit, he got out and handed his car keys to the valet. Confidently, he strutted into the eatery with a casual, 'I-own-the-world' type of walk that the rich instinctively did so well.

Arrogant jerk, Christina thought, as she double-parked nearby. So, he liked to have lunch at the very exclusive Carbiri's, did he? The place was such an 'in' spot that you had to book your table months in advance—if you were an ordinary person. 'Special' people like Havenwood could probably get in with one phone call and a huge tip.

Christina adjusted her camera lens and began taking pictures of the front of the building. Might as well get comfortable, she thought. These rich folk usually had three hour lunches and she'd probably be here for sometime.

Suddenly, before the valet had even had a chance to park the Ferrari, an angry Bill Havenwood came stalking back out with a tall, gorgeous redhead in tow. The mystery woman, wearing lemon-colored silk pants and matching silk shirt with her cropped short red hair, was the epitome of high fashion and money.

"Hello, this looks interesting," Christina mumbled, as she began clicking away with her camera. Who was this woman?

A girlfriend? Certainly not a wife. Through her research, Christina knew Havenwood was single and had never been married. Maybe she was a relative? A cousin? No, this was girlfriend behavior, Christina sensed, as she continued taking the pictures.

Suddenly, the woman said something to Havenwood that made him even angrier. She then frantically wrapped her arms around Billy's neck and tried to kiss him. Abruptly, he pushed Miss Redhead away and said something to her that forced her to shout something back at him. Dismissing her, Havenwood walked to where the valet was holding the driver's door open for him and got in. The Ferrari's engine roared to life and he squealed away.

Wow! What had that been all about? Christina had managed to capture the entire scene on film and she'd analyze it later. But right now, she needed to keep her focus on that Ferrari and its rich boy driver.

Christina quickly started her car. She couldn't lose him—no matter what. Stepping on the gas, she sped down the street and ended up three cars behind him. Being bright red, the Ferrari was easy to keep in sight.

Suddenly, he braked at the intersection ahead and turned left. It took Christina three seconds to reach the same stop sign. Looking to her left, she spotted the Ferrari making a right turn onto another street. She could still catch him, it wasn't too late—if only the traffic wasn't starting to get so heavy. Quickly making a left-hand turn, Christina barreled down the same street but a large van suddenly pulled out in front of her, blocking her view.

"Oh no." She couldn't lose him now, she just couldn't.

Agitated, Christina rolled down her window and strained her neck, trying to look around the van. She could barely make out the red speck of a car up ahead turning left onto yet another street. At least she hadn't lost sight of him. If only this damn van would move out of her way.

Frustrated, Christina beeped her horn but the van remained in front. Owing to the heavy traffic, she couldn't pass it. All she could do was follow as closely as she could and pray for an opportunity to get around it. Suddenly, as the traffic lessened, the van picked up speed. Relieved, Christina did likewise. Now all she had to do was to somehow pass it.

Suddenly, the van flashed its turning signal.

"Yes." Christina was euphoric. Triumphantly, she stepped on the gas and her car surged forward. The van quickly pulled into the left lane but Christina's jubilation was short-lived because there—directly in front of her—was the Ferrari—stopped behind a long line of cars. Shocked, Christina slammed on her brakes. Her tires squealed with effort as her car slid forward trying to stop. But she didn't stop—and she smashed into the back of the Ferrari.

The sound of metal crashing against metal was deafening.

Christina was violently catapulted forward, saved only by her seatbelt as her car's front end completely smashed into the back-end of the Ferrari, crumpling it like an empty beer can.

The accident lasted a microsecond but to Christina it felt like an eternity—with steel smashing against steel, glass and plastic popping and breaking.

Then silence.

Dazed, Christina let out a deep breath. Was she all right? Was she hurt? Taking a split second to feel her body, she confirmed to herself that she was fine.

"Thank God," she whispered in relief.

Refocusing on the situation, she slowly looked up—through her cracked windshield—past her own mangled car—to see Bill Havenwood climbing out of his own twisted wreck.

And he was coming towards her.

"Oh God," she whispered in panic. He was going to recognize her and then—Christina suddenly gasped in shock as she remembered something else.

She didn't have any car insurance.

CHAPTER 9

IT HAD BEEN such a stupid, stupid, stupid thing to do. Last month, Christina had used the money allotted for her car insurance to pay for her rent. She'd never done that before, but the funds she'd earned on a photography assignment hadn't arrived in time. Her insurance had been due but so had her rent. And she didn't have enough to pay for both. So—she chose.

She chose wrong.

Her insurance had expired and she shouldn't have been driving. But she'd been expecting that assignment check any day now and she really didn't think anything was going to happen.

Christina stared straight ahead at the damage on both cars. This accident was clearly her fault. How was she ever going to pay for all of this? Her savings were nil and her cash flow was poor—very poor. But all thoughts of money quickly evaporated when her eyes flew back to ' *him*' approaching her car.

And he was getting closer—

And closer—

And closer—

And all at once, Christina was fourteen again—that shy, scared fourteen again with everybody laughing at her—including 'him'. Especially *'him'!*

Bill Havenwood stuck his head into Christina's half-lowered driver's window.

"Are you all right?" he inquired. Deeply concerned, his eyes ran over Christina's face and then down her body, looking for signs of injury. He was clearly shaken too.

Christina, with her hands still clenched on the steering wheel, slowly turned to look at him. His face was inches away and her eyes glued onto his. Did he recognize her? Did he? No—there were no sparks of recognition. Suddenly, he was speaking again.

"Are you hurt?" Worried, Bill looked her over again. "Do you feel any pain? Can you move?" he anxiously asked.

Wide-eyed and in shock, Christina just kept staring at him. His eyes were greener than she remembered, but that arrogance was still stamped on his handsome, movie star face. Or was that the confidence that came with maturity?

"Do you... know... your... name?" Bill was speaking very slowly now.

"I... I..." Christina stammered, too mesmerized to say anything else.

"You... what?" Bill tried to encourage her.

Christina just gave him another blank stare. Her brain felt like it was in a fog and she couldn't put a complete thought together. What was the matter with her? Why couldn't she snap out of it?

"That's it." Bill stepped back from the car and pulled out his cell phone. "I'm calling an ambulance." He started dialing.

As soon as Christina heard the word 'ambulance', she snapped out of her trance. She was fine and she knew she didn't need any medical attention.

"No," she blurted out.

Unbuckling her seatbelt, she reached for the handle and tried to push her door open. But the frame had been bent and the door wouldn't budge. She gave it a hard push with her hand but it was stuck.

"I don't need an ambulance," she shouted at Bill who was calling 911. "I'm fine." She kept pushing at the door. "I'm okay."

Bill lowered his phone and approached Christina's car again. "What did you say?"

"I said I'm fine." And with that, Christina gave the door one good shove with her foot. Violently, it swung open and hit Bill full on in the chest and groin area.

"Ahhhh." Screaming, Bill dropped the phone and hunched

over in extreme pain. Within seconds, he collapsed onto the pavement and curled up into a fetal position, all the while hugging his private parts.

Bewildered, Christina jumped out of her car and stood over him, looking down at his writhing, Armani-clad body.

What should she do? Help him up? Comfort him? Loosen his tie maybe? But thoughts of concern lasted only a nanosecond before she remembered who this guy was. He was her avowed enemy—the target of her revenge plan.

Suddenly, she smiled to herself. Served him right. In fact, here at her feet, was the great Billy Havenwood and she loved it. She wasn't that gawky, insecure fourteen year-old anymore. She was a thirty year-old woman who was older, wiser—and stronger. And she was going to be the one in control of this situation from now on, not him.

"Sorry," she mumbled, but she wasn't one bit sorry. "Did I hurt you?"

"No, I'm… fine." Bill whispered breathlessly, as he used her smashed car hood for leverage and slowly stood up. "I—just need a moment to catch my breath. That's all."

Christina bit the inside of her lip to keep from smiling. Here was the great Bill Havenwood slumped over her car hood because she had hit him—accidentally, of course—in the billionaire family jewels. Oh, who would have thought her revenge could have begun so quickly?

Suddenly, an ambulance appeared on the scene along with the police. A crowd of onlookers had circled around them by now and the emergency vehicles had a difficult time trying to get through. Christina waved at them.

"Over here. Someone's been injured." She pointed to Bill, who was slowly straightening up away from the car.

"No, I'm okay." Bill limped a few steps as the paramedics came rushing over. One of them put his hand on Bill's arm.

"Sir, where are you hurt?" he inquired.

"I'm fine, really."

Christina butted into the conversation using her 'concerned' voice. "No, you're not fine." She addressed the paramedic. "I think he hurt…" Christina lowered her tone and pointed to Bill's groin area, "…his package." A few of the women onlookers snickered. None of the men did.

Bill gave an embarrassed laugh. "Nothing to worry about." He took a few more tentative steps. "See? I'm walking it off."

"Sir, if you'd like to go to the hospital?" The paramedic wasn't convinced.

"No… no hospital needed, really."

Inside, Christina was laughing to herself. Was Billy's face actually turning red? Beet red? Yes, it was. Uncomfortable, was he? Well, she'd only just begun. She turned back to Bill.

"Maybe you should go. Have them take a look."

Bill turned to her. "I think… you've done enough, thank you," he gritted through his teeth.

Raising her shoulders in a 'whatever' gesture, Christina walked to where the two cars were sandwiched together and where a police officer was already inspecting the damage. She looked down at the mangled mess. How was she ever going to pay for this?

Her junk-heap-of-a-car was totaled—a complete write-off. And his expensive red Ferrari? Well, the backend had been flattened like a tortilla—and she didn't have any insurance to pay for any of it. But did she care? No. In fact, it was even funny. This was the funniest, damn thing she had ever seen in her life.

Suddenly, Christina burst out laughing—and she couldn't stop. Her attitude was irresponsible, crazy and mad; she knew it. And she also knew that she'd cry about this later on, but right now, the enormity of her predicament and its consequences had been shoved to the back of her mind. She was on such a high for having got the better of Bill Havenwood that nothing else mattered. She was just going to enjoy the moment.

Bill stared at Christina in amazement. She was laughing? She was actually—laughing? He'd met some crazy women in his time, but this one was a true wacko—even if she was beautiful and attractive—and very hot.

He approached her in disbelief, still limping all the way. "What's so funny?" he piped up.

Christina tried to stem her giggles. "Delayed shock or something." She looked back at his car. "Sorry about your—car." She burst out laughing again.

Bill followed her gaze and looked down at the Ferrari. For the first time since the accident, he saw the extent of the damage. Earlier, he'd been too preoccupied with whether this crazy woman had been hurt or not that he hadn't even taken a good look, but now that he had—

"Oh my God, my car!" Bill was stunned. "Look at what you did to my car."

Christina stopped laughing but still couldn't help smirking. "It was an accident."

"It's… it's… unbelievable!" Bill's voice began to rise with astonishment and anger. "There must be thirty, forty thousand dollars worth of damage here."

"What?" That wiped the smile off of Christina's face and it suddenly wasn't funny anymore. "You can't be serious."

"This is a Ferrari. Do you have any idea what repairs and parts cost on something like this?" Bill was now yelling.

"It wasn't my fault," Christina started to yell back.

"Oh, it was your fault, all right. I was stopped and you hit me. Where in the hell did you think you were going?"

"I… I didn't see you. There was a van blocking my view and…"

Bill put his hands up, stemming her words. "Lady, I don't need this today, of all days." He looked at his watch. "Great, now I'm late too." Angrily, he turned back to Christina. "Thanks a lot, sweetheart." Limping back to where he had dropped his cell phone earlier, he picked it up and dialed. "Hi Charlotte, it's me. I know I'm late but tell the old goat that I've just been in a car accident." He pulled the phone away from his ear but kept talking into it. "What? I can't hear you. The phone's breaking up." He slammed the phone shut, and then limped back to where Christina was standing.

Flabbergasted, Christina looked up at him. "There's no way this'll cost thirty, forty thousand dollars. You're just trying to s... scare me."

"Think so? Now why would I do that?" Bill was very irritated. This had not been a good day for him so far and it wasn't over yet.

"Because... you're mad I ruined your stupid car and... and..." The full impact of what had happened finally hit Christina like a shovel to the face. Thirty to forty thousand dollars? It couldn't be! Where was she going to get that kind of money?

"And what? Look at it. Look at my car. You know, I think it could even go as high as fifty grand." Bill shook his head as he reached into his wallet for his driver's license.

"Fifty...?" Christina's eyes wandered back to the smashed, red metal. She was in trouble. Serious, serious trouble. Trouble like she'd never been in before. What was she going to do?

Bill looked over at Christina and saw how badly shaken she suddenly seemed to be. Maybe she had been hurt in the accident after all? He should really calm down and find out.

He didn't even know why he was yelling. Sure, his car had been smashed, but it had happened. Yelling about it and making a scene wasn't going to change anything.

His tone of voice softened and he put a comforting arm around Christina's shoulders. "Maybe you should sit down and have one of the paramedics look you over."

Christina looked at his hand touching her arm and she flinched. Billy Havenwood was actually touching her; pretending he was concerned about her welfare; pretending to be nice. What a phony!

"Hey, I don't need your sympathy," she spouted. The tough, in-control Christina was back.

Bill let go of her as if he'd just touched a hot stove. Raising his hands up in surrender, he backed off. "Sorry, it won't happen again." Miffed, he walked away to where one of the officers was standing.

Another police officer, Officer Robbins, a twenty-year veteran, approached Christina. "Ma'am, can I please see your driver's license and insurance?"

"S… sure." Christina went back to her own mangled heap and grabbed her purse. She handed her license over and waited anxiously for the next question.

"And your insurance, please?"

A huge lump of fear suddenly lodged in Christina's throat. "Well… I… don't have any." She quickly shut her eyes as if that would save her from any fallout.

Officer Robbins, who'd heard and seen everything, calmly shook his head and silently began to write in his notebook.

"Did I hear right?" Bill's voice boomed through Christina's thoughts. Slowly, she opened her eyes to see him standing in front of her with his arms folded over his chest.

"You don't have any insurance?" he asked again incredulously.

Christina squeaked out a little, "No."

With anger flashing from his green eyes, Bill turned to Officer Robbins, "I'm not paying for this."

"Sir, please calm down."

"This wasn't my fault."

"Sir, please."

Bill shut up and Officer Robbins walked away to his squad car to call into dispatch.

Taking in a calming breath, Bill stared at Christina. "Who doesn't have insurance? Everybody has insurance. You can't drive without insurance."

"I was going to pay it but I didn't have enough money. Somebody like you…" Christina gave him a disgusted up and down appraisal, "… would never understand that."

"Oh, I understand, all right. I understand you should have been taking the bus."

She couldn't argue with him there—but she was going to anyway. "I don't appreciate your tone of voice."

Stupefied, Bill laughed out loud. "Tough." This was one crazy, beautiful loony bird, he thought to himself.

Christina raised her chin in defiance. "In fact, I think you owe me an apology."

"I owe you what?"

"An apology for your rude behavior just now." Christina knew she was pushing it too far but she wasn't going to let him get the better of her no matter what she had to say.

Bill shook his head as if to get the cotton balls out of his ears. "You want me to apologize to you? To you?"

"Yes."

"Honey, it ain't gonna happen." Bill couldn't believe her gall. If he weren't so angry, he'd almost have to admire her. "Let me ask you something? What do you do for a living?"

"What's it to you?"

"I'm just curious how you're going to pay for this disaster." Bill pointed to the wreckage.

Christina held her head up proudly. "I'm a photographer."

"Like for babies and puppies?"

"No, I'm on assignment right now for Streetwise."

"What's that?"

"It's a local magazine."

"Streetwise? Isn't that the newspaper you get at clubs—for free?" Bill emphasized the word 'free' as if it disgusted him. He shook his head. "A starving artist with no money. Well, I guess my insurance company will be suing you for damages then."

"Probably." Christina lifted her nose in defiance.

"Oh—you can bet your sweet little ass they will." Suddenly, he flashed her a confident smile, giving her the same head-to-toe appraisal she'd given him moments earlier.

"That's something I never bet, Mr...?" Christina pretended not to know his name.

"Havenwood. Bill Havenwood."

Admiration and interest kept shining in Bill's eyes as he studied Christina. She may be exasperating but she had spunk and that intrigued him. As a matter of fact, a lot about this woman had instantly intrigued him and he didn't know why.

She was pretty, but he knew lots of pretty girls. She was smart—he could tell. But so what? He knew lots of smart girls too. No—there was something original and unique about her, an almost Dr. Jekyll and Mr. Hyde quality. One second, she seemed to be innocent and naïve—and the next cunning and strong. He couldn't figure her out. But whatever it was, he liked it. He liked it a lot.

He gave her another rakish smile. "And you are?" Bill let the question hang in the air.

"I'm what?" Christina played dumb. What a jerk! He was actually flirting with her.

"Your name? What's your name?" He asked again.

Suddenly, Christina's heart started pounding against her ribs. Her name, what if he recognized her name? Then he'd know she was that little nobody from high school. But wait! So what if he recognized her? It could just be a coincidence, right? Two former schoolmates meeting by accident—literally. And he'd never in a million years figure out that she'd actually been following him. Besides, her name would be on the police report anyway—

"You don't know your name?" Bill teasingly prodded.

"Christina. Christina Matteo."

There, she'd said it. Did he remember her now? Christina searched his face for any spark of recognition, but there was none. Her name hadn't rung a bell in that alcohol-damaged brain of his at all. She refocused on what he was saying.

"Well, Christina Matteo, you'll be hearing from my insurance company." He smiled then—that smile someone gives you when they know they've got you cornered.

Christina shot him a dirty look. "I'm in the book," she decreed, before turning to leave.

"You'd better get a good one. A lawyer, I mean."

She turned to glare at him. He was smiling again—that damn, superior smile. Boy, she'd love to smack that off his face.

Coyly, she smiled at him. "Are you going to sue me for personal injury too?"

"What?"

"In case 'it's' not working." Christina pointed to his private parts.

The smug look was instantly wiped off of Bill's face. "Don't worry your pretty little head. Everything's fine down there," he announced proudly.

"Well, I did hit you very hard and I've read that when that happens to a man, he may not be able to—function properly. But it's nothing to be embarrassed about. It happens to a lot of men," Christina gave him her best fake smile of concern. Take that, you lowlife, she thought.

Bill returned her smile and limped closer. He leaned into her face and whispered, "I'm not worried. Know why? Because it's—functioning—right now, thanks to you, Ms. Matteo. You can take a look, if you don't believe me."

Christina glowered into his green eyes as he continued to smile at her with those perfect white teeth of his. The cad! He was enjoying this and getting turned on by the game—her game—and getting turned on by her.

She was repulsed. "Mr. Havenwood, I wouldn't turn you on if I was on fire and you were the nearest faucet."

He laughed then—a good, hearty, laugh. He was truly enjoying himself. Christina thought that last crack would have insulted him, but it hadn't.

Damn it. Well, she wasn't going to stand here and spar with this creep any longer. Dismissing him, she turned and walked to the police cruiser. But she could hear his laughter following her—just like all those years ago—and it sent chills down her spine.

Christina approached Officer Robbins. "Excuse me, but his car? Can that really be fifty thousand dollars worth of damage?"

The officer looked back to the accident scene. "Probably."

Christina bit her lip hard. So Havenwood hadn't been lying. Where was she going to get that kind of money?

The colossal jam she was in finally registered in Christina's brain and she suddenly felt faint. Not only was she now without a car herself, but she owed all that money for his car too? She should never have started this revenge thing. Never. It had been a big mistake. But at least he hadn't remembered her. She was pretty sure of that. But Christina didn't know whether to feel relieved or insulted. Had she been that forgettable?

Bill Havenwood had gotten the better of her in the past.

He had done it again today—for the second time in her life.

CHAPTER 10

IN THE END, Christina was charged with careless driving and driving without insurance. And as for the damages to Havenwood's Ferrari? She'd been told by Officer Robbins that she would probably be taken to court and have her wages garnished for a very long time. She'd then avoided Havenwood while the tow trucks were removing the mangled cars and had taken pictures of the accident scene with her camera. After all, they might help her in court.

Christina had felt his eyes on her the whole time she was shooting the frames, but she didn't acknowledge him with a look of her own. She just couldn't deal with him anymore that day. She'd had enough.

After finishing her film and without so much as a backward glimmer, she caught a cab to the Streetwise Magazine office. She needed to speak to Jenny. She'd know what to do and what to say to make Christina feel better.

*

"You did what?" Jenny's eyes bulged out as Christina recounted the days' events. The two were sitting in the small lunchroom having a coffee.

"I didn't mean to."

"Chrissy, oh my God!"

"It's not that bad."

"It's bad."

Christina's face fell. "I know. And no I-told-you-so's, okay?"

Jenny studied her friend's dejected face and her tone of voice softened. "If you needed money for insurance, why didn't you come to me?"

"Because it's embarrassing and I'm not borrowing money from you. Besides, you're barely making it yourself and you've got Taylor."

"I knew this was going to lead to disaster. I had a feeling."

"Why don't you think he remembered me?"

"Chrissy, you were only at that school for three weeks before you left. It's probably not even listed on your school records."

"But what he did to me…?"

"Listen, you look different now and Havenwood was drunk twenty-four seven. I doubt he'd remember the name of that school, let alone you."

"I guess you're right."

"You sound disappointed." Jenny was trying to figure out what was going on in Christina's brain.

"Jenny, no way. You know how I feel about him." Christina took a gulp of her coffee without even tasting it. She wasn't disappointed. She hated that man. How could Jenny even think that?

"All I know is that you're not indifferent to him. And one thing my marriage to Derek taught me is that the opposite of love is indifference, not hate. Love and hate are actually this close." Jenny brought her index finger and thumb together in front of her face.

Christina suddenly burst out laughing. "Me? In love with rat bastard, Havenwood? You're crazy." Trust Jenny. She could always be counted on to bring a smile to your face. Christina sobered a little. "Jenny, what am I going to do? I don't have that kind of money."

"First thing, get some legal advice. I'll give you the number for Stanley Moore, the lawyer we use here at the magazine. Second thing—you are giving up your revenge plan, right Chrissy?"

Christina thought about it for a second. Should she?

"Chrissy!" Jenny was shocked at her friend's silence.

"Yes, yes, it's over. I don't want to even hear Bill Havenwood's name again. The whole thing was a huge mistake."

"Good. I'm glad to hear it." Jenny was afraid for her friend. This wasn't over yet and she feared that when it was, Billy Havenwood would hurt Christina all over again.

For her part, Christina didn't say anything to Jenny about Havenwood making a pass at her. It was too ridiculous to even think about. He was just being a man.

CHAPTER 11

BILL HAVENWOOD WAS dreading this—a meeting with his father. Or should he say a castration?—because that's what it felt like whenever he was summoned to the inner sanctum of his father's palatial office at Fido Foods.

Bill nervously glanced at the gilded mirrors and crown molding inside the private elevator as it silently whisked him upwards. Only the best for his old man.

Even though both Bill and William Sr. lived in the same house, neither spoke to the other. If there was anything that needed to be discussed, William would have Charlotte, his secretary, set up an appointment in his office with his son.

And Bill had better be there—on time and without excuses— or else it would be one more grievance added to the long litany which he would rant and rave about.

The elevator doors parted and Bill stepped out into a dark green, carpeted outer office. The lighting was low in the room— better to show off the two Renoirs on opposite walls.

Charlotte, a slim, well-maintained woman of sixty, rushed out from behind her desk and hugged Bill briefly before releasing him.

"Thank God you're all right. We were so worried," she said in a breathless, concerned voice.

"You mean 'you' were worried."

"I mean 'we'," Charlotte was adamant.

At that moment, the office door behind Charlotte was yanked open and William Havenwood Sr. stood there, glaring at his son. "You're late," he barked in his British accent before slamming his door shut again.

Bill sighed. Yes—he was definitely coming out of that office a eunuch today. First, that crazy, beautiful broad had damaged 'the goods' and now his old man would finish the job. Taking a deep breath, he turned the doorknob to his father's office and entered.

Inside, Bill took no note of the richly appointed office or the large expanse of windows which overlooked the city. He only had eyes for his father who stoically stood, with hands clasped behind his back, beside his ornate cherry wood desk.

"It wasn't my fault. I was rear-ended and…" Bill started to explain.

"Sit." The word was spoken as a trainer would to his dog.

Bill let out a breath as he took a seat in one of two wingback chairs opposite the desk. Here it came—the lecturing—the recriminations—the disappointment in his father's eyes, yet again. Well, he was immune to all of that. And numb. He had been for a very long time.

"Punctuality is the mark of a successful man," William enunciated every word as he began to pace the room like an angry leashed tiger with its tail lashing back and forth.

"Only thing I'm successful at is spending your money. Does that count?"

"Don't be smart."

"No, I'm never that," Bill gave a half laugh.

William looked his son over. "At least you're in one piece."

"Wouldn't want to ruin your fun."

"Meaning?"

"Well now you can rip me… to pieces."

William stopped his pacing and glared at Bill. "Charlotte was crazed with worry. Why didn't you call back?"

"I didn't think…"

"No, you never 'think', do you? Or should I say you only 'think' of yourself."

"Like father, like son."

"Not quite. I don't exactly start my day at noon and spend my nights screwing around."

"No, you just screw people during the day," Bill said as he returned his father's glare.

"It's paid for your lifestyle all these years and I haven't heard too many complaints from you, have I?" Bill remained silent. "Have I?" Bill again said nothing. William answered his own question. "No, I haven't. Well, all that's about to change."

"What do you mean?" Warily, Bill swiveled his head to look directly at his father. What was the old goat up to now?

"You're cut off."

"What?"

"No more cars. No more trips. No more allowance. You're to pack your bags and be out of my house within twenty-four hours. I've had enough of your lazy, irresponsible ways."

Bill was floored. What the hell was going on here? No more Havenwood money? It couldn't be. His father had threatened many times before but he'd never gone this far.

"Look, I don't know what this is about but…"

"And you're out of the will too." Like a man possessed, William marched over to his desk and retrieved several papers from a drawer. He threw them at his son. "I've set up the Havenwood Trust. When I'm gone, all my money's going to charity. All of it."

Slowly, Bill glanced at the papers clutched in his hands. They were legal papers all right, signed and witnessed, detailing what his father had just said.

William looked around his office and shook his head in disgust. "All this…" His hand swept the room and he shouted. "Everything… everything that I've bloody worked hard for all my life will be given away when I'm gone. I have no legacy. I don't even have any grandchildren to leave it to, thanks to you."

Bill was speechless. This couldn't be happening to him. He needed that money. He couldn't live without that money. Especially now, when there were people counting on him to… well, he couldn't think about that now. He needed to focus on changing his father's mind.

William stared at his son with contempt as he continued his

speech in that proper British tone. "My son, my only son… look at you. You're thirty years old and what have you done on your own? Absolutely nothing, that's what. Well from now on, you're going to stand on your own two very expensively shod feet because I've footed your bill for far too long."

Bill stared hard at his father who was now standing proudly behind his desk. Studying William's face, he thought he could actually see a glimmer of excitement in that old, devilish puss of his.

Well, he wasn't giving up without a fight. His spirit wasn't broken by a long shot, and if that's how the old man wanted to play it, then fine, he would too. He also had Havenwood blood in him and he hadn't survived this long under his father's thumb without some smarts of his own. Bill took a deep calming breath. Be steady and think clearly, he thought to himself.

"If you're mad about…" Suddenly Bill's face turned even paler than it already was. Could his father have found out about what he was really up to? About…? Nah. Impossible. He continued his previous train of thought. "If you're mad about my timekeeping here at the office, then…"

"What timekeeping?" His father started pacing again. "You're never here. You show up at one in the afternoon, stay three bloody hours, accomplish nothing of value, and leave to party all night long. I should have fired your useless ass a long time ago."

"But you didn't."

"No, I didn't. I kept hoping, praying this was just a phase, that you'd change. I kept telling myself, he's young, he'll learn. He'll become more responsible."

"I am responsible."

"For what? I gave you one thing, one damn bloody thing to do and you screwed it up."

"You'll have to be a bit more specific," Bill smirked sarcastically. But it wasn't funny. None of this was.

"This." William grabbed a folded newspaper from his desk and threw it at Bill's chest. He didn't appreciate his son's smart mouth.

Unfolding the newspaper, Bill looked at the article. The head-line screamed "Your Dog Food Pays For This", and below that was a picture of oil oozing into a lake. Scanning the text, Bill saw that it linked Fido Food and Samco Oil with the leaking pipeline problem.

"You were put in charge of P.R. It was your job to see that noth-ing like this would ever get into the press," William continued angrily.

"It's only The Bulletin; it's not like it's The Times." 'The Bulletin' was a small, radical newspaper put out by one of the larger national environmental groups. It was rumored they had ties with the Guardians of Mother Earth Organization that had been picketing lately outside the Fido building.

William frowned. "Not yet, it's not. But that's how these things start and before you know it, our name is being dragged through the mud."

"Don't you mean oil?"

"My… aren't we clever today? Too bad you weren't clever enough to stop this before it went to print." William pointed to the newspaper still in Bill's hand.

"I'll make a few calls and…"

"You'll do nothing.

"But…"

"You're fired and out of my life for good."

"You don't mean that." Bill was getting very worried.

"I most certainly do mean it," William stated emphatically. "Now get out."

Bill sat there looking shell-shocked. What could he do? What could he say? There must be something. There had to be.

"Out! Now!" William shouted at his son with all the force he could muster, snapping Bill out of his reverie. The old man wasn't getting away with this. Not if he could help it. But he needed time to think and it had to be away from this hellhole.

Bill stood up slowly. The impeccably cut designer suit gave his movements grace as he fluidly threw the newspaper and will back down on his father's desk. He looked squarely into William's eyes. "Fine, if that's the way you want it." He turned and began walking to the door.

A glimmer of sadness briefly crossed William's determined facial features. "It's not the way I want it." Bill stopped dead in his tracks and turned to look at his father. "It's the way it has to be," William continued, his hard business face now firmly back in place.

Father and son stared at each other and in that moment, Bill knew he still had a chance. If only he knew how to get through to that crusty old heart of his father's. But he didn't know. He hadn't known for a long time. All Bill knew was what he had been taught. No showing of real emotions—just games, lies and deception. It was the Havenwood way. And that's how he was going to play it. But how? Think, Bill, think.

And in a flash, he knew the answer. Grandchildren. The answer was grandchildren—or at least the possibility of grandchildren. The old bastard had mumbled something about wanting a legacy. If only he could convince his father that there was a chance for a grandchild in the very near future, Bill could buy some time. And if he could buy some time, he knew he could eventually convince dear papa to embrace him back into the Havenwood fold—and back into the money.

Bill had one eye blink second to take a shot at it. It was now or never. "I'll be out of the house by tonight. I know where I'm not wanted." Bill stared at his father who was still standing expressionless behind his desk. Not one tick of emotion. Not one. God, the old man was good. But he, the son, was going to be better. "See you around, pops." Bill turned and strode to the door. "Oh and by the way…" he stopped and looked back at his father, "… you'll understand if I don't send you a wedding invitation?"

"Wait." William imperially commanded.

Innocently, Bill stared back. Yes—there was now genuine interest stamped across the old devil's sour mug.

"What wedding?" William inquired.

"I was planning on telling you today but…"

William rudely interrupted his son. "What wedding and don't make me ask again."

Bill bit the inside of his cheek to keep from smiling. The old man was definitely interested and this ploy just might buy him the time he needed to change his father's mind.

"I'm getting married."

William was very suspicious. "Really? Who's the lucky bride?"

"Well, Stephie…"

William burst out laughing. "I should have known you'd pick that money-hungry tramp. You can't even be trusted to make a responsible decision in your own personal life." He flopped down in his chair, as he continued to laugh and regard his son as a joke.

Bill didn't like to be regarded as a joke. "I wasn't going to say, Stephie." Yes, he had been. Now what? Who was he going to say it was? "I was just going to say that Stephie and I have called it quits. We haven't even seen each other for awhile." If you could call that afternoon 'awhile'.

"Is that right?" William didn't believe a word of it.

"Yes, and since then, I met someone else and I love her and I'm going to marry her."

"Who?"

"You don't know her."

"Well, I would if you told me her name." William was losing his patience.

Who? Who the hell was Bill going to say? His mind was drawing a blank. He had to stall.

"She's… different. A serious sort of girl."

"And she wants to marry you? You?" William laughed again.

"Yes. She's crazy about me."

"Or crazy about the money she thinks you have."

"She's not like that."

"Everybody's like that," William looked directly at Bill with accusatory eyes. "It's amazing what people will do or say when large amounts of money are involved."

Bill wasn't really paying attention to his father's suspicions. He was too busy mentally trying to come up with a name. Who could he say was his beloved bride-to-be? How about Rachel from the country club? No. William hated her father. Maybe Melissa Crawford? No, William hadn't been too thrilled with her drug-bust a couple of years ago, even if the charges had been dropped. What about...?

"I'm waiting."

William's loud and impatient voice barged into his train of thought. Bill focused again on his father's face. "For what?"

"The name, damn it; the name—if there is one."

"Of course there is. I wouldn't lie about something like this." He would and he was. "And I don't appreciate you thinking that I would." Bill was still scanning his brain for a name. Maybe he should just make one up? "Her name is..."

And that's when Bill saw it. Looking down at the carpet in front of his feet was the piece of paper the officer at the accident had given him with that crazy woman's name and information on it. It must have fallen out of his jacket when he'd made his way to the door.

Thank you, heaven.

Casually picking up the paper, he stole a quick glance at it before stuffing it back into his pocket. Christina. Christina Matteo. That was it. The name he needed. A name his father had never heard of—and a name about which he could spin any story he wanted—and a name that belonged to a real live person. After all, the best way to tell a lie was to tell as much of the truth as possible—and change only what you needed to change. His father had taught him that one.

Bill looked directly into William's eyes. "Her name is Christina. Christina Matteo."

"So why haven't you mentioned—this Christina—before now?"

"Because I..." Why? What was the reason? "I didn't think you'd approve. She's not from your social circle."

William smirked. "I may be a bastard, but I'm not a snob. What does she do?"

"She's a photojournalist at Streetwise Magazine."

"What? A reporter? You're involved with a bloody reporter?" William was outraged as his eyes bulged out in shock.

Oh no. Bill had put his foot in it. He hadn't seen that one coming. Stupid move. Of course, his dad hated reporters, or at least the ones that weren't on his payroll. Bill had to do some damage control and do it fast. "She's not a reporter. She just takes pictures of club happenings and musicians and events and... stuff like that." Smooth, Bill, smooth. Don't blow it now. "Streetwise is just a free music newspaper. You know, rock and roll and fashion and... stuff."

Seconds ticked by as father and son stared at each other.

William broke the silence first. "So, you've already asked her to marry you and she's accepted?"

"I love her; she loves me. What else is there?" Bill was starting to feel anxious. Had his father bought it? Watching William sitting there with his arms folded across his chest, Bill couldn't tell.

William watched his son squirm. No. He wasn't buying any of this. His son was lying and he knew it. He hadn't built a billion dollar empire by being an idiot, even if his son seemed to think so. He eyed Bill suspiciously. "You're telling me all of this now, when I've thrown you out. Coincidental, don't you think?"

Bill innocently shrugged his shoulders. "I would have told you today but..." He let the sentence hang in the air.

William stood up and Bill betrayed himself by instinctively taking a step back. Damn it. His father could still get to him. Here he was—thirty years old—and he still felt ten in front of his old man.

William's shrewd eyes didn't miss anything. "I want to meet this Christina. Bring her over for dinner tonight."

Bill had no intention of actually producing the real 'Christina Matteo'. He was just going to create an imaginary 'Christina

Matteo' as an excuse until he could think of a better way to change his father's stubborn, bull-headed mind. "I can't," he spouted.

"Why not? Is there something you're not telling me?"

"Christina's out of town for the next couple of weeks on assignment for the magazine."

"I thought you said it was a local newspaper. What does she have to go out of town for?"

Bill had better get his story together. He was making mistakes and his father was just too sharp not to catch them.

"She's… photographing some band on the road; recording their tour. I think they're called…" Bill's eyes scanned the office. "Paperweight. A new up and coming group. Very hot right now." His dad wouldn't know 'Paperweight' from the 'Stones'.

William stared at Bill. "Well then, I guess I'll meet Christina when she gets back."

"I think you forgot something? You threw me out, remember? So you're not a part of my life anymore. In fact, when I leave here, I'm going straight home to pack my bags."

"Why don't we put all that unpleasantness on hold for awhile? At least, until I've met Christina?"

Bill smiled. It was exactly what he wanted to hear. Two weeks. He had two weeks to come up with something better. And he would. "All right, we'll wait for Christina to come home and I'll introduce you."

And with that, Bill turned and walked out of the office and towards the elevator. Charlotte had already left for the day.

Bill had won round one. He was still in his father's good graces—well not really—but at least his credit cards weren't going to be cancelled and he still had a magnificent multi-million dollar roof over his head. But more importantly, he could still get his hands on some cash—some desperately needed cash. People were depending on him—and he wasn't going to let them down, no matter what he had to say or do.

No matter what.

As Bill walked through the downstairs lobby, he pulled out his cell phone and dialed.

"It's me. I just came back from seeing the old man and he's threatening to cut me off." Bill paused as he listened to the other end. "I know, I know, don't get excited. I'll keep getting you the money somehow. I won't let you down, I promise."

A worried and pensive Bill shut his phone and strode to the exit doors.

*

William sat behind his ornate desk and calmly reached for his phone. He dialed.

"Get me everything on a Christina Matteo, a photojournalist at some rag called Streetwise Magazine, and get it to me now," he barked.

He replaced the receiver and stared hard at the closed door through which Bill had exited moments before.

CHAPTER 12

CHRISTINA WAS ENSCONCED in a tiny cubicle in a corner of the Streetwise Magazine office, downloading a series of photographs she'd taken that morning but her mind was not on her task. It had been three days since the accident and Christina had heard nothing from Bill Havenwood's insurance company. She was worried, very worried.

She'd spoken to Stanley Moore, the attorney for the Magazine and he'd confirmed all of her most horrible fears. She was definitely liable for all of the damages on Havenwood's Ferrari and she'd be lucky—damn lucky—if he didn't sue her for personal injury too—or for mental anguish—or for— Christina blocked the rest of Stanley's speech out of her mind. She just didn't want to think about it. In one sunny afternoon, her life had become a Greek tragedy and it was all Havenwood's fault.

That scumbag was just bad luck.

Suddenly Sue, one of the magazine's editors, put her head over her cubicle wall. "Christina, there's a Mr. Havenwood here to see you," she announced, before disappearing again.

Havenwood??!!

Shocked, Christina's hands started shaking and her breathing increased. Okay, here it was. The moment of truth when she'd find out how much the damages on that maggot's Ferrari were going to be. Or maybe he was here to tell her he was going to sue her for one million dollars in personal damages—or maybe two million—or ten? Oh, why did he have to be here at all? Why couldn't he just let his insurance company contact her?

Forcing her legs to move, she resolutely walked out into

the reception area. But as she entered, she stopped dead in her tracks. There—waiting for her was Mr. Havenwood all right—Mr. William Havenwood Sr., Bill's father, impeccably dressed in his Brooks Brothers navy suit and gray ponytail. Christina immediately recognized him from the pictures she'd taken of him outside his house days ago. But what could he want with her?

He came forward and extended his hand. "You're Christina, aren't you?"

"Y… yes." Christina was wary as she shook his hand. She briefly looked over his shoulder to Jenny who was sitting at the reception desk. Jenny shrugged her shoulders.

"I'm so glad to meet you," he smiled at her.

"You are?"

"Of course. My son's told me everything."

"He has?"

"You sound surprised."

"Well I… guess he would tell you." Christina was baffled. Why should William be so interested in the accident? Unless the Ferrari was his? "Look, I'm sorry about what happened…"

William halted her speech. "Say no more, Christina. I know I should have been told right away, but I suppose my son wanted to surprise me. And he did, the little devil."

Christina looked again over William's shoulder to Jenny who was completely engrossed in the conversation. Jenny again raised her shoulders in ignorance.

"Mr. Havenwood…"

"William, please." William smiled at her and Christina was thrown off balance. Why was he being so nice to her if she owed him or his son all that money?

"William," Christina smiled back at him. "Why are you here?"

"I want to invite you to the house for dinner, tonight, if you're free."

"Dinner?" Christina squeaked in disbelief.

"Yes, so we can all sit down together and discuss… the situation."

"Dinner?" Christina's voice was getting higher.

"Don't you think that would be the best course of action?"

"Well… I suppose…"

"Can you make it tonight?"

"Well… I…"

"Good." William was clearly in control. He pulled out a business card and started scribbling on the back of it. "Here's the address to my home and we'll say eight?" He handed the card to a perplexed Christina.

"I'm sorry, I don't have a car and…"

"Then I'll send my driver to pick you up; and I'll look forward to tonight." With that, William smiled again at Christina and then acknowledged Jenny briefly with a nod before striding out of the building.

Christina suddenly remembered he didn't know her address so that his driver could pick her up. She ran after him and opened the front door just as William was about to get into his limo.

"Wait." He paused to look at her as his chauffeur held the car door for him. "Mr. Havenwood, you don't know where I live."

William looked at her for a hard second before mysteriously replying. "But I do." He then got into the long black car, as did the chauffeur and drove away.

*

Inside the limousine, William grinned to himself. So, his son thought he could outwit him, did he? Think again.

William had had a background check done on Christina Matteo and had learned everything. She had been the other party in Bill's car accident from a few days ago and before then had never met his son. They were strangers to each other and William could tell by her puzzled behavior just now that she had no idea what Bill was up to.

Well, let's see what sonny boy would do tonight with the appearance of his 'so-called' fiancée returning early from her 'so-called' out-of-town assignment. How clever would he be then?

And how far was he really prepared to go with his little charade? William planned on finding out.

It was time someone taught that demon spawn of his a lesson.

*

Christina slowly came back into the office.

"What was that all about?" Jenny asked a shell-shocked Christina.

"I don't know but I feel like I've been bull-dozed with a steam-roller like they do on Saturday morning cartoons."

"You look it too." Jenny giggled. "And, of course, you're not going there tonight."

"Why not?"

"Chrissy!" Jenny was shocked. "Let Stanley Moore handle it. Don't get anymore involved with Billy Havenwood than you already are. He's bad news."

"But Jenny, aren't you curious what this is all about?

"No."

"I am. And why did he send his father? Why didn't he come here himself?"

"Exactly. Something's wrong here and I don't like it."

Christina lifted her nose in defiance. "I am going tonight and I am going to find out what those Havenwoods have up their perfectly tailored sleeves. I need to know what they're think-ing regarding the accident. It's always better to know what your enemy is planning rather than have no clue and be broadsided."

Besides, what about her revenge plan against Havenwood? Maybe she should think about resuming it? After all, she was being given a golden opportunity here to step into Billy Havenwood's private world—see where he lived, who his family was and maybe even learn his secrets. She couldn't pass this up.

"Then I'm going with you." Jenny went to retrieve her purse.

"No!" Christina shouted the word. "This is my mess and I'm cleaning it up." Besides, she wouldn't be able to put her revenge plan into action if her friend was there. Jenny believed that Christina had given up that idiotic scheme and that's how Christina wanted it to stay.

"But…"

Christina was determined. "No, Jenny." She looked at the concern stamped on her friend's face. "Don't worry, I'll be fine."

Jenny shook her head and sighed. "The last time you said that it cost you $50,000. What's it going to cost you tonight?"

CHAPTER 13

HER STOMACH WAS doing somersaults—Olympic, gold medal somersaults.

Here she was, in a short, black cocktail dress and pearls, in the back of a stretch limo, being chauffeured by a uniformed gentleman named Summers, on her way—to her execution. She felt like Marie Antoinette, in the lap of luxury and about to have her head chopped off.

Oh why, had she agreed to go? She should have listened to Jenny and let Stanley Moore handle this. She should have said no. She should have—

It was too late for 'should haves' especially since they were now pulling into the mansion's long, circular drive. Christina's eyes scanned the car's plush interior, wondering if it came with a barf bag, because she could use one about now.

The limo came to a full stop in front of the house's front doors. In about five seconds, she would again be face to face with him—Billy Havenwood. And she would actually be sitting down and sharing food with him. Could she do it? Could she act civil and refrain from what she really wanted to do… which was to scratch his eyes out? More importantly, if she had to eat with him, could she keep her food down?

Oh no, there it was again. Her stomach performed another gymnastic stunt—a triple backflip followed by a mid-air lunge followed by a nosedive into the black pit of hell. God, she wasn't feeling well at all.

Summers swung open her car door and gallantly offered Christina his hand. Taking it, Christina smiled her thanks and stepped out. The coolness of the fresh night air took her by surprise and she inhaled deeply. Oh, that felt good.

She turned her eyes to the entrance of the mansion. He was waiting for her behind those massive, double doors. What would he say? How would he act? Would he remember her? And what about this invitation to his house? Why was she here at all? Something about this whole thing didn't feel right.

As Christina ascended the steps to the front doors, they suddenly and magically opened. It's him, it's him, she thought as dread coursed through her system.

But it wasn't him. It was William, elegantly dressed in a tuxedo. "Christina, welcome. I'm so excited about you being here that I had to greet you myself," he proudly announced.

"Thank you for inviting me, William," Christina smiled tentatively as she entered the lavish home. The foyer floor was an elaborate pattern of black and white marble, and ornate vases and sculptures glittered in every direction. To Christina, it was all a blur.

"You look beautiful tonight," William gushed before looking down at her left hand and frowning. "But where's your ring?"

"Pardon?"

"Your ring? You're not wearing one?"

"Well, I… " Christina was baffled. What did it matter what jewelry she'd worn? Was there some cocktail dress bling bling etiquette she didn't know about? "I'm sorry, I don't know what you mean."

"Doesn't matter; we'll ask my son when he gets here."

"Bill's not here?"

"No, running late, as usual… and undependable, as usual but that's no surprise to you, is it?"

"No," a stunned Christina squeaked. Did he know that she knew Bill from way back? Knew all about his lazy, irresponsible ways? Was this more than a meeting to talk about the accident?

William took her arm and led her into a huge living room filled with French provincial furniture, gold-gilded mirrors and more priceless antiques. This room was called the salon and it reeked of taste and wealth.

"Would you like a martini, my dear?" he asked, as he walked to a drinks trolley where a prepared martini shaker sat.

"Yes, thank you." Christina looked around at her opulent surroundings. This was all so strange—so very strange.

William turned to her. "Please Christina, sit." He indicated the elegant settee couch in front of her. "I want you to consider this… your home." He turned back to pouring out the drinks and he smirked to himself as if enjoying a private joke.

Christina sat gingerly on the love seat and admired the exquisite paisley-print fabric. This was nothing like her charity shop, orange couch. And her entire dumpy apartment could fit in this one room alone.

William handed her the martini. "Being a photojournalist must be very exciting." He sat down on the couch opposite to hers.

Christina was surprised. "How do you know what I do?"

"My son told me."

"He did?"

"Of course, why wouldn't he?"

Christina thought about it for a moment. "Well, I guess he would. I mean you'd have to know if you're worried about the money."

William laughed out loud. "Well, you don't pull any punches. Direct and honest. I like that." He took a sip of his own drink. "When you're as rich as I am, Christina, you're always worried about 'the money'.

"Let me reassure you William that I'm a hard-working, responsible person who always pays her debts. I'm not a deadbeat."

"Unlike my son," William mumbled under his breath. He looked up and smiled at her. "So tell me then. What do you think of pre-nuptial agreements?"

Stunned, Christina paused a moment. What did pre-nups have to do with accident claims? "I… think they're a good idea, if you're the one with the money."

"And if you're the one with no money?"

"Then they're a good idea after you've seen a good lawyer."

William laughed again. He was certainly enjoying himself. "Beautiful and smart." He looked beyond Christina's shoulder as he watched Bill enter the room. "I can see why my son wants to—marry you."

Christina, who'd been in the middle of sipping her drink, suddenly choked on hearing his words and spluttered alcohol all over her dress. She lapsed into a coughing fit.

What the hell had he just said?

"Oh my." Smirking, William launched to his feet and handed Christina a napkin. "Are you all right, dear?"

Christina nodded. "Fine. Th…thanks." She tried to clear her throat.

Angry, William glared at Bill who was approaching them. "It's about time you showed up. Lost your watch?"

"You said dinner was at 8:30 and I'm on time so…" His words faded as he spotted Christina on the couch. His face, suddenly, turned white—deathly white—and he froze in shock.

Christina returned the stare. Billy Havenwood! She was finally meeting him again. The flip-flops in her stomach returned. Or was that the martini hitting the spot? No, it was him. Her breathing instantly picked up speed to match her racing heart. But wait! She wasn't going to be intimidated by this creep ever again. She'd made that promise to herself and she was keeping it. Slowly, she forced herself to stand up, prepared for an attack.

Her eyes never left his face.

Nor his, hers.

Christina raised her chin. "Hello there," she dared him.

The room went silent as all three of its occupants stared at each other—Bill with shock—Christina with wariness—and William with humor.

Bill, suddenly, let out the breath he'd been holding in a single whoosh mixed in with, "What the…" He stopped as he noticed his father watching the proceedings like a vulture about to swoop in on a corpse. He quickly regained his wits and smiled at Christina. "Christina, this is a surprise. What are you doing here?" God, what did the old man know, he thought to himself? Had he found out about the lie? Were the big guns trained on Bill now?

"Your father invited me. I thought you knew." Christina was taken aback. What was going on? And what was that niggling thought in the back of her brain that was trying to push its way through the thick, London fog her mind had become when 'he' had walked into the room?

"No, I had no idea," Bill smiled sweetly as he turned to William. "You didn't tell me… dad."

"Didn't I?" William innocently looked back at his son—as innocently as he could ever remember being—which was never.

"No. I would have remembered," Bill gritted his teeth behind a phony smile.

"No matter." William sipped his drink. "I thought we could all have dinner together and discuss… things. Why? Is there a problem?" He challenged his son.

"No, no problem." Bill grinned back, trying to appear cool and unruffled.

Christina wasn't really paying attention. She was trying to remember something William had said when his degenerate off-spring had walked in and she'd lost her focus. Something about her? Or was it about Bill? Or about her and Bill? Something about—suddenly, Christina gasped loudly. It was about her and Bill—and their marriage! Her stunned eyes swiveled to William.

"What did you…?" She never finished the sentence because at that instant, Bill rushed forward and pulled her tense body to his, planting a big, passionate kiss on her lips. Taken by surprise, Christina just let it happen. Two seconds later, Bill pulled back from her bewildered face.

"Sweetie, I need to speak to you in private." Smiling at his father, he grabbed her wrist and dragged her towards the French doors, which led outside into the gardens of the estate. If they were being chased by a pack of tigers, they couldn't have moved any faster.

Christina was so flabbergasted by what was happening that she didn't even think to snatch her wrist out of his hand. Her mind was completely focused on valiantly trying not to spill the contents of her martini glass.

Too late. The alcoholic concoction left a trail of spots across the expensive carpet as her drink sloshed from side to side.

In a millisecond, they were outside and Bill marched her further away from the house and out of view of William.

William watched them leave and then burst out laughing. He lifted his glass high in the air in a mocking toast. "Thank you, dear boy. I needed that." He continued to laugh as he made his way to the drinks trolley for a refill.

*

Christina was marched across the vast expanse of green lawn like a parent marching a three-year-old away from the candy aisle. And she, still holding onto that damn martini for dear life, was too confused to do anything about it. Her brain felt like it had been put in a blender.

They reached the edges of the large, Romanesque swimming pool and Bill finally released her wrist. He was breathing heavily and beads of sweat were starting to form on his brow. He frantically searched Christina's eyes.

"Look, whatever my father told you, I can explain."

Christina stared into those gorgeous, devious, evil, green eyes of his—and she was transported back in time to that crushing day at Cloverdale High. She was frozen.

Bill, too, was frozen as he stared back at this beautiful creature that now had the power to explode his privileged world apart. He waited for some response from her, anything that would tell him to proceed with his explanations and damage control.

They each held their breaths as the moment stretched to infinity.

Suddenly, Christina's brain synapses began to fire up again. Had William actually said something about her marriage—to his son? And had Bill actually called her 'sweetie'? And—oh my God—had he actually 'kissed' her with those vile, disgusting, drunken, 'who knows-where-they've-been' lips of his? She stared at Bill in total shock.

Bill was still waiting for Christina to say something. His eyes searched her face and he became frantic at her silence, "Christina?"

And on hearing her sweet name coming out of his filthy mouth, Christina instinctively did the only thing she could think of—

She threw the rest of her martini into his damn, handsome face.

*

And there Bill stood—in the middle of his beautiful gardens, beside the glittering, moonlit swimming pool—with alcohol dripping down his face.

Actually with gin and dry vermouth dripping down his face, if you wanted to get specific. And Bill wanted to get specific. He desperately wanted to get specific. In fact, in that instant, he desperately wanted nothing more than to put his tongue out and taste that delicious, enticing, alcoholic concoction—my God—it was all over his face. He could smell it—he could almost taste it.

He hadn't been this close to it since—well—since—

Bill stared hard at Christina who was warily watching him but his mind was on the alcohol instead. Should he put his tongue out and taste it? Just one lick? Who would know? Who would—? He had one millisecond to make a life-altering decision and he knew it. His tongue was so close—so close to it! He only had to—

And that's when it happened. Bill instinctively did the only thing he could think of— he jumped into the swimming pool.

CHAPTER 14

CHRISTINA WAS FLABBERGASTED. Had that moron actually jumped—fully clothed—into that gigantic swimming pool? Well, what else could you expect from a drunken fool?

She had come tonight to find out about the money she owed and as of yet, she hadn't heard one peep from either father or son. Something else was going on between those two and she wasn't going to stick around to find out what.

To hell with the both of them!

Christina plunked her empty martini glass on a lounge chair and started marching across the lawn. She was getting out of here and they could bloody well sue her for the money.

As Bill came up for air, he saw Christina quickly walking away. Oh crap! Was she going to look for his bastard father?

He had to move and move fast.

With swift, smooth strokes, Bill swam to the edge of the pool and hauled himself out of the water. His Armani suit was sopping wet and—oh great—he'd lost one of his custom-made shoes in the pool. But he couldn't waste any time thinking about that. He just had to catch that woman and plead his case. Or stop her from talking to his father at least, until he could plead his case. If there was one thing he could do right in this world, it was to bullshit talk his way out of anything.

Bill scanned the grounds. There she was—still marching across the property towards the salon doors. Thank God for large estates with expansive grounds.

He started racing after her, moving as fast as anyone could in a drenched suit and one shoe. "Christina, Miss Matteo, wait!" he yelled as he limped after her. "I can explain. Please."

Christina heard Bill calling after her but she didn't stop. She was getting out of here and no one was going to prevent her from doing that. God, why did these rich people have to have these large estates with expansive grounds? She felt like she'd walked a mile already.

Bill picked up his pace and was practically running after her. "Christina, just give me a chance!" He shouted after her.

If she made it back into his monster-of-a-father's lair, it was going to be all over for him. She would deny Bill's story and he'd be on the streets by midnight. Well, not the streets exactly—but definitely in a very, very cheap motel—the kind one lived in when you didn't have any credit cards or savings or anything. After all, what money he had made or could get his hands on this past year had gone to—but he couldn't think about that now. He just had to stop that blasted woman somehow.

"Fifty-six thousand dollars." Bill suddenly, yelled out.

Christina stopped, rooted to the spot.

He continued, as he limped closer to her. "My insurance company called today with the repair estimate. Quite a chunk of change, isn't it?"

Slowly, Christina turned to face him. Damn the man! She'd been serious about leaving this hellhole but now the enormity of the jam she was in came flooding back to her. She was in deep, deep trouble—the kind of trouble that can last for years and ruin your life.

Bill threw her his most charming, model-perfect smile as he inched closer to her. "My insurance company will be calling you—about the money, I mean."

Christina stared Bill down and did not return his pearly white smile. "I don't have it."

"That's not my problem." Bill leaned into her as if about to share a secret. "It's yours," he whispered into her face. Christina remained silent as she glared daggers at him, but he went on.

"Let's see, how long would your wages have to be garnished for you to pay off fifty-six thousand dollars? What are we talking here—twenty, thirty, forty—years?" Bill smiled again. "You get the fifty-six thousand dollar picture, don't you?"

Christina had had enough. "Let's cut the cute bullshit. What do you want?"

Bill laughed at her directness. "You scratch my back? I'll scratch yours?"

Christina's eyebrows shot up. "Right now, the only thing I'd be willing to scratch on you, are your eyes out."

Bill laughed again. The woman was quick and witty, and in spite of the mess he was in with his father, in spite of the fact that he desperately needed this woman's help—in spite of everything—he was enjoying himself. He hadn't had this much fun since, well since, the last time he'd met this hot babe when she'd smashed his car days ago. She'd turned him on then and she was turning him on now.

There was just something about her that attracted him so much. She was cool, calculating and strong, not to mention beautiful. She wasn't intimidated by his position or his wealth—he sensed it—and that was refreshing. But until he figured out what was really going on in that pretty, clever little head of hers, Bill knew he'd need to be careful—as careful as a snake charmer, if he wanted her to dance to his tune.

Christina's nerves were now at a breaking point. Here he was laughing at her again. Well, it was time to wipe that damn smile off of that handsome, devil face.

"Your father mentioned something about you, me and marriage..." Bill stopped laughing and Christina innocently continued. "I don't know where he got a ridiculous idea like that, but I'll go ask him."

She turned to walk towards the house but took only one step before Bill's hand latched onto her arm and stopped her. "Wait." His tone was imperious as his eyes bore into hers.

Christina returned the stare. "You've got exactly five seconds to explain everything before I march back into that house and get my explanations from your father." Disgusted, she looked down at his hand gripping her arm.

Bill's gaze followed hers and he quickly released her. Running his hands through his still wet hair, he let out a tension-filled breath. It was the moment of truth for him.

"Look… my father and I don't see eye to eye about things, about anything really. And he's very upset with me right now… for certain reasons. A week ago, the day of our accident actually, he threatened to cut me off. Out of the will, out of the money, out of his life."

"So what does your dysfunctional family life have to do with me?"

"Bottom line? He wants me to settle down and provide him with an heir."

Christina stepped back, putting space between them. "Wait a minute. I don't like where this is going."

Bill smirked. "Don't worry. It's not what you think."

"Then tell me what I 'should' think and make it fast because I'm two seconds away from getting the hell out of here."

"Look, Christina, it's just that I needed to stall for time to get back into that old goat's good graces and the only thing I could think of was if I told him I was getting married."

"And you told him you were getting married to me?"

Bill nodded. "I was on the spot and he hates all the women I know. The accident had just happened. You were fresh in my memory and your name just kind of popped out. I had no intention of ever producing the real Christina Matteo. I just needed a name I could spin some stories around. I wasn't ever going to involve you in this, I swear."

"Then why am I here?"

"I'm not sure. Why are you here? Did my father ask you to come?" Christina nodded and Bill turned pensive. "That sneaky bastard," he mumbled to himself.

Christina watched him like a hawk. So—Billy boy was in

trouble, was he? She continued, "He came to my workplace. I thought he wanted to discuss the money I owed you. Apparently not."

"No, not quite. My father owns the Fido Foods conglomerate and he has a lot of resources at his disposal. He probably had you checked out. That's how he knew where you worked."

"Then he probably knows I'm the one you were involved with in that accident which means he knows everything—that I'm not your fiancée and that you're scamming him." There, that should put a good scare into this bum, Christina thought.

Bill's heart skipped a beat. Did his father really know everything? Was Bill's head on the chopping block?

"Did he say anything about our engagement before I came in? Anything at all?" Bill anxiously asked.

Christina had an impulse to wildly lie and tell him that his father did know it all but she needed to play it cool and see where this evening was going to lead. Maybe she could be the one to spill the beans to William about Bill and watch the creep get thrown out on his sweet, marble-chiseled ass. Now that would be poetic justice. But she did no such thing as she turned her eyes back to his worried face. "No, not until you showed up."

Relieved, Bill let out a deep breath.

*

Inside the house, William was at the dining room window watching the show. The two, his son and that girl, had been out there on the lawn talking for a while now. His son was probably begging for her help and would probably use the money she owed him as a bribe to ensure that help—and she, of course would agree.

He didn't blame her or his rotten son, really. It's what he would have done if he were in his son's shoes. But then again, he, William Havenwood Sr., was much too smart to ever find himself in a predicament like the one his idiotic son was in. If he were going to lie, he would have tied up all the loose ends right away and brought the girl on board as soon as possible. He would have left nothing to chance.

"Bentley?" William called out.

A stodgy, British butler dressed in a black and white butler's uniform appeared. "Yes, sir?"

"Another martini, please; act two is about to begin."

"Yes, sir."

Bentley quietly disappeared and William returned to his post at the window. He laughed to himself. This evening was turning out to be more fun than a corporate takeover. And he didn't feel an ounce of sympathy for Bill. His rotten, lying son deserved it all.

CHAPTER 15

BILL WAS WORRIED. How much did his evil father know? His frantic eyes refocused on Christina. "I need your help."

Christina studied his desperate expression. If she played the upper hand she was holding, she might get out of paying for those damages to his stupid car and might also be able to be the one to spill the beans to dear papa Havenwood about the scam his little boy was pulling. Debt free and revenge—wrapped in one tidy, Armani package. Sweet.

"Okay, Mr. Havenwood, what do I have to do and what's in it for me?" Christina challenged him with a show-me-what-you've-got smile. Might as well play that upper hand and see what he puts in the pot, she thought.

"I need you to pretend to be my fiancée."

She played it cool. "For how long?"

"Six months."

"What?" Outraged, Christina almost yelled the word.

"Four months."

"No way!"

"Okay, okay; one month. I need your help for one month."

Christina pretended to think about it. That was better. She might be able to put up with this jerk for a month. Anymore than that and they'd have to lock her up for murder. His.

"And what exactly would I have to do in that month?"

"Not much, really. Just a few dinners with my father where we'll act like the happy couple." Bill gave a little nervous laugh.

Christina was not laughing. *Act like the happy couple???* God, was this going to involve touching—him? It was time to spell some things out to this lunkhead. "I'll put up with some hand holding and maybe a hug or two, but no kissing, got that?" When those drunkard lips of his had touched hers earlier, she would have tossed all her cookies if her stomach hadn't already been empty.

"If I don't kiss you in front of my father, he'll think it strange."

"Forget it. I'm outta here." Christina turned to leave. She was banking on how desperate he was and it worked because he balked.

"Okay. No kissing on the lips… but maybe a peck on the cheek every once in a while?" Bill pleaded. "Look, we have to make it believable for the old demon because he'll be looking for any signs of trouble between us that he can find."

Christina folded her arms across her chest. The scoundrel did have a point—some form of affection was always expected from an engaged couple, even she could see that. "Okay, a couple of pecks on the cheek but don't make a habit of it."

Bill was relieved. "I won't. You can trust me, Christina."

Christina almost laughed out loud. Trust him? Was he kidding? He was one of the biggest assholes she'd ever met and he was asking her to trust him? That was rich—Havenwood rich.

Christina continued to act cool. "So, we've discussed what I have to do, now you tell me 'why' I have to do it?"

"I'll pay for the damages on the Ferrari, fifty-six thousand dollars worth, and we'll call it even."

"I want it in writing," she quickly demanded. If she was going to make a pact with the devil, then she wanted that devil's signature on paper. Christina trusted Bill Havenwood as far as—never.

Bill smirked. Man, she was all business. He admired her for that—and respected her too. "All right, I'll see a lawyer in the morning." Bill extended his hand out. "It's a deal then?"

Christina looked at his outstretched hand as if it was a rattlesnake about to bite her. This was it. The moment she'd been dreading. If she shook on it, she wouldn't go back on her word. She wasn't built like that. She may hate Bill's guts and she may eventually tell his father everything, blowing his rich man's world apart, but for now, she'd pretend to be engaged to him and fulfill her end of this devious bargain.

Christina extended her hand out and placed it in Bill's. "Deal." They shook on it.

Suddenly, Christina felt as if a cosmic, electrical shock had surged from his hand into hers and for one split second, she felt an overpowering physical pull towards him. She hadn't imagined it. It had been real—like the pull the sun exerts on the planets. It frightened her and Christina gasped. She quickly pulled her hand out of his and looked up at him. Arrogant bastard! He'd felt it too. She could tell because he was smiling.

Bill had indeed felt the same physical pull towards her and he'd never felt anything like that with any other woman in his life before. This was going to be a very interesting month, he thought to himself.

*

Still spying at the dining room window, William watched the two shake hands.

"So, the appetizers are over and now for the main course," he threatened, as he smiled wickedly.

*

Christina faced the still wet-from-his-jump-into-the-pool-Bill.

"Okay, let's get this miserable, God-forsaken evening over with." She announced as she turned and marched towards the salon doors.

Bill quickly caught up to her and suddenly, grabbing her hand, linked his fingers through hers. Christina stopped and looked down at their intertwined hands. She tried to pull free but he wouldn't let her.

"What the hell are you doing?" she demanded.

Bill gave her a devilish grin. "I thought we could practice

the love thing a little before we go in and face Satan." He was so enjoying this. "Wanna try the pecking-on-the-cheek-thing too?"

Christina had had just about enough of his nonsense for one night. She glowered at him. "Mr. Havenwood, keep your… pecker… to yourself."

Bill burst out laughing. "I don't want to sound conceited but not very many women have said that to me."

With his movie star good looks and money, Christina didn't doubt it.

He continued, "And to hear my wife-to-be say it, well, kind of spells trouble for our marriage, don't you think… darling?"

Christina gave one good yank and broke free of his grip. "Keep laughing. I'm sure your father will see the funny side of this mess too."

Bill stopped laughing. He paused and turned serious. "Okay, here's the plan. I'll do all the talking. Any questions he asks, I'll answer. You just follow my lead."

"Really? So how did we meet and how long have we been dating?" Christina asked.

"Hmmm…" Bill rubbed his chin as he began to think. He had to get this right if he was going to fool that smart old coot.

Christina pressed on, "Come on. We have to get our stories straight if we're going to make this work."

"I'm thinking, I'm thinking." Bill was stumped. "I did tell him we kind of 'crashed' into each other when he asked me last week but I didn't mention the car accident."

Christina rolled her eyes. Maybe it was about time she took control. "If you told him that we 'crashed' into each other, then we'll say I was coming out of a store… Bloomingdale's… with packages and I didn't see you and I ran right into you. That happened…?" Christina's paused to think, "…let's say that happened three months ago. We've been dating for three months. Now about the car accident, we'll say we'd had lunch together and when we were driving away in our separate cars, I was following you too closely and smashed into you. A quirk of fate. We'll laugh it off.

Now what else? Let me think…" Christina paused to think some more.

During her entire speech, Bill had been gawking at her with respect and admiration. She was smart, beautiful and—crafty, he thought. He was going to have to watch himself with this one.

Christina resumed her litany. "Okay, we'll say we got engaged last week. You asked me to marry you. I said… 'yes'." Disgusted, she eyed Bill up and down. "If your father asks when we're getting married, we'll say a year from now because that's how long it takes to plan a wedding. After a month, we'll break up and tell him I changed my mind because I feel I'm not ready. That way the fault for the breakup is mine, not yours and your father won't blame you. How's that? Have I covered all the bases?"

Bill gave her a big smile. "Wow, what a good little liar you are, Miss Matteo. You're definitely going to fit into this family."

Christina gave him a cold stare. "For one month."

Bill smiled at her again. "For one month." Here he was—in one of the biggest messes of his life—and he had been in some doozies before this—and all he could think about was how much fun this woman was. He hadn't been bored for one millisecond and he couldn't wait to find out more about her. Oh—and had he mentioned how incredibly sexy she was too?

Christina, on the other hand, couldn't wait to get out of his presence. She needed quiet time, by herself, to think more about this little plan of hers. Revenge always had to be planned out to the smallest detail if it was to work successfully. Billy Havenwood didn't want to make any mistakes in front of his father regarding his little scam, and she didn't want to make any mistakes in front of Billy. It took a scammer to scam a scammer, and she was going to be the best of the lot.

CHAPTER 16

CASUALLY, WITH MARTINI in hand, William walked back into the salon just as the happy couple was walking in through the French doors.

William smirked, "Why, there you two lovebirds are. I'd almost given up on you."

On seeing his father, Bill awkwardly slung his arm around Christina's shoulders and pulled her close to his side.

"We haven't seen each other all day." He glanced down and gave Christina a 'lover's' smile before turning back to his father. "You know how it is. Or maybe you don't?" He dared his father.

William sipped his drink while eyeballing his deadbeat son. "You're all wet," he smirked slyly. "What the hell happened to you? Christina push you into the pool?" He laughed.

Bill pretended to laugh too. "Don't be ridiculous. I fell in. It was an accident." Tension engulfed the room as they glowered at each other.

Both men knew it hadn't been an accident.

Christina was becoming uncomfortable with Bill's heavy, wet arm still wrapped around her shoulders. She could feel heat emanating from his body into hers and she was suddenly aware of him as a living, breathing, attractive male.

And there was that pull again—like two magnets coming together. It was craziness. She must be going mad. And to top everything off, pressed up against the big lug as she was, her dress was getting wet from his still sopping suit.

Gritting her teeth, Christina plastered a fake smile on her face and looked up at Bill. "Darling, you're getting me wet."

Aware of his father's laser sharp focus on them both, Bill gazed down at his 'fiancée' and cockily replied, "I should hope so." He gave her a wink.

William rolled his eyes as he continued to sip his martini and Christina gritted her teeth even more. "You should really go get changed," she continued. She pushed at him trying to get out of his embrace but had no luck. He was hanging on tight.

"She's right. You're dripping on my Aubusson rug," William piped in as he approached the couple and wrapped his arm around Christina's other shoulder. "Get changed and I'll keep my beautiful daughter-in-law-to-be company. We have so much to talk about." He gave his son a sly smile as he tugged Christina to his side.

Bill glared back at his father as he reluctantly let Christina go. "Be gentle... dad," he gritted. "Christina's not used to our family ways and I don't want you scaring her away."

"But of course, dear boy. I promise to be on my best behavior. This lovely creature has graced our home and I will do everything in my power to make sure she's treated... the way she should be... treated." William gave his son an enigmatic smile.

Bill was suddenly uneasy. He didn't trust the old vulture and he didn't want this girl hurt by the apocalyptic war that had been waging for years between his father and himself.

Bill lowered his eyes to his fiancée and gave her a little smile, "I'll be back sooner than you think... sweetie." He then gave William a tight smile before calmly walking out of the room.

*

The second Bill was out of the room, he raced towards the opulent staircase. He shot up the stairs, taking them two at a time, all the while unbuttoning his jacket and loosening his tie. Running down the upstairs hallway, he sprinted into his bedroom and started yanking off his wet clothes. No time to lose. Who knows what could be said down there without him.

He threw his jacket, pants, shirt, and everything else

haphazardly around the immaculate, richly decorated chocolate brown suite as if he was stripping down to a fast forward button.

Naked, he started rifling in his massive closet for his dinner jacket and pants. He needed to hurry. His whole life could right now be exploding downstairs.

*

The minute Bill was out of the room, William, steered Christina to one of the couches.

"Please sit my dear and I'll get you another drink." He moved to the drinks trolley and started pouring another martini. He gave her a sly sideways look. "How long have you and my son been seeing each other?"

Poised and cool, Christina pasted a smile on her lips. "We've been seeing each other for three months."

William studied her as he approached with the drink. She's calm and composed, he thought to himself. Not a flinch or nervous tick. She had looked directly into his eyes and lied to his face with the expertise of someone like—well someone like himself—an accomplished, sophisticated liar. What talent! Oh—he liked this girl and his respect for her was growing by leaps and bounds. His moronic son didn't realize it but he would have his hands full with this one.

William gave her a wide smile as he sat down opposite Christina. "So for three whole months my son has been keeping you a secret. I wonder why?" he quizzed.

Christina sipped her martini and skillfully looked at him, "I don't think it was so much 'keeping it a secret', William. It was just that we, Bill and I, needed time to find out where the other one stood in this relationship... before we made any formal announcements."

"And did you find out?"

"Oh, I think we each now know where the other one stands," Christina cryptically replied. "And we're both going into this new phase of our relationship with our eyes open."

William smiled inwardly to himself. She's weaving the truth into her lies, he observed. How brilliant was that? A master's stroke. He couldn't have done any better himself. If he weren't playing dumb, he would have right now stood up and given her a standing ovation.

"Yes, that's so important... to know the temperature of the water before one jumps in," William nonchalantly replied, all the while coolly studying Christina.

"And I bet the water can get very hot around here," Christina remarked as she casually sipped her drink.

"What do you mean?" William was suddenly even more interested.

"Only that I know there's friction between you and your son. Bill has told me a little about it and I sensed some tonight," Christina parried. There take that, Mr. Havenwood Sr.!

She wasn't going to meekly sit here for who knows how much longer, waiting for that jackass-of-a-fake-fiancé to return and be grilled by his father as if she was on the witness stand. She needed that fool here to help her with her answers and for him to listen to what she was saying so that they could both keep their stories straight. And the only way to put an end to William's questioning was by doing some questioning of her own. Didn't they say that the best defense was a strong offense? Christina was no mouse and she was going to be the one in control of these two snarling tigers, father and son, not them in control of her.

She innocently continued, "You two don't get along?"

William gave a little exasperated laugh, "My son and I each think we're right. But we can't both be right, now can we?"

"And you think Bill is wrong?"

"Well, I'm not saying he's wrong, but one of us is and it isn't me." William finished his martini in one gulp. He knew what Christina was up to—the girl was giving as good as she was getting. Oh, she was definitely a formidable opponent and he liked that a lot. What a breath of fresh air to have come into this house!

He smiled at her then. "What do you think, Christina? Which one of us is right then and which one's wrong?"

"Well, from what I can tell, you're both right and you're both wrong."

"A cryptic answer for a cryptic question. What do you mean exactly?"

"Only that you're two very strong, stubborn personalities and you're each 'right' when discussing your own lives but both 'wrong' when discussing each other's."

William laughed uproariously. "How diplomatic of you." He was impressed and he was rarely impressed by anyone or anything these days. He was far too old and had seen far too much to be so. But this girl—she was different.

And she certainly wasn't afraid of him. He could tell. Everyone in his life was afraid of him—his employees, his business rivals, even his imbecile-of-a-son—but not this young lady. She didn't fear him at all and he found that invigorating. Christina Matteo was definitely a worthy opponent and he so loved the 'fight'.

Christina, on the other hand, was starting to feel a little hot under the collar. Oh—where was that idiot? And why was he taking so long?

*

The 'idiot' was, at that moment, flying down the staircase at breakneck speed. He had cleaned himself up as best he could and was wearing a black dinner jacket and pants, and white shirt and black tie.

Bill ran through the foyer and skidded to a stop at the closed salon doors. He steadied himself as he straightened his tie and ran his fingers through his still damp hair. He hadn't had time to run a hair dryer through it and the best he could do was just to comb it back. Luckily for him it was already drying in places. Unbeknownst to him, dressed as he was in black tie and slicked back hair, he looked liked a 1940's debonair, movie star hero.

Taking one last deep breath, he put his hands on the doorknobs and slowly turned them. The double doors parted and he nonchalantly sauntered in, as if he hadn't a care in this world.

His eyes quickly sized up the situation. Both his father and Christina were seated on opposite couches and seemed engrossed in each other's company. Oh, he prayed everything had gone all right.

William was the first of the two to see him. "So the prodigal son returns," he wisecracked.

Christina, having had her back to the doors, turned around and when she saw Bill dressed as he was, her stomach did a somersault. Bloody hell, the bastard was handsome, she thought to herself. But then again, most devils were. But why had her traitorous stomach fluttered like that when this Beelzebub had walked in? It was empty, of course. That's why. She hadn't had a thing to eat all night.

William and Christina both rose as Bill walked further into the room. Bill came to stand beside Christina.

"Everything all right, sweetheart?" he enquired, as he studied her face for any signs of trouble or a secret signal or anything. He was worried.

Christina smiled at him, "Of course. Your father's been a perfect gentleman."

"I treated her with kid gloves," William piped in. "She's very charming, Bill, and very beautiful. You've found yourself a diamond in the coal, a jewel-of-a-girl." Oh—how he was going to enjoy challenging the both of them with this monstrous lie of theirs. What fun!

Bill was wary. "Then you approve of us getting married?" he questioned, placing a protective arm around Christina's shoulders.

Christina's stomach fluttered again. Damn it! What was wrong with her? She needed to remember who this was—Billy Havenwood, High School Asshole—the one who'd been responsible for the most traumatizing day in her life and who was now forcing her to participate in one of his devious schemes for his own benefit—that's who. Don't be fooled by the looks of the outside of the package, it was the inside that mattered. Beautiful garbage—that was what Bill Havenwood was, and she needed to remember that. Christina's racing mind was pacified.

She focused back on the conversation between father and son. William was speaking.

"Why, of course, I approve. To think that one day soon this house will be filled with grandchildren." William approached Christina. "Welcome to the Havenwood family, my dear." He bent and kissed her on both cheeks. "You are exactly what I needed." His eyes became watery.

Christina was surprised by this show of emotion from William. Was he about to cry with happiness? "Thank you, William," she accepted.

Bill had also seen the unshed tears in his father's eyes and was stunned. His father never cried! In fact, he never remembered having seen him cry. Never. You have to have a heart to cry and his father didn't have one. But hey, if his impending marriage brought tears to dear old dad's eyes, that could only mean one thing. Bill was back in the Havenwood billion-dollar fold. He was secretly elated and he smiled at William. "Christina and I are very happy that you're happy, dad."

William pasted on a phony smile. The glistening eyes with unshed tears had been a nice touch, he thought to himself. At least those theatre days in London when he'd been a teenager hadn't gone to waste. And the best way to win in any game was to disarm your opponent with kindness and acceptance—a trick William had used successfully many times in business. Then as soon as your adversary has let his defenses down, you go in for the kill.

Who the hell did his brainless son think he was dealing with anyway? William was almost insulted to think that his son believed him to be that stupid to fall for such a scam.

Getting married indeed! His son was an irresponsible, alcoholic, hard partying, hard living mess who would never come within sniffing distance of marriage. Marriage would put a crimp into that boy's lifestyle. After all, how would he explain a wife to all of his many slut girlfriends?

William graciously smiled at the couple again. "Shall we go to dinner then?" he invited politely.

CHAPTER 17

THE GILDED, ORNATELY decorated dining hall was as impressive as the rest of the house. It had been decorated in French Rococo style and the massive dining table could have easily seated twenty. Seventeenth century Dutch paintings hung from the walls, and taste and elegance abounded everywhere.

Fine bone china and sterling silver flatware adorned the antique table. Two silver candelabras sandwiched a centerpiece of fresh flowers and the lights from the candles glistened off of the crystal glasses. The room was not only a feast for the stomach but also for the eyes.

William was seated at the head of the long table. Bill was sitting on his left and Christina to his right, allowing the couple to face each other. The shrimp cocktail appetizers had been served and the trio had just begun to eat.

Bentley, the stodgy butler, was pouring wine into their glasses. As he approached Bill's glass, Bill quickly covered the top with his hand and stopped him.

"No thank you, Bentley. I'm driving Christina home later."

"Very good, sir." The butler nodded and moved away.

Christina had witnessed the little exchange and was surprised. Billy Havenwood had actually refused alcohol? That was something she'd thought she'd never see.

And when had drinking and driving ever stopped him before? She remembered all the stories she'd heard in school about his legendary drinking and driving exploits—disgusting as they were—and that had been before he was even old enough to drive! Maybe tonight, he was trying to impress his father by being on his best behavior. Yes—that was it.

But William had noticed nothing. He was completely focused on Christina. "My dear Christina, you're already doing me good. I can't remember the last time my son and I actually sat down together for dinner," he observed, as he popped a shrimp into his mouth.

"Fourteen months, twenty one days and..." Bill looked at his watch. "...Sixteen hours," he commented in a blasé voice.

William cocked an enquiring eyebrow at him as if to say how the hell would you remember that? Bill sarcastically smiled at his father, "The dinner party you gave for the Latimers? It was over a year ago."

"Well, well, so it was. A whole year." He quickly turned back to his daughter-in-law-to-be. "Christina, can you believe that? My son and I haven't dined together for more than a year." He gave Bill a look of disgust. "And yet I'm home practically every night. After putting in a hard days' work, I don't have the energy to go gallivanting elsewhere."

Bill pretended to ignore the cutting remark about his lifestyle as he aggressively started attacking his own shrimp cocktail.

Christina studied the two. What a pair they were! The room was practically suffocating with bad karma. And here she was—stuck between them—in a disaster of titanic proportions that was just beginning.

She swiveled to William, "William, you have an incredible home. It's lovely."

"Why thank you, my dear but I'm afraid all the credit belongs to my dearly departed wife."

Shocked, Christina eyed Bill. "Your mother is dead?"

A pregnant three-second pause permeated the room.

Damn, damn, damn, Christina thought. She'd made a mistake; a big one. If she were truly Bill's fiancée, she would know whether his mother was alive or not.

"She lives near Phoenix. That's dad's idea of a joke," Bill replied. Oh no, he thought. Had his dad caught that one?

William had indeed caught 'that one'. He pretended to be confused as his gaze wandered from one to the other and back again. He chose to focus on Bill, "My dear boy, you've been dating for three months and you've never told your fiancée whether your mother was alive or not? But how can that be? These are things lovers talk about when they first get together." William gave his son his complete attention as he waited for an answer.

Another three-second pause swept the room as Bill's thinking processes froze. Christina, on the other hand, began to smile inwardly. At first, she'd been shocked by her faux pas but then she remembered she was here to get revenge on this nightmare-of-a-man. And although she may have agreed to his devil's one-month bargain, there was nothing in it that said she was supposed to make it easy for him. Christina innocently looked at Bill, waiting for him to bail them out of this predicament.

William persisted, as he scrutinized his son, "Well?"

Bill turned to Christina, "But darling, I've told you about mother. About how she and dad divorced five years ago and she went to live on the commune in Arizona? Don't you remember?" Bill's eyes implored her to agree with him.

He was sweating again, Christina thought to herself. How wonderful! She turned to William, "You know, I completely forgot. Bill did tell me. It must have slipped my mind with all the excitement of getting engaged." She turned back to Bill. "We'll have to invite her to the wedding, honey bunny."

"Of course, sweetie pie," Bill readily agreed.

William turned back to Christina, "Yes, it's true. My loon-of-an-ex-wife left all this to go live like a hippy in the desert. How crazy is that?"

"Maybe the desert's not as hot as hell?" Bill cracked slyly, as he bit into a shrimp.

"If this is such a 'hell', then how come you're still here?" William tersely responded.

"Because I'm the devil's son. It's in my blood to stand the heat," Bill angrily shot back and the two glared at each other.

The tension was suddenly broken when Bentley and an under butler walked in to serve the main course of beef bourguignon, steamed green beans and mashed potatoes.

They expertly removed the appetizer dishes and served the meal before quietly disappearing. Both father and son slowly turned away from each other and focused on the hot food in front of them.

Christina casually speared a green bean and addressed William. "Bill mentioned that you owned Fido Foods. It's unbelievable to think that dog food did all this." She let her fork sweep the luxurious room.

"Yes, isn't America wonderful? I came here with nothing, but I worked hard and I made something of myself."

Ignoring his father, Bill addressed Christina, "Fido Foods is my father's flagship company but he owns many, many others. He's a very busy man."

William gave his son a sideways dirty look, "Yes… and unfortunately industriousness is not hereditary."

"Maybe it skips a generation?" Christina slyly piped in as she dug into her mashed potatoes.

William burst out laughing. "My sentiments exactly," he said. He turned to his son and poked him in the arm. "She's charming, absolutely charming." He was almost giddy with excitement.

Christina could tell by the sour expression on Bill's face that he didn't appreciate her catty remark. Good. She was here to stir things up anyway.

She addressed William again, "They say that behind every great fortune there's a great crime. Is there, William? A great crime, I mean?"

The room fell silent. Bill stopped midway to putting a forkful of beef bourguignon into his mouth and smirked at his father. "More like many, many smaller crimes instead," he cracked sarcastically.

William looked from one to the other. Silence. Suddenly he burst out laughing again and he was laughing so hard that he had to dab his wet eyes with his napkin.

"Oh Christina, pardon my French but you do have balls."

His laughter subsided as he gave Bill a dirty look. "At least one of you will have them in your marriage." Bill glowered at his father but didn't say anything. William turned back to Christina. "Tell me, Christina how did you and my son meet?"

"I was coming out of Bloomingdale's loaded with packages. I didn't see Bill on the sidewalk and we kind of crashed into each other."

"And I picked her up… literally and figuratively," Bill interjected. "I took one look at Christina and knew I was in love. She was the one for me."

William raised a skeptical eyebrow at his son before turning to Christina. "And what about you, my dear? I suppose it was love at first sight for you too?

"No."

Bill choked on a green bean and both father and fiancée stared at him. He took a sip of water and tried to push it down his throat.

Christina continued, "What I mean to say is it wasn't love for me right away but he was so persistent, that it came on gradually. Before I knew it, I was involved." She gave Bill a small, tight smile.

William took a sip of his wine. She was doing it again—twisting the truth with the lie. How clever this girl was.

William's eyes scanned the both of them. "Like a bad rash, you mean? You don't know it's there until it starts itching?"

Christina laughed, "Something like that." She refocused her gaze on her fiancé. "And then when Bill proposed, I had no choice. I had to say 'yes'. Who knows what my life would have been like, if I'd said 'no'."

Oh, she is good, William thought as he continued to sip his wine and watch the two of them. His useless son was no match for this smart female.

"Tell me, Christina, are you marrying my son for his money?" There—let's see how she answers that one, William thought, as he put a spoonful of beef bourguignon into his mouth.

Bill nervously looked up from his food. Oh no—how was she going to answer that one without sounding fake if she denied it or greedy if she acknowledged it?

Composed and collected, Christina gave William an unruffled sideways look. These two bozos were not going to fluster her—no matter what was thrown her way. That was a promise to herself.

"Of course," she replied, as she too calmly put a forkful of the beef concoction into her mouth.

"How interesting," William's head swiveled in his son's direction.

Bill uncomfortably glowered at Christina. "Dad doesn't know you're joking, sweetheart." He gave her a secret eye signal as if to say 'what the hell are you doing?'

"But I'm not, my love." Let him panic, Christina thought. She swiveled her gaze back to William. "What I mean to say, is that I do… love… your son very much William and the money is just a part of who he is." God she'd almost choked on the word 'love'.

Relieved, Bill gave his dad a small smile. "She loves all my parts."

"Even the defective ones?" William quipped.

"You mean the ones I inherited from you?"

"Not bloody likely. More from your mother's side of the family, I'd say."

Bill turned to Christina. "Mom's side is more… fun."

William refilled his glass as he also addressed Christina. "Yes… the crackpot side. Let's hope your future children… my beautiful grandchildren-to-be… don't get stuck with those rotten genes." He sat back in his chair and perused Christina. "So my dear, you're marrying for love and money. Blunt, honest and to the point." He gave Bill another forceful jab to the arm. "I do like this girl."

Christina laughed. "Now the real question you should have

asked me William was this. If my little love pot over here…" she cagily glanced at Bill, "…were to lose everything tomorrow, would I still marry him?"

The room went silent.

Intrigued, William quipped, "And would you?"

Bill's eyes darted nervously to her face. What the hell was going to come out next out of that perfectly shaped, luscious mouth of hers?

Christina let him sweat it out for a few seconds more before answering. "Of course I would. How could I resist a handsome face like that?" She gave her fiancé a little laugh. Bill visibly relaxed and Christina continued as she addressed him directly, "Besides, we don't need money, darling. We have our love to live on."

Bill pulled at his collar as if it was suddenly strangling him. "That's so romantic, lovebug. I wonder where Bentley is with the dessert."

William snickered. He was having a blast tonight. Although this girl may have struck a devious bargain with his lying, idiotic offspring, it was obvious she wasn't going to make it easy for him. Attuned to every flinch, fidget and nervous tick from his son, William was in heaven. Oh—if only he could have had this entire evening videotaped so he could have replayed it over and over again!

At that moment, Bentley the butler walked in with a bottle of French champagne elegantly cradled in a sterling silver ice bucket.

"Ah… time for a toast," William announced.

As Bentley began to pour the champagne, he reached for Bill's glass and Bill again stopped him, covering the crystal flute with his hand.

"No thank you, Bentley," he said.

"How can we toast to your impending nuptials without champagne?" William demanded.

"I'm driving Christina home later."

"Oh, don't be daft," William rudely interrupted. "One sip won't make a difference, not to your pickled constitution anyway."

Slowly, Bill removed his hand and Bentley filled his glass with the bubbly.

"Now…" William raised his glass high in the air as he stood up. "A toast to the happy couple."

Bill warily looked at Christina before standing up too.

Slowly, Christina followed suit and pasted another phony smile on her lips. God—how much more was she going to have to endure this evening?

William gave a big grin as he focused on Christina. "My dear, you are a breath of fresh air that has swept into this old house and I approve most heartily. For once, my son…" he gave Bill a look of disgust before turning back to Christina, "…has done something right."

"Gee thanks… daddy," Bill sarcastically piped in.

"Shut up," William barked at Bill before again turning to Christina. He raised his glass even higher in the air. "To Christina and to your upcoming marriage. May it bring the both of you all that you wish for—love, joy, togetherness…" he slyly eyed them both before continuing, "…honesty, truth and intimacy."

Christina squirmed a little as she suddenly felt a twinge of guilt. Love, honesty, truth and intimacy? These were the things that real lovers would be toasting to and here she was—toasting to a big lie. Maybe this wasn't right—lying like this, fooling this old man? Maybe—?

And then she turned her gaze to Bill—and suddenly, she remembered everything. Billy Havenwood, revenge and the accident money she owed him, that's why she was doing this. And she was determined to go through with it no matter what it cost her—no matter what.

Christina raised her glass even higher in the air and gave William a wide confident smile. "Thank you, William."

Bill was feeling a bit uncomfortable himself. Yes, he was ecstatic that things were going so well with his old man and yes, it looked like he was back in the money but—well—he just had this feeling of impending disaster to come.

He looked up to see Christina studying him. She smiled and saluted him with her raised glass. He returned the gesture. Yes, things were going very well and this beautiful woman had helped him pull it off. He couldn't have picked a better partner-in-crime if he'd advertised for the job. She was gorgeous, witty, clever—and smart. Very, very, smart. Smart enough to handle his bastard-of-a-father and that was saying a lot.

William continued his speech. "Christina my dear, here's to you and my son. May you both be very happy together and produce many grandchildren." He toasted them both with his glass before taking a sip of his champagne.

Christina received the toast graciously and took a sip of her drink.

Meanwhile, Bill was suddenly eyeing his drink as if it was a snake. And no venom could have been as deadly as that champagne was to him right now. In fact, he'd be safer drinking the venom. His hand holding the glass started to shake slightly. God he wanted to drink it, he wanted to very badly. But he couldn't, not after—everything.

Eyeing his father and Christina, Bill brought the glass up near his lips and pretended to sip as he turned away from them. He turned back and was relieved to realize that neither of them had witnessed the 'fake' sip. He quickly put the tempting glass of bubbly down on the table.

William turned then and eyeballed his son, "Well?"

"Well what?" Bill inquired.

"Go and kiss your bride-to-be and seal the bargain."

"What?"

"Give her a kiss, you moron."

"I… I…"

"Go on."

Bill nervously stole a quick glimpse of Christina. Yes—she was mad—steaming mad from the look on her face. Should he dare?

"You do know how to kiss, don't you?" his father bullied.

"Of course, I do," Bill angrily retorted.

Wickedly, William turned to Christina. "I hope he doesn't need step-by-step instructions on your wedding night too," he chuckled.

Bill's gaze was still focused on Christina and he gave her a sheepish 'I-have-no-choice' kind of smile.

Christina was not amused. This was not part of the bargain but how were they going to squirm out of it without getting Williams' suspicions aroused? A kiss between an engaged couple was no big deal but there was no way she was going to let that imbecile give her that kind of kiss. What was she to do? And oh no, was he actually starting to walk around the table—coming towards her?

Bill was scared as he stiffly inched around the massive, mahogany table slowly. What was she going to do if he tried to kiss her? Would she call this whole thing off and tell his father the truth? He turned to William, who was standing there with expectation on his face.

"You know it's not a true engagement until the happy couple seals it with a kiss of love," his father innocently proclaimed.

Damn him, Bill thought, as he faced his evil father. He then looked at Christina who was silently warning him with her eyes to not try anything—or else. What was he to do? If he didn't kiss her, his father would know something wasn't right and throw him out. And if he did kiss her, Christina would break their deal and his father would throw him out.

He was trapped and his whole life was about to blow up in his face in the next five seconds.

Bill nervously approached Christina like a condemned man shuffling to the gallows. He smiled uneasily as he started to lean into her—getting closer and closer to her lips. He was so close he could smell her heavenly perfume—he was now only a fraction of an inch away now from those lush, pillow soft lips of hers—he could almost taste them—

And that's when it happened—Christina sneezed.

Stunned, he looked at her, not quite realizing he was being thrown a lifeline. She sneezed again and this time Bill backed away.

"Sorry, sweetie but you're wearing that cologne again. Did you forget that I'm allergic to it?" Christina artlessly remarked.

"What?"

"Your cologne. I'm allergic to it. Remember?" Christina fumed to herself. God, maybe his father was right—maybe he was a moron.

"Right, my cologne. You know passionflower, I did forget. Sorry." Bill quickly pressed a speedy kiss on her cheek and moved like lightning back to his side of the table.

"Well, that wasn't much of a bloody kiss," William cracked.

Bill looked at his father and shrugged his shoulders as if to say 'oh well.' William rolled his eyes upwards and sat back down. On the outside he looked disappointed but on the inside he was in seventh heaven. That had been the funniest display he'd seen all year. He'd wondered how they were going to get out of kissing each other and now he knew. And it had been all the girl's idea, of course—not his useless son's. She was the clever one in that unholy union.

Oh, what a fabulous time he was having. To watch his son sweat with nerves as he approached her angry visage—what fun! William never wanted this magical, enchanting evening to end.

Christina, on the other hand, couldn't wait to get out of there. There had been no way in blazes she was going to allow that swine to kiss her on the lips again and she'd come up with the fake sneezing fit at the last millisecond.

William was speaking to her again and Christina focused on him. "Sorry, William?"

"I was saying about your engagement ring. I can see my son has 'forgotten' about that too."

"I didn't forget. We wanted to tell you first," Bill smiled at his dad.

William ignored him. "Tomorrow Christina, you will…"

At that moment, Bentley stoically walked in. "Excuse me, sir. A telephone call from Mr. Downey for you." He gave a slight bow.

"Ah yes, I was expecting that call." William apologetically smiled at Christina. "Excuse me, my dear. I shan't be a moment." William rose from the table and walked out of the room. Bentley followed and closed the door behind him.

Christina's phony smile evaporated as she angrily turned to Bill. "Mr. Havenwood, I thought we'd agreed to no-kissing-on-the-lips," she enunciated through her gritted teeth.

"What did you want me to do? This old man was expecting a display of affection and if we'd been a normal engaged couple, it would have been no big deal."

"But we're not 'normal', are we?"

Bill paused for a second as he studied Christina. Should he dare? Why not? "I think we might have to reconsider the 'no-kissing' thing."

"Excuse me?"

"Look, Miss Matteo, if we're going to fool this old geezer, we might have to give each other a kiss on the lips… once in awhile… maybe a couple of times, if the situation calls for it… like an emergency… like it was tonight." Bill watched Christina intently as he cringed inwardly waiting for the bomb to detonate.

But it didn't as Christina returned the stare. Even she had to admit the fool did have a point. But that didn't mean she wasn't going to go down without a fight.

Bill was wary and he continued. "I mean you can't go on sneezing forever, can you?" He gave a nervous laugh.

"It won't be forever. It'll only be for one month, remember?"

"Right… one month." Bill paused. Might as well bring out the big guns. He continued, "For which you're getting paid fifty-six grand."

The mention of the sordid, dirty money seemed to hang in the air between them like polluted smoke.

Bill continued, "Look, if this plan is going to work I need a few 'things' from you to make it believable to my father and 'kissing and hugging' like two people in love is one of them."

If she wasn't willing to do that, then this entire deal might as well blow up in his face right now. Maybe it hadn't been the smartest thing he'd ever done—to bring these points up now when his father could come back at any second but it had been a hard, nerve-racking evening on him too and Bill was getting tired. He almost wanted it to be over—one way or another.

Christina studied him. His father had been wrong. Billy Havenwood did have balls—to bring this subject up now when his father could come back at any minute and she could tell him everything? William Sr. didn't see it but his son was just like him. He was ruthless, manipulative and cold, as Christina knew first hand from that awful day years ago—and she would never forget that, no matter how much charm he oozed now.

"Let's get one thing straight, Mr. Havenwood. I will not prostitute myself."

"But you are taking my money."

Christina's eyes bored into his. "I owe you fifty-six thousand dollars. It would take a lifetime for someone like me to pay that back. So this is about survival, not greed. Do I make my position clear?"

"Crystal." Bill gave a little smile. He had to admire her. She did have spunk—loads of it—and she was also very beautiful, all fired up like this—so alive—so magnetic. Now if he could only get her to kiss him.

Christina, on the other hand, was so steaming mad, that she wanted to launch her plate of food at him and wipe that smarmy smirk off of that handsome face. But the bozo did have a point. There might be moments when they would have to 'play' the happy couple-in-love for his father's sake—and that meant kissing him, however revolting that was to think about. If her revenge plan was to move forward, she'd have to do this. So, she'd just close her eyes and think of England.

"Don't forget, I want to see a legal contract tomorrow with all the details, financial and otherwise spelled out," she postulated.

"Does that mean you're agreeing to comply with my 'terms'?

"Only when absolutely necessary so don't make a habit of it, capice?"

"Loud and clear, madam." Bill smiled to himself. Well, well, well—he had actually gotten his way with her—of sorts. It was a start anyway.

God, Christina hated that smile on him. Gloat all you want, Mr. Havenwood. You may have won this battle but you are definitely not going to win the war.

She sarcastically smirked back at him. "But no kissing tonight, darling. I have a headache from your cologne, remember?"

Bill burst out laughing. She was becoming more and more intriguing to him as the minutes of life ticked by.

The door opened and William came back into the room and addressed Christina as he sat down. "I do apologize Christina for having to take that call."

"What did Downey want?" Bill casually asked, as he sipped his water.

"Maybe if you'd show up for work more and sit in on meetings, you wouldn't have to ask."

Bill sarcastically commented to Christina. "Stephen Downey is my father's VP and right-hand man. He shows up for work everyday."

William glared at his son. "We're discussing strategy on how to fight those damn ecological terrorists that have been hounding me for months."

"You mean The Guardians of Mother Earth?"

"Yes, that's the damn bunch." William was clearly exasperated.

Christina watched the two carefully before piping in, "I've heard of them. Quite a persistent group."

"I'm sure they're no match for the great William Havenwood," Bill chimed in.

"I'm sure they're not!" William added forcefully. "Now

enough about those ruffians. We need to discuss you, my dear. Tomorrow, you'll have your bags packed and ready by noon when my chauffeur will pick you up."

"What bags?" Christina was confused.

"You know… your things."

"I'm sorry, William, what are you talking about?" She turned to Bill who was equally confused.

"You're moving in here, of course," William stated as he refilled his wine glass.

"What?" Shocked, both Christina and Bill had spoken the word together.

"Yes. You're a member of this family now and you'll live here until your wedding and then after your wedding, of course."

"No, I don't think so, William."

"No? No?" He turned to Bill. "What does she mean 'no'?"

"Christina and I may be getting married dad but we're not moving in together… before the wedding," Bill stiltedly explained.

"But of course you are. Isn't that what all young people do nowadays?"

"Not Christina. She's very… traditional." Bill's eyes landed on her face and implored her to help him. God, things were going badly again.

"Yes, William. I don't believe in… living in sin. It's either marriage or 'nothing' for me." She emphasized the word 'nothing' as her eyes trained back onto Bill's panicky face.

"My dear, I will not have a future Havenwood living in a dump. Summers, my chauffeur told me how you were living when he came to pick you up tonight."

Bill jumped in, "I'm going to move Christina into a better apartment until the wedding."

"Nonsense. Christina will live here starting tomorrow." William was firm.

"But William, I… I can't. We can't live together… without vows," Christina stammered.

William sighed with resignation and grabbed her hand,

squeezing it protectively like a father would to his daughter. "Your ethics are admirable my dear, especially in this day and age."

At that moment, one of the under butlers walked in pushing a trolley cart with coffee cups and dessert plates with pieces of chocolate mousse cake piled high with whipped cream. He began to serve.

William pushed back his chair and stood up. "Unfortunately, I've got some calls to make but you two enjoy your dessert," he pointed to Christina. "And you I will see tomorrow when you move in here."

"But… but…?" Christina was speechless.

"Dad, I thought it was settled. Christina and I are not going to live together before the wedding."

William turned to his worried son. "And you won't be. She'll have the bedroom next to yours. It's a huge house, after all." He turned to a stupefied Christina. "You're one of us now, my dear and this is where you belong." William gallantly lifted her hand to his lips and kissed it. "Till tomorrow then." He gracefully walked out. The under butler followed him and the 'engaged' couple was left alone.

Feeling as if she'd just been battered, bruised and bullied, Christina lifted her gaze to Bill. He gave her a little apologetic smile and lifted his hands in the air as if surrendering.

"I had no idea, honest." Slowly, he could see anger creeping into her face and Bill began to stammer. "There… there was nothing I… I could do." Silent, Christina kept giving him a deadly look. "You've seen the way he is. Once he makes up his mind, that's it." Still no response from her. "I know this wasn't part of our bargain but… maybe we can make it work? What do you say?" Bill held his breath.

Still giving him the evil eye, Christina slowly stood up from her chair.

"Is that a 'yes'?" Bill squeaked.

Cupping both hands together, Christina scooped up some of the Chocolate Mousse cake from her plate and began to walk around the table towards Bill with it. Bill watched her progress and knew what was coming—but he was rooted to his chair. She came to stand beside him with the gooey, creamy confection.

He looked up at her then. "You wouldn't dare."

As if on cue, Christina smashed the cake onto his head—pushing it down hard—making sure it was deeply imbedded into his hair. Pieces of it fell onto his expensive dinner jacket, but Bill just sat there and took it like a gentleman. A part of him knew he deserved it for putting her through so much this evening.

He looked up again at her angry face. "Hope you don't want coffee with that too," he quipped.

Christina was so mad at him she couldn't even speak. Grabbing a linen napkin she roughly cleaned her hands of the creamy mess, reached for her purse and started walking towards the door.

"Christina, wait!" Bill jumped up, brushed off as much of the gooey mess as he could and ran after her.

*

Spying, William had his eye plastered to the scant two-inch opening of his study door that overlooked the foyer. He suddenly saw the dining room door being flung open and Christina marching away. She had her purse and she was heading for the front doors—and boy, did she look livid.

William snickered to himself. Wonder what she'd said to his conniving son when he had exited the room? Giddy, he watched as she threw open the massive front doors and stalked outside. She was on the move and there was no stopping her.

A blink of a second later, he witnessed his deceitful progeny spring out of the dining room and charge after her.

And what the hell was that on his head and smeared onto his jacket? Could it be? Yes it was! Cake. It was the chocolate mousse cake—and his son looked bloody ridiculous.

William shut his study door and burst out laughing. The girl had hit him with the cake! Oh, what a perfect topper to a wonderful evening.

William devilishly giggled to himself. "The family that lives together, sticks together… and sticks it to each other," he mumbled.

What a bumpy ride this was going to be for his son. And when that ride was over, so would be the Havenwood gravy train.

CHAPTER 18

BILL'S JAGUAR WAS slowly crawling beside Christina as she was purposefully marching down the long drive away from the house. The driver's window was down and Bill was pleading.

"Christina, please let me drive you home."

Christina was so angry with him, with his father, with the entire situation that she didn't want to look at him, hear him or speak to him. All evening long, she'd been railroaded into doing things she didn't want to do and now, these two assholes were expecting her to move in and live with them in that huge house— 24/7 for an entire month???!!!

It had been one thing to pretend to be a 'couple-in-love' for a few dinner dates with his father but now this creep expected her to do it 24 hours a day for thirty days under the laser-sharp eye of his commandeering, overbearing father? How would she survive that?

Christina kept walking.

"You can't walk home. It's almost midnight," Bill continued his pleading.

Christina didn't say anything. Her anger had neutralized her vocal cords.

"Christina, get in the car… please."

Bill studied her furious face. He couldn't blame her, really but he should have known his devil father would do something like this. He should have known his father would push and push and push until he'd gotten his way about everything. He was always trying to control Bill's life and Bill should have expected him to try to control Bill's marriage too.

"Let me drive you home, and if you don't want to say anything to me then you don't have to," Bill continued.

Christina reached the end of the drive and walked through the open gates. She opened her purse and retrieved her cell phone. She was calling a cab and getting the hell out of here.

Bill stopped his car beside her. "You know, it'll take a cab an hour to reach this place. Do you really want to wait an hour until 1 a.m. in the middle of nowhere?"

Christina put the phone to her ear and Bill heard her say, "Hi, I'd like a cab at 14025 Wickingham Drive." She paused, then exploded, "What? An hour?" Angry, her eyes flashed to Bill and he smiled. "Never mind. Thank you," she barked into the phone before slapping it closed with one push.

Bill reached over and opened the passenger door invitingly. Christina glared at him as she reluctantly plopped herself into the plush seat. She slammed the door shut and stared straight ahead through the windshield, refusing to look at him.

Bill studied the beautiful creature beside him. "I know you don't want to talk to me but you're going to have to tell me where to take you. I don't know where you live."

Christina gave him a deadly fierce look. If looks could kill, as the old adage said, he'd have been incinerated to burnt toast right about now.

Then, reaching into her purse, she pulled out a small pad and pen and wrote the words, 'twenty-third and sixth' on it. She shoved it in front of Bill's face.

Bill looked at the paper and then at her set expression. "The silent treatment still on?" he asked. Not answering, Christina stared straight ahead. "Okay then," he surrendered. He put the Jaguar in drive and squealed onto the street.

Christina gave him a sneaky look from under her lashes. She knew that not speaking to him may have been childish and immature but it was the only thing making her feel good right now—so what the hell!

*

They had been driving for twenty minutes and neither of them had spoken a word. Christina sensed rather than saw his eyes dart towards her several times. She knew he was worried. She would be too, if she were in his position. Good. Let him worry. Let him panic. Let him suffer. It looked good on him. But then anything would look good on that handsome mug.

Suddenly, Bill reached over to turn on the radio and his arm accidentally brushed her leg. Christina felt the physical sparks again—almost as if he'd given her a static shock. She quickly pulled her leg away from him.

"Sorry," he mumbled.

So—he'd felt it too, she sensed. The damn car was too small anyway and they were sitting too close to each other. And God— the heat inside the Jaguar was getting to be unbearable. Christina felt like she was on fire. She reached out to her passenger door, fumbling for the window button. Suddenly, the window magically slid down half way and she turned to Bill who gave her a big grin.

Christina gave him a full-on glare before turning her frozen face away. She heard him sigh with frustration.

Suddenly, Christina's calculator brain started to add a few things up. When William had first mentioned the "moving-in thing", she'd been furious. Things were quickly spiraling out of her control and she'd felt like a bed sheet on a clothesline, being pulled by the wind.

But, thinking logically—if—she were to move in with those dastardly Havenwoods, she would have complete and total access to Bill's life—to his routines, his secrets, his everything. It would be so much easier to dig up dirt on the bum if she was inside the nest rather than if she was outside looking in. What if this 'moving-in thing' was actually a blessing in disguise?

Christina instantly made up her mind. She would definitely move in tomorrow and with the unlimited access to his life that alone would give her, she could dig up enough manure on Billy Havenwood to bury him.

Bill turned onto Twenty-Third Street and in seconds he pulled over to the curb outside her apartment building. As he shut off the engine, Christina was already fumbling for the door handle.

"Do I get a goodnight kiss?" Bill sarcastically cracked.

Ever so slowly, Christina turned her head towards him, exorcist style and gave him another chilly glare.

"That looks like a 'no'," he continued, half to himself. "So, are you moving in tomorrow?" Christina kept glaring at him. He was clearly becoming frustrated as he let out a quick breath. "Say something," he said in exasperation.

Christina paused, for effect. "There's cake in your hair," she enunciated before opening her door. In a flash, she was out of the car and walking towards her building.

Panicking, Bill scooted out and looking over the top of his car, shouted after her, "I'll come by tomorrow. We'll talk then."

Christina pretended to ignore him and just kept walking. Let him wait for his answer. Why should she make this easy for him? She reached her front doors and disappeared inside.

Frustrated, Bill slapped the roof of his car before getting back in. Tomorrow, he was going to have to use every ounce of charm, fast-talking and brains he had to convince Christina to help him. But would she? Or was this the end of the Havenwood billion dollar line for him?

He revved up his Jaguar and pulled out into the city traffic. Crap—he wasn't going to sleep a wink tonight.

Meanwhile, as Christina entered her apartment, she threw her hands up joyfully in the air and shouted, "Yes" to the heavens. This was going to work! Her revenge plan was actually going to work! It was time Bill Havenwood paid his dues.

Wow—revenge really was sweet and she could almost taste it.

CHAPTER 19

BILL HAVENWOOD WASN'T the only one who hadn't slept all night. Christina hadn't either but for very different reasons. Ideas and plans had raced through her mind and she'd spent the night detailing everything in her journal. By morning, she had a clear picture of what she was going to do to make the big jerk suffer.

By 9 a.m., Christina left a message for Jenny at the Streetwise Magazine office to meet her at Napoleon's Restaurant for lunch. Jenny and her little daughter Taylor lived in the same apartment building as Christina. She had knocked on Jenny's door this morning but her friend had already left for work.

*

"I'm engaged." Christina blurted out the words in a rush.

Both Jenny and she were seated at a small table near the back of ritzy Napoleon's. Being lunch hour, the chi-chi eatery was already suffocating with patrons.

Stunned, Jenny froze with her wine glass poised in mid-air. "But you haven't been on a date in months."

Christina sheepishly rolled her eyes as if to say, 'you never know'. Dawning crept into Jenny's eyes. "Is it Stanley Moore? Have you been secretly dating Stanley Moore?"

"Stanley?"

"I knew he had the hots for you. And then he offered to give you free legal advice about your car accident and it all adds up. Good ole Stanley."

"Jenny…"

"He's a good catch you know, being a lawyer and a good one at that." Jenny took a big sip of her wine.

"It's not Stanley. It's… Bill Havenwood."

Jenny spit out her wine, spraying it onto Christina's blouse. "What?" Jenny choked out.

Other patrons turned their heads to stare at the commotion.

Christina lowered her voice. "Before you start screaming, hear me out." She eyed Jenny as she wiped at the stain.

And for the next ten minutes, Christina gave Jenny a blow-by-blow account of what had happened and her devil's bargain with Bill Havenwood. When she'd finished, Christina studied Jenny's face. "Well?" she tepidly inquired.

"I don't like it," Jenny announced. "You're the one who's going to get hurt, not him."

"Not this time, Jenny. I've got the upper hand."

Jenny shook her head 'no'. "Guys like him always win in the end, Christina. And from what you've said about the father, he sounds just as bad."

"Are you going to support me or lecture me, because I'm telling you now, I'm going through with this, no matter what."

"Chrissy, please, think about it some more…"

"No more thinking. Are you going to help me?"

Jenny scrutinized her friend's determined face. She sighed. "You know I will. So what do you want me to do?"

Christina reached into her purse and pulled out a key. She gave it to Jenny. "This is a spare key to my apartment. Just keep an eye on the place and pick up my mail. I may have a few bills that need to be mailed out on certain days so my checks won't bounce, so I'll leave them on the kitchen table for you. I'll come back and forth during the month, but I may not be able to get back to the apartment everyday."

"Anything else?"

Christina wrote the Havenwood address on a napkin. "This is where I'll be. If you need to reach me, call me on my cell. Don't come by the place, whatever you do. Billy Havenwood might recognize you. You were at that school a lot longer than me and he might remember you."

"That's true. I was there for almost six months before I left."

"Right. He doesn't remember me but if he sees you, it might trigger some neurons in that booze-soaked, fried brain of his and then he might connect you to me and game over."

"Got it."

Content, Christina smiled. "Now, let's eat this overpriced slop before it gets cold." She pointed to her plate.

Jenny laughed. "I'm sure it tastes better than crow which is what you'll be eating if this thing backfires on you."

*

After lunch, Jenny went back to work and Christina went back to her apartment, but not before stopping at a newsstand to buy ten different magazines.

On entering her flat, Christina checked her answering machine for messages. There were none. So, Havenwood hadn't called and it was after 1 p.m.? Interesting. But Christina wasn't worried. She knew he would call.

Now—to begin her plan…

Christina dumped all the magazines she'd bought onto the table. She then retrieved scissors, glue and an envelope from a kitchen drawer, and went to work. Christina was going to send Billy Havenwood a blackmail letter through the mail—with cutup magazine alphabet pasted together to form sentences on paper—just like they did in the movies.

And why was she doing this? She needed to know whether he truly did have secrets—and this was one way to flush it out of him.

Christina reasoned that she'd send him this anonymous blackmail letter and watch his reaction. If the only secret he was hiding was their phony engagement, Bill would show her the letter so that they could compare notes on who might have sent it. If he didn't show it to her, then—bingo—she'd know he definitely did have more secrets to hide… and she'd find them.

It was quite clever—her little plan. And it would work too. Christina was sure of it.

CHAPTER 20

HER PHONE RANG after 3 p.m. Christina knew who it was before she even answered it. "Hello?"

"Christina, it's Bill Havenwood."

She knew that. "Hello, Mr. Havenwood." She made herself sound cool.

"I was wondering… would you have dinner with me tonight?" Christina didn't respond. "Christina?" He sounded anxious—and nervous.

"Why?" She was going to make this as difficult for him as she could.

"I've been to a lawyer and had an agreement drawn up…just like you wanted. I've got a private table at Carbiri's and I can pick you up at 7."

So, he'd done what she'd asked. He really was desperate. "No thanks. I'll make my own way there."

He breathed a sigh of relief. "Great, see you then."

"See you then."

Christina shut her cell phone.

So—a private table at Carbiri's? La di da, he was sparing no expense.

*

They were seated opposite each other at a private booth away from prying eyes. Carbiri's was full but the crowd was reserved and elegant. Everybody was minding his or her own business.

Christina had taken a cab there and on her way, had mailed her 'blackmail letter' to Bill. She figured that if she were to move into the mansion tomorrow, he should receive the letter the day after that—and she'd be there to see what he'd do and how he'd react.

Now, sitting across from him, Christina's heart fluttered a little. Dressed in an expensive suit and tie—another Armani probably—Bill Havenwood looked every bit as handsome as he had the night before. And she'd seen the admiring glances from some of the women that had passed by their booth.

Bill was speaking again and Christina re-focused on him.

"I managed to keep my old man at bay by telling him you needed more time to pack before moving in," he said.

"And what did he say to that?"

"That you'd better be there by tomorrow."

Christina gave a little laugh. "Does your father always get what he wants?"

Bill gave her a steady look. "I don't know. You tell me."

Christina smiled. She was playing her part so well, she was proud of herself. "Mr. Havenwood, last night I…"

He interrupted her. "Can you please stop calling me Mr. Havenwood? My name is Bill." He sounded irritated.

"I know what your name is." And it wasn't Bill, it was 'asshole', Christina thought to herself.

He gave her a smirk of resignation as he read her mind. "You don't like me very much, do you?"

"Do I have to?"

"No, you don't. You just have to pretend to love me."

The air in the booth sizzled with tension as she studied him with a disgusting look—the kind you'd give a bug you've just squashed under your shoe. Bill knew she didn't like him—he could see it in her eyes—but he didn't care. He was so damned attracted to her right now he could barely sit still.

She was beautiful and smart and something else—he couldn't quite put his finger on.

Yes—he was attracted to her all right and he'd had enough experience with women to know that despite her feelings of dislike towards him, she was attracted to him too. He had caught the fleeting glances she'd given him last night and just now, when she'd thought he wasn't looking. And he could feel the chemistry between them—even sitting like this across from each other in a public restaurant—it was there—whether she was willing to admit it to herself or not.

He reached into his jacket pocket and pulled out the legal contract he'd had drawn up that morning and a ring box. He placed them both in front of her.

"I went to a very discreet lawyer that my father has never heard of and had that drawn up this morning as my lady commanded." He carefully studied her reaction.

Christina reached for the document and unfurled it.

She quickly scanned the contents. Even though Christina wasn't a lawyer, she could make enough of it out to know that it clearly spelled out the terms of the bargain that they'd agreed to last night—her month-long 'engagement' to him in exchange for cancellation of her $56,000 debt.

As she was scanning it, she spotted the last clause. It basically said that if his father were to discover the contents of this agreement through any means of hers, the agreement would become null and void and she'd have to pay Bill the money after all. So— the degenerate didn't trust her completely, did he? Well, Christina had no intention of telling William about this little agreement but she had every intention of telling him anything else she might find out about his son.

Christina reached into her purse for a pen and signed the document.

Bill was surprised. "Don't you want to take it to a lawyer first?"

"Why? Shouldn't I trust you?" She gave him a full-on glare.

He gave her one of those Havenwood sly smirks that she hated so much. "You can trust me, Christina."

Christina smiled back. "Good, I'm glad…Bill." She was proud of her Oscar-worthy performance so far tonight.

And had he actually smiled at her when he'd heard her call him by his first name just now? Interesting. Maybe she should start being nicer to him and have him lower his defenses? After all, you could catch more flies with honey—or in this case, a big cockroach named Bill Havenwood.

She refolded the contract and handed it back to him.

Unbeknownst to them both, a very interested pair of female eyes was secretly watching them from across the room.

When the woman saw Christina sign the document, her cat eyes narrowed dangerously. And they turned even more deadly, when she saw Bill open what looked like a ring box…

*

"What do you think?" Bill was holding the open ring box in front of Christina.

The box was marked Tiffany's and the square cut diamond ring inside looked to be about six carats. It was vulgar, flashy and ostentatious, not Christina's style at all.

She raised her eyes to him. "How much did that thing cost?"

"$250,000."

"What?" Christina gasped.

Bill smiled at her stunned expression. It was the first time he'd really seen her at a loss for a smart, witty comeback.

"It's what my bastard father would expect a Havenwood to wear… and he'll also choke on the bill when he gets it. It's a win-win situation for me," Bill laughed.

"But…" The cost of the ring had thrown Christina off her game. With that kind of money, she could put a down payment on a house, buy a car, take a trip, so many things. "It's so expensive!" she gushed.

Bill laughed again. "Not to me."

Christina raised her eyes to his. "What's a quarter of a million to a billionaire, right?"

"Something like that, especially when it's daddy's money."

To her, that kind of money could change her life but to him it was a piss in the ocean. Well, let's see what it'll mean to you, Billy Havenwood, when you end up with nothing by the end of this month.

And he didn't completely trust her about the ring either. She'd read the clause in the contract that stipulated the ring would have to be returned intact when the engagement had been terminated otherwise she would be liable for its replacement cost. It hadn't said what that cost was. She was already in debt to him for fifty-six grand. She certainly didn't want to add another two hundred and fifty thousand to that. Christina was going to have to be very careful with this extraordinary piece of jewelry.

Bill popped the ring out of its box and reached across the table for her hand.

"What are you doing?" Christina tried to pull her hand free but he was holding on tight.

"Making it official." He started to slip the ring on her left hand.

"I can do it myself, thank you." Everything was suddenly becoming too real for her and she was feeling uncomfortable.

"No, I'll do it." Determined, he finished slipping it on and admired his work. He raised his twinkling, teasing eyes up to hers. "How about a kiss?"

Christina tugged her hand out of his grasp. "Go to hell."

Bill laughed uproariously. "And it's official. We're engaged."

Bill was thrilled with how well everything had gone tonight. He'd been prepared to have to beg for Christina's help but once again she'd completely surprised him. She'd agreed to everything without a hiccup and the entire evening had progressed smoothly.

It was obvious she'd done some thinking of her own over-night and come to the realization that she would benefit from this arrangement as much as he would. There was something in it for him and there was something in it for her.

Smart girl.

He studied her now as she studied the enormous glittering rock on her finger. She was even more beautiful tonight, if that was possible, and seeing her like this—with his ring on her fin-ger—gave him goosebumps, good goosebumps. What would it have been like if this had been a real engagement between them, if she'd agreed to marry him for real, if he was going to have the promise of a family of his own?

Nah, that was nonsense. He'd never really thought about marriage before—hell he'd never really thought about anything before—except for the booze. But now, today, when his head was clear—he was suddenly thinking about it.

Bill gave his 'fiancée' another admiring perusal. Wonder what she looked like naked with only the ring on, he thought to himself?

Christina chose that moment to look up at him.

"We're now bound together, you know," he teased.

"For one month."

He smiled at her attempt to keep everything business-like. He admired that about her. Every woman he'd ever known had been a pushover and they'd spoiled him, made him soft. Not this one. He'd have to be the one to fight for anything he wanted from her. And want did he want from her? Deep down, he didn't really know.

"When do you want Summers to pick you up tomorrow?" he questioned, breaking his line of thought.

Christina pretended to act shocked. "You mean my fiancé isn't going to carry me across the threshold himself?"

His smile dropped. "I've got appointments tomorrow. Sorry." And he did have a lot to do—commitments he didn't want any-one finding out about.

"Three in the afternoon should be fine. I'll be ready then."

Christina had seen the change in him, how he'd gone from smiling to dour and evasive when he'd had to answer for his time tomorrow. Yes—there were secrets there to be uncovered. Christina was elated to know her intuition had been right all along.

*

When Christina had been reading Bill's legal document, William Sr. was also reading a copy of that very same document in his company office. A private detective named Mackenzie was standing in front of him.

"Any problems getting this?" William inquired of the P.I.

"Nothing that your money couldn't handle," he coldly responded.

William continued reading the legalese. It was all spelled out in black and white, the nefarious deal his nincompoop son had made with the girl. And he would bet his last dollar on earth that it had been the girl's idea to get it all in writing. She was smart enough not to trust his irresponsible son and it was obvious she wanted her interests protected. Good for her! William admired that.

William looked up at the detective.

"Good work, Mackenzie. Now get back to our other little project and get me as much dirt as you can on those Guardians of Mother Earth scum."

"Whatever you say, boss."

"Have you found out anything new?"

"Only that they have a secret source of funding, but we suspected that."

"Any ideas who that might be?"

Mackenzie shook his head. "Whoever they are, they've cleverly concealed their identity behind several offshore banks but it's only a matter of time before we find out."

"Well, make it sooner rather than later. They're costing me money and they're making me look bad in front of the public."

The detective gave a subservient nod before walking out. William frowned before returning to the document in his hands.

*

The coffee was being served by one of the Carbiri waiters and Christina took the opportunity to study the restaurant's interior.

She could see why this place was so expensive. The ambiance was refined, the wait staff was discreet and the food was excellent.

The waiter moved away and she refocused back on the big jerk sitting in front of her. The meal had gone well. The food had been delicious and Billy Havenwood had acted the perfect gentleman. He hadn't even had a drop of alcohol all night. His wine glass had remained untouched and he had sipped only water. He obviously was on his best behavior and if Christina hadn't known what he was like, he could have easily fooled her into believing what a caring, sincere, gentleman he was, instead of the drunk she knew him to be.

"You didn't touch your wine tonight? Not to your liking?" Christina inquired innocently.

Bill's eyes lowered to the wine glass in front of him before quickly returning to her face. "I'm driving. You can't take a chance with even one drop these days," he casually responded.

What bullshit, Christina thought. Who was this lush trying to kid? Her, obviously.

Suddenly, out of the corner of her eye, Christina saw a tall, willowy redhead with the gorgeous face of a model come barreling down on them. She instantly recognized her as the woman Bill had been having the argument with outside this very same restaurant last week when Christina had initially been tailing him with her car.

The redhead approached the table and as she came closer, Christina saw her face more clearly—beautiful but cold and at the moment, very, very angry. Bill hadn't seen her because she was coming up behind him.

"Who the hell is this?" the redhead snarled at Bill's back as she gave Christina a look of disgust.

Bill literally jumped up from his seat as he stood to face her. "Stephie, what are you doing here?" He was clearly stunned to see her.

Stephie—or whoever the hell she was—put her hands on her hips, confrontation style, and glared into his eyes. She was as tall as he was and just as beautiful. They made a very handsome couple together, if a little too perfect.

She ignored his question. "Tell me who this bitch is," she growled, raising her voice loud enough so that the other patrons began to crane to see what was going on. Even the waiters stopped their serving duties to watch.

And Christina was loving every moment!

Bill sensed that they'd become the center of attention.

"Stephie, calm down. This isn't the place for this," he patiently intoned, trying to diffuse the awkward situation.

The redhead's eyes swiveled to Christina's left hand where the huge diamond ring was glistening under the candlelight.

"Where'd you get that?" she snarled at the other girl.

"Bill gave it to me. We're engaged." Christina coolly responded.

Bill briefly closed his eyes as he prepared for the storm to come.

Stephie swiveled her furious gaze back to Bill's face. It was one thing to suspect what that 'ring' was but to have it confirmed by this little nobody was something else.

She'd sat at her own table all night watching the pair of them until her nerves had reached their stretching point and against her cousin's advice—the person she'd been having dinner with—she had jumped up and marched towards their table.

Bill put his hand on her arm and tried to steer her away from the table. "Stephie, stop this. We'll talk tomorrow."

She threw his hand off as rage boiled up within her. "So you've been fucking her and me at the same time?" she snarled at him at full volume.

Bill remained silent but his face was turning beet red.

Christina giggled to herself. Oh, what fun this was! How embarrassing for him, being confronted by his jealous girlfriend and in his favorite restaurant! Maybe they'd throw him out and ask him never to come back? Oh, she could only hope. She secretly giggled even more.

"Stephie, please…" he began again but the redhead interrupted him.

"Mummy was right about you. You really are a prick!"

And with that pronouncement she hauled back and gave him a hard slap across his face. Whack! Some of the patrons gasped. Bill just stood there and took it.

That must have hurt, Christina thought as she smirked to herself. His left cheek was even now turning more red than it had been a few seconds before.

"Feel better?" Bill calmly intoned.

With a look of pure hatred, Stephie turned and marched away—out the door.

Bill looked around the room. Everyone was staring at him and it would probably make the gossip rounds by tonight. He'd made a big mistake in conducting his private business with Christina here at Carbiri's, where he was known and where his 'crowd' hung out.

He sighed as he held out his hand to her. "I think we should go."

"What? No dessert?" Christina cracked.

"'I think we were the dessert," Bill mumbled, as he stared at all the interested faces.

*

He had insisted on driving her home.

Christina studied him as she sat beside him in the small confines of the Jaguar. He'd been silent since they'd left the restaurant.

"You should put some ice on that when you get home," she threw at him.

He threw her a quick glance as he drove. "Look, I'm sorry you had to be a part of that."

"I'm not. I enjoyed it."

"You what?" Bill was shocked.

Christina giggled. "I've only ever seen that happen in the movies. It was fun to see it happen in real life."

Bill laughed and gave her a quick look of admiration before turning back to his driving. "You really are a cool customer, Christina Matteo."

Christina shrugged her shoulders. "I'm only here for a month, remember? It's really none of my business what you or your girl-friend do."

"So you're telling me, I can see all the women I want this month while we're engaged?" He was curious to see how she would respond.

"You can have a harem for all I care, Bill Havenwood."

"Really?" He smiled. He'd never had anyone 'not' be inter-ested in him before. This was certainly different.

"Sure," she continued. "Just like I can have a harem too."

"What?" His smile dropped and Bill experienced the first pangs of jealousy. He'd never been jealous before and he didn't really know what this feeling was.

"You can't really expect me to stop having my own… relation-ships this month, can you?" Christina innocently asked.

"Yes I can. I'm paying you fifty-six grand to 'stop having rela-tionships'," he angrily threw back at her.

"Funny? I didn't see that in your contract tonight."

"It's implied." He gritted between his teeth.

They reached the outside of her building and he pulled up to the curb.

"Don't worry. I'm discreet. Unlike you," Christina parried back.

Bill gave her a long, hard look. "I'm sorry about Stephie. We'd been seeing each other off and on for the past two years but it's been over for awhile."

"So don't tell me, tell her," Christina quipped, as she opened the car door.

Bill reached for her arm and stopped her. "Is there… some-one?" He had to know. For some reason, he just had to know.

A few seconds ticked by as Christina studied him. "Thank

you for the...entertaining... evening Mr. Havenwood," she slyly smiled at him and got out of the car.

He was so much fun to tease and it was best if she kept him slightly off balance where she and her affairs were concerned.

Bill watched her as she entered her building. He'd never met anyone like her before. Cool, calm, collected and smart enough to handle his wicked father. Yes, this was definitely an intriguing woman and he had one month to get to know her better!

CHAPTER 21

IT WAS 7 p.m. and Christina was sitting at the Havenwood's massive dining table with William seated at the head of it to her left. And she was in the hot seat. William was asking her questions—lots and lots of questions.

And where was her big jackass of a fiancé? Who knew!

Christina had no idea where he was or if he was even coming home tonight. She hadn't heard anything from him since he'd dropped her off last night.

Summers, the Havenwood chauffeur, had promptly shown up at her building today at 3 p.m. and had driven her and her suitcases to the mansion. One of the maids—and there seemed to be an army of them—had shown her to her sumptuous bedroom next door to Bill's and had even helped her unpack. Her name was Tilly and she'd told Christina to ask for her personally if she needed anything.

There'd been a large bouquet of roses on a side table near the floor to ceiling windows in her bedroom, and a card with her name on it propped up against the vase. She'd torn it open and read, 'Welcome home'. It had been signed by William.

She then looked around the enormous room and spotted a goldfish bowl on her bedside table. A small goldfish was swimming inside and there was a little tag propped up against the glass. All it said was "Samson".

Christina approached the little fish and bent down to stare at him.

"I guess we're going to be bunkmates, Samson," she said to the fish.

Nice touch, Christina thought. Ever the sophisticate, William had thought of everything. But from Bill there was nothing. Not a card, not a letter, not a phone call. And he hadn't shown up for dinner either.

He'd told her last night that he was going to be busy today. Christina had thought he meant he wasn't going to be there for her arrival. But surely he'd show up for dinner on their first night living together as future husband and wife, wouldn't he?

But he hadn't.

And when 7 p.m. came and went, and it was time to sit down to dinner with William, Bill was nowhere to be found.

And William was now grilling her!

"So Christina, you don't know where my son is?"

That was the fifth time he'd asked her that all ready.

"Sorry William, it's been a hectic day with me moving in here and everything. I must have missed his call." Christina lowered her eyes to her soup. Where the hell was that swine and why had he left her to deal with his father on her own? She was getting angrier by the minute.

"But how can you miss his call? You're a photojournalist on assignment. Surely you have voicemail?" William declared.

"I do, but I forgot to check my messages today. Bill's probably working late."

"I left the offices at 6:15 and he never showed up for work today."

"Well… I'm sure he'll be here soon."

William grunted as if he didn't believe her. "So tell me, Christina, when do you and my son want to get married?"

"Like we told you last time, probably in about a year." Oh, where was that idiot? How dare he leave her to fend for herself with his overbearing father!

William grunted again and began to dig into his steak. "And how do your parents feel about Bill? You've introduced him to them, I take it?"

"Well… not yet."

"What? Why not?"

"They're retired and live in Florida. Everything's happened so fast that we haven't had a chance to see them yet," she smiled apologetically.

Outwardly, Christina was acting calm and pleasant but inside her emotions were a seething cauldron about to boil over. *Oooohhh—where was he, damn it????*

"So you don't know where my irresponsible son is tonight?" William repeated.

Again with that same question…

And on and on it went all night long—questions thrown left and right at Christina as if she was being cross-examined on the witness stand.

'Where would you like to get married? How many children do you want? How many guests would you like to invite? Are you going to continue with your career once you're married? What are your parents' names? What does your father do? So you really don't know where my son is tonight? What do you think about…?'

And on—and on—and on.

When William finally excused himself after the coffee, Christina let slip an audible sigh of relief. William caught the sigh and smiled inwardly to himself. He did feel sorry for the girl—a little—but she had signed up for this job and he wanted to see what she was made of.

He'd been impressed, as he knew he would. She'd fended off every question, had answered what she could and expertly evaded what she couldn't—and had kept a cool head throughout the whole ordeal.

William hadn't expected his irresponsible son to show up for dinner. He never did. And he also knew Bill wouldn't let Christina know where he was. His son was untrustworthy, lazy, immature and stupid. He was probably right now out partying with his friends and getting drunk. Wonder what she'd say to Bill when he finally showed up? Christina didn't strike William as the type to take any crap from anyone, let alone his party boy son.

"Goodnight, my dear." William bent down and gave Christina a kiss on the cheek. "I'm very glad that you're here now." He gave her a fatherly smile and walked out.

Christina took her napkin from her lap and wiped her forehead with it. She had actually been sweating. Sweating!

Oh!!! Was she furious! Raging, volcano furious! That idiot had left her alone to deal with his mess and he hadn't even had the common courtesy to let her know where he was or when or if he was coming home.

And where in all probability was he?

Christina would bet he was with that tramp, Stephie from last night. Probably trying to explain and calm her down. Telling her this was all a ruse for his father's sake. That it would only last one month and the little 'nobody' who was helping him really didn't mean anything to him. And maybe—they were, right now, having sex together, however disgusting that was to think about.

Christina hadn't believed that phony story he'd told her last night about breaking up with that witch. Sure, they'd had an argument last week, as Christina had witnessed but Stephie didn't seem to think it was over.

So they were right now having sex, were they, while Christina was left to hold up his end of the scheme? How dare he? How bloody dare he? Boy, was she mad tonight!

And there was going to be hell to pay tomorrow!

What Christina didn't realize was that these were her first pangs of jealousy too.

*

It was 7 p.m. that same night and Bill was sitting in the audience waiting for the Alcoholic Anonymous meeting to begin. He looked at his watch. This was the time his father usually had dinner. Hopefully, Christina had gotten the phone message he'd left for her at her apartment saying that he wouldn't be home for dinner and to avoid his father like the plague.

He'd wanted to talk to her again before Summers came to pick her up but today had been especially hectic for him and when he'd called her, she hadn't answered. He'd also left several messages for Stephie to call him back. Although, they'd been over for a while now, he still felt bad about what had happened last night at the restaurant and wanted to explain things to her in person.

But she never returned his calls today and knowing Stephie, she probably wouldn't. Maybe it was best that things be left as they were. He would be the 'bad guy' in all this and she could feel good that she'd escaped the clutches of a 'prick', as her mother had put it.

At that moment, a man in a wheelchair came in and headed straight for Bill. It was Jake Monroe, Bill's high school drinking buddy, the same Jake that had pulled the cruel joke on Christina all those years ago.

"Hey Bill, meeting started yet?" he asked as he locked his chair wheels into place.

"Nah, we're still waiting for Greer to show up," Bill answered, as he forlornly watched Jake handle the levers on the wheelchair. It was obvious the two were still the best of friends.

Jake looked up and caught Bill's guilt ridden expression. "It's okay, you know. I've accepted it," he told him.

"But I haven't. I hate seeing you like this," Bill replied forcefully.

"It's been over a year and a half since the accident. I've come to terms with it."

Bill shook his head. "It was all my fault."

"I was the one driving drunk, Bill, not you. You weren't even in the car."

Bill gave a sarcastic smirk, "Only because you'd already dropped my pathetic drunken ass home. You know it could have been me driving drunk that night just as much as you. I'd done it many times before."

"But it wasn't. It was me. My fault. Not yours. I was the one who made that decision that night. I just thank God nobody else was involved in that smashup...except for that tree," Jake laughed, trying to cheer up his friend.

Bill wasn't having any of it. "I'll never drink again," he adamantly stated.

"Remember, don't say 'never'. Take it one day at a time. We won't drink today, only today."

"No, I won't drink today," Bill agreed, as he looked with anguish at his friend. "All the drunken crap we've pulled over the years, all the wasted time, the blackouts, the disappointments we caused everybody...do you think there's hope for two drunks like us, Jake?"

Jake laughed, "I'm living proof, buddy. I should have died in that crash but I didn't. It's my second chance at life... and look at you, this is your second chance too. We've both been sober for over a year and a half, we're working the program and we're trying to do some good in this world. There's hope, man, there's hope."

Bill smiled at his friend's positive attitude. "How are the guys holding up?"

"You can ask them yourself tonight. We're all meeting at the secret location."

"The warehouse on Shelley Ave.?"

"Yeah, at midnight. We've got to discuss strategy."

Bill laughed, "You know, my old man is about to have a coronary with the guys picketing outside his building. Keep up the good work."

Jake laughed too. "GME was your idea... and with your money funding us and your inside knowledge of how your father is running his operations, we've been very successful so far."

"The Guardians of Mother Earth may have been my idea but we're all in this together," Bill corrected him. "You, me and the guys. We all believe in this cause and we have to stop my evil father from pumping that oil through those decrepit pipelines in the Russian Arctic. It's an environmental disaster over there."

"Hey, you don't have to preach to the choir," Jake laughed again.

"We just have to stop people like him, we have to. This planet is too precious to let greed destroy it. And you know he won't listen to anything else. Hurting his public image and hurting his bottom line are the only ways to get him to stop."

"How's the girl working out?" Jake inquired.

"Christina? She's helping me, although she doesn't know the full extent of how or why. But as long as she's there pretending to be my future wife, my old man will let me stay and allow me access to all the money I can get my hands on. Which reminds me…" Bill patted his jacket pocket with his hand, "…I've got more greenbacks here for you and the guys… and there's more coming through some of those private accounts I set up in the Caribbean."

Jake looked uncomfortably around, "Bill… this… isn't like… stealing, is it? I don't want you to do anything illegal."

Bill lowered his voice so that the other AA members in the room couldn't hear anything. "No Jake, it's not. This is my money that he gives me, along with the salary I earn working for him. You know he's always given it to me and he never asks what I do with it. He just thinks I piss it away like I've always done in the past."

Jake laughs again, "Yes, we did have some fun times together."

Bill laughed too. "Yeah… the ones we remember in between all the drunken blackouts."

"What's this girl Christina like?" Jake was curious. The few times his friend had mentioned her name this past week, his face had always lit up. He knew Bill very well, having been friends since high school and he knew when his friend was more than casually interested in a woman.

"She's…" Bill's face broke out in a smile, "… different."

"Good different… or bad different?"

Bill quickly remembered the car accident, the drink in his face and the cake she'd smashed on his head—and he laughed out loud. "The jury's out on that one," he answered Jake.

At that moment, Thomas Greer came in and headed for the podium. Everyone took their seats and the meeting began.

"My name is Thomas Greer and I'm an alcoholic," he stated.

"Hi Thomas," everyone replied.

"We'll start tonight with…" he stopped as he saw Bill raise his hand, "Yes, Bill?"

Bill stood up. "My name is Bill and I'm an alcoholic."

"Hi Bill," everyone again replied together.

"I… I just want to say that I almost had a drink this week," Bill's words gushed out as if he was expelling some bad junk food he'd just eaten.

"What happened?" Thomas Greer questioned.

There were no gasps in the room and no one was passing judgment on Bill. At one point or other, they had all been there and would probably be there again.

"I had a martini thrown in my face," Bill replied.

"By a woman, Bill?" someone in the audience piped up.

"Yeah." Everyone laughed. Bill continued, "I almost took a taste. It was so close… and I wanted to so badly…"

"But you didn't," Jake confirmed.

"No. I jumped in the pool to wash it off."

Again, everyone in the room laughed and some even clapped.

*

Click!

Tucked into her luxurious, wrought iron four-poster bed, Christina had just heard Bill's bedroom door open and close shut. She looked at her bedside clock. Bloody hell! 4:10 a.m.!

Where had he been until 4:10 a.m.? With that rich bitch, that's where! Christina closed her eyes again and tried to go back to sleep. She'd get him tomorrow. She'd get him good.

CHAPTER 22

CHRISTINA LOOKED AT her watch. 7:30 a.m. So, lover boy had probably only had about three hours sleep so far, had he? That was enough.

She was standing outside his bedroom door, dressed and ready for her day. And he, lazy bum that he was, was probably in there, sleeping. From what she'd gleaned from the staff at breakfast, Bill would probably sleep until noon before getting up. He apparently always came home very late and slept all morning. Well not today! She'd make sure of that.

Christina knocked on his door and waited for an answer.

Nothing.

She knocked again.

Silence.

Gingerly, she tried the doorknob and it turned. Should she go in? Why the hell not? She was supposed to be his fiancée anyway, in case anybody saw her.

She pushed the door open.

There he was—in bed, sprawled on his back, naked to the waist with the top sheet covering his lower half—and in a very deep sleep. Christina stomped in and shut the door.

Furious, she studied him. Look at how relaxed he looked, she thought to herself. He must have had a good night while she had had to endure hours of torturous questioning by his relentless father. Christina's anger went up another notch.

"Bill? Bill Havenwood?" Christina loudly gritted through her teeth.

There was no response. He was, obviously, in a very deep

sleep—a drunken deep sleep, no doubt. And look at how good he looked—with his hair ruffled like that and his naked muscular chest rising and falling ever so gently as he softly breathed in and out.

Christina approached the bed and peered into his handsome face. He looked so rested—probably from all the cheap sex he'd had last night with that Stephie. Christina's anger suddenly went through the roof.

"Hey! You!" She poked his chest with a hard finger. "Wake up!"

Bill made a soft moaning sound but didn't awaken.

Christina was seeing red—and green—with fleeting thoughts of him and Stephie together, in each other's arms while she'd been trying to save him from his inquisitive father.

She looked around his chocolate brown room. On a tall pedestal by the window sat an ornately decorated Oriental vase. It looked expensive and perfectly suited for what she had in mind. Crossing the room, she picked it up and took it to Bill's private bathroom. She filled it up with water and carried it back to the bed.

Then—with one good swing—Christina suddenly launched all the water in it at Bill's sleeping form. Whoosh!

The water landed on his face, on his chest, on his bed. With a startled gasp, Bill bolted upright.

"What... the... fuck!" he yelled as, dazed, he looked around the room trying to get his bearings. Water dripped from his face and chest, and his hair was plastered to his head. A water stain was slowly creeping outwards on his top sheet, soaking the bed even further.

Breathing heavily, his eyes focused on Christina who was standing in front of him holding his treasured Ming Vase.

She threw the expensive item at his chest and he anxiously caught it with both hands.

"This is your piss pot, I believe," she enunciated through gritted teeth.

Bill was stunned. "What... is going on here?" he yelled at her.

With hands on her hips, Christina yelled back, "Next time you want to party all night, leave word with me so that I can make arrangements not to be here all alone stuck with your father and having to make excuses for your sorry ass."

Bill wiped the water from his face. "What are you talking about?"

"Last night was my first night here in this godforsaken gilded cage and you left me all alone to deal with your overbearing father. Do you know how many questions I had to answer at dinner?" Christina began to parrot William's questioning. "How many children do you want? When do you want to get married? What do you mean you don't know where your fiancé is? That's strange. Why don't you know?" She re-focused her angry eyes back to Bill's wet face. "I went through hell last night having to answer for you to your damn family and you didn't even bother to call me to let me know you weren't going to show up!"

Bill looked at her furious face. Yes, she was steaming mad and her fury was being hurled at him in full force but boy, did she look hot!

He took a deep breath. "Christina, I did call you. I left a message on your answering machine at your apartment."

"Well, I didn't get it." Still livid, Christina crossed her arms in front of her. "Yesterday was very hectic for me having to pack and move to this billionaire hellhole."

"Look, I'm sorry. I said on the message that I wouldn't be here and for you not to have dinner with my father, to plead a headache or something and I would square things with him today."

Christina studied his pleading face. Was he telling her the truth? Had he left her the message? Some of the steam went out of Christina but she was still angry with him.

Bill sensed the indecision in her and he quickly threw the sheet off and jumped up from the wet bed. Wearing only a pair of boxers, he stood in front of her still cradling the expensive vase in his arms.

"I'm sorry but I'll make sure that from now on you'll know

when I'm going to be late so that we can co-ordinate our stories for my old man, okay?" He held out his hand to her as if he wanted to shake on the deal but she ignored it.

"Don't let it happen again," she decreed highhandedly.

Bill gave her a slight smile of admiration. She really did look cute when she was trying to be bossy.

"Did you get my present?" he questioned.

"What present?"

"Samson."

"Samson? You left me Samson?" Christina was floored. She thought William had left the little goldfish.

Bill nodded. "I know we're all strangers to you here, and I wanted you to have at least one friend in this house that you could trust completely."

Christina's mouth actually fell open. She quickly shut it. That was just about the nicest, sweetest, most thoughtful thing anybody had ever done for her—and it had been Bill Havenwood who'd done it!

He wasn't supposed to be like that. He was a selfish, drunken, party boy who stepped over people for kicks. He was her enemy and he had no right to be nice. No right at all!

She looked into his smiling eyes. "You... you... asshole!" she yelled at him before storming out the door.

Now it was Bill's mouth to gape open in shock. What had he said?

*

Christina marched down the huge staircase, still fuming to herself. As she reached the bottom, she spotted the day's mail on the foyer table. Picking up the pile, Christina rifled through the stack. Junk mail, bills, letters and—there it was—her blackmail letter to Bill Havenwood. Christina smiled to herself. The real games were now about to begin.

CHAPTER 23

AN HOUR LATER, Christina was walking the estate grounds, talking to Jenny on her cell phone.

"Oh Jenny," she giggled, "When she slapped him in front of the whole restaurant, it was… magical."

Jenny was at work at Streetwise and she was giggling too. "I'm sure he deserved it."

"He did, the cad." Christina confirmed. "Anyway, I'm coming into the city tonight, so let's have dinner."

"Great, come by for some mac and cheese. Bet you can't get that at the Havenwood's."

Christina laughed again, "I'll be there."

*

Bill had been watching her from his upstairs bedroom window.

He had showered and dressed, but was still very tired from his late night. He usually slept until noon on the nights he was busy with GME meetings like last night, but this morning he'd found it difficult going back to sleep considering he'd had a pot of water thrown on him.

He smiled at the thought of it. Wow, had she ever been angry with him. His domineering father did have that effect on people and if you weren't used to it, as he was, then you could find it overwhelming.

Bill watched her walk the grounds, laughing as she talked on her cell phone. God, she looked beautiful—like an angel—and mesmerized, he couldn't take his eyes off of her.

But who the hell was she talking to? Was it her boyfriend?

Was it one of her 'relationships'? Bill was suddenly in a fit to find out.

*

Bill reached the bottom of the stairs just as Christina was coming back inside the house.

She defiantly looked at him, "I'm not apologizing, you know."

"Didn't ask you to but you could thank me," he parried.

Christina was aghast. "For what?"

"For Samson."

Christina eyed Bill with disdain. So, 'Samson' had been a thoughtful gesture, so what? Probably part of his plan to keep her in line in their devious scheme. No—she'd never thank him—for anything.

Christina shifted her eyes from his face to the foyer table. "Is this today's mail?" She innocently picked up the stack. "Hope you don't mind but I'm having my mail forwarded here."

"Why would I mind?"

She began to rifle through the pile and Bill watched her with hungry eyes—the eyes of someone who can see what they want right in front of them but can't quite have it.

"I saw you talking on your cell outside. Was it your boyfriend?" Bill blurted out, as if he couldn't help himself.

Christina looked up from the letters. "My boyfriend? Why do you think it was my boyfriend?"

Bill experienced what felt like a punch in the gut. So she did have a boyfriend! "Just a hunch," he tried to sound casual but failed miserably.

"Well, I don't ask you about your special friends so you don't ask about mine, okay?"

Bill wasn't going to be put off that easily. He'd ask again tonight. "I've rescheduled some appointments so I'll be home for dinner tonight. You won't have to put up with my father alone."

"Sorry but I've got plans."

"With your boyfriend?" Bill accused.

God, he was beginning to sound pathetic even to his own ears, like some jealous high school geek who was being rejected by the most popular girl in class. That had never happened to him in his entire life—ever!

"Are you going to answer me?" he pressed on, when Christina didn't answer. High school geek be damned, he just had to know.

Christina gave him an enigmatic Mona Lisa smile—neither confirming nor denying. She lowered her eyes back to the mail. "Here's one for you." She casually handed him her 'blackmail letter' and went back to rifling through the mail.

With his mind on her 'boyfriend', he absentmindedly ripped the envelope open and then—froze. In his hands, was a letter with the words "Liar, Liar, Pants On Fire" pasted on it with letters cut out of a magazine. He blanched and quickly scanned the envelope for a return address. There was none.

Who'd sent this? And what did they want? Money, obviously. This was an extortion letter but who'd done this? Did they know about his phony engagement scam or worse... did they know about his involvement with The Guardians of Mother Earth?

Christina saw the color drain out of his face. "Anything wrong? You look like you've seen a ghost," she asked as if she cared.

With worried eyes, Bill looked at her. "No, everything's fine." He quickly stuffed the letter into his jacket.

Bingo!

And that's when Christina knew for sure that he had more secrets than their phony love match. If the only secret Bill had was their engagement scheme, he would have shown her the letter and they would have compared notes on who could have sent it.

But he hadn't. He had acted guilty and hidden the letter away from her. And that meant that "Liar, Liar, Pants On Fire" had been telling many lies about many different things—and he just didn't know which 'lies' the blackmail letter were referring to. Now all Christina had to do was find out what they were.

At that moment, Bentley, the head butler, approached the couple and handed Bill a portable phone. "Telephone for you, sir. It's Mr. Havenwood."

"Thank you, Bentley." Bill took the phone and mumbled "Hello, dad" into the receiver. He paused to listen to what his father had to say and then exclaimed in a frustrated voice, "No... I wasn't still sleeping! I've been up for awhile."

Cristina couldn't help giggling. William certainly knew his son well. She refocused on the one-sided conversation she was hearing.

"Okay, I'll ask her." Bill paused. "All right then, we'll be there!" exasperated, he shouted into the phone. Hanging up, he turned to Christina. "My father wants to see us in his office this afternoon."

"What about?"

Bill shrugged his shoulders, "Wouldn't say but we'll find out what that devious swine is up to. I'll pick you up at 1."

"No thanks. I'll meet you there myself. Your father said I could have the use of the BMW. Wasn't that thoughtful of him?"

"Yes, he's so lovable," Bill sarcastically chimed in.

CHAPTER 24

THE PRIVATE ELEVATOR was whisking Christina to the top inner sanctum of the Fido Foods office building. When she'd arrived ten minutes ago, she had had to cross the GME picket line outside the building where other media had been filming the spectacle too.

Teddy, the GME protester she'd spoken to last week, recognized her and yelled out, "Hey, honey, you haven't crossed over to the dark side, have you?"

"I don't take sides, Teddy. I only photograph the truth," Christina shouted back.

"Well, come back and photograph this... my salute to those greedy Havenwood criminals." He threw his middle finger up in the air, indicating a "screw-you" type of gesture. The other protesters followed suit.

Christina laughed, "I'll come back with my camera, I promise."

Teddy yelled, "Yeah, all right," and threw a victorious clenched fist up in the air.

Christina had then entered the glass and steel building, been cleared through security and had been ushered by a guard to William's private elevator.

As the elevator doors opened into William's private offices, Christina felt like she was entering the Holy of Holies. She'd been greeted by Charlotte, William's private secretary and had been invited to take a seat on the opulent couch. 'It would only be a moment', she'd been told, and 'would she like some coffee or tea?' Christina shook her head no and thanked Charlotte.

Sitting on the plush sofa, Christina was now able to take a

better look at her lavish surroundings. Everything about the place screamed taste and money—lots and lots of money.

The elevator doors opened again and Bill walked out, gorgeous and debonair as usual. The scoundrel didn't have a hair out of place. Christina stood up as he made a beeline for her.

He smiled. "You look amazing, dumpling." He secretly rolled his eyes indicating that Charlotte was watching and began to bend down as if to give her a kiss.

Not bloody likely, Christina thought to herself, as she put a restraining hand on his arm. Kissing for his father's sake was one thing but kissing for everybody else? No way in hell!

"Sweetheart, I think I'm catching a cold. Don't get too close or you'll… get it… too," she emphasized the words 'get it' as if to warn him of the consequences of foisting himself on her.

He understood the message and backed off. "I'll have to take better care of you, honey bunch," he teased before turning to the secretary. "Is he ready for us, Charlotte?"

"Yes, sir. Go right in," she replied, as she watched the couple closely.

Bill knocked on William's door and on hearing his father say, "Come in," he took Christina's elbow and ushered her in.

William was sitting behind his ornate desk and there was a woman of about fifty seated opposite him on one of the wingback chairs. They both rose.

"Mindy, this is my son Bill and his beautiful fiancée, Christina Matteo soon to be a Havenwood," he announced proudly.

They all shook hands.

William continued, "Bill, Christina… this is Mindy Soames." He paused for effect. "Your wedding planner."

Both Bill and Christina swiveled shocked eyes at him.

"Our… what?" Christina stammered.

William came around the desk and put a fatherly arm on Christina's shoulders as he led her to a couch.

"Mindy is going to help you plan your wedding, Christina,

my love." He pushed a stunned Christina down before taking a seat himself.

Bill began to protest, "But dad…"

"Sit," he ordered Bill as he pointed to a chair opposite the couch. Bill did as he was told.

Mindy, carrying a folder of papers, took the other chair beside Bill's and began her presentation. "Now Miss Matteo… may I call you Christina by the way?" Bewildered, Cristina nodded her consent. Mindy began to read off of a notepad. "St. Patrick's has been booked for six weeks from this Saturday as has the country club. The couture house of Baldora has been advised and they're waiting for your arrival. The flowers…"

"Excuse me, but…what are you talking about?" Christina had finally come out of her stupor.

"Your wedding arrangements," Mindy clarified.

"My… what?"

William jumped in, "Your wedding, Christina. It's all been arranged—the church, the reception, your dress. All that's left is that you need to decide your menu, the invitations have to be chosen and your bridesmaids, and oh…" he snapped his fingers as if remembering something, "Mindy needs your guest list from your side of the family and you'll have to be registered and choose your china pattern and your honeymoon destination…"

"And the flowers, Mr. Havenwood, for the tables and the church?" Mindy chimed in.

"Of course," William agreed. "You and Christina will decide all that together."

"But dad, Christina and I are getting married next year," Bill piped in, as he took in Christina's angry expression.

"Oh, nonsense," William decreed.

Christina jumped in, "William, Bill and I need time to properly plan everything…"

"Oh, pooh," William gleefully announced, in his proper British accent. "I have money, my dear, lots of it. And money can make anything happen whenever you want it to."

"Dad, this is something Christina and I should decide ourselves," Bill firmly announced.

Suspiciously, William turned on his son. "Why don't you want to marry now? Do you and Christina love each other?"

"Of course, we love each other. What kind of question is that?" Bill's words rushed out.

William turned to Christina, "And you my dear? Do you love my son?"

The room fell silent as everyone waited for her answer.

Bill eyeballed Christina, as fear coursed through his veins. With one small 'no', she could walk out of this mess, and his world would blow apart.

William watched the both of them closely. What fun he was having! The church and the country club had indeed been booked and Mindy was actually a topnotch wedding planner. She knew nothing of the games all three of them were playing. Everything would proceed as if a real wedding was going to take place in six weeks time.

William knew from the copy of Bill and Christina's contract that their deal was only for one month. If this sham went on that long, they could simply call the wedding off at the end of the month and tell everyone that the happy couple had changed their minds. But he would bet all the Microsoft stock he owned that his weak, pathetic son would crack under the pressure before then—or Christina might kill him first, if her furious face was anything to go by. William bit the inside of his lip to keep from laughing.

The room was still silent. Everyone was waiting for Christina's answer. Slowly, she turned to her nincompoop fiancé and gave him a loving smile. "Of course, I love him," she gushed.

What was she going to say? She still owed him that money and her revenge plan was progressing very nicely, even though she hadn't dug up any dirt on the jerk yet. She saw Bill visibly relax.

William nodded, "Good. You'll be married in six weeks and I won't take no for an answer."

"William, I don't think…" she began but William interrupted her.

"And your engagement party will be at the house in three weeks time."

"Our… what?" Christina glared at Bill who gave her a weak smile.

William continued, "Your engagement party, dear. It's bad form if you don't have one. We'll be inviting all the right people, of course. As my future daughter-in-law, you'll be living in their world now, Christina and you will be treated with respect."

Engagement party??? *Engagement party!!! She'd have to put up with that too!!!???* Suddenly, Christina's anger went into overload and she turned to Bill. "Can I speak to you for a moment—darling?" she gritted.

Bill was wary. "Of course—pumpkin pie."

The two rose and walked out of the massive office and into Charlotte's outer office. The secretary was nowhere to be seen. Bill closed his father's office door, separating them from a perplexed Mindy and a satisfied-looking William.

As soon as the door shut, Christina furiously rounded on Bill. "You never said anything about wedding plans," she hissed at him.

"I had nothing to do with this."

"A few dinners with your father, you said. A couple of kisses on the cheek, you said. Only for one month, you said. Well, everything 'you said' has been wrong."

"Christina, I had no idea he was planning this, I swear it."

"I'm not going through with wedding plans. For God's sake, he's booked a church. He's set a date even, and the country club. He's talking about my dress."

"Look, everything's set for six weeks from now. In a month's time, we'll tell him we've changed our minds and the wedding's off. Until then, why don't we just humor the old man? Nothing's going to come of it."

"Are you crazy?" Christina almost screamed at him. "We can't 'pretend' plan a wedding."

"Why not?"

"Because… because it's deceitful and a big lie."

"And what have we been doing up until now?" Suddenly, Bill inched closer as if some force was pulling him to her.

Christina, immediately, felt his presence envelope her and she gazed up into those gorgeous, green eyes of his—and her voice, suddenly, softened. "Those were little lies. This one would be big."

"So? We're the only ones who'd know and I'm not telling. Are you?"

Bill gazed at her beautiful face. He was so close he could smell her musky perfume and it was lulling his brain. His problems were fading away, being replaced by his strong, primitive attraction to her. What would it be like to kiss—to really kiss those lush, rosy lips of hers? He could almost feel an electrical current attaching his lips to hers.

Christina stared back at him. She felt like she was being drugged by his aura as she too began to feel the same imaginary current pulling the both of them together. A small censor in her brain began to warn her that what she was experiencing was crazy and dangerous and not part of her plan, but she couldn't quite remember what that plan was. All she could think of was 'him' and what it would be like to give into that pull that was drawing her like a magnet to his lips.

Christina tried to break free of the spell he was weaving. "I… I…your father wants… a party…"

Bill's eyes devoured her, as he absentmindedly answered, "He does?"

"Yes…three… three weeks time…" she stammered but she was in a fog and he was hypnotizing her with his essence. Instinctively, she took a step closer to him.

Suddenly, the door from William's office opened and they both heard William shouting, "What are you two doing out there?" as he came out to see.

And in the split second that it took William to come out of his office, Bill made his move. Not able to resist the physical attraction he felt for her any longer, he grabbed Christina by the arms, pulled her against his chest and began to kiss her with abandon.

Surprised, Christina moaned a small protest before giving in to her passion too. In that moment, she didn't know anymore who she was and she certainly didn't know who he was. The kiss deepened as his hands began to travel slowly down her body and around her back. They lowered even still to cup her derriere and draw her closer—into him.

Responding to him, her hands crept up his chest and wrapped themselves around his neck, pulling him closer—into her. They were both on fire and on autopilot, no longer thinking, and no longer in control. Like two pieces of a jigsaw puzzle, they had locked into place. It was right. It was safe. It was home.

From someplace far away, they heard William giggle, "Excuse me" before retreating back into his office. As he closed his door shut, it made a 'click' sound and it was that sound that finally penetrated Christina's passion-drugged brain. She snapped out of her fog and suddenly, the enormity of what she was doing came roaring at her like a hurricane.

She was in Bill Havenwood's arms—Bill Havenwood, for God's sake—her enemy, the man she hated most in the world, the one who had caused the most traumatic day of her teen life—and she was returning kiss for kiss, wanting more, wanting it all. With a strangled cry, she pulled out of his arms and pushed at his chest with all her might.

Just as dazed from the kiss as she had been, Bill stumbled back. With all the women he'd been with, and he had to admit there had been many, he'd never felt anything like that in his whole life. Never. And it had been just a kiss, just a damn kiss! He was as confused and shocked as she was, if for very different reasons.

Both were still breathing heavily as they continued to stare at each other.

Oh God, what had she done? Christina's hand came up to cover her swollen, kiss-ravaged mouth and she could still taste him on her lips.

She, Christina Matteo, had allowed this filthy swine to kiss and fondle her in the middle of a public office and she had enjoyed every hot, fiery second of it. And what was worse, she had kissed him back. In those moments, when she'd been in his arms, she had wanted nothing more than to drag him down on the couch opposite the desk and make love to him—and the consequences be damned! Christina locked her shocked eyes into Bill's.

"Say something," he pleaded, trying to figure out what she was thinking.

"I'm...I'm going to be sick," Christina's pallor suddenly turned gray.

Bill was a little insulted—well a lot actually. He smirked, "The kiss wasn't that bad."

"No, you don't understand. I'm really going to be sick!" Christina's hand clamped onto her mouth.

"What?"

Panicking, Christina shouted at him, "I need a bathroom now or else..."

Too late! In a flash, Christina vomited all over Bill's Armani blue suit.

Stunned beyond belief, Bill looked down at the mess on his jacket. What the hell had happened here? One minute the kiss—and the next—this? He looked back up at Christina just in time to see her eyes roll back in her head and faint dead away into his arms.

CHAPTER 25

CHRISTINA WAS LYING on a beach—a white, sandy, hot beach—and she was wearing her favorite bikini, the one with the tiny cherries plastered all over. The sun was shining its healing warmth on her body and the ocean breezes were fanning her skin back and forth, back and forth, back and forth. She couldn't remember the last time she'd felt this good. It was a perfect day and she never wanted it to end.

Suddenly, there was movement beside her. She turned her head and saw Bill Havenwood lying there—naked, tanned and perfect. He gave her a smoldering look and without saying a word, he rolled onto her and covered her body with his. Skin plastered to skin, he began to kiss her, a deep, penetrating kiss that reached down to her soul.

It felt yummy.

It felt delicious.

It felt hot.

Especially hot. Christina was on fire and it was for him… only for him… all for him.

She never wanted him to stop. Her hands began to travel over him, feeling every square inch of his skin—as his were doing to her—and the cool ocean breezes continued to fan them both.

His hands slipped her bikini top straps off and they began their slow descent down to her breasts. It felt so good to have him touch her like that—so good.

From somewhere off in space, Christina heard a distant, far away voice—a very, very angry voice—shouting at full volume…

"What in bloody, all mighty hell did you do to her?"

It was William's voice, but what was William doing on the beach?

She heard another voice, equally angry, yelling back, "Me? You were the one who was pressuring her with all your damn wedding plans."

Wait. That was Bill's voice! But how could Bill be speaking if he was, right now, kissing her? That didn't make sense.

And then Christina heard a woman's voice say, "Maybe we should call an ambulance?"

Ambulance? Who needed an ambulance? That was odd.

Oh well, whatever, she thought as she kept on kissing Bill's scrumptious lips. She just couldn't get enough of him—nor him her. And all the while those cool, comforting ocean breezes continued to gently fan their overheated bodies…

"Once again you have royally screwed up! Can you be trusted to do anything right?" Christina heard William's furious voice say.

"Your marriage wasn't exactly a raging success, so stay out of this! This doesn't concern you." It was Bill again and he was livid.

"If it's in this family, it bloody well concerns me," William angrily responded.

Father and son were both shouting at each other, a full-blown fight. But how could Bill be arguing with his father if he was passionately kissing her—wait a minute— *Bill Havenwood was kissing her?*

With an anguished gasp for air, Christina's eyes finally fluttered open. She found herself stretched out on the couch in William's office and there were two Fido Foods Annual Reports being fanned over her body, cooling off her hot skin. One was being held by William and the other by Bill.

"She's coming to," she heard a worried Bill say. She focused her blurry eyes on him as he crouched down to her level. "Christina?" he whispered softly. "Are you feeling better?"

Both William and Mindy lowered their faces to peer into hers.

Christina's eyes flitted from one to the other. "What… what

happened?" she croaked. God, her throat was parched and some-one had put a wet washcloth on her forehead.

Bill tenderly pushed her hair off of her face. "You were sick and then you fainted."

"Faint… fainted?" she stammered, as she gazed into his eyes. That wasn't possible. She had never fainted in her life, not even when she'd broken her arm skiing at nineteen.

Bill nodded. "Do you want to go to the hospital?"

"Hospital…?" Confused, Christina briefly closed her eyes and the memories of what had happened came flooding back to her. She'd been kissing Bill Havenwood—Bill Havenwood!! And she'd enjoyed every second of it! How could her body betray her like that? Ashamed, she groaned out loud.

"That's it, I'm taking you to the emergency," Bill ordered.

"No! I'll be fine," she pleaded. Ashamed, she could barely look at him, as she covered her face with her hands.

"You're not fine." Bill was very worried. He'd never had any-one faint in his arms before, although the 'being sick part' was nothing new to him from all of the drunken nights he'd had over the years with his friends.

"Maybe she's pregnant?" William, wickedly, piped up.

"No, she's not pregnant," exasperated, Bill shouted at his father. But wait, what if she was? What if her boyfriend had got-ten her pregnant? Suddenly, he felt a fury of white, hot jealousy consume him. Unsure, he turned back to Christina. "Are you?" he questioned forcefully.

Christina lowered her hands from her face and glared at Bill. "No! No, I'm not pregnant!" she retorted, just as forceful as him. What bozos they were, the pair of them!

She saw Bill visibly relax. Of course, he would. A pregnancy would definitely put a glitch in his devious plan to scam his father. Her eyes lowered to the vomit stain on his suit and suddenly it all came back to Christina. She'd thrown up—on him? How embar-rassing! No one had ever seen her throw up before, let alone be the recipient of that honor. But—if it did have to happen—might as well be on this scumbag.

Suddenly, Christina felt a giggle rise up in her throat. It bubbled out, followed by another giggle and another…

"Sorry… sorry… about your suit," she said to Bill before bursting out in a fit of laughter. This was just about the most ridiculous mess she'd ever gotten herself into, and the most embarrassing and the most humiliating. Christina continued to laugh and couldn't stop.

"My God," William said, "She's becoming hysterical." And at that remark, Christina laughed even harder.

That's when Mindy, the wedding planner took charge. "Okay, you two," she addressed the men. "Out of here."

"I'm not leaving her," Bill stated.

"Yes you are." Mindy was adamant. "This is nothing more than bride-to-be jitters. I've seen it a million times. I'll take Christina into Mr. Havenwood's private washroom and fix her up." She patted Christina's hand. "You'll feel better once we splash some cold water on your face."

Bill squeezed Christina's other hand gently. "I'll be right outside if you need me," he softly told her.

"Me too," William announced from over Bill's shoulder.

Bill rose up from his crouching position, glared at his father and walked out. His father glowered at him too, before following him.

*

In William's private bathroom, Mindy was patting Christina's face with a wet towel.

"I'm sorry, Mindy," Christina sheepishly remarked.

"Honey, if I had a quarter for every time a bride threw up and fainted on me, I could quit this lousy job and buy myself a Trump Tower penthouse."

Christina giggled. "I guess it comes with the territory."

Mindy smiled. "You know, your man out there really loves

you, and your father-in-law too. I saw how worried they both were when you were out cold. I thought they were going to come to blows."

Bill Havenwood in love with her? How ridiculous was that? People really did see what they wanted to see.

Mindy continued speaking as she grabbed a brush from the counter and started to comb Christina's hair. "Now, I don't want to put anymore pressure on you but we don't have much time to plan this shindig so how about if I come by tomorrow… if you're feeling better, of course."

Christina sighed deeply, "Sure, why not?" Might as well get this over with. She'd make some silly decisions about flowers and food, and get William off their backs for awhile.

*

Both Bill and William were in Charlotte's outer office, pacing like two expectant fathers waiting for the baby to be born.

Bill gave his dad a dirty look as he passed him again for the fiftieth time. This was all his fault, the bastard. His old man shouldn't have been making wedding arrangements behind their backs.

William glared back at his son. This was all Bill's fault, the bastard. He shouldn't have been forcing himself on that sweet girl. William knew his womanizing son had been attracted to her from the get-go, but if he was pressuring her into doing anything she didn't want to do, there'd be hell to pay.

The door opened and a refreshed Christina and Mindy emerged. Both men rushed over to her.

"Are you feeling better?" a concerned Bill asked.

"My dear, you gave us all a fright," William quickly added.

Christina put her hands up. "I'm fine. I just want to go home and rest."

"I'll drive you," Bill replied, as he wrapped a protective arm around Christina's shoulders.

At his proximity, Christina felt her cheeks flush as she blushed at the memory of his devastating kiss. She could feel his body heat start to envelope her again and it was making her dizzy.

She quickly moved away.

"I'll drive myself. The BMW is outside," she affirmed

"No, you're not well enough to drive and the BMW will be driven home by one of the employees here," Bill was adamant and Christina could see he wouldn't budge.

Still feeling weak, Christina reluctantly agreed and said her goodbyes to William and Mindy.

*

As William's private elevator descended, Bill studied Christina's gray pallor.

"You're not fine, you know," he piped up.

"I am fine."

Standing so close to him, in the small elevator, Christina began to feel the physical attraction she seemed to have for him. Her body was such a traitor, she thought, as she could still feel the imprint of his fiery kisses on her lips. She took a step away from him and her still wobbly legs made her stumble.

"That's it!" Bill firmly announced and as the elevator doors slid open, he scooped her up in his arms.

"What the hell are you doing?" Christina shouted, trying to wriggle down.

"I'm not having you fainting all over the place again," he shouted as he carried her outside, through the GME protesters and through the media cameras that began to click away at the boss' son carrying a woman.

Christina fumed, as he carried her to his Jaguar. "You're making a spectacle of us," she yelled.

"I don't really give a big hot damn." He opened the passenger door and gently lowered her in. He then took off his stained jacket and threw it into the trunk before getting in himself.

Christina was really angry now. That display hadn't been necessary. He could've easily had his car driven to the back of the building and they could have gotten in there. What had he been thinking?

She gave him a quick look. He'd rolled up his shirtsleeves and was now maneuvering the car into traffic.

"How much did you pay for your suit?" she asked reluctantly, afraid to know the answer.

He glanced at her before returning his attention to his driving. "$5500."

"Ohhhh no! You're not going to add that to my tab too, are you?"

"No, I'm not. You really do have a low opinion of me, don't you?"

Christina didn't answer him and there was silence in the car for a full minute. And in that minute, Christina was again becoming aware of him as a man. What was the matter with her today?

"I'm sorry about throwing up on you," she said. She wasn't really sorry but she had to say something to break her treacherous thinking.

Bill laughed. "Christina, it's not the first time, believe me."

"What do you mean?"

"I mean that I've got a PhD in vomiting."

And at that Christina laughed, the first genuine laugh she'd ever had in his presence.

Bill glanced at her. God, she looked beautiful when she laughed like that. He returned his gaze to the traffic. "I'm sure you've heard my father allude to my partying days?"

"I guess."

"Well, what he didn't tell you was about the one time I came home so drunk, I threw up all over him." Christina burst out laughing again. He continued. "And his suit was custom-made and cost $10,000."

Christina laughed even harder as she pictured William's stoic face as he stood there with vomit all over him.

Bill laughed too because she was laughing and he was

somehow making her happy. He didn't know why but it just seemed to matter to him that he was the one bringing her such joy.

Christina caught herself, as her laughter subsided. What the hell was she doing, enjoying his company? She'd better stop it right now. She had a revenge plan to execute on him and she needed to be focused on that.

*

He had insisted on carrying her into the house, up the stairs and into her bedroom—and he wasn't taking 'no' for an answer.

He had then placed her gently on the bed before leaving to get Eudora, the head maid who'd been with the Havenwoods since before Bill had been born. Eudora had helped Christina undress and get into bed. She'd then been royally propped up against a mountain of soft pillows and left to rest.

Christina was now on her cell phone to Jenny letting her friend know that she'd have to reschedule their mac and cheese night because she'd been sick that day.

Jenny was worried about her friend. "Chrissy, I'm coming over," she was saying on the phone.

"No," Christina shouted the word. "You know you can't. He might recognize you."

"But..."

"Don't worry, I'm already feeling better." Christina had told her friend about being sick all over Bill, which had elicited a giant laugh from Jenny but she'd said nothing about the kiss that had preceded it.

There was a knock at the door before it opened and Christina saw Bill come in, carrying a tray of food.

"I've got to go. We'll make it tomorrow night, okay?" Christina was careful not to mention her friend's name, as she said goodbye to Jenny.

Bill gave her an eyeful, as he positioned the tray in front of her. "Your boyfriend upset about you canceling tonight?" He tried to sound casual.

Christina was evasive. "I didn't cancel, just rescheduled." She looked down at the food in front of her.

Bill smiled proudly. "I made it myself. Plain toast and flat ginger ale for your upset stomach."

"I see you have a PhD in cooking as well as in vomiting," Christina cracked.

Bill laughed. "Actually, I do. Mom made me learn how to cook. She said I'd need those skills one day when my father would throw me out on my spoiled, rich ass."

In spite of herself, Christina laughed. "Did she really?"

"Oh yes. She had Eudora teach me. And I can do laundry too. Separate the whites from the dark and the prints. I know when to use hot water, when to use cold and when to use bleach. I'm very accomplished, you know." There—that brought another smile to that enchanting face of hers, Bill thought.

"Your mother sounds like a very smart lady."

"She left my dad, didn't she?"

Christina detected a hint of sadness there, but if true that might mean he was actually human? She pushed the food tray to the side. "I'm not hungry, right now. I think I'll just get some sleep."

Bill gave her a quick smile. "If you need anything, you can reach me anytime on my cell." He reached into his pocket and handed her his business card.

Christina mumbled a "thanks". Need him? Need him for what? There was nothing she'd ever need him for.

He bent down and gave the goldfish bowl on her bedside table a tap on the glass. "Watch over her, Samson," he said to the little fish.

He straightened, gave her a smile and walked out.

Christina breathed a sigh of relief. He was making her uncomfortable and she refused to examine why.

CHAPTER 26

IN SPITE OF herself, Christina did sleep. What with the tension of meeting the wedding planner, the disgusting kiss she'd shared with the louse and the 'being sick-fainting' episode, her energy levels had been severely depleted.

She finally woke up at 11 p.m. later that night.

Something had been digging into her cheek and she'd awoken to find that her diamond engagement ring on her left hand was sandwiched between her face and her pillow.

Damn Bill Havenwood! He wouldn't even let her sleep in peace!

Irritated, she pulled the ring off her finger and slapped it beside Samson's goldfish bowl. The diamond twinkled at her in the lamplight. That thing was worth $250,000 and if she lost it, she'd really be screwed. Christina reached for it and slipped it back on. She couldn't afford to take that chance even if she found wearing rings cumbersome. They'd never been her favorite piece of jewelry.

She looked over at Samson swimming back and forth in his bowl. "Trapped in a goldfish bowl, are you Samson? I know exactly how you feel," Christina sighed.

Throwing her blanket off, Christina slowly got up and tested her legs. They weren't wobbly anymore. She took a few steps. Yes, her strength was back.

She thought back on the day's events and it was time to face facts. Christina knew exactly why she'd gotten sick.

This hadn't been a flu bug or food poisoning. She'd gotten sick because Bill Havenwood had kissed her—and she'd kissed him back—and the strong physical attraction she seemed to have for him disgusted her mentally, emotionally and physically.

That was it in a nutshell.

Bill Havenwood had been responsible for making her the laughing stock of the school. He'd ruined her reputation with that sexual disease letter. He'd orchestrated an entire class to throw condoms at her and he'd been the cause of her parents sending her to boarding school for four years.

Because of his drunken antics, she'd been sent away from her friends, her parents and her home.

Did she still hate him? Christina felt a tickle in her solar plexus. Hell, yes—even though she now seemed to want him in her pants too! But why? What was this all about?

She was probably starved for physical contact, that was it. She hadn't been involved in a relationship for over a year and her traitorous body was just responding to his male proximity. And the creep was movie star handsome, there was that too.

Yes—that was it.

Happy with her logical explanation, Christina's stomach, suddenly, rumbled. She was hungry. After all, what she'd eaten that day had ended up allover his designer suit.

Putting on her silk robe, Christina left her bedroom and headed for the kitchen. There was always lots of food in the two massive refrigerators the staff kept stocked there.

The house was quiet as Christina made her way down the curving staircase. As she passed William's office, she noticed the door was slightly ajar and she suddenly could hear angry voices coming from inside.

It was William and Bill.

And they were yelling…

And they were yelling—about her.

She stealthily plastered herself in a dark alcove where she could listen and not be seen. Inside the room, William and Bill were standing facing each other with William's ornate desk wedged between them.

William was yelling at his son. "My fault? How in blue blazes hell is Christina getting sick today my fault?"

"Stop pushing her with all your damn wedding plans. For Christ sake, you booked the church... the church... without even talking to us first! How do you think that makes her feel?" Bill yelled back.

"I'll tell you how it should make her feel—elated, elated... that's how. If you two are as in love as you say you are, she should be thanking me for pressuring your lazy, noncommittal ass to the altar. Do you think I'm going to leave this all up to you?"

"And what the hell is that supposed to mean?"

"You know exactly what it means. You either want to get married or you don't. And I'm not going to have you string that girl along until you decide what you want to do." William was shouting now at full volume.

"You don't decide my life for me, old man and you don't decide Christina's life for her either, so back off!" Bill growled like a menacing dog.

William was taken aback by his son's words. Bill had never spoken to him in this tone before. He'd never stood up to him in such a forceful, 'stand-my-ground' stance. It was the first time William had seen Bill act like a man and refuse to be bullied by him.

And it was all because of the girl.

That little slip of a girl.

Interesting.

Very interesting.

William wasn't finished yelling at his son just yet. "What happened to Christina today wasn't my fault, it was yours!"

"My fault?"

"Yes, yours. Don't think I didn't see you pawing her out there like one of your damned, cheap girlfriends."

Outside the office, Christina began to blush. It was surreal. It felt like they were talking about someone else. But they weren't, they were talking about her.

Bill was yelling again, "We were kissing. It's what engaged couples do. Has it been that long for you, that you've forgotten... dad?"

"Watch your smart, damn mouth! I'm still your father."

"I know who you are; you don't have to remind me."

"Well, let me remind you about this. That girl upstairs is wearing your ring. Make sure you don't hurt her with your foolish ways."

"And what the hell do you mean by that?"

"I mean that for once in your life, stand up and be a man."

"And what's that dad? Two point five kids and a retirement plan? I don't conform to cookie-cutter molds and you never... in your entire miserable, selfish life... understood that about me."

"You're wrong! I've understood that quite well. Why do you think I've put up with and financed your lazy, irresponsible, drunken antics all these years? But this time it's different. If you truly love her as you say you do, then by Jove I want to see you shape up, start showing up to work everyday and stop whoring around at night."

"Meaning?" Bill was fuming.

"Don't think I don't know you're always coming home in the wee hours of the morning, drunk after a night of debauchery with who knows how many of your cheap, slut women."

"Jealous, dad?"

Christina could almost picture Bill smirking.

"If I was younger, I'd put my fist in that smart mouth of yours," William retorted.

There was a pause and then Christina heard Bill threateningly say in a soft voice, "Just try it."

There was another long pause as the two men stared each other down.

"Don't threaten me," William broke the silence first.

"No, that's your department, isn't it, dad? Threats, lies, and deceit. Well, I may be a lazy, drunken bum but at least I'm honest with myself. I know who and what I am and I don't pretend to be anything else."

"Meaning I do?"

"You are a ruthless savage hiding behind a veneer of sophistication. Look at you. You don't give a damn about me or anyone else. You certainly never cared about mom."

"Don't bring your mother into this! She left me," William shouted.

"No, dad. You left her a long time before she ever walked out on you. You were never there for her."

"I was building a business… something you wouldn't know the first thing about."

"Yeah, I guess we lazy, drunken bums don't qualify as CEO material."

William wagged his finger at his son. "You listen to me. If you love that girl as you claim, then you'll change your ways and show her some respect. Otherwise, call it off now. What's it going to be?"

William was trying to get his immature, irresponsible son to break under pressure but the boy didn't seem to be budging. William was surprised. His offspring seemed to be made of tougher stuff than he'd thought.

Interesting.

Very interesting.

"If the lecture's over, I'm leaving," Christina heard a seething Bill grit through his teeth before he walked to the office door and pushed it open with a fierce shove.

The door swung wildly open and slammed against the opposite wall, missing Christina by inches. She gasped softly in shock before slinking even deeper into the shadows.

She then heard William yelling after his son, "Where the hell are you going?"

Bill was striding towards the front doors. "Out and as far away from this fucking hellhole as I can get!" he threw back so loudly that Christina was sure the entire house must have heard it.

He then strode out of the house and seconds later, she heard the roar of the Jaguar engine rear up and the car squealed away. The house was silent.

Wow, Christina thought. What she'd heard had been incredible. The way Bill had stood up to his father—for her—believing William to be the cause of her illness today. But that didn't make sense. Bill Havenwood was a selfish, worm-of-a-dirt-bag who would never jeopardize his standing with his moneybags father to protect someone else, especially someone like her, a pawn he was blackmailing into doing his bidding.

That wasn't like him at all. He must be up to something and Christina would find out tonight. In fact, if Mr. Maggot had just zoomed away in his Jag, now would be the perfect time for her to snoop in his bedroom for clues. She doubted he'd be back soon, not after the way he'd stormed out.

Quietly, Christina disappeared into the dark shadows of the foyer.

*

Dumbfounded, William sat down at his desk. He'd never witnessed such a display from his son before. Bill had actually stood up to him like a man, especially if that 'man' was protecting his 'woman'. It was almost as if he really cared for Christina. Did he? Did his son have feelings for her?

One thing was certain—the girl had spunk, smarts and courage, and she seemed to be bringing out those same qualities in his son.

Interesting… very interesting.

*

Christina entered his chocolate brown, masculine bedroom. Her eyes scanned the massive room, which was being illuminated by two table lamps on either side of his bed.

She moved quickly to the bedside table on the left. Opening it, she began to rifle through it. There was the usual stuff—cough drops, tissue box, aspirin, some quarters—and a couple of smut magazines. Christina rolled her eyes. Figures, she thought to herself.

She quickly moved to the other bedside table. She opened it and found it filled with books. But wait—Bill Havenwood didn't read. What was he doing with books? She remembered hearing the stories in high school about how he was always too busy partying to study. After she'd left the school, Jenny had told her the rumor was he'd even paid people to write term papers for him.

She pulled out some of the books. There were some on politics, some on the environment and others on business and—good God—there was even a Bible. *A Bible???* Maybe Hell had actually frozen over! Christina shook her head in disbelief.

Very strange.

Closing the drawer, she moved to his armoires. Socks, underwear, belts—the rogue kept a pretty clean ship, but that was easy to do when you had an army of servants picking up after you.

She slid open his closet doors and Christina gasped. There must have been fifty designer suits in there, not to mention his other clothes. His closets ran the length of the room and since his room was huge, so were they. She took a deep breath. She was going to check every pocket in every jacket, shirt and pair of pants if it killed her tonight. She just had to find something on him, she just had to.

On the 36th suit jacket pocket, she found a piece of paper with an address on it. 1625 Shelley Avenue. It probably meant nothing but Christina decided to keep it.

She finished going through all of the pockets. Other than some matches, a tissue and some change, there was nothing else.

Christina then moved to his private bathroom. Other than more aspirin—probably for his daily hangovers—his colognes, shaving stuff and a couple boxes of condoms—again Christina rolled her eyes—there was nothing there either.

Well, this fishing expedition had been a dud! If Bill Havenwood had any secrets—and Christina was positive he did—they weren't hiding in his room. Quietly, she slipped out.

*

She couldn't sleep that night.

She was too well rested from the sleep she'd had after being sick to feel tired now. So she was wide-awake when she heard him come home at 4:50 a.m.

The mother-of-all-fights he'd had with his father happened around 11 p.m. Where had he been this whole time?

With Stephie, his rich-bitch girlfriend, that's where!

And they'd probably been having sex all night long, wrapped in each other's arms; kissing and caressing and making love. Christina felt a tidal wave of jealousy sweep over her. And the feeling was so overpowering that she couldn't kid herself any longer.

This was jealousy! Pure, pea-green jealousy! But why was she feeling this way? And about him, of all people? She hated him! It didn't make sense. She must be insane.

CHAPTER 27

SITTING IN THE breakfast room the next morning, Christina was reading the newspaper and having her coffee. It was almost 11 a.m. and her deadbeat, debauched fiancé was still in his room, sleeping. That was understandable, considering his all-night sex session with his country club slut, Christina jealously mused.

Eudora, the head maid, came in carrying a fresh pot of coffee. "And how are you feeling this morning, madam?" she sweetly inquired in her soft Irish accent.

"Much better, thank you," Christina answered her.

"I'm glad, madam."

"Eudora, what was Bill like as a child?" Christina casually asked.

If you want to know anything in one of these grand houses always ask the servants and Eudora had been with the family so long that she probably knew everything. Maybe the maid would let some clue or secret slip? It was worth a shot.

"Oh, madam, little Billy was a wonderful child, so sweet and kind, and very sensitive," Eudora gushed.

"Really?" Christina was surprised.

"Oh yes, mum. But he was always getting into mischief where Mr. Havenwood was concerned. Why I remember one time when…" And for the next ten minutes Eudora regaled Christina with stories of her 'sweet' little Billy's exploits in the house. Several were quite funny and Christina laughed in spite of herself.

Eudora continued, "And there was another time little Billy flushed all of Mr. Havenwood's silk ties down the loo." The maid laughed uproariously. "He couldn't have been more than seven, the holy terror. He said he wanted his dad to stay home and if he didn't have any ties, he couldn't go to work." She shook her head at the memory and smiled. "Why it took the plumber five hours to unplug it."

Christina laughed at that. Eudora was such a sweet old lady and Christina was developing a fondness for her.

The maid continued. "Oh my… was Mr. Havenwood furious with him that day." She then turned to Christina and became serious. "It's not my place to say, madam…but I'm saying it anyway. Master Bill is a sensitive soul and Mr. Havenwood never appreciated that about him, but I know that you're good for him. You're strong and you'll be an ally to him in this house. He loves you very much madam. I've seen the changes in him since your arrival. Together you make a good team and your love for each other will bring out the best in him. Now, I know he's had his problems… I'm not blind… but he's a good man with a good heart. Be kind to him. There, I've said my piece." Eudora folded her hands in front of her and nodded as if she'd just gotten off her chest what she'd been dying to say for days now.

Eudora may have been sweet and nice—but she was no fool. She knew her little Billy was up to something regarding this 'engagement'. And she knew they weren't sleeping together, that was for sure. She knew who slept in what bed and those two were definitely not sleeping in the same bed. As head maid, she knew it all.

But she'd liked Christina on first meeting her. The girl had been so kind and respectful to all of the staff and there hadn't been a demanding diva bone in her body. That meant a lot in Eudora's eyes.

And when she'd seen how her little Billy had acted around the girl—so smitten—always asking where she was, if she'd come home, if she was all right, if she needed anything—and how worried he'd been when she'd been ill last night—well, Eudora thought her little Billy had indeed been struck by Cupid's arrow and this girl was 'the one' for him.

Now if they would only sleep together everything in their relationship would right itself, she was sure of it! She wasn't too old not to remember the power of love.

Christina stared into the wise, knowing eyes of this little, sweet Irish woman standing so stoically in front of her—and she felt awful! This kind woman believed that her and Bill were in love and that she, Christina, would be the best thing in the world for him.

In reality, the opposite was true. She, Christina, wasn't here to 'love' Bill but to destroy him. And he didn't love her either. He was using her so that he could keep his sticky fingers in his father's bank accounts. No—there was no 'love' here.

"Thank you, Eudora. I'll...I'll keep in mind what you said," Christina stammered awkwardly.

Maybe she should have told the maid to mind her own business and that she didn't take personal advice from the staff, but Christina wasn't like that. She couldn't be rude to this sweetheart. She knew Eudora only wanted to see her 'little Billy' happy.

The maid nodded again, satisfied that she'd spoken her mind and that the girl had listened. Now if they would only sleep together...

Bill walked in then—showered, shaved, and handsome as always—and a guilty Christina did something she would never, in a trillion light years think she'd do. She got up, threw her arms around him and gave him a light kiss on those devastating lips of his.

She pulled back slightly and looked into his stunned eyes, "You're finally up, you sleepy head. I hope I didn't tire you out this morning."

Eudora, who was looking on, giggled at the display.

Christina bent her lips to his ear and whispered softly, "Make it look good for her."

Never one to miss an opportunity, Bill's mouth slanted into a lazy, sensual half-smile as he wrapped his hands possessively around her waist and said, "Why don't we go back to bed and find out?"

And before Christina realized his intent, his lips swooped down and captured hers in a soft, slow, deep kiss. Conscious of Eudora's scrutinizing gaze on them, Christina had no choice but to respond. At least, that's how her brain rationalized her passionate response.

Eudora giggled again. "Well, I'll leave you two lovebirds alone now. I'm sure you don't want an old lady hanging around." She teetered to herself as she left the room.

Christina heard her leave and she should have stopped the kiss right then—but she didn't.

She went on kissing the bastard…

For one bloody second too long…

But he was such a damned good kisser…

And he smelled so good…

Regaining her wits, Christina brought her spike heel down hard on Bill's instep.

"Ahhh…" he yelled as he pushed her away and started massaging his foot, "Was that really necessary?"

Still shaken up by how much she'd enjoyed his disgusting kiss, she backed away. "Yes, it was. You didn't have to take advantage of the situation."

"Advantage? You kissed me first, remember?" Bill poured himself a cup of coffee.

Sure, he'd taken advantage—and why shouldn't he? He'd enjoyed every electrifying, sizzling second of that kiss and he was going to take any crumb she'd throw his way. He wanted her that badly.

This had become more than just a scheme to stay in his father's good accounting books. He wanted her, plain and simple. That was becoming more important to him than even his father's money—and that scared the hell out of him.

Christina sat down and pretended to read her paper. She didn't want him to see how badly his kiss had affected her.

Nonchalantly, she turned the pages and replied, "I didn't want to disappoint Eudora. I like her and for some strange reason, she seems to think the sun shines out of your ass."

Bill laughed as he sipped his coffee, "Maybe it does. Care to find out?"

"Watch it… you'll not only be drinking that coffee, you'll be wearing it too."

Bill laughed again as he reached for one of the newspaper sections. "Anytime you want to put on a show for Eudora's sake, please feel free. My body is at your disposal."

Suddenly, Christina's mouth hung open as she stared at a photograph in the newspaper. She turned furious eyes to Bill and screamed, "Oh my God!"

"What?" He quickly came to peer over her shoulder at the open newspaper on the table. There—on page six—was a picture of him carrying Christina in his arms outside the Fido Foods building yesterday. The caption read, 'Billionaire's Son's Shotgun Wedding!'

Christina began to read the blurb aloud under the photo. "Bill Havenwood, son and heir of billionaire industrialist, William Havenwood carries his bride-to-be, Christina Matteo to his car outside the Fido Foods building. Inside sources say that Miss Matteo fainted yesterday and had to be escorted out. She is pregnant with Bill's child and that's the reason for the quickie wedding that's to take place in a few weeks time at St. Patrick's Cathedral. Officials at the company had no comment and would neither confirm nor deny the report."

Livid, Christina zeroed in on Bill and stood up with such force that Bill jumped back as her chair toppled over. She grabbed the newspaper and shoved it at him.

"Do you know…how many people are going to see this? My friends, my co-workers, my cousins…my… parents?" She screamed the word "parents" at him.

"I thought you said your parents live in Florida?" Bill was staying calm in order to keep her calm. It wasn't working.

"Have you ever heard of a telephone?"

"Christina, it's not that bad."

"Not that bad? Not that bad?? Do you know how many explanations I'm going to have to make now? How many people are going to ask me about my pregnancy and my impending marriage… to an asshole like you?"

"Correction… a rich asshole. And I am taking responsibility for the baby by marrying you; that is something." He threw her a big smile.

"This is all a big joke to you, isn't it? Just a good ole time, for a few laughs until you can get your hands on daddy's money."

"I never joke about daddy's money," Bill drawled, as he calmly sipped his coffee.

"What am I going to tell these people? That it's all a scam?"

"You can't say that, we've got a deal." Bill was suddenly tense.

"I know what we've got. You think I want them to know that I would sink so low as to go along with a lying, scumbag ruse like this? Well, I don't."

Bill let out a silent breath of relief. He contemplated her anxious face. "I am sorry, you know."

"Save it." Christina turned to leave.

"Where are you going?" Bill wasn't quite sure what she'd do next. Knowing her, as he'd come to know her these past few weeks, Christina Matteo was capable of anything.

"To plan our wedding, sweetie pie. I've got an appointment with your father's fucking wedding planner!" She screamed the words at him before disappearing out the door.

Bill looked at the newspaper photograph again. Yes, this certainly complicated everything. He again read the blurb under the picture. "Inside sources say…"

And who the hell were these 'inside sources'?

*

'Mr. Inside Source' was at that moment, sitting in his office, looking at that same newspaper picture of his son carrying his bride-to-be. He laughed to himself. He was brilliant, just brilliant.

And the part about the pregnancy and the quickie, shotgun marriage had been a stroke of Havenwood genius on his part. What a clever spin on the whole rotten affair!

He wondered how his conniving son had reacted to the picture this morning. And what about Christina? William was sure she'd hit the roof and blamed Bill for getting her deeper in a mess that was only supposed to have involved the both of them and William.

He laughed again to himself. The pair of them were either going to crack under this new pressure or become stronger partners-in-crime.

William thought about it for a second. No, they'd crack. Christina would leave him—his son's scheme would backfire—and William would have the immense pleasure of throwing Bill out on his spoiled, soon-to-be-poor, ass.

CHAPTER 28

WHAT AN AFTERNOON she'd had! After Christina had stormed out of the breakfast room, she'd found Mindy, the wedding planner, waiting for her in the salon. For the next hour, Mindy bombarded Christina with hundreds of questions about decisions that needed to be made for the wedding and the engagement party.

How many guests? What menu would you like? Which flower arrangements? Which invitations? And on—and on. Within thirty minutes, Christina had developed a major headache. She couldn't deal with any of it. This was all pretend and within a month's time, this whole thing would be called off anyway, so what did it matter which flowers or invitations or menus were chosen. It was all fake.

The wedding planner droned on and Christina had reached her limit. "Mindy?" she interrupted. "I'm sure William has given you a budget of what to spend for the engagement party and the wedding?'

Mindy nodded, "It's the first thing I always ask my clients."

"Good. In that case, I want you to plan everything. I… can't handle all this pressure right now."

Mindy was aghast, "But my dear…"

Christina was firm. "No, I insist. You decide and I'll agree to it all. And as for the guest list from Bill's side, you can get that from William and as to my side of the family, just leave me some blank invitations, about 20, and I'll mail them out myself." She was going to throw them in the garbage, that's what she was going to do.

"Are you sure, my dear?" Mindy was still unconvinced.

"Yes. This will be such a relief to me." Christina gave Mindy her sweetest smile.

The planner nodded sympathetically. "All right, then. But you'll have to go for your gown fittings and pick out your china patterns."

"That I'll do. I promise."

After Mindy had left, Christina had gone back to her room for a nap. Her headache had gotten worse and she really needed to rest. But that's when the phone calls began. One after another, her cell phone never stopped ringing.

First, it was Jenny wanting to know what was going on about the photo, then some of her Italian cousins called and then some of her work colleagues. The only call she didn't get was the one she dreaded most—her parents.

The calls came quick, all congratulating her and wanting to know about the 'baby'. The baby part she told them wasn't true, only a rumor spread by the newspaper but she accepted the wedding well wishes with gratitude. What else could she say? She couldn't very well deny that too and have it get back to William.

This was all that creep's fault, Bill Havenwood! He had screwed her over in high school and he was doing it to her again.

This had to be the worst mess she'd ever been involved in. She'd had to lie to friends, family and co-workers. Everyone was now expecting a real wedding and they'd all begged for invitations, considering it would be one of the social events of the season.

She was marrying into New York royalty, they'd told her; and what a lucky girl she was, they'd told her; and her husband-to-be was one of the most eligible bachelors in the country, they'd told her; and get a good lawyer before signing any pre-nups, they'd told her…

Ohhhh—that swine!!! He had it coming—and she was going to deliver!

*

Jenny was gushing over Christina's engagement ring that she'd slipped on her own left hand. The diamond glistened in the small apartment.

"Is it really worth $250G's?" Jenny asked, wide-eyed.

"Yes," Christina sighed.

"He must like you a lot to trust you with something like this," Jenny surmised.

"But that's the whole point. He doesn't trust me. I had to sign over my life in that blasted contract if I should ever lose it," Christina frowned.

Little 8-year-old Taylor came over, "Can I try it on too, Aunt Chrissy?"

"Of course you can, honey."

Jenny interrupted, "Later, darling. Right now, you go set the table. Mommy has to discuss something important with Aunt Chrissy."

Taylor's face showed disappointment as she disappeared into the kitchen. Jenny pushed Christina down on the couch and plopped herself down beside her.

"Okay, I want major details. Have you seen him naked yet?"

"Jenny! What kind of question is that?" Christina had already told her friend everything that had been happening except for her physical attraction to the sleazeball.

"Is he big or small? I betcha he's big."

"Jenny!"

"Come on, Chrissy, you're living together. You're bound to have seen him naked."

"We have separate bedrooms and separate bathrooms. Why would I have to see him naked?"

Jenny gasped, "Oh my God, he's seen you naked?"

Christina laughed. "Nobody's seen anybody naked."

"Oh." Jenny was disappointed. "Have you kissed him yet?"

"Jenny!" But this time, Christina blushed and her shrewd friend caught it.

"You have!"

"He kissed me, all right?"

"And you kissed him right back, didn't you?" Christina remained silent. Jenny smiled and continued. "I knew it. I knew you liked him on account of how much you hated him."

"Jenny, stop this. He's a super rat, alcoholic scumbag and you of all people know what he did to me."

"You had a crush on him in high school before he pulled that prank on you, admit it."

Christina wasn't admitting anything. "Everybody had a crush on him back then, even you."

"Not me. I liked his buddy, Jake."

Christina was shocked. "Jake Monroe? That drunken idiot?"

Jenny nodded, "He was cute. Has Bill ever mentioned him now?"

Christina shook her head. "No. They've probably lost touch over the years."

"Probably." Jenny took a moment to assess her friend. "I know you better than you know yourself, so you listen to me. Love and hate are the flip side of the same coin; be careful which side you land on. I don't want to see you get hurt."

"Jenny, stop being such a mother hen."

"And if you like him and you think he likes you, grab him. I saw his face in that newspaper today. He wants you badly, mark my words."

Christina was skeptical. "And you could tell all this from a blurry newspaper picture?"

"Of course. Men don't carry women like that unless they really care for them. So forget about all this revenge business, forgive him for the past and marry the prick for real. He's a good catch."

"Marry Bill Havenwood?" Christina burst out laughing. "You're crazy!"

*

Driving the BMW back to the mansion that night, Christina was still laughing to herself. Marry Havenwood for real? What an imagination Jenny had!

Bill Havenwood was a drunk, lazy, good-for-nothing womanizer that never showed up for work—even his own father said so—not to mention the fact that she detested him and had vowed revenge on the idiot.

But on the plus side? Wait—there was no plus side.

Okay, he was rich but he wasn't really. His father was. And that meant he and his 'wife' would always have to dance to the old man's manipulating tune.

Okay, he was drop dead gorgeous but looks fade over time. The heavy drinking and constant partying would probably take their toll and he'd end up bald and fat—and still drunk.

There was this physical attraction thing she seemed to have for him. Every time she was within his orbit, she felt an intense magnetic force that pulled her to him. It disgusted her, of course. How could she be attracted to such a slime?

And this morning—when she'd kissed him for Eudora's sake—she really shouldn't have done that. But she'd acted on instinct—and every instinct in her body kept wanting him.

What would sex with him be like, Christina wondered, as she let her mind wander? Probably incredible and delicious, if his passionate, sweet kisses were anything to go by. She gave herself a small shake. Yuck—now she'd grossed herself out!

Stop it, Christina. You have a job to do. Focus on that.

She reached into her pocket and pulled out the slip of paper she'd found in Bill's jacket pocket when she'd been snooping in his bedroom last night.

1625 Shelley Avenue, it said.

Okay, she wasn't too far from that area now. It might be a good time to go and have a look. What was 1625 Shelley Avenue and what did it have to do with Bill Havenwood?

*

1625 Shelley Avenue was an old, empty, abandoned warehouse.

Christina parked the BMW under a streetlamp for safety purposes. This wasn't the best part of town and it was almost 10 p.m. at night. Stepping out of the car, she began to take pictures of the building with her camera.

Approaching it, she peered through the dirty windows.

Not much in there. She could make out an old desk and several chairs. The rest of the cavernous interior was bare.

She moved to one of the doors and pulled. It was locked—of course.

Why would Havenwood have this address in his pocket?

Was his father's company thinking of buying it? Did they own it already? Was the property it sat on valuable?

Taking a few more pictures, a disappointed Christina went back to her car. This had been another dead end. Damn!

*

It was almost 11 p.m. and Christina turned onto the road that led to the Havenwood mansion. Getting closer, she suddenly spotted Bill's Jaguar zooming out of the front gates and accelerating away. Where was he going again at this hour? Pressing her foot on the gas, Christina took off after him.

Keeping a safe distance behind other cars, she followed him into the city, undetected. But city traffic was heavier and Christina soon lost him. The Jag disappeared.

Where had he gone? And why was he always going out at night—sometimes at 7 p.m. and sometimes at 11 p.m.? Was he seeing his snooty girlfriend? Was he drinking, clubbing and partying with friends?

What was really odd, though, was that not once, since she'd been at the mansion, had she seen him come home drunk. She'd never even smelled any alcohol on him. If he was partying, he hid the effects very well.

Well—whatever he was up to, she was going to get to the bottom of it—no matter if she'd have to spy on the louse 24/7.

She pulled a U-turn and headed back to the mansion.

What Christina didn't know was that there'd been a mysterious car following her all night long, too.

CHAPTER 29

HER CELL PHONE was ringing. Christina opened one eye and looked at her beside clock. 6 a.m. Who was calling her this early? She reached for her phone and croaked out a sleepy, "Hello," into it.

"Christina, oh my God, your Aunt Sylvia just called! She told us that you're pregnant??!"

Jumping jelly beans! It was her mother.

"Mommy!" Christina bolted upright.

"Why didn't you tell us? I had to find out from that cow?" Gabriella was clearly upset.

"Mommy, it's not what you think…"

"And you're getting married too?"

"Were you going to send us an invitation even?" That had been said by her dad, Nunzio, who'd been listening on another extension in their Florida condo.

"Pop, I was going to tell you, but…"

"When's the baby due?" her mom interrupted.

"Mommy, there is no baby."

Her mom gasped in shock. "Oh my God, you lost the baby? Oh my poor Christina…"

"Mommy, I didn't lose the baby. There is no baby." Christina was now shouting. "The newspapers got it all wrong."

Her mom was confused. "But are you getting married? Sylvia said she saw your picture in the paper."

Christina paused. What was she going to say? That it was all a scam—that she was doing it for money? This entire mess was spinning out of control and it was all Havenwood's fault! Her anger at him soared as she re-focused on her parents.

"Yes mommy, I am getting married." Christina crossed her fingers, hoping that would cancel her lie.

"And who's this Havenwood? What's he do?" Her father jumped in.

"He works for his father's company, Fido Foods."

"Fido Foods?" Her father was impressed. "We did some construction work for them. They're big."

"When's the wedding? We have to invite your aunts, uncles, cousins…" Gabriella started rattling on.

"Mommy, nothing's been decided yet." Hopefully, in a couple of weeks, this fiasco would be over and she'd just tell everyone that the wedding was called off.

"Okay, we're flying back tomorrow to start planning everything."

"No!" Christina shouted. "Just wait until I give you the date."

"But Christina, we want to meet our son-in-law and his family too," her mom insisted.

"Don't push me, mom. Just wait until things are more settled, okay?" That's all she needed, to have her parents show up and create more of a disaster than this was already turning out to be.

Gabriella sighed, "Okay then. But you call and tell me what's going on. I don't want to find things out from Sylvia anymore."

"I promise mom." Relieved, Christina sighed. Saying goodbye to her parents, she shut her phone.

Bill Havenwood! That moron was really putting her through a meat-grinder and she'd had enough!

There'd been a message on her voicemail last night from Mindy, the wedding planner. She'd said that the engagement party was set for the following Saturday on the mansion grounds and the caterers would soon set up the tents—and now, this morning— *this???*

Yanking off her bedcovers, she donned her silk robe over her baby doll p.j.s and marched to the door. She was going to give that jerk a piece of her furious mind before telling him to take his devil's bargain and shove it!

Christina was so mad that she didn't even bother knocking on his bedroom door. Too enraged to care whether he was sleeping or naked or what, she threw his door open.

His bed was rumpled but he wasn't in it. She could hear the shower running in his bathroom. Stomping inside his bedroom, she slammed his door shut. Crossing her arms across her chest, she waited for the asshole to appear.

She didn't have to wait long. She heard the water shut off. A minute later, the bathroom door opened and he appeared with a towel wrapped around his mid-section.

His hair was wet and slicked back, and his chest was chiseled. His body looked lean—not thin—but lean. The bastard obviously worked out, but that was easy to do when you never showed up for work and spent your nights partying, Christina bitchily mused.

Bill suddenly spotted her—near his bed—dressed only in a flimsy robe and who knew what underneath, obviously fired up about something. God—she looked magnificent! All his senses sprang to life. He wanted her so badly, he ached for her but he wasn't going to do anything to scare her off so Bill calmly walked into the room as if it was the most normal thing in the world to have her show up there.

"Good morning, Christina. What can I do for you?" He gave her a sensual smirk. He knew exactly what he 'wanted to do' for her. He'd been thinking of nothing else for the past few days.

"Our deal is off." Christina yanked off her ring and threw it at him. It bounced off his firm chest and fell to the floor.

Bill's stomach lurched at her words. He studied her angry face before picking up the ring. The diamond glistened in the room's light as he held it up. "We have a contract."

"You can take your contract and shove it! I'm outta here. Today." And with that Christina turned and started marching towards the door.

Bill, quickly, grabbed her arm and spun her around to face him. "Tell me what's happened," he forcefully demanded.

"Go to hell!"

"That's exactly where I'll be if you leave me." Christina didn't realize that he meant more than just the consequences of losing his father's money.

"I'm not playing your game anymore, so let go of my arm," Christina spouted through her gritted teeth.

But he didn't let go, he was hanging on for dear life. "What's changed between yesterday and today? Did my father say something to make you upset? Because if he did, I'll…"

"I haven't seen your father since yesterday morning."

"Then what? Tell me." He was shouting now.

"I don't have to tell you anything except that our contract is null and void."

"No." His voice was firm. His hand slid down to her wrist and brought her left hand up. Before she realized what he was doing, he'd slipped the ring back onto her finger.

She went to yank it off again but he stopped her. She was now trapped in his arms and he wasn't letting go. She could feel the steel strength rippling through his muscles.

"Let me go now."

"Did your boyfriend say something to you last night? Is that what this is all about?"

Bill was still under the mistaken impression that she'd had a date with her mysterious 'boyfriend' as he'd overheard her making plans with Jenny when she'd been sick.

"That's none of your business." Christina had no intentions of correcting him.

He yanked her left hand up between them. "The only ring I see on your hand is mine. Where's his? If he truly cared about you, he would have helped you out in whatever jam you were in and not let you handle it all on your own."

"Leave him out of this." God—what was she saying? This was insane. There was no boyfriend and he was making her crazy.

Bill, on the other hand, was jealous—white hot jealous. He suddenly knew he wanted Christina all for himself and he wasn't a man who shared.

He yanked her closer to him. "So how come your white knight boyfriend isn't saving you from my evil clutches, then?" he threw at her.

"Because... because... fifty-six grand may mean nothing to you, but it's a lot of money to people like us. But you wouldn't understand, living in your cushy world, always having everything handed to you on one of your father's sterling silver dinner platters. What do you know about it?"

Christina tried to yank her hands out of his grip but he was holding on fast.

"I know this. If you leave today, my father's gonna throw me out. And if he does, I'll have nothing and I won't give a damn if my insurance company sues your pretty, little, well-shaped ass to get their money. And your wages will be garnished for the next sixty years, make no mistake."

Bill was desperate and he was going to say whatever he had to, to stop her from leaving. This was more than just losing his father's money. He didn't want to lose her either.

Christina stared back into his determined, gorgeous green eyes and knew he meant every word. "You really are a bastard. You always were and you still are."

"What do you mean by that?"

Oops—she'd slipped up. How did she know he used to be a bastard if she'd only met him a few weeks ago?

"I... mean that I've heard the stories about you...from your father about your drinking, your partying and your army of girlfriends."

"You wouldn't by chance be jealous of my harem?" He gave her a half smile, as his eyes glued themselves to hers.

He was still holding her strong against his chest and Christina felt his heat suddenly engulf her body. Or was that hers engulfing his? She didn't know anymore and her breathing began to synchronize with his.

But in a flash, a light bulb went on in her brain. What the hell was she doing here—in his bedroom—in his arms—dressed in a flimsy baby doll and robe, and he—half naked?

This was too intimate, too dangerous. It wasn't that she didn't trust him—she didn't trust herself.

"Me? Jealous of your easy conquests? I don't think so. Now let go of me," she bravely retorted.

Bill stared deeply into her eyes. Did she really have no feelings for him? He wasn't sure. He did know however, that she wanted him as much as he wanted her—whatever she said. He'd had enough experience with women to know that. When they came anywhere near each other, they were both on fire. He could feel it.

Suddenly, he released her and she took a step away from him. But her kitten heel on her right slipper caught in the carpet pile and Christina lost her balance. She began to fall backwards.

Quick as ever, Bill reached for her to prevent her fall, but she was already on a downward trajectory and pulled him with her. Luckily, his bed was positioned behind them and they both fell on it, with Bill on top of Christina.

They were both stunned at how fate had made them end up this way—on the bed and in each other's arms. He had his arms around her waist, from trying to break her fall, and she had her arms around his neck, from trying to grab on.

They stared into each other's shocked eyes. How had this happened?

Christina didn't know who started first but they both suddenly burst out in a fit of laughter and they couldn't stop.

They just kept laughing and laughing… together.

And it was the most erotic thing they'd ever both experienced.

They stopped laughing suddenly—and gazed into each other's eyes. A moment of unspoken understanding passed between them. Christina knew she had a fraction of a nanosecond to make a decision. Here she was, lying on his bed, in his arms and already her legs were itching to wrap themselves around him.

He lowered his lips to hers but stopped an inch away.

His eyes flirted upwards to hers and he was silently asking her for permission to go on. What did she want to do? It was clear what he wanted. Christina could already feel him getting hard underneath his towel.

So—what did she want? Should she give in to her desire and make love with him? Or should she stop this right now?

Christina was almost at the point of no return but not quite.

Suddenly, her rational, logical brain began to function.

Was she crazy?

This was Bill Havenwood, her avowed enemy. She'd promised to exact revenge on him for what he'd done to her and she never broke promises to herself. NEVER. She had more respect for herself than that.

Besides, it wouldn't be making love—it would be having sex. And there was a world of difference in that. She was worth more than a cheap lay.

But those tempting lips of his looked so delicious—and soft and hard—all at the same time, promising her pleasures like she'd never experienced with anyone before.

A moan escaped her lips before she uttered the word, "No."

Bill remained still. He'd watched her thoughts race across her beautiful face when she'd been trying to decide. He knew he'd almost won—almost—and he wanted her so badly. But he released her and rolled away.

She got up and started walking to the door.

"Christina?" At the anguished way he said her name, Christina turned to him. He was sitting up on the bed, focused on her. "Are you leaving?" He was asking her whether she was going to continue with their deal or not.

"I don't know," she replied softly. She was so confused right now and needed to retreat to her own bedroom to think.

"Don't go. I need you," his voice sounded hoarse and strangled as the words spluttered out of him.

Christina had the oddest sensation that he wasn't just talking
about her helping him get his father's money.

Suddenly feeling unsettled, she walked out without answering him.

*

Christina sat on her bed and she was shaking very badly.

This last encounter with him had really shaken her up. How
can you want someone so badly yet hate them at the same time? It
didn't make sense.

When she was away from him, she could think clearly and her
revenge plan came back to her thoughts. But when she was physically anywhere near him, all those thoughts went out the window
and her brain became mush. What was the matter with her?

Now that she'd had time to cool off after that upsetting phone
call from her parents, Christina realized that she'd have to see this
month through to its bitter end. She couldn't afford to have her
wages garnished for the insurance money. That debt was hanging
over her head. If only she could come up with something to hold
over his?

She needed to concentrate more on her revenge plan, that's
what she needed to do. She wouldn't think about why she'd been
shaking, or why he seemed to affect her in this way, or why she
wanted him so badly—that was all nonsense anyway. She'd think
about her revenge plan instead.

Christina calmed down and the shaking stopped.

*

Bill sat on his bed and he was shaking very badly.

This last encounter with her had really shaken him up. He
slicked his wet hair back with his hands. It was time to face facts,
however hard that was going to be.

He loved her.

But how can you love someone who doesn't even like you back? She may have wanted him physically, but Bill knew she didn't really like him. How can you love someone like that?

What an idiot he was!

When she'd announced that she was leaving, Bill had felt like he'd been punched in the gut. What would this house be like if she left? If he would never see her smile again? Or hear her laugh? Or see her scowl even? If he would never kiss her again? Or smell her intoxicating perfume? Or feel her soft skin? Or see her beautiful face?

She fascinated him.

She enchanted him.

She challenged him.

She excited him.

It sometimes felt like he'd known her all his life—that missing puzzle piece that clicked into his soul. If she walked out of here, she would leave behind a big, gaping hole in his life—and she didn't even know it. How in the hell could she have wormed her way into his heart in so short a time? How—damn it?

Bill had no idea. All he knew was that he loved her and she was going to walk out of his life today—maybe. And if she stayed until the month was up, she'd walk out of his life then. Either way, she was walking—back into the arms of someone else that she cared for because Bill knew she didn't care about him.

If he ever needed a drink, it was right now. He could bury all of these feelings in booze and not have to deal with any of them. And it would certainly stop this shaking.

He reached for his phone and began to call his Alcoholics Anonymous sponsor. He desperately needed to talk to someone; otherwise he'd make a beeline for the drinks cabinet downstairs in about two seconds flat.

CHAPTER 30

OVER THE NEXT few days, Christina avoided him like the Black Plague. Or was he avoiding her? By the third day, she wasn't sure. All she knew was that whenever they saw each other, the only words that passed between them were a polite hello and a polite goodbye.

She'd been prepared to follow him on his nightly expeditions but he hadn't gone on any. Lately, he'd been showing up for work all day and coming home at night for dinner. After dinner, he'd stay in. The entire staff had been gossiping about nothing else.

Apparently, even William had noticed and had made a pleasing comment about it to Bentley, the butler. One of the maids had overheard it and the remark had quickly made the rounds of the house.

Although Bill had now been showing up for dinner, Christina had not. After her unsettling encounter with him in his bedroom, she needed some alone time to strengthen her resolve against him, and pleading a headache, had had her dinners sent up to her room.

Concerned about her, both Bill and William had each, on separate occasions, come up to ask if she was feeling unwell.

Lying to their faces, Christina had simply told them that it was that time of the month and she had cramps. That had instantly shut them both up and they'd scurried away like cockroaches.

Christina had also had several dress fittings with the House of Baldora for her wedding dress and engagement party dress. William had insisted that she choose whatever she wanted from sketches, no matter the cost.

For her wedding dress, she'd picked a simple white sheath that molded to her body perfectly; and for her engagement party dress, Christina had chosen a white Grecian style dress with tiny crystals beaded throughout. She hadn't asked what the costs were. She didn't want that on her guilty conscience too. Although she'd didn't feel guilty about what she was doing to Bill, she did feel terrible about fooling everybody else.

The preparations for the engagement party on the Havenwood grounds had also begun. The household staff had been getting the house ready; flower arrangements had begun to arrive, as had the tents and settings. Parties didn't happen very often at the mansion anymore—not since Mrs. Havenwood had divorced Bill's father five years ago.

Everyone was excited and giddy—everyone, except Christina. She felt like a big, fat phony.

*

Bill was sitting at the boardroom table, with Vice-President Stephen Downey. Both were waiting for William to arrive.

Bill's thoughts wandered to his 'fiancée' and he half-smiled to himself. These past few days he had avoided Christina like the Black Plague.

Ever since he'd faced himself in the mirror and admitted how deeply he'd fallen for her, he couldn't bear to be near her because it only brought home to him that he could never have *her*—because she didn't want *him*.

Maybe he could do something to change her mind? Or say something? Bill had racked his brain these past few days but had drawn a blank. You can't make someone love you. It doesn't work that way.

William walked in and took his seat at the head of the boardroom table. "Gentlemen, I'm going to make this meeting brief. I want to discuss our strategy for combating these dastardly Guardians of Mother Earth terrorists that have been hounding us," he began, speaking in his proper British accent.

"Maybe we should call a meeting with one of their leaders and see how we can resolve this," Bill piped in.

"Are you mad? I'm not giving into them. They don't dictate to me how I run my blasted companies," William shouted at his son.

"The bad P. R. we're getting is affecting our sales and our share prices are down. Maybe we should…" Bill retaliated.

"Maybe—nothing! I'm not about to let everything I've built be destroyed by a bunch of unemployable crybabies who couldn't organize a piss in a brewery. We're going to fight fire with fire and I've come up with a plan to crush those imbeciles."

"Which is?"

William gave his son a wicked smile. "First off, I'm going to start by hiring detectives. I want all of those damn activists put on 24-hour surveillance. I want to know who they are and where they sleep. Who knows, maybe they live in glass houses too? Second… I'm going to plant spies inside GME. They'll pretend to be fellow environmentalists, willing to do anything for the cause. Not only will I get inside information, but I'll also make sure they stir up a batch of 'trouble' stew." He laughed, pleased with himself.

"How clever of you," Bill sarcastically remarked.

"I'm not standing for their nonsense any longer," William said before turning to his VP Stephen. "Downey?"

"Yes sir?" Stephen was sitting at attention.

"I suspect that someone from one of my companies is feeding those hoodlums inside information. I need you to ferret them out."

"Of course, sir," Stephen quickly responded.

Bill was nonchalantly doodling on the report in front of him. "What makes you think that?" he casually asked.

"Because they know too many details about my activities and how my businesses are run, things only an insider would know." William turned to his VP, "Stephen, get started on my ideas immediately."

"Yes, sir."

"You may go. I need to speak to my son in private," William

waved his VP away. Stephen obediently rose from his seat and left the room.

Bill folded his arms across his chest and disappointed, glared at his father.

"Don't look at me like that," William began. "I'm doing this for us."

"There's a better way, dad."

"Like what?"

"Like maybe these people have a point! Those pipelines are disintegrating and that oil is leaking into the environment. We're destroying the Russian Arctic."

"And what would you have me do, huh? Do you know how much money I would lose if I refused to pump oil through that pipeline? It's not my fault if the whole damn Russian infrastructure is falling apart." Frustrated, William pounded the table with his fist.

Equally upset, Bill stood up. "You wouldn't exactly be forced to line up at the food bank," he threw back.

"That's not the point and I didn't call you in here to discuss my ethics."

"Or lack of them," Bill retorted.

William eyed his son. The boy had developed some balls lately. He'd been standing up to William's bullying tactics—and William knew it was because of the girl.

William had enjoyed the game he'd been playing with the both of them—manipulating them by adding more and more pressure to their steam cooker of a phony 'engagement.' Time to turn up the heat.

"I want to discuss Christina with you," William interjected.

Bill was immediately wary. "What about her?"

"I like the girl. She's got spunk and she's exactly what you need to wake you up." He snapped his fingers in front of Bill's face.

"I'm glad you approve. Was there anything else?" Bill was playing it cool.

"Just this. If you don't marry that girl, you're out." William smiled to himself.

William knew perfectly well they were going to officially 'break up" before the month was out. Why not put more pressure on his lying, deceitful son and make the game more fun until then?

"Was that all you wanted to say to me?" Bill glowered at his father.

William nodded. "That's all."

Bill walked out of the room.

William watched his son leave. The boy hadn't shown a flicker of fear. He'd remained cool, the way a real man would.

Interesting.

That girl was truly having an effect on his son, a positive effect. Bill had even been showing up at the office lately and had actually worked! He'd been involved in meetings and put in his suggestions. And William had been impressed with how smart some of those suggestions had been.

Interesting.

His son had also been having dinner with William lately. Although they'd barely spoken two words to each other throughout the meals, they'd still sat down together—and that was something.

Also interesting.

And the boy had been staying home at night and William had actually caught him reading a book in the mansion's library one evening. He couldn't remember the last time he saw his son pick up a book, let alone read one!

Doubly interesting.

Yes, William was convinced the girl had brought about this change in his son. But what would happen when, at the end of the month, the two would part ways? Well, true to his word, William was prepared to throw Bill out. That might make him more of a man.

But what if—they didn't break up?

What if the girl stayed?

What if his son were to actually marry Christina? What then?

Very interesting idea.

William needed to think about this some more.

CHAPTER 31

CHRISTINA WAS TAKING pictures of the GME protesters outside the Fido Foods office building. Teddy, the hippy 60's throwback that she'd met last time, came over.

"Hey, you're back," he happily greeted her.

"We needed more pictures for our magazine story. So, how are you guys doing? Making any headway with corporate America?" she asked.

"Yeah, man. We've been getting a lot more media coverage and as a result, Fido Foods sales are down and so are their share prices. We're winning the battle."

Christina was impressed. According to what she'd learnt from Robert, the reporter at Streetwise who was writing the story to accompany her pictures, GME was a well-organized, well-financed machine that seemed to know what they were doing. They may have looked like a bunch of misfits but they were anything but.

"I'm going to take a few more pictures. Thanks for your help, Teddy," Christina smiled at him.

"Anytime, man." Teddy smiled back before rejoining the protest line.

Christina began to snap more photos. So her Billy and his dad were losing money over this? Served them right, if they were polluting the environment for cash, as GME claimed. As Christina continued to take her pictures, someone else was taking pictures of her—from far away, with a zoom lens.

*

Tall, red-headed Stephie, Bill's former girlfriend, was sitting with her model legs crossed on the couch in Drummond Sinclair's office and was jealously studying the photos of Christina Matteo that were in her hands.

"So tell me everything about her," she purred.

Drummond Sinclair studied Stephie's cold face. She was absolutely beautiful, but dangerous if crossed—and Bill Havenwood had definitely crossed her. As a private investigator for over twenty-five years, he'd been involved in many love-gone-wrong cases like this. In fact, 'love-gone-wrong' was his middle name as were the words 'straight cash' but he'd never seen a more gorgeous, breathtaking woman that had been dumped than Stephanie Hartwell.

"We know there's more to this engagement than love. And she doesn't trust him, because she's been following him while we've been following her," Drummond explained.

"Really?" Stephie's eyes widened with interest.

Drummond nodded. "We're currently in the process of acquiring their pre-nup agreement and we'll know more then."

Stephie was surprised. "Bill's lawyer is willing to sell you that?"

"No... not quite. He used a different law firm and we've got an insider there who can get us a copy."

"Which means you'll need more money?"

Drummond smiled, "I told you when you started this, Miss Hartwell that it wasn't going to be cheap."

Stephie's eyes narrowed. "I don't care what it costs or what you have to do... just get me everything on Christina Matteo and get it to me now."

"We may have to... 'investigate'... inside her apartment," Drummond cagily informed her. "And we may have to... 'liberate'... any interesting things or information we may find there. Do you have any problems with that?"

Stephie took out her wallet and started counting out hundred dollar bills. "None whatsoever, Mr. Sinclair," she replied.

As Drummond Sinclair greedily watched her count out the

money, he thought to himself that there really was no fury like a woman scorned.

CHAPTER 32

CHRISTINA STARED AT her reflection in the mirror. Was that really her?

There she was, at the couture house, standing on a platform in her wedding dress. The simple, white sheath had been beaded with seed pearls and the overhead lights picked up their luster, creating a twinkling effect. She looked magical.

And she couldn't take her eyes off of herself.

There was someone else who couldn't take his eyes off of her—Bill. He was watching her from the shadows, having arrived five minutes before. She looked incredible, he thought to himself. And gorgeous, and magnificent, and desirable... and she belonged to someone else.

He felt that familiar punch to the gut. This wedding was all make-believe. None of it was true—except his love for her. That was the only true, good, clean thing in this entire mess.

Bill approached her.

"You look beautiful," he said, as his eyes devoured her.

Christina was surprised at seeing him there. "What are you doing here?"

"I got a message from Genghis Khan to meet you here, then take you to Beacon's to register."

Christina gave a small laugh, "And his lordship must be obeyed."

Bill laughed himself, "Or else it's off with my head and other male body parts."

His eyes shifted from hers to their reflection together in the mirror. Christina's eyes followed his. Dressed in one of his designer suits and her in her wedding dress, they definitely made a very handsome couple.

Bill smirked, "Isn't it bad luck for the groom to see the bride in her dress before the wedding?"

"I don't think we have to worry about that."

"No, we don't." He gave her a polite smile. "I'll wait for you outside." He turned and left.

Christina watched him leave. The oddest thing—he'd been very quiet lately. What was he up to?

*

Mindy, the wedding planner met Christina and Bill at Beacon's where they registered for their bridal gifts. Christina felt so uncomfortable at having to perpetuate this monstrous lie of theirs in the real world that she picked out her choices in ten minutes flat. Whatever the Beacon's representative suggested, she agreed to. Bill had stood beside her—very sullen and again very quiet.

Outside the store, Christina was about to walk away, when Bill grabbed her hand. "Have lunch with me?" he asked.

Christina paused. She didn't want to, but maybe he'd let something slip over pasta and drinks that she could use against him in her revenge plan. So far, she had nothing and their contract would expire in ten days time.

"Sure," she responded.

He took her to a very trendy outdoor café. They were given a bistro table near the sidewalk, enabling them to watch the passersby while under the shade of a large, yellow-striped awning.

While they were both studying their menus, Christina was secretly studying him. He was in a funny mood today, but she'd sensed a change in him ever since their encounter in his bedroom.

She kept eyeing him. Wow—was he ever handsome. He'd removed his jacket and rolled up his white shirtsleeves. With his hair smoothed back and his Hollywood action-star looks, Christina noticed several women passing by, staring at him. He didn't appear to notice the female attention he was getting. His hypnotic green eyes remained glued to his menu.

The waiter came by to take their order and he turned to Christina first.

"I'll have the pasta primavera and a glass of white wine, please," Christina ordered.

He scribbled her request down, and then turned to Bill. "I'll have the same but with mineral water instead."

The waiter nodded and left.

Christina looked him over. Mineral water? No wine??? That was strange. She knew he was driving, but one glass with his meal was allowed. After all, he was a big guy and one glass wouldn't affect him.

"You don't like wine?" Christina broke the silence.

Bill suddenly burst out laughing. "I love wine. It's one of my favorite drinks actually. But not… today."

She continued, "Your father seems excited about our wedding. Are you back in his good accounting books?"

"For now, but I'm sure you've noticed that he and I have our differences."

Christina smiled, "Oh, I've noticed." Curious in spite of herself, she turned serious. "Has it always been like this…between you two?"

"As far back as I can remember; except for my younger years when I was shipped off to boarding school. Then we had no relationship."

"So why do you stay? For his money?" she just had to ask.

"Sometimes I think I keep taking his money because that's all he ever wants to give." Bill gave her a big grin but she sensed there was a lot of pain behind it.

This was getting too personal—and Christina didn't like it one bit. How was she going to get through the rest of their lunch together?

But the rest of their lunch went well. They stayed on neutral topics of conversation—the weather, the economy, the New York Yankees—and Christina was surprised to discover that he was quite intelligent. He was up on all the latest news and his comments were smart and thoughtful.

At the end of their meal Christina excused herself and went to the powder room. She was putting on her lipstick at the mirror when the door opened and a tall redhead glided in. It was Stephie, Bill's rich bitch girlfriend. Christina was instantly jealous. What was she doing here?

The bitch made a beeline for Christina.

"Small world," Stephie remarked, as she started applying her own lipstick at the mirror beside her nemesis.

"Stephie, right?" Christina sounded calm but what she really wanted to do was claw the other woman's eyes out. God, why was she feeling like this? It didn't make sense.

Stephie finished applying her lipstick and turned to Christina. "Honey, let's cut the chit chat. He loves me. He always has and always will. The only reason you're in his life is to please his father so he can keep having access to his money."

Christina was shocked. "Who told you that?"

Stephie laughed smugly. "Who do you think?" She looked down at Christina's engagement ring. "Nice rock. Too bad it's a loaner—for one month only."

Christina was stunned speechless. How did she know that?

Stephie read her mind. "How do I know that? Bill told me. He tells me everything. We're still seeing each other, you know."

Damn it! Christina had suspected as much but it was one thing to have a suspicion—quite another to have it confirmed.

That louse! So he was hopping from this bitch's bed and was now trying to get into hers?

"So if he loves you, why are you wasting your time with me?" Christina bitchily replied.

"Honey, I know women and I know my Billy around women. I'm sure he's already made a pass at you, but he means nothing by it. He's a spoiled, little, rich boy who always wants what he can't have. But once he's had you, he won't want you anymore. He always comes back to me. In fact, he's never left. He was just in my bed this past week."

Stephie knew exactly where to aim her arrows of lies and malice.

And Christina believed every word. Oh, that big jerk, she swore to herself! She'd actually been softening up to him over their so-called, bonding lunch. What an idiot she'd been!

"Really?" Christina gritted the word out.

Stephie smiled. She knew she was causing maximum damage with her remarks.

"Yes… really." She mocked Christina. "Sex with him is always fun. He's so inventive and good. He's told me he can't wait to be rid of you so we can stop all this sneaking around and go public again with our relationship."

Stephie turned to leave. She'd accomplished what she'd set out to do—to play on Christina's insecurities where Bill was concerned. She knew all about their deal together, having read a copy of their contract, and her private investigator was still on the case digging up more dirt on this little mouse. And the rest—the fact that they hadn't slept together yet but Bill wanted her? Well—call it woman's intuition but she'd guessed right.

"Oh, Stephie?"

Stephie turned back to the little mouse.

Christina gave her a smug look back. "Our deal may have been for one month and Bill may prefer you over me, but his daddy holds all the cards… all the credit cards… and his daddy likes me. He likes me a lot. In fact, he'd like nothing better than for me to marry his son. And you know what? I'm going to."

What Christina was saying was all nonsense, but Stephie wasn't the only one who knew how to throw arrows.

"You bitch!" Stephie snarled.

"You see, Miss Stephie…these past few weeks, I've discovered that I like being a Havenwood. I like the money, the prestige, the big house. I'm not giving any of it up to go back to my barely-making-it existence. And whether Bill likes it or not, I am marrying him. His daddy will make sure of that. And he can keep sleeping with you all he likes. In fact, I'd prefer he not come to my bed anyway. That way I can have access to all his money and not have to work that hard for it."

Stephie's hands were clenching in anger by her side. "You slut!" she threw at Christina.

"No, I don't think so. You'll be his slut. I'll be his wife."

And with that, Christina walked out with her head held high.

Take that, you bitch!

Furious, Cristina marched back to their table. Ooohhhh… that prick, she thought to herself. So, he couldn't wait to get rid of her, could he? So, he'd been sleeping with that slut only days ago, had he? So, he'd been talking bad about Christina behind her back too?

No, she didn't give a damn about the Havenwood money. And no, she had no intentions of actually marrying the bum, as she'd told Stephie—but she was going to get something on him to destroy his life for good, as originally planned.

As Christina approached the table, Bill rose from his seat.

"I've got a few errands to run. I'll see you back at the house," Christina tartly replied. She was so angry—and jealous—she could barely stand to look at him.

"I'll drive you," he quickly offered.

"No, thanks," she gritted, before walking away.

Bill felt like he'd just been bulldozed. What the hell had happened? He'd thought they were having a nice lunch. He'd thought they'd even shared a few genuine moments without all of the deception bullshit.

He racked his brain. Had he done something to offend her or said something? When she'd gone to the washroom, had she made a call to her boyfriend? Had he upset her? This was the first time in his entire life he'd actually fallen in love with someone—and it was sheer hell!

Bill sat back down to pay the check and he noticed the waiter bringing martinis to the next table. Man… he would love one about now, but he was in recovery and he wasn't going back to that other life no matter what. But he really needed to go to an AA meeting tonight. He needed it bad.

CHAPTER 33

IT WAS 6 p.m. and the pre-sunset sunlight shone through the clouds onto the magnificent Havenwood estate. Christina had tucked herself underneath an oak tree with a book propped in her hands. Should anyone see her, she appeared to be enjoying some fresh air and a good read.

She wasn't reading though. She was spying—and waiting for her prey to emerge from the house. She'd seen Bill drive up in his Jaguar about a half hour ago. Christina had then quickly grabbed her book and headed outdoors.

She was going to wait for him to leave the house and then she was going to follow him. And she wasn't going to lose him tonight, no matter what. Her car keys to the BMW were in her pocket, and her purse and camera were already in the car.

And if he went to see that tramp Stephie, Christina would be there with her camera too. Maybe William wouldn't appreciate photos of his son in the arms of his mistress weeks before the wedding? Maybe she could use that against him—because so far she had nothing. His goody-two shoes, stay-at-home act that the house had been gossiping about wasn't fooling her.

Christina checked her watched. 6:20 p.m.

Suddenly, she saw him coming out of a side entrance. Dressed in casual jeans and a polo shirt, he was heading for his car. Christina's heart beat faster. Ready to follow him, she got up from her sitting position. Scooting behind the oak's tree trunk, she secretly watched as he got in his Jag and zoomed away.

As Bill's car reached the front gates, Christina ran at full speed to her BMW. Having left the doors open, she slid in, revved up the engine and took off after him, keeping enough of a distance between them so that he wouldn't spot her.

And of course... Stephie's detectives immediately began to follow Christina, as soon as they saw her car coming out of the Havenwood gates too.

*

Christina had been following Bill for twenty minutes.

She'd stayed a safe distance behind and managed to keep the Jag in sight. She really didn't think he'd spotted her—or so she had hoped.

Suddenly, Bill slowed and parked in front of a low-rise building whose sign read 'Kingston Community Center'.

Christina parked her car a block away and reached for her camera. With her zoom lens, she began snapping pictures of Bill as he got out of his car. He went to stand in front of the community center's doors, obviously waiting for someone.

Was he waiting for Stephie? But why here? This was just an average, middle-class part of town, not his style at all.

Spying through her camera lens, she suddenly saw someone in a wheelchair approach Bill. The man said something to Bill, who laughed, and then he and Bill shook hands. Furiously, Christina snapped more pictures. Who was this person?

And he was in a wheelchair, paralyzed. Who did Bill know who was in a wheelchair? He only ran around with the perfect, beautiful people, like he had in high school.

And from the way the two of them had greeted each other, it was obvious they were friends. Christina adjusted her lens and zoomed in on the mystery person's face.

Suddenly, she gasped. Good God! She knew that face. Maybe he was a little older and a little plumper but it was Jake Monroe, Bill's best friend from high school. Christina continued taking pictures as the two men disappeared inside the building.

Stunned, Christina lowered her camera. Jake Monroe—after all these years—Jake Monroe! And he was in a wheelchair! What had happened to him? And what were those two doing here at this community center? Christina needed to know more.

Locking her camera in the trunk, she grabbed her purse and crossed the street. On entering the building, she found herself in a long, empty hallway with various doors on either side leading to rooms. It reminded Christina of a school.

Quietly, she crept down the hall. All the rooms were empty except for the one at the far end. The doors to that room had been propped open and she could hear someone giving a speech. The man said his name was Roger and he was talking about 'falling off the wagon' on a business trip, and how ashamed he was at losing control.

Christina was shocked! My God—could this be an AA meeting? Quickly, she peeked into the room before pulling back out of sight. She'd spotted about fifteen people in there—and one of them was Bill. He was sitting at the end of a row of chairs and Jake Monroe was in his wheelchair beside him.

Bill Havenwood was at an AA meeting?? And so was Jake Monroe? Two of the biggest, drunken, partying boozers she'd ever met in her life—and they were here—getting sober? But Bill Havenwood was a drunk!

But was he? He used to be. She knew that. But since she'd met him again, had she ever actually seen him drink? Christina racked her brain, trying to think of all the meals they'd shared. No, she hadn't.

And when she'd thrown the martini in his face and he'd jumped in the pool—was that why he'd plunged in—to wash the alcohol from his face because it was so tempting? And she'd never seen him come home drunk and had never smelled any alcohol on him either.

But if he had stopped drinking, why didn't William know? Why hadn't he told his dad? It could have scored him some serious brownie points with the old man.

Suddenly, Bill's voice pierced her thoughts. He was addressing the man named Roger. "We've all been there, Roger. Look at me. I'm tempted every day. You don't think I want to go back to the way it was? Where I can use booze to numb all my feelings so I don't have to feel the hurt or pain anymore? I want to—believe me. But I won't because I don't ever want to go back to the way it was—the way I was. You came here tonight and admitted it before it got out of hand and that's good. Just start working the program again. And if you fail a hundred times, you can win a hundred times if you just keep trying. That's all I have to say."

Christina heard Bill's chair scrape the floor as he sat back down and the others started to clap for him. She was flabbergasted. This couldn't be her Bill Havenwood, could it?

Undetected, Christina slipped away back down the hallway and out the door. Crossing the street, she retrieved her camera from the trunk and got inside her car. Dumfounded, she just sat there. Was her Bill Havenwood a recovering alcoholic? Had he stopped drinking? And Jake Monroe too?

Christina's brain went into overload. If Bill Havenwood didn't drink anymore, then he wasn't the same person he'd been in high school—the person she hated—the monster of her nightmares. He was a changed man. But—just because he'd decided to get sober, didn't mean he didn't deserve to pay for his past sins, did it? No—her revenge plan was still on.

But—when he'd stood up and talked about feeling pain and hurt? Could that be true? No—Christina suddenly reasoned— bastards didn't feel pain. They caused it. Bill Havenwood was still an asshole—just a sober asshole. But, he didn't drink anymore— and neither did Jake—that was something!! In spite of herself, she was impressed.

She didn't realize it, but her heart had softened towards him. That hard shell of protection she kept herself wrapped in where he was concerned, began to melt away.

She'd gone soft on the bastard—a little.

CHAPTER 34

JENNY HAD BEEN staring at the photograph of Jake Monroe for the past five minutes without saying a word.

Christina couldn't stand the silence any longer. "Well? What do you think?" The two were sitting in Jenny's living room.

Jenny shook her head in disbelief. "This… it's just too incredible for words."

"I know. Imagine that, they're both sober and in AA."

Jenny kept staring at the photo. "He still looks cute, though." Her expression suddenly turned sad. "I wonder what happened to him?" She was referring to Jake being in a wheelchair.

"Do you think you can get Brad at the office to run his name through the archives?" Christina inquired.

Jenny nodded. "I'll do it first thing." Jenny studied his picture again. Suddenly, she brought her eyes up to Christina and nervously bit her lip.

Christina quickly noticed. "What is it?"

Jenny's eyes flitted around the room. "I have to tell you something but you're going to be mad."

"Jenny, don't be ridiculous; you can tell me anything."

"I went out with him." The words came out in a rush and Jenny kept biting her lip.

Christina was confused, "With who?"

"Jake Monroe."

"What?" Christina put all of the 'shock and awe' she felt into that one word.

"It was one time." Jenny said defensively.

"Oh my God!"

"It was back in high school."

Christina couldn't believe what she was hearing as she put her hands up to her head. "What happened?"

"It was six months after you'd left. You were already in boarding school. I met him in the library. We… reached for the same book and…" Jenny paused.

"And what?"

"Well…" Jenny began to fidget with nervousness. "I smiled at him. And he said I could have the book and he said he'd seen me in class and…"

"And what…?" Christina prompted.

"Well… he said I was cute and maybe we could go to a movie sometime."

"Was he drunk?"

"Chrissy, are you implying a man has to be drunk to want to go out with me?" Jenny laughed, trying to diffuse the situation.

"Jenny, you know what I mean."

Her friend stopped laughing. "No, he wasn't. And Billy Havenwood wasn't anywhere in sight. You know it was Havenwood who was always the bad influence on Jake. Whatever he said or did, Jake went along with it."

Christina nodded, "I know, you don't have to tell me."

"Anyway, we went out… once. It was just a movie and some tacos. And a week after that, you know my dad got transferred and we moved to Chicago and I never saw him again."

Christina shook her head, trying to process this new information. "So how come you never told me?"

"Because, it was no big deal and I figured you'd be mad. I know what those two had done to you and I never saw him after that, so what was the point?"

"Jenny, you should have told me." Christina was reproaching her friend.

"I know, but I was scared. I'm sorry."

Relenting, Christina hugged her friend. "I'm your friend and

I'll always be your friend, no matter what, even if you do have bad taste in men."

Jenny laughed as she pulled back from Christina's arms. She had unshed tears in her eyes. "Thanks, Chrissy. I feel so much better now that that's out after all these years."

"So, tell me everything that happened on your date."

"Well, it was just that, a movie and some junk food."

"Did he drink?"

"No. He was actually sober. And he was sweet and funny, and he acted like a gentleman. Havenwood wasn't around. Jake said he'd gone away on some trip with his rich parents."

"Did you kiss him?"

Jenny blushed. Even though she was older now, had been married and had a child—that kiss had been her first and it still made her blush.

"Yes."

"And...?"

"It was sweet. He walked me to my door and kissed me goodnight. Nothing fancy, but... it was nice. He said maybe we could see another movie that weekend but then you know, we found out about the transfer and that was that. I never saw him again."

"Jenny, you're full of surprises."

Her friend laughed, "I have one more surprise for you. We talked about you on our date."

"What?"

Jenny nodded. "I brought your name up and told him you were my friend and I didn't like what they'd done to you."

Christina perked up even more. "What did he say?"

"He said it had all been Bill's idea. And he didn't even remember your name. Jake kept referring to you as 'the girl under the bleachers' because that's where you confronted them that day, remember?"

"How could I forget?"

"He said that Havenwood was so mad at you... the girl under the bleachers... because you told him to 'go f... himself' and no 'chick' had ever said that to him before. He said that Bill told him the next day he was going to find you and make you eat your words."

"What did he mean by that?"

Jenny shrugged her shoulders. "Jake didn't know. You never came back. Your parents shipped you off and that was that. That's why I didn't want you to start this again. I didn't want you getting hurt."

"But Jenny, I'm the one who's now making him eat his words, not the other way around."

"But Chrissy, if Bill doesn't drink anymore, he's a changed man. He's not a kid, he's an adult now. Maybe you should stop all this revenge business?"

"What are you saying?"

"I'm saying, forgive him and if he really is sober and you like him and he likes you, then give him a chance. Maybe you could even grow to love him and…"

"Jennifer Susanna Lewis, have you lost your mind?" Christina was shocked and angry at her friends' words. "You know how much I hate him! How could I ever love him?"

Jenny clasped her friend's hands in hers and stared deeply into Christina's eyes. She wanted her friend to listen to every word she was about to say. "Chrissy, there's a bond between the two of you… call it karma… call it fate… call it whatever… but it's there. I want you to look in your heart and if you can say to yourself… honestly… 'I don't like him, I could never love him and I want nothing to do with him'… then fine. But if you even have an inkling that you might have feelings for the bum…" Jenny gave a little laugh, "…then think about what you're doing. Is it worth it to possibly lose him by making him pay for something he did when he was a stupid, drunken kid? If you've got feelings for him, you've got to explore them because if you don't and you throw him away, you may have thrown away someone you could have loved and who could have loved you back. And in this cruel, lonely world, that's hard to find. Believe me, I'm still looking."

Christina yanked her hands out of Jenny's. "I know what I'm doing, Jenny."

Jenny studied her friend. She knew Chrissy had heard every word she'd just said, but was being stubborn by refusing to admit her true feelings for Havenwood. She sighed. Sometimes, we really all did have to learn things the hard way.

*

It was after 1 a.m. when Christina finally left Jenny's apartment. Because it was so late and she didn't want to drive back to the mansion at that hour, she decided to sleep at her own apartment downstairs and go back to the Havenwood's in the morning.

She did call the house though and left a message with one of the staff saying she was going to be staying in the city that night. All the staff, including William, had been so nice to her and she didn't want anyone to worry if she didn't show up.

Christina now lay in her own bed and looked up at her ceiling. Her thoughts went back to what Jenny had said.

Fall in love with Bill Havenwood? Ridiculous!

But—she did have that physical attraction for him—she had to admit that. But that was just lust; nothing deeper. But love Bill Havenwood? Was there anything to even love about him?

Well—he had stopped drinking. That was admirable. And he had given her Samson, the goldfish, so she could have a friend in the house. That was nice. And he'd stood up to his demanding father over her—when she'd fainted in William's office and when she'd overheard their argument later that night.

And that day, when she'd fainted and been sick all over him, he'd seemed so worried about her, so caring—the way he'd picked her up in his arms and carried her to the car—God—she could still feel the butterflies in her stomach—the way his arms had felt around her—so protective and strong—electrifying.

Damn Jenny! She was the one who had put these stupid thoughts in her head. Fall in love with Bill Havenwood and marry him for real? How insane was that! She'd have to change her name to Mrs. Bastard. Christina chuckled to herself. Mr. & Mrs. Bastard. Now that was funny.

Anyway, tonight she was in her own bed and it felt wonderful. Her bed may have been lumpy and her apartment may have been dumpy but it was all hers—and it was home.

Christina fell asleep and had one of the most restful nights she'd had since this entire mess started.

*

Bill was lying in his bed, staring up at the ceiling. He'd just spent one of the worst nights he'd ever had and he hadn't slept a damn wink.

All night long, he'd been thinking about her—with him, her boyfriend, whoever the creep was—in each other's arms, having sex—all fucking night long. That's why she hadn't come home last night. That's why she'd called and said she was spending the night in the city.

She was spending it with him!

Bill seethed with jealousy. He didn't want anyone to touch her—anyone except him.

Bill had come home after his AA meeting and had quickly gone looking for her. He always did. He just had to know where she was and what she was doing at all times. He was beginning to feel like a puppy dog always looking for its master—but he just couldn't help himself.

Eudora had told him that Miss Christina wasn't in. And so, like the complete idiot he'd become over her, he waited up, and waited, and waited. It was after 1 a.m. when one of the night staff had told him that she'd called and wasn't coming home that night. And that's when the images of her in someone else's arms started running through his brain.

Where was she? Who was she with? And what the hell were they doing together?

Yes—this had been one of the worst nights Bill had ever spent and he hadn't slept a damn wink.

CHAPTER 35

THAT VERY SAME morning, Christina was in the BMW driving back to the mansion when her cell rang. It was Jenny calling from the Streetwise Magazine offices.

"Chrissy, Brad ran Jake Monroe's name through the computer and found out what happened to him."

Christina sighed, already knowing what her friend was going to say. "Let me guess, drunk driving?"

Jenny sighed on the other end. "Yeah, about a year and a half ago. He was driving drunk and smashed into a tree."

"Was Bill there too?" For a split second, Christina felt her stomach turn over with fear.

"No, he was alone."

Christina sighed with relief. But why should she be relieved that Bill hadn't been there—that he hadn't played a part in his friend's accident? She pushed the feeling away.

*

Christina was walking through the foyer towards the staircase when Bill came out of the salon. He'd been waiting for her to come home this morning—and he was roiling, fuming mad. He appraised her. She looked so beautiful, so rested, so relaxed. That made him madder.

"Oh, Miss Christina?" He used Eudora's pet name for her.

Christina turned and spotted Bill standing in the open salon doorway. What was he doing here? She'd thought he'd have left for the office by now, as he'd been doing all week.

They stared at each other for a blink of a second.

Bill smiled at her. "Can I see you for a moment, please?" His smile didn't reach his eyes.

Christina was suddenly wary as she sensed tension emanating from him. She walked past him into the salon and he closed the door behind them.

She turned to him. "I thought you'd left for the office by now."

"Fuck the office! Where were you last night?" Bill shouted at her through gritted teeth. He was beyond the point of social niceties, having spent all morning thinking about her and her damned boyfriend—together.

Christina was taken aback by the anger in his voice, but cool as ever, didn't show it. "Excuse me?"

His steely eyes were trained on her. "You heard me."

"What's this about?"

"Answer me. Where were you?"

"I heard you the first time."

"Then tell me."

"I don't have to tell you anything. You're not my keeper."

Christina started to walk past him to leave, but he grabbed her arm and stopped her. He pulled her to him, their faces inches apart.

"Did you sleep with him?" he angrily accused her.

Maybe he should be handling things differently—and maybe he should be calming down—and maybe he should be acting rationally—but he'd spent one hell of a night and morning imagining all kinds of crazy things about her and it was all coming out now.

When she remained silent, he asked her again, "Did you sleep with him?"

Suddenly, Christina realized that Bill was insanely jealous of her 'phony' boyfriend and thought she'd spent last night with him. So that's what this was about.

Anger shot through her system like wildfire. How dare he

be angry with her when he'd been sleeping with that tramp, Stephie only days ago!

"How dare you ask me that? You have no right!"

"That ring on your finger gives me a right." He still held her close and Christina began to feel the heat between them.

"We both know what this ring means. It means nothing... which is exactly what you're entitled to know about my business," she shot back at him.

His eyes bore into hers. "Let me spell out a few truths, Miss Christina. I want you, and you want me."

The words were naked and raw, and hung between them like a knife. Neither had said those words out loud before, but now that they'd been said, they couldn't be retracted—or denied. Christina wanted to deny them—she tried to deny them—but couldn't. She just stood there within inches of him, with her heart beating wildly in her throat.

She gave him a half smile. "Spoiled, little, rich boys always want what they can't have." She was repeating Stephie's words.

Bill gave her a sensual smile back as he bridged the inches between them even more by pulling her closer still and whispering in her ear, "I may be spoiled... and I may be rich... but I'm no boy."

Christina felt his hot breath delicately fanning the inside of her ear—and instantly desire shot through her. Heat rose from her toes to the top of her head and she was on fire—for him.

He continued to hold her close. "And I'm not little," he softly whispered. His words, so close to her ear, were wrapping themselves around her like a snake. She was speechless and she briefly shut her eyes for a second. It would feel so good to give into him right now—she wanted him that badly—and her revenge plan, be damned!

Bill pulled back so that he could stare at her luscious lips. Some of the anger was beginning to leave him as he focused on them. He was so close—he could almost taste them.

Sweet, soft, delicious—and they had been kissing someone

else all night long—and who knows what else she'd been doing to him—with them—all night long. His anger returned and determination flared in his eyes.

"Admit to me that you want me." He was going to get an admission out of her if they had to spend all day in this damn room.

"I'm admitting nothing." She may have desperately wanted him, but she still had some self-respect left and if she admitted it to him, it would be like betraying herself.

He confidently smiled at her, "Then I'll kiss it out of you. Kisses don't lie."

And with that, his lips swooped down on hers, ever so softly, ever so gently and it was Christina's undoing. If he'd taken her lips in anger, she could have pushed him away. But this gentleness from him was the key that unlocked her heart. Slowly, she began to respond to him.

As he sensed her response, his lips grew harder, more demanding and deeper. He let go of her arm and his hands traveled slowly up to her breasts. She felt so good to him—and he wanted her like he'd never wanted anything in his life.

And when he felt her hands snake up his chest and entangle themselves into his hair, he knew he had her. She was his. She may not love him—but she wanted him. He could taste it on her lips and in the way her body had locked into his. He could feel the tremors of desire shooting through her. And he could feel the heat they generated together.

But he made a mistake.

He got greedy.

He just had to hear her say it. He needed to hear the words. He pulled back from her lips and stared into her luminous eyes. "Tell me you want me and not him."

Christina felt like ice water had just been thrown in her face. What the hell was she doing? And how close had she come to giving him her body, her soul, her dignity, her everything? She needed to put a stop to this—now. She needed her righteous anger but where was it?

She looked into his gorgeous, green eyes. "Is that how you kiss your slut?" she threw out. There it was—her righteous anger.

Bill was taken aback, "What are you talking about?"

"Answer me. Is that how you kiss… her?" Jealousy flared through Christina at the mere thought of Stephie.

Bill shook his head in amazement. "Who?"

Christina pulled out of his arms, putting space between them. "I know all about your girlfriend, so don't play dumb."

"Girlfriend? There is no girlfriend."

Christina ignored him. "You disgust me. You think you can go from her bed to mine and back again? Think again."

Bill ran his fingers through his hair in frustration. This really was the most trying, difficult, impossible female he'd ever met in his life—and he loved her. Why did he have to pick this one to love? His eyes refocused on her angry face. "There is no girlfriend. There hasn't been anyone since before I met you."

"And you expect me to believe that?"

"Yes, I expect you to believe that because I'm telling you the truth. I swear it."

Christina was suddenly unsure. He seemed so adamant, so convincing. Was he telling her the truth? But then that meant that Stephie had been lying—which was very possible. Big bitches like her were always good liars. But the other woman had known too many details about Christina and Bill's secret deal that only Bill could have told her. No—he was the one who was lying, not Stephie.

"Go back to your rich-bitch lover, Mr. Havenwood and leave me alone."

Christina walked to the closed door but quick as a flash, he was there before her, preventing her escape.

He glared at her. "There is no one…except you. Only you."

Bill desperately wanted her to believe him. But he wasn't

going to go all the way and tell her how deeply he felt for her. He couldn't bear it right now to have his love thrown back in his face too.

Christina was back to being her cool and in-control self again. Not believing one lying word coming out of that hot, sensual, experienced mouth of his, she looked at him as if he was a used gum stuck under her shoe.

"Move out of my way before I scream the place down."

Bill paused, as he continued to devour her with his eyes. He had been so close—and he'd blown it. He gave a small laugh at his own stupidity before opening the salon door for her and gallantly waving her out with his hand.

As she passed him with head held high, he caught a whiff of her perfume—the one that had tattooed itself into his brain—and he felt his desire for her flare up again. What was he, a high school boy that a mere whiff of her could make him hard again?

As he watched her well-shaped ass walk away from him, he shook his head at the mess he was in. He wanted her and he really had no chance in hell of getting her.

*

Furious, Christina stormed into her bedroom and slammed the door shut. How dare he, damn it! Accuse her of sleeping around, when he was guilty as sin! And then he'd made that pass at her, forcing his kisses and hands on her…

But no—he hadn't really forced anything on her, had he?

She could have refused him at any point during that encounter, but she hadn't. She had wanted more. In fact, when she was in his arms, she'd forgotten about everything—her revenge plan, her dignity, who he was, who she was. If he hadn't broken the spell by asking her to admit her desire for him, she would be, right now, in this very bed of hers, having sex with him—and loving every moment of it.

Christina moaned out loud at her own stupidity. Thank God

he had spoken up. Thank God she had come to her senses. And thank God she had walked away from him.

Suddenly, Christina felt like she couldn't breathe. This was all too much for her and she needed to get out of here.

Grabbing her purse, she headed for the door. She needed fresh air, sunshine and shopping. Retail therapy would make her forget about the mess she was in—with him.

CHAPTER 36

HE FELT LIKE the biggest jackass on the planet. Bill was sitting at the Fido Foods boardroom table. His father had called an afternoon meeting and all of the executives were there. Everyone was listening to William's lecture on improving sales—except him. Bill's thoughts were on her. He'd been so jealous this morning that when she'd finally come home, he'd exploded.

In his favor, he didn't have any experience with what jealousy felt like. He'd never really been in love before so he'd never been jealous. All of his past relationships had been casual and fun—and if anyone had wanted more than that, he usually broke it off. No woman had ever brought out in him the range of emotions like this one had. And no woman had ever made a jackass out of him either—like this one had.

But she was right.

He had no business asking her where she'd spent the night. It wasn't like they were really engaged. They only had a deal between them and he had no rights where she was concerned.

If she wanted to sleep with every Tom, Dick, Harry and Joe, that was for her to decide—even if it killed him inside. And it would kill him, because he loved her.

William noticed his son was not paying attention. He was instead doodling on the sales report and his head was down.

Hastily, William ended the meeting and all the executives filed out. The only one who remained seated was Bill. Lost in his thoughts, he hadn't heard his father dismiss everyone.

William studied his son's bent head. He knew what was going on. He had a suspicion that Bill had fallen for the girl—and fallen hard. Bentley had called him this morning with the news that Bill and Christina could be heard yelling at each other in the salon. Apparently, Christina had spent last night elsewhere and Bill had demanded to know where she'd been.

That had resulted in a major fight that could be heard through the closed doors. His son had thought Christina had spent the night with her lover and his son had been wild with jealousy this morning.

That could only mean one thing, William reasoned. His son had fallen for her, maybe even loved her? He certainly was attracted to the girl; even William had noticed that. And the girl had been good for his lazy, good-for-nothing son. Look at him. Bill was actually sitting in the Fido Foods boardroom taking a meeting—even if his mind was elsewhere. When had Bill ever shown up for work on time, let alone a meeting?

William's calculator brain fired up. What if—the girl was to marry his son for real? William liked Christina a lot. She had grit, sass and smarts—and seemed to be shaping up his son whereas all of William's efforts had failed. Maybe the love of a good woman really did work miracles on a man? It certainly seemed to be working for his lazy, drunken, bum-of-a-son.

William had given up hope of his son finding a woman to love and settling down. All Bill had ever been interested in was partying, drinking and whoring—and nothing William said could change his ways.

But this girl had.

Of course, Christina didn't come from wealth and her parents were middle class, working people. And of course, William would have preferred his son to marry into some pedigreed, old money, Mayflower family, but beggars couldn't be choosers—and he'd begged his son enough times to smarten up to no avail.

Maybe this girl was the one?

Besides—middle class, working blood was good for breeding strong, ambitious grandbabies—and he certainly wanted those. And if his son married the girl for real, William would get those grandbabies in spades. Christina was definitely good breeding stock.

At that moment, Bill looked up from his doodling and seeing that everyone had left, mumbled a 'sorry' and got up from his chair.

William folded his arms across his chest. "You had a fight with Christina, didn't you?"

Bill went on the defensive. "Who told you that?"

"No one told me." Yes, they had. "You didn't hear a word I said throughout the meeting."

"Does it really matter? You never take my suggestions anyway."

"Son?"

Bill was suddenly wary. He couldn't remember the last time his father had called him 'son'. "Yes?"

William came over and put a consoling arm around his son's shoulders "Son, you're going to be a husband soon and I think it's a father's duty to talk to his offspring about the birds and the bees."

"I think I know all about that stuff, dad."

William smirked. "Yes, I'm sure you could give me lessons, but that's not what I'm talking about. The birds and the bees have to do with the facts of life. And the facts of life are this—when you marry a woman and she becomes your wife, you the husband, must learn to grovel."

"What?"

"It's called groveling. You get down on your knees and beg for forgiveness, even if you were right and she was wrong. Now, groveling is an art form and you will perfect it as your marriage continues, so don't expect to do it right the first time."

Bill burst out laughing. "That has to be the most insane thing I've ever heard you say." And about the nicest, he added to himself. He couldn't remember the last time his father had been nice to him. "I bet you never groveled with mom."

"Then you, sonny boy, would be wrong. You weren't privy to

everything that went on in our marriage and if your mother were here right now, dressed in one of her hippy, gypsy outfits, she'd tell you that I groveled many times."

"I don't believe you."

"Believe it. Now, go back home to Christina and grovel. Beg for forgiveness. She'll listen, I promise."

Bill gave his father a slow smile. "You're pretty smart for an old, conniving coot."

William smiled back. "That's about the nicest thing you've ever said to me."

Giving his father a look of newfound respect, Bill walked out.

William watched him walk out. Sure, he knew all about their scheme to deceive him—and sure he'd done everything to have their scheme backfire; but now there was going to be a change of plans.

Suddenly, he wanted the girl to marry his son for real. And he wanted his grandbabies. He desperately wanted his grandbabies. And she was good for him—and he'd be happy with her.

William wasn't a complete ogre. Deep down, he loved his son very much and only wanted the best for him. It was just that they, father and son, usually disagreed on what that was.

Yes—those two were going to marry and he, William, would bring it about, but how?

He could try to offer Christina money but he knew she wouldn't be interested. He'd already seen that she wasn't interested in anything the Havenwoods materially had—which of course, was another gold star in her favor. So, what could he do?

William needed time to think—and to plot—and to plan.

CHAPTER 37

HAVING SPENT THE day shopping, Christina was in her bedroom at the mansion trying on her new slingback shoes. There was a knock at her door.

Opening it, she saw Bill sheepishly standing there with a bouquet of flowers.

"Christina, I'm sorry."

She slammed the door hard in his face. She was still fuming about what had happened that morning and the last person she wanted to see right now was him. He knocked again. She ignored the knock.

He pleaded through the door. "Christina… please, open up. I want to apologize."

"Go away!" She yelled back.

"I'm sorry about what happened, what I said. You were right. I had no business acting that way." The door remained closed and there was silence on the other end. "Christina?" Had she even heard him, Bill wondered?

There was a pause and then he heard her say, "I'm listening."

"Can you please open this door so I can at least apologize to your face?"

More silence, and the door remained closed. Bill nervously shuffled from foot to foot. He'd never had to work this hard for a woman before and he wasn't sure what she wanted from him.

He racked his brain. "Okay, I was a jerk."

Suddenly, he heard her say, "And…?"

"And… a jackass and I'm sorry."

"Keep going."

Defeated, Bill sighed. "And you were right and I was wrong."

Slowly, the door opened and she stood there with a snotty expression on her beautiful face.

Bill launched then into his prepared speech. "Christina, you were right. We have no claims on each other and what we each do in our private lives doesn't concern the other. I'm sorry." She continued to stare at him as if he were a gob of spit on the sidewalk. Bill cleared his throat. God, he was nervous. He was actually nervous around a woman. That had never happened to him before. "I… was wondering… if you'd go out to dinner with me tonight?"

Christina's eyes narrowed. Suddenly, she snatched the flowers from his hand and announced, "Pick me up in an hour and a half." Then she slammed the door back in his face.

Stunned, Bill stared at the closed door. So, this was what his father had meant by groveling. A slow smile crept along his face. Pathetic? Maybe. But she'd said 'yes'.

*

Christina slipped on her new black stiletto shoes and stood up. She went to stand at the full-length mirror and studied her glamorous reflection. Her hair was up, her makeup was perfect and she was wearing her new black halter dress that she'd just bought this afternoon. The dress molded enticingly over her curves and if there was ever a dress that was made for sex, it was this one. Christina knew she looked good.

Satisfied with her appearance, she glided to her dresser to spritz on perfume. She really shouldn't have accepted this invitation, but when he'd asked her he looked like a little boy waiting for a present from Santa and not knowing if he was going to get one. Something in her had cracked and she'd instinctively said yes to him.

She smiled when she thought about his apology. Bill Havenwood had actually apologized to her about something?

Amazing! And from the awkward way he'd said it, it was obvious he hadn't had much practice but it looked good on the jerk.

There was a quiet knock at her bedroom door and she checked her watch. An hour and a half to the minute, and not one second more. Good. He was treating her like a lady.

Christina opened the door and her breathing stopped.

Wow—did he look good. He was wearing a black tuxedo and black tie—and he looked like one of those heroes on a romance book cover. The expensive fabric of his dinner suit skimmed over his lean physique, making him look like a big, black jungle cat with power stored in its muscles—ready to pounce on its prey. He looked deliciously dangerous—and Christina began to feel heat creep into her face. Maybe this dinner hadn't been such a good idea, after all?

She stammered a little, "I'll… I'll just get my purse." She walked away from him to her bed to get her clutch.

As he stood at her open door, Bill hungrily watched her walk away from him. That dress on her did amazing things to her ass—and he immediately felt his longing for her spring into action. How the hell was he going to get through an entire meal without touching her? He needed a cold shower, that's what he needed.

She turned to him then and he immediately pasted a gentlemanly smile on his face. If she knew what he was thinking right now, she'd slap his face and slam this door back on him again.

"Shall we go?" he offered politely.

She politely smiled back, "Why not?"

They walked side by side out of the house and to his parked Jaguar—each physically aware of the other.

CHAPTER 38

BOTH CHRISTINA AND Bill were sitting in a very dark, intimate corner of the small restaurant. The table held one lit candle that cast a romantic glow about them.

Christina could tell that this place was very understated but very expensive. Only the rich could truly appreciate eating here where the decor, the food and the ambiance were elegant, simple but nevertheless cost a fortune. Bill Havenwood certainly had good taste.

She glanced at him as he was studying the menu. Their conversation in the car had been on neutral ground, mostly about the weather. But the weather wasn't what she'd been thinking about. She'd been thinking how handsome he looked and she'd remembered how soft his lips felt and how electrical his touch had been on her body.

He looked up then and caught her staring at him. Hiding her embarrassment, she stammered, "I… was thinking about how everyone thinks we're engaged and yet this feels like our first date." Oh no—why had she referred to this as a date?

He laughed. "Well, my father always says I do everything backwards."

In spite of herself, she laughed too. He really did have a good sense of humor about things. That was one of the first things she'd noticed about him these past few weeks. Oh no—why had she just admitted something positive about him in her own mind?

Bill admired her beautiful face. She looked mind-blowing when she laughed and her eyes lit up like that, just mind-blowing…

Christina continued, "Your father does have an opinion on

everything." She suddenly looked into his eyes, "Do you hate him for it?"

"No, I just don't like him very much sometimes. And he doesn't like me. We're two different peas in the same Havenwood pod."

Christina sensed the pain behind his remark. "I'm sure he loves you," she replied.

"Are you? Because I'm not." Smiling, he tried to hide his hurt feelings.

Christina sat back in her chair and studied him. "You and your father care more about each other than you're willing to admit. Take it from me, an impartial observer. I hadn't been in that monstrosity of a house more than a day before I saw that. And besides, Eudora thinks so too and she's been with you forever. So you have that on two good sources, one new and one old…although I don't think Eudora would appreciate being called old."

"Thanks for saying that. It means a lot to me." He smiled at her then—one of his devastating, pearly-white, movie star smiles—and butterflies fluttered in Christina's stomach. Oh no—why had she said something nice to him that made him feel better?

Bill suddenly patted his jacket pocket. "I almost forgot." He pulled out a small, blue box with the words Tiffany on it. "This is for you." He placed it on the table.

Christina looked at it as if it was an explosive device about to detonate. "What is it?"

"Open it," he challenged her, his eyes intent on every expression crossing her stunning face.

Slowly, Christina opened the box. Inside was a platinum stickpin encrusted with real diamonds. It was about three inches in length and the shimmering stones cascaded down the platinum metal.

Her stunned eyes fluttered up to his. "This is… for me? To keep?"

He nodded yes. "When I saw it, it reminded me of you."

"Really? Why?"

Bill had a bad boy twinkle in his eyes. "Because it's sharp and dangerous. And for some strange reason, you always seem to enjoy 'sticking it' to me," he laughed, "But in a very beautiful way, of course, hence the diamonds."

Christina giggled. She appreciated his humor and was flattered by his comments. He had described her to a tee. She glanced at him from under her lashes. "I like that description of myself, Mr. Havenwood."

"I figured you would," he cagily replied. Any other woman would have taken his comments as an insult but not this one. He'd known that she'd get a kick out of it.

As Christina took the pin from the box, Bill gallantly reached for it and said, "Let me."

Gently, he pinned it high up on her shoulder, letting his fingers linger there a second too long as the diamonds glistened in the candlelight.

"Beautiful," he softly commented, his eyes glued to her face.

Christina's hand instinctively went up to touch the piece. She wasn't sure she liked this. The way he was looking at her and the way he'd placed the pin on her dress made her feel like an animal who'd just been branded by its owner—his to keep forever. But the feeling gave her goosebumps—sexy, tingling goosebumps. No—she didn't like this at all.

"You didn't have to do this, you know," she said.

"I know, but the best way to say I'm sorry is with diamonds. It's the Havenwood way," he laughed.

At that moment, the waiter approached their table with a bottle of wine. He expertly filled Christina's glass, then left. He hadn't filled Bill's. Obviously, Bill was a regular customer here and they knew he didn't drink alcohol.

Suddenly, Christina just had to know why. The words spilled out before she even knew what she was saying. "You don't drink anymore, do you?"

Surprised, he looked at her for a few seconds. "No, I don't."

"But your father—he's always saying how you're coming

home drunk and how you're drinking all the time—but you don't?"

"My father doesn't know everything about me, although he thinks he does."

"When did you stop?"

"About a year and a half ago. I've been sober for eighteen months." He looked at her, desperately wanting her to understand. "I'm a recovering alcoholic, Christina. I'm in AA."

"But... why haven't you told your father? It would ease a lot of the tension between you."

"Because there are certain things I shouldn't have to tell him. He should love me enough to notice on his own, like you just did."

Suddenly, Christina felt very guilty. She'd only found out because she'd spied on him—not because she'd 'noticed'.

"How long had you been drinking?" Christina already knew the answer.

"All my life, since I was a kid. I'm a drunk, Christina, always have been, always will be, but today I choose not to drink. That's all I can do. One day at a time. Does the fact that I'm a drunk disgust you?" Bill held his breath as he waited for her answer. He just had to know what she thought and how she felt.

"Yes, it does," she answered him honestly.

He felt like he'd been punched in the stomach. "You don't pull any punches, do you?"

"I'm not going to sugar coat my answer for you but I will explain it."

His gaze was so fixed on hers that a nuclear explosion couldn't have taken him away from her. "I'd appreciate that," he said.

"Just because I don't like your behavior, doesn't mean I don't like you." She gasped—stunned at her words. God, what had she just said? Like him? She didn't like him. But the words had just popped out of her mouth.

He smiled wickedly, "So, you're saying you like me?"

"What I mean to say is... you're not your behavior." She

stopped. What had she just said again? He wasn't his behavior? Then if that was the case, she shouldn't be blaming him and trying to get revenge for his 'drunken behavior' in the past?

Christina was becoming confused. The intimacy of the restaurant, him being nice to her, the diamond pin, the honesty about his drinking, her attraction to him—everything—was making her confused about her feelings for him.

She looked at him and he smiled—one of his lopsided, devastating smiles. "Thank you for that," he said.

"What happened—that you stopped drinking, I mean?" her words came out in a breathy whisper. He was having a hypnotic effect on her and she couldn't seem to snap out of it.

Bill pulled back emotionally, as he was forced to recall Jake's accident. "Eighteen months ago, a very good friend of mine smashed into a tree while driving home drunk. He was paralyzed and he'll spend the rest of his days in a wheelchair and it was my fault." Christina could see the raw pain in his eyes and she had the strongest urge to wrap her arms around him. But she didn't. She just sat there.

"But you weren't in the car?" Christina already knew he hadn't been.

"I almost was. Jake had just dropped my drunken ass off home and in fact, that night, I'd been insisting on driving but Jake wouldn't let me. He felt I was drunker than him." Bill gave a harsh laugh. "So you see, I have to take a lot of the blame for him not walking again. And when I saw him in the hospital with all those tubes—and he almost died, I knew it was over—my drinking. I had to change." He looked up at her then and his eyes were shining with unshed tears. "Dance with me?" he asked softly.

Bill needed to feel her again, to have her arms wrapped around him so that her goodness could wash away all the pain he was reliving at this moment. "Please?"

Christina knew he was asking her to help him forget the pain of Jake Monroe's accident and the part he'd played in it. He was asking her for comforting and for absolution. Could she give it to him? She didn't want to—but the tormented way he was looking at her now, she couldn't help herself.

Before she had a chance to rationalize her actions, Christina clasped his hand and led him to the dance floor.

Wrapped in each other's arms, they slow danced for the next half hour—oblivious to where they were. In their own private world, they clung to each other, each washing away their past sins—hers as well as his. When the music finally stopped, they walked back to their table, hand in hand.

The rest of the evening, including the food, was wonderful—almost magical. Their conversation was light and funny—and Bill was charmed by everything she said. He was also thrilled because he knew that somehow he'd gotten through to her, on some level.

And Christina?

She was confused and astounded. What had happened? She'd actually enjoyed herself with him tonight. They'd talked and laughed, and had seemed to have a lot in common. Her feelings toward him had made a drastic 180-degree change. Something in her had been washed away and she couldn't quite get her bearings. She felt lost.

They drove home and he walked her to her bedroom door.

"Goodnight, Christina."

His head lowered to her lips and he gave her a very gentle, sweet kiss. Sure, Bill wanted more from her but he wasn't going to do anything that might push her away. He raised his head, smiled and disappeared into his own room, closing the door behind him.

Christina was stunned. She'd expected another pass from him, but was she relieved that it hadn't happened? Slowly, she walked into her room and shut the door.

Suddenly, she stopped as realization dawned on her. The 'Bill Havenwood' she'd had dinner with tonight wasn't the 'monster Bill Havenwood' from her nightmares.

Jenny had been right. He'd changed. He wasn't the same drunken kid he'd been. Tonight, she'd seen how sorry he was for his past mistakes and she'd felt for him—she'd wanted to forgive him.

And she had. She'd forgiven him for what he'd done to her all those years ago. She didn't hate him anymore. In fact, was she falling for him? Was she in love with Bill Havenwood? But how could that be?

Oh God—she *was* in love with him. She was in love with— *the bastard!!!!!*

Christina ran to her bathroom and spent the next half hour hunched over the toilet, throwing up her $250 a plate dinner.

At that same time, Bill was next door in his own bathroom taking the longest cold shower he'd ever taken in his life.

CHAPTER 39

CHRISTINA HAD SPENT the next morning hiding in her room until 'he' had left for work. She just couldn't face him—not after she'd admitted to herself that she was in love with him.

After she'd been sick last night, she'd crawled into bed. Emotions always affected her like that and admitting such a soul-debilitating thing as her being in love with Bill Havenwood had turned her world upside down. But how had this happened?

Looking back, she realized that her feelings for him had been slowly changing these past few weeks. She'd come to see that he was a human being—with faults and flaws, and with sweetness and kindness and a sense of humor, and as Eudora had told her, a good heart. He wasn't the two-dimensional childhood creep whose image she'd carried in her heart all those years. He was a man—a very attractive man who laughed and smiled and charmed—and who hurt and felt pain and regret.

Tears started to fall down Christina's cheeks. Loving him was the most horrendous thing that could have happened to her. She didn't want to love him—but she did.

And he didn't love her.

Sure, he wanted her, but so what? That was lust, not love. She was just the means for him to keep his rich lifestyle, and to amuse himself with for the course of the month. She'd leave here in little over a week's time and he'd never think of her again. After all, he'd have his father's money again and he'd have Stephie—so what would he need her for?

Christina stood at her bedroom windows and looked out over the manicured grounds. Everything was set for the engagement party tomorrow night—guests would be arriving, champagne would be flowing, and she'd have to accept congratulations while standing by his side with a phony smile pasted on her lips—and it would all be pretend. How was she going to get through it?

Suddenly, she couldn't wait for the engagement party to be over with. After that, she could avoid Bill for the following week and then their deal would expire. She'd be able to leave here, go back to her own apartment and forget all about him.

From her vantage point at the window, Christina saw Eudora down below in the gardens. Maybe she'd go have a chat with her? She desperately needed to talk to someone right now.

Outside, Christina approached Eudora who was on her knees in the dirt planting herbs.

"Good morning, Eudora," she smiled at the older woman.

"Good morning, mum; I'm just planting herbs for the kitchen," she replied in her Irish accent.

"But doesn't Tom, the gardener usually do that?"

Eudora cackled. "I don't trust Tom with my herbs, Miss Christina. No sir, I do this myself."

"Let me help you," Christina said, as she too got down on her knees.

Eudora was aghast. "No mum, you shouldn't be doing this type of work. You'll get all dirty, you will."

"Nonsense, dirt can be washed away," Christina was adamant.

Eudora smiled. She liked this sweet girl a lot; now if only things would smooth themselves out between her and Master Bill. She'd heard all about their huge fight the day before—the screaming and the yelling. Why, the whole house had heard it and had been talking about nothing else. Jealous, he was, they all said. And why shouldn't he be? He was in love with this girl. Of course he should be jealous.

And if there was another man involved in her life, then he should be putting his foot down and causing a scene. A little screaming and yelling was good for a relationship, if love was behind it. And she knew her little Billy loved Christina. Now, if they would only show each other how much and sleep together, she thought to herself. Even though they'd gone out together last night, they'd both slept in their own beds when they'd come home. As head maid, Eudora knew it all.

For the next twenty minutes, Eudora showed Christina how to make a hole in the soil and place the herb plants inside. And Christina enjoyed herself immensely. It was nice being out in the sun, getting some fresh air and forgetting about her predicament.

Christina sheepishly looked over at the matronly maid. "Eudora?"

"Yes, mum?"

"You've been here a long time, haven't you?"

"Since I was a wee lass myself."

"About Bill's other girlfriends…"

Eudora sat back on her haunches and gave Christina a cautionary look. "Are you sure you want to go there, Miss Christina?"

Christina looked Eudora square in the eyes with a determined look of her own, "Yes."

Eudora shook her head from side to side. "All right, but I don't gossip, you see. I'll only answer questions I think you should know as Master Bill's future wife; you understand?"

Christina nodded respectfully. "Yes, ma'am."

"All right, then. What is it you want to ask?"

"Bill's last girlfriend… I think her name was Stephie?"

Eudora raised her eyebrows, not confirming or denying.

Christina quickly continued before she lost her nerve. "Did you ever meet her?"

"He brought her here a few times, yes."

"And what did you think of her?"

"She was very beautiful, but she was all wrong for my little Billy."

"Why was that?"

"My personal opinion, mind you, but she was selfish and cold. She was more in love with the Havenwood name and money than she cared for Master Bill. I didn't like her at all."

"Do… you think he loved her?" Christina anxiously bit her lip.

Eudora suddenly realized that the girl didn't know how much her Billy loved her. "Master Bill loves you, dear," she reassured.

"I know that…" Christina awkwardly smiled, trying to cover up the truth that he didn't love her at all… "But do you think he loved her back then?"

Eudora folded her arms across her chest. "No, I don't. Master Bill did not love her, mark my words."

"But she was very beautiful." Christina stated it as a fact.

"Yes, but not as beautiful as you. And I know Master Bill thinks so too."

Christina smiled at the old woman. If she only knew the truth of how things really were between her, Stephie and Master Bill.

"Do you think he still sees her? I mean… as a friend?"

So that's what this was about, Eudora thought. Miss Christina thought Bill was still seeing the tramp.

"No mum, he does not. That evil woman is out of his life for good. And he has you now. He loves you and he's going to make you his wife. Of all the women he's had over the years…oh… excuse me, madam…" Eudora stopped talking, suddenly embarrassed at how much she'd revealed.

Christina smiled, "That's all right, Eudora, I know Master Bill was always popular with the ladies." She gave the old maid a wink.

Eudora giggled. "Yes… well… he never asked any of them to be his wife and that says alot about his love for you."

Christina smiled again at her. Eudora was so sweet—and such a romantic—and had no idea of what was really going on. "Thank you, Eudora. You've been a big help to me." No, she hadn't.

"My pleasure, mum."

For the next half hour, Christina and Eudora finished planting the herb garden together. When Christina stepped back into the house, she realized that her hands were dirty from digging in the soil, so she went into the main floor powder room to wash her hands.

After turning on the taps, she removed her engagement ring as she always did when washing her hands and put it on the sink counter. But her mind wasn't on what she was doing. It was on Master Bill and Stephie—still sleeping with each other behind her back—and she washed her hands automatically without thinking.

After drying them on the guest towel, she left the bathroom— and left her $250,000 diamond ring behind on the counter, forgetting to put it back on—in fact, forgetting all about it.

*

Later that afternoon, William was working in his office when his secretary, Charlotte buzzed him on the phone.

"Bentley is here to see you, sir," Charlotte said.

William was very surprised. What was his head butler doing here? "Send him in."

The door opened and Bentley stoically walked in. Worried, William arose from his chair.

"Bentley? Has something happened?"

"No sir, not to worry."

"I thought you'd already left to visit your sister in London."

"No sir, my flight's in two hours. In fact, I'm on my way to the airport now."

"Then why are you here?"

"Well sir… I have a delicate matter to discuss with you."

The butler reached into his pocket and pulled out Christina's engagement ring. "I found this in the first floor powder room this morning." He handed it to William and continued. "Madam must have forgotten it there, and by the time I found it, she'd already left the house. I came here to give it to Master Bill but he's not here and I have to go to the airport to catch my flight so I'll give it to you instead to give to Madam."

A wicked smile played on William's lips as he fondled the

expensive ring. "Does anyone at the house know that you found this?" he asked.

Bentley was taken aback. "Why no, sir. I didn't tell anyone. I wouldn't want to embarrass Madam and I felt that as head butler, this is something I should personally take care of myself."

"You did well, Bentley. I don't want to embarrass my daughter-in-law either. Thank you for bringing this to me. I'll see that she gets it." William's scheming brain was already putting two and two together—and coming up with a marriage.

Bentley continued, "Again sir, I'm sorry to be leaving you at such a time, what with your son's upcoming wedding but my sister's in the hospital and I have to go to her."

"Of course, Bentley. Think no more of it. And in fact, instead of a two week leave of absence why don't you take four—all paid for of course."

Bentley was thrilled. "Why, thank you, sir. I appreciate that." He shook William's hand. "I'll be off, then."

William smiled at his head butler, "Have a good flight, Bentley."

"Thank you, sir." And with that, Bentley left.

William held the bauble up to the light. The diamond cuts in the ring sparkled like fireworks.

Yes—the gods had answered his prayers. He didn't need to come up with a plan to marry those two. Fate had done it for him. All he had to do was seize the opportunity.

William knew that Christina was liable for the ring's value should it ever be lost. It was all in that blasted agreement she'd signed with his son. And if she hadn't been able to pay for the car damages, how could she ever repay $250,000 for the ring?

She couldn't—unless she married his son, of course, and the debt was forgiven. But would Bill use this to get her to marry him?

Yes, William reasoned. The boy wanted the girl that badly.

William walked to his secret wall safe, opened it and plopped the ring inside. Of course, he would tell no one he had the ring, not even his son. The only other person who knew was Bentley and he was off to England for four weeks and by the time he returned, his son and the girl would be married. For all intents and purposes—the $250,000 engagement ring was lost—and Christina was liable for it.

Yes—things were going his way and he didn't even have to play dirty this time.

CHAPTER 40

CHRISTINA HAD RUN a few errands that afternoon including meeting Mindy at the couture house for her engagement party dress fitting. The seamstresses had finally performed their magic and the dress was to be delivered to the house that evening. Christina had changed back into her street clothes and had met up with Mindy in the lounge area.

Mindy was frowning. "My dear, I must ask you something. I noticed you're not wearing your engagement ring. Is everything all right between you and Bill?" The question had been bothering Mindy since Christina had walked in.

Christina brought her left hand up and suddenly realized her ring was missing. "Oh, my god…" she squeaked, as panic flashed in her eyes.

"My dear, are you saying you don't know where it is?" Mindy was worried. Weddings had been called off because of things like this.

In a frenzied state, Christina shook her head 'yes'. That ring was worth a quarter of a million dollars and she was responsible for it. Where was it? Quickly, she scanned her memory. Had she lost it here, at the couture house? Or at the mansion? Or at any of the ten errands she'd run today? Oh no!

She was in trouble again—big, big trouble.

Mindy put a comforting arm around Christina's shoulders and pushed her down on the couch. "Honey, let's stay calm. Now, I know you didn't have it on when you came here because I noticed that right away. Did you have it in the car?"

Christina closed her eyes and tried picturing her left hand on the steering wheel when she'd driven to all her errands.

"No, I don't think I had it on."

"Good. Did you have it on when you left the house?"

Again, Christina tried to picture what she'd done this morning. "No," she excitedly told Mindy. "I'm positive. It wasn't on my hand when I left the house. But I did have it on this morning because I remember taking my shower and then putting it back on… or was that yesterday? Oh Mindy, I'm not sure." Her voice was desperate.

"Then it's at the house. Call the staff and start an immediate search. I'll drive you home."

"Thank you." Christina hugged the wedding planner. What would happen if they couldn't find the ring and she had to pay for it, like it said in that damned contract? Where would she get that kind of money? She didn't even have $500 in her bank account.

This was bad—really bad!

On the way home, Christina called the house and spoke to Eudora. The maid said she and the staff would immediately begin a search, leaving no cushion unturned.

Christina asked if maybe the ring had fallen in the dirt when she was helping Eudora plant the garden. Eudora said she didn't know but if they couldn't find it in the house, she would uproot every plant herself if she had to.

Christina hung up and her heart was beating wildly. She just had to find that ring, she just had to.

*

Bill came home early that day.

He just had to see her again, to be near her, to talk to her, to kiss her even—if he got lucky. He hadn't thought about anything else.

He walked in the front door and immediately noticed some of the maids and under butlers scurrying across the foyer. As he passed the open doors to the salon he saw Tilly, the young maid, overturning cushions on the couches.

She was looking for something and he sensed that the whole house was in a frenzy—but over what?

Bill walked into the salon. "Tilly, what's going on?"

Surprised, Tilly stood up and stammered, "Sorry, sir but… I… think you should ask Madam Christina."

Bill's interest perked up even more. Christina? What was she up to now, he thought? "Tilly, I want you to tell me."

The young girl looked down at her shoes. She was nervous.

Bill continued. "Don't worry; I won't say anything about who told me. You can trust me." He gave her one of his radiant, movie star smiles and the girl melted.

"Well, sir… Madam Christina… has lost her engagement ring and the entire staff is looking all over the house for it… sir." She did a quick curtsey and scurried out of the room.

Bill froze. What??!! Christina had lost the ring???

She'd lost the ring…

A smile spread across his sensuous lips as his brain began to calculate at lightning speed. If she couldn't find it, she'd be liable for it—which meant that she'd be in debt to him for a quarter of million dollars—money she didn't have.

That meant that now he could call the shots—and he could make her do what he wanted—which was to marry him, of course. God help him, he wanted her that badly that he was willing to sell a piece of his soul to get her.

Maybe forcing her to marry him would send him to hell but he didn't care. He loved her and he didn't want to lose her. And if he had to play the upper hand he'd just been dealt, he would. He was a desperate man and he would do what he had to in order to keep her.

He knew that Christina didn't love him. And he would keep his love for her to himself. He couldn't stand to have that thrown in his face—and she would, if cornered. So he'd play the villain and blackmail her into marrying him for the money she owed for the ring.

She would hate him, of course…

And curse him, of course…

But she would marry him.

May God forgive him—because he knew Christina never would.

CHAPTER 41

BILL KNOCKED ON her bedroom door. At the speed of light, a frazzled-looking Christina yanked it open and stared at him.

Bill's eyesight went beyond her shoulder into her room. He could see clothes strewn everywhere and drawers open with their contents spilling out. The place looked like it had been hit by a tornado—and that tornado's name was Christina.

She looked desperate, panicked and frantic. He could see it all in her eyes—and in the way she was keeping her left hand hidden behind her back.

She smiled at him. "You're home early today."

Bill studied her face. She was scared. Good. That's exactly how he wanted her to be if he was going to pull this off. He played it cool. "Were you busy?"

"No… just a little spring cleaning," she laughed to hide her nervousness.

He let his eyes slowly wander again beyond her and into the room. "It looks like you'll need to do a spring cleaning after your spring cleaning," he teased, quirking an inquiring eyebrow at her.

Christina turned her head briefly to look at her room. It was a complete disaster. She'd been so anxious about finding the ring that she'd pulled out clothes, shoes, bedding—everything in an effort to find it.

But she hadn't found it.

And neither had the staff.

And now he'd come home.

She turned back to him with a fake smile on her lips. She needed to get him out of here before he discovered what was really going on. "You know how it is…can't decide what to keep. Was there something you wanted?"

"Now, there's a loaded question," Bill slyly retorted.

"Did you need to ask me something?" Christina innocently asked. Oh God—he was acting funny—did he know already?

Bill didn't answer but glued his eyes to her face. He took a few slow steps into the room, like a big, powerful animal stalking its prey, and Christina—the prey—took a few steps back. She was still keeping her left hand hidden.

"What are you hiding behind your back?" he asked her in a silky voice.

"Nothing," she quickly responded—too quickly.

"Show me," he demanded, his eyes never leaving her face.

On the defensive, Christina became indignant. "How dare you come into my room and…"

In one swift move, like a rattlesnake striking, he grabbed her left arm and yanked her hand up to his face. His eyes glittered with confidence—and Christina realized that he knew! Was he going to make her pay for it? Of course he was. She may have fallen in love with him, but she knew he wasn't in love with her–and $250,000 was alot of money, even to a Havenwood.

Bill watched her panicked thoughts race across her features. He gave her a wicked smile as he powerfully held her left hand up. "Where is it?" he demanded.

Christina was mesmerized by the dangerous look she saw in his eyes, but she straightened her spine with courage. "I've misplaced it, but it's here somewhere. I'll find it." Her wild eyes glowered at him as she tugged at her hand. He released her and she quickly stepped away from him, enabling her to breathe again.

"Are you sure you'll find it?" he smoothly asked.

Christina raised her chin in defiance. "Of course. It's here. I know it."

Bill stealthily approached her, but this time Christina stood her ground. He wasn't going to intimidate her, no way.

But he was. He was scaring her very badly. And he was acting differently too. Where was the sensitive, thoughtful, tortured soul that she'd had dinner with last night? The one with the sense of humor, the one who'd protected her against his father, who'd cared for her when she'd been sick—the one she'd fallen in love with? Where was that Bill Havenwood?

He'd disappeared and the bastard was back!

Christina watched as a self-assured Bill crossed his arms in front of his chest. "So... what are we going to do about this situation?"

"The staff's looking, I'm looking... there's nothing for you to worry about."

He burst out laughing. "Oh, I know there's nothing for me to worry about."

Christina didn't like the way he was laughing at her. "What do you mean?"

He came closer—into her face. "I mean this. We have a contract and you're responsible for the value of that ring, a quarter of a cool million."

Christina looked him square in the eyes. "You know I don't have that kind of money."

Bill's eyes roamed over her beautiful face. He could smell that intoxicating perfume again. She was standing here, so close to him that he could almost taste her and although he knew she was frightened out of her wits right now, she was acting brave, defiant, and bold. He admired her for that—almost as much as he loved her. He could have relented and told her not to worry—that the ring was insured and she wouldn't have to pay him back, but he was a desperate man—and desperate men do desperate things.

He nodded. "Yes, I know."

"So?"

His hand snaked out and she flinched, unsure of his intentions. But all he wanted to do was to gently brush away a strand of her hair that had fallen across her beautiful face. Bill just couldn't stop himself from touching her. He wanted her badly and he was going to have her—no matter what he had to do, no matter what he had to say.

His movements mesmerized Christina. She could feel his whisper soft touch across her cheek as he brushed the hair back behind her ear. He was so close to her that she began to breathe faster—and this time it wasn't due to fear. She wanted him badly and she loved him—but he didn't love her. She pulled away from him.

"I guess you'll have to take me to court, but I'm warning you, you can't get water out of a dry well."

He laughed at that. "Your well's not dry, Christina. In fact, I'm sure you have what it takes to quench my thirst."

The rational part of Cristina didn't like the way he said that—the other half, the part that was on fire for him—did.

She stared him down. "I'm going to find that damn ring if I have to tear this colossal mansion down brick by billionaire brick, so you can die of thirst for all I care Bill Havenwood," she sneered at him.

The rogue had the audacity to laugh at her again. He seemed to actually be enjoying her predicament.

He stopped laughing. "Here's the deal. If by the end of this month when our contract expires, you can't produce the ring, you're going to marry me… for real."

Christina's jaw dropped. "What? I'm not marrying you."

"You will. And when you do, your debt will be cancelled. A wife can't owe her husband money, now can she? After all, what's mine will be yours." He paused. "And what's yours will be mine."

Christina saw the hunger for her reflected in his eyes.

"Why are you doing this?" she croaked out.

"Because I…" he stopped, then gathered his wits about him again. "Because, if I make you my wife, my father won't kick me out of the money and maybe… you won't kick me out of your bed. It's a win-win situation."

Anger shot through Christina. It was suddenly all so clear. This was the real Bill Havenwood. Here was the bastard who'd pulled that prank on her in high school, the one who'd threatened her under the bleachers that day, the one who'd blackmailed her into helping him scam his father—and now he was blackmailing her again.

And the Bill Havenwood that she loved?

He didn't exist.

Her love for him had been based on a lie—an image of him that she'd created in her mind. She'd almost forgotten her golden rule—with men, what you see is what you get, and she saw a bastard.

How stupid had she been to think herself in love with this creep? Thank God she hadn't done anything about it. Thank God she hadn't said anything to him. And thank God she hadn't slept with him. He was a user and he was using her to further his own ends. It was all about what he wanted—and he didn't give a damn about her.

The war was back on.

Christina threw him a dirty look. "Just because you'd make me marry you, doesn't mean I'd let you touch me."

"Maybe not, but my odds improve."

He smirked at her then, that damned Havenwood smirk she remembered from high school. Oh what a fool she'd been to imagine that he'd changed.

"I wouldn't bet on it," she threw back at him.

Bill inched closer and whispered in her ear. "We'll see… Mrs. Havenwood."

Christina pulled away from him. "I'm not marrying you."

He smiled that confident, cocky smile of his. "You will. And one more thing? Your lover? He's history. You're never to see him again. You'll be my wife and I don't share."

"What about you and your lover? Stephie is it?" How dare he forbid her to see her so-called lover when he had that slut on the side!

"I don't know who you've been talking to, but I've told you

before, she and I were over before I met you. So you see, I'm all yours."

He planted a swift kiss on her lips and before Christina had a chance to push him away, he'd already stepped back.

Disgusted, she wiped his kiss off her lips with the back of her left hand—the one with the missing bauble.

He gave her a devilish grin. "Find your ring and you're free. Otherwise, you're mine. You can go back to tearing the house apart now."

Angry, Christina rounded on him. "Get out of my bedroom," she seethed.

Bill was cool. He knew he'd won. "Ahhh… now is that anyway for a wife to talk to her husband?"

"I'm not your wife."

"You will be." He gave her a confident grin and with that, he turned and walked towards the door.

"Oh, Mr. Havenwood?" He turned back to her. "You said last night that you and your father were two different peas in the same Havenwood pod. You were wrong. You're just like him."

It was the first time since he'd walked in here that Bill's eyes glittered with anger. It was a parting shot from her—and it was a good one.

"That's about the worst thing you could have said to me," he spit out at her.

"But true," she threw back at him.

With one last withering look at her, he walked out.

And Christina went back to tearing her bedroom apart. The ring just had to be here—it just had to.

*

Bill was coming down the stairs when he saw Geoffrey, one of the under butlers, scurrying across the foyer.

"Geoffrey, has the ring been found yet?" Bill called out to him.

Geoffrey stopped his march. "Not to my knowledge, sir."

"Tell the staff that if it's found, I want it brought to me, not to Christina, is that understood?"

"Yes, sir. To you." The under butler nodded and left to spread the news.

Bill was going to stack the deck in his favor and if that meant playing dirty, so be it. If that ring was found, she was out of here, but if it wasn't, she was his. And he wanted her—anyway he could get her even if that meant he had to play the part of a bastard.

It disgusted him that playing a bastard came so easily to him. Maybe she was right and he was more like his old man than he cared to admit. Maybe the manipulating, conniving Havenwood blood did course through his veins after all.

He smiled to himself. But he would bet he was the first Havenwood in their whole sordid line of cutthroat, thieving ancestors, who was actually thrilled about losing a quarter of a million dollars.

CHAPTER 42

IT WAS 8 a.m. Saturday morning, the day of the engagement party. Everything had been set—the tents, flowers, champagne; and the festivities were to take place on the mansion grounds that evening. Everyone was excited—everyone except the bride-to-be.

She was standing outside the door to Jenny's apartment in tears. She knocked tentatively. A sleepy Jenny opened the door and was shocked to see her friend there.

"Chrissy, what are you doing here so early?" she asked.

With watery eyes, Christina sobbed, "Jenny… I'm in trouble."

Jenny gasped as she yanked her friend into the apartment before closing the door. "Oh my God, you're pregnant with Bill Havenwood's baby! I knew it! I knew this was going to happen!" She declared, as she pushed a despondent Christina into a kitchen chair.

"No, not that kind of trouble! Why does everyone think I'm pregnant?" Exasperated, Christina threw her hands in the air.

"Then what?"

Tears started falling down Christina's cheeks again. "I think I'm going to have to marry him… for real."

"What?"

Christina nodded. "I… lost the ring."

Jenny gasped. "The one that was worth…?" She glanced down at her friend's bare left hand.

Christina nodded. "And the big jerk found out and he's saying that if I can't find it, I have to pay him back, but I don't have that kind of money and he says he's going to sue me unless I marry him."

"You don't remember what you did with it?"

Christina shook her head 'no'. "And everybody's been look-ing, but nobody's found it. I can't marry him, Jenny, I just can't." She buried her face in her hands.

"So Havenwood wants to marry you?" Jenny handed her friend a tissue as Christina nodded 'yes'. "Did he say why?"

"Sex and money."

Jenny gasped. "What?"

"He said his father wouldn't kick him out of the money if he married me and… he wants me."

"Really?" Grinning, Jenny sat back in her chair. "So, Havenwood is in love with you. Go figure."

Frustrated, Christina stood up and began to pace the small kitchen. "I said sex Jenny, not love. He wants to have sex with me because I'm a challenge to him, that's all."

"Are you sure? Men don't usually marry…"

"Yes, I'm sure! God, don't read more into this than that."

Jenny's eyes narrowed on Christina. "And do you want to have sex with him?"

Christina was indignant. "How can you ask me that?"

"From the look on your face, very easily." Jenny kept her eagle eyes trained on her friend. "Are you going to answer me?"

With an exasperated moan, Christina began to shout, "Yes. Yes, I want to have sex with Bill Havenwood. I've been wanting to have sex with him since the first day I met him again. He's hot and he's gorgeous and every time he pierces me with those beau-tiful green eyes of his, I want to rip his clothes off and feel him moving inside me. I want to know what sounds he makes when he comes and what his naked body feels like plastered on top of mine, and mine on top of his. There, I said it! Are you happy now?" Defeated, Christina plopped down into her chair.

Jenny shook her head from side to side. She knew this was going to happen. "Are you in love with him?" She asked softly.

Christina looked away as she whispered, "Yes, but he doesn't love me."

Jenny wasn't so sure. From what Christina had told her about how he'd been acting around her, she suspected Havenwood might have stronger feelings for her friend than she cared to admit.

"Maybe he does," Jenny pushed.

"Jenny, no!" Christina shouted the words. "Besides, I'm in love with a Bill Havenwood that doesn't exist. I thought he'd changed… with the AA and everything, but he hasn't. He's still the same rat he was in high school, only now he's a sober rat and I refuse to love that creep."

Jenny sighed, "Okay. I'll help you out of this mess."

Thrilled, Christina hugged her friend. "Thank you, Jenny. I knew I could count on you."

Jenny smiled. "Here's what you do. You can't find the ring so you tell him you have no choice but to marry him. That'll lower his defenses. Then you have to put your revenge plan back into action and find something to hold over his head."

"But Jenny, I've tried and there's nothing."

"Listen to me. Is there anything… a name, some tidbit of information you've come across that I can check out for you at the office?"

Christina's eyes opened wide. "Yes." She rifled through her purse and pulled out the paper with the 1625 Shelley Ave address on it. She showed it to Jenny. "I found this in his jacket pocket. It's just an old abandoned warehouse. Can you find out who owns it and if it has any connections with Fido Foods or Samco Oil?"

Jenny was already copying the address on her notepad. "Consider it done… but I still think he loves you."

"Jenny!"

"All right, my lips are sealed. Now let's get to work. We'll outwit the big rat together."

Christina giggled. It was the first time since yesterday that she began to feel hopeful again.

*

Christina was at her bedroom window looking down at the twinkling lights of her engagement party on the mansion grounds. It was 7:45 p.m. and guests had begun to arrive. Limousine after limousine had been crawling up the circular drive, dropping off their distinguished passengers.

She was waiting for the slimeball to pick her up.

According to William, she was to make a grand entrance on Bill's arm when most of the guests had arrived. William had also arranged for hair and makeup people to come to the house and turn his future daughter-in-law into more of a goddess than she already was. Christina smiled. Those had been his words, not hers.

That afternoon, when she'd been in the middle of being primped and plucked, there'd been a knock on her door. It was Geoffrey, one of the under butlers. He handed Christina two small boxes marked Tiffany's and an envelope with her name on it. She recognized Bill's scrawl.

Ripping open the envelope, Christina pulled out the note. It read, 'We can't have an engagement party without an engagement ring or a wedding without...' He'd left the last part blank.

Christina opened the first box and gasped. Inside was the most beautiful ring she'd ever seen. Whereas her last ring had been big and showy, this one was a simple five karat design with one perfect square-shaped diamond in the middle and two heart-shaped diamonds on either side. It was tasteful and elegant—and exactly what she would've picked out. She loved it. Damn him! He was getting to know her so well—and she didn't like that at all. She slipped it on and it fit perfectly, glistening on her hand. Wonder how much this one cost?

She then opened the second box. Inside, was a diamond eternity band with perfect diamonds circling the band. It was her wedding ring—and Christina felt her stomach heave. Was that because she was disgusted at having to marrying him—or excited? For one split second she wasn't sure.

But the wedding date was still three weeks away. She now

had Jenny helping her and they'd find some dirt on him before then. Christina's stomach calmed down and she placed the wedding band back in the box.

"I hope you kept the receipt Bill Havenwood, because that's one ring I'm never going to wear," she mumbled to herself.

The makeup and hair people had left and Christina stared at her appearance in the full-length mirror. Her hair was pinned up with tiny crystals placed throughout the style. As she moved her head, her hair seemed to shimmer like an angel's.

Her couture dress was a white, chiffon Grecian toga-style floor length that molded itself perfectly to her womanly shape. It also had crystals beaded throughout. As she moved, it too shimmied and sparkled. She looked like she'd come down from the heavens—and she felt it, too.

The only jewelry she wore was her new engagement ring and the platinum stickpin the worm had given her during their dinner date. She'd placed it high up on the dress near her shoulder. What had he said when he'd given it to her? That she was sharp and dangerous? Sharp and dangerous indeed! He didn't know how sharp or how dangerous, but he'd find out soon enough. He'd also said that she enjoyed 'sticking it' to him. Yes—that was coming too. She smiled to herself. Wonder what he'd say when he saw her dressed like this?

There was a knock at her door. It was him.

She glided across the bedroom and her heart was beating at the speed of light. Why was she feeling like this about seeing him—and having him see her? She opened the door.

It wasn't him. It was William.

"Change of plans, my dear. I've decided I want to introduce you to the New York phonies myself," he announced.

William was dressed in a black tuxedo and looked every inch as handsome as his son, if only older. With his ponytail tied at the back and his suave British accent floating out of his mouth, he was the epitome of class.

"I'd be honored," Christina smiled and placed her hand through his arm.

"Christina, you look a vision," William gushed as they walked down the hallway. "I couldn't have asked for a more perfect daughter-in-law than if I'd picked you out myself."

Which he had, of course, he devilishly thought to himself.

CHAPTER 43

THE ENTIRE HOUSE and grounds were lit up like a Christmas tree. Waiters in black and white uniforms were serving champagne and hors d'oeuvres to the two hundred plus guests in the back gardens and pool area where huge tents with tables had been set up. A small orchestra was playing and a few couples were already dancing. The mood was soft, elegant and posh. The cream of New York high society was here, all the movers and shakers of the moneyed class. There wasn't a 'have-not' in the entire well-heeled bunch.

Dressed in a black tuxedo that molded to his lean physique, Bill was pretending to listen to Jonathan Simons, a boring banker that was trying to interest him in some stock deal. But he was keeping an eye on the French doors leading out of the mansion. He was waiting for 'her' to appear.

His father had insisted on being the one to escort her out, even though Bill had objected. He wanted to be the first person to see what she looked like tonight. He wanted to have a quiet moment with her before this damned debacle began and maybe find out what she thought of her new engagement ring. He wanted to touch her, to smell her, to kiss her even—well maybe not kiss her—he didn't think there was much chance of that now that he was blackmailing her into marrying him—but he could still hope, couldn't he?

Bill shook his head at himself. Look at how pathetic he'd become! The Bill Havenwood who had always been able to get any woman he wanted into whatever position he wanted was now giddy about 'maybe' getting a little kiss from this one—if he was lucky. When had he become such a fool over a woman?

Ever since this one had crashed into his life, that's when.

Bill kept his peripheral vision glued to the doors as he continued to humor Jonathan by pretending to listen.

And then—she magically appeared.

Bill's eyes widened with desire as he saw her float outside on his father's arm. She looked spectacular and he saw several men in the crowd swivel their heads in her direction. She seemed ethereal, from another world, as her dress sparkled with tiny stars.

And she was going to be his.

He felt like a little boy who'd been promised an ice cream cone and couldn't wait to get his hands on it—and his tongue. He smiled to himself as the sensuous images ran through his brain.

Yes, he definitely wanted to eat his fill.

Two other bankers approached him and Bill greeted them warmly. Tonight, he was going to be the perfect host. This was their party—his and Christina's—and he wasn't about to do anything that might embarrass her in front of this hypercritical, snobby crowd.

She was all that mattered tonight.

For the next half hour, William paraded Christina in front of New York's elite, introducing her to everyone that mattered.

And they all treated her with respect. She was going to be a Havenwood after all and William had a lot of power in all circles—business and political.

Bill, on the other hand, worked the other side of the party, greeting everyone, making small talk and making them feel welcome. He shook so many hands he felt like he was running for office. These snobs were going to give his marriage their blessing if it killed him tonight. Not that he cared two pence what they thought, but he cared for her sake. She was going to be accepted by them if he had to kiss every rich-bitch matron at the party and bullshit with every pig businessman and politician already lining up at the buffet table.

It was all for her.

CHAPTER 44

CHRISTINA WAS FEELING overwhelmed. So many faces, so many names—how was she going to remember them all? William had just finished introducing her to the hundredth black tuxedo. She'd stopped seeing faces fifteen minutes ago. Now all that registered in her brain was what they were wearing.

On coming outside, she'd spotted Bill standing by the pool talking to some man. Her eyes had gone to him of their own volition as if her radar was set to his frequency, but she'd quickly looked away before he noticed. As always, he looked magnificent. His aura radiated outwards and attracted every female within his parameters. Yes, the devil was definitely good-looking.

And as William showed her off to his cronies, she had an almost sixth sense of where Bill was at all times. She could even feel his magnetic presence when her back was turned to him.

Oh, why did he have this power over her?

But the jerk was blackmailing her again—and that made her mad. And when she got mad—she got smart. She was going to be the captain of this Havenwood ship and it was going to sail where she steered it, not him.

Christina refocused on William who was leading her to the pool area.

"Everyone loves you, my dear," William gushed.

"You mean they all love your money, don't you William?"

William laughed. "That too. You're too smart for this crowd, Christina. But that's what makes you so perfect for becoming a Havenwood." He gave her a wink.

Too late, Christina realized that William was taking her to

where Bill was standing. They reached him and her heart started racing as Bill turned his green orbs on her.

"You look very beautiful tonight, Christina," Bill admired, as his eyes devoured her.

Christina blushed, unable to stop herself.

William became impatient. "Yes, yes, Christina always looks beautiful. Never mind that. Now you two listen. I've introduced Christina to everyone. You both now need to show them how much in love you are. They've all got their beady little eyes on you now. So you…" He pointed to his son. "Dance with your fiancée and stay close to her for the rest of the evening. And watch your drinking tonight. I don't want to have to explain any drunken antics to this snotty bunch of reptiles, got that?"

"Right dad, no drunken antics from me tonight." Bill smiled at Christina and she couldn't help smiling back as they shared their secret that Bill was now sober.

"Good." Pleased, William nodded. "Now, go dance with Christina."

Bill took Christina's hand and led her to where several other couples were already dancing. As they began to move to the music, she looked up at him and gave him one of her warmest smiles—and he was dazzled. Was she beginning to soften up to him?

"I've decided I have no choice but to marry you… you prick," she purred.

No, she hadn't, Bill thought—but her agreement to marry him sent triumphant shivers up his spine. He returned her smile with one of his own radiant grins.

"That's not exactly the speech of a loving bride, but I'll take it."

She smiled again for the sake of their guests. "Most grooms aren't scheming swines like you, sweetheart. I despise you, you know."

Bill laughed as he danced even closer with her. "So you do have feelings for me, sugarplum."

"And they're quite strong feelings. I'm actually surprised at how passionate I am about my loathing for you."

Bill dipped and twirled her. "As long as you're passionate about me beloved, then I'm the happiest man in the world."

Obviously, she wanted to play this light and witty for the benefit of their audience and Bill had no objections. He wasn't happy about her confession just now that she detested him, but he was forcing her into this, so it was to be expected. But maybe—she'd eventually change her mind once they were married? Maybe? But tonight he would take whatever crumbs she was willing to dish out, even if they were poisonous.

Christina inched closer to him and disengaging her hands from his, she let them slide up his chest and wrap around his neck. This brought their bodies together as they continued to shimmy to the romantic music. A jolt of instant desire shot through Bill as her soft curves cupped themselves to every angular feature of his, and he briefly closed his eyes hoping that his body wouldn't betray him by showing every snob at this party how much he damned well wanted her.

"There, that's better," she whispered as she lovingly began to caress his cheek with her gentle hand. "Do you think all your friends are enjoying the show now, sweetie?" She smiled up at him, her full lips pouting enticingly.

"Baby, if you keep grinding against me like you're doing now, I'm going to put on a show for these assholes like they'll never forget."

She laughed at him then but didn't move away. "We both know you'll do nothing to embarrass yourself in front of your moneybags father. So don't focus on what I'm doing with my body to yours… focus instead on all the money you'll be getting if you pull this off."

Bill took a deep breath as he got control of himself. "That's a little 'hard' to do right now." He emphasized the word 'hard'.

Christina ran her finger across his lips while temptingly licking hers. "I know you want me."

Bill was completely mesmerized. He couldn't have walked away from her if his pants were on fire—which they were!

"Yes," he gasped out. "I haven't made a secret about that."

She smiled into his eyes, "Well, you'll never have me because I hate you, you louse."

Bill bent down to her ear and whispered, "Them's fightin' words, darlin'."

"Bring it on, you swine," Christina's laughter twinkled out.

Bill laughed as he spun her around before yanking her back to his overheated body.

Two society matrons had been watching the couple, as had everyone else at the party. They whispered to each other about how much in love Christina and Bill were, and what a lovely couple they made.

Bill gazed at his beautiful bride. "So tell me, do you like your new engagement ring, you little hellcat?"

Christina dared him with her eyes. "What are you going to make me sign over this time if I lose it? A kidney, maybe… or my firstborn?"

"Your firstborn? Now there's an idea." Those piercing green eyes of his glinted dangerously down at her.

Her heart skipped a beat, as for one split second, the thought of having his baby sent a thrill through her, but she quickly made it go away. She glanced at her new ring, sparkling on her left hand. "The ring is beautiful. You have exquisite taste, Mr. Havenwood."

"I picked you, didn't I?" His eyes darkened as they devoured her beautiful features and Christina again felt that thrill shoot through her.

But the lowlife wasn't getting her tonight. She was going to get him.

She rubbed her hand across his cheek again as the orchestra played another tune. "The month's not over yet, sweetie and I might still find my first ring. If I do, I'm gone and you can go to hell," she said, with her most winsome, loving smile.

"That's 'if' you find it and you haven't yet… so I'm still in the running for your sweet affections."

"We'll see," she mysteriously replied.

"What about your white knight boyfriend? Have you broken it off yet?" Bill jealously asked.

"I still have a few weeks left before I have to take vile vows with you and a girl can sow a lot of wild oats by then."

Another surge of jealousy coursed through Bill. So, she was still sleeping with the scumbag, was she? He quickly got control of himself and gave her a movie star grin.

"My darling, if there are any wild oats to be sown, I'll do it for you. I'm very good at—farming."

In spite of herself, Christina was impressed with his witty comeback. He had such an amazing sense of humor, damn it!

"Are you now?" she coyly replied.

"Definitely. In college, I majored in drinking, vomiting and—farming. I got my degree in all three. I'm not good at much in this world Christina, but in those three subjects, I'm a Nobel Prize genius. And since I'm not drinking or vomiting anymore, I'm now putting all of my energies into—farming."

"Why am I not surprised, honeybunch?"

Bill laughed at her. He was so enjoying this little game of hers. "Let's see. I'm good at tilling the soil and planting my seeds…"

"From what I've heard, you've planted your seeds far and wide," Christina cattily interrupted him.

"Don't believe everything you hear, my little milkmaid—at least half of it anyway," he replied, as his hands moved down to her derriere and began to softly caress both cheeks.

That felt so good, Christina thought, that it angered her even more. With her arms still around his neck, she began to play with the back of his hair as she sensed everyone's eyes on them.

She wickedly smiled up at him. "Farmer Bill? The only thing you're good at—is spreading manure."

He laughed then—a deep throaty laugh—that resonated throughout her body. It filled her up, as if they were indeed having sex. Every molecule in her greedily lapped up the tingling vibrations he was shooting out. Oh, why did he have to have this effect on her?

All of New York high society watched the couple and there wasn't one person there who didn't believe that Christina and Bill weren't deeply in love. It was in the way they were holding each other as they danced—and the way they were softly speaking to each other like lovers—and in the way they smiled as they stared deeply into each other's eyes.

Yes, those two were in love—it was so obvious.

There was also someone else who had been watching the pair intensely—a tall, willowy redhead named Stephie. She was standing on the outer perimeters of the crowd where she wouldn't be seen. She hadn't crashed this party tonight to cause a scene. No—she had come tonight to do another kind of damage.

Jealous rage roiled through her system as she watched them dancing so close to each other. She knew how Bill looked when he was having a sexual relationship with someone, and it was obvious those two were now screwing each other. It was in how they were moving in sync together—and in the way they were holding each other—and in the way that little mouse was caressing his cheek.

She may not have been sleeping with Bill when Stephie had met her at the restaurant that day, but she definitely was now. And they were going to be married—and that little whore was going to be his wife—Mrs. Havenwood—mistress of this house and his fortune.

That should have been her!

Seething with anger, Stephie moved away and quietly disappeared into the house. She stealthily climbed the staircase on her way to Bill's room. She had visited this mansion many times when she'd been seeing Bill and she knew it like the back of her well-manicured hand. After all, she had expected to be his wife one day and in charge of all of this. And it had been taken away from her by that little tramp.

Well, she wasn't going to roll over and let the both of them do this to her. Her detectives were still on the case, digging up dirt. They were even now in the process of breaking into the little mouse's apartment to see what they could find there. Drummond Sinclair had also found out that although the wedding was only three weeks away, Bill hadn't yet booked a honeymoon. So, Stephie decided to do it for him. With a wicked grin, she pulled out three airline tickets from her purse.

Quietly slipping into Bill's bedroom, Stephie opened his night table and placed the tickets inside. She smirked. Now, if she could only get that little bitch Christina by herself for a few moments, her plan would be complete.

CHAPTER 45

WHEN THEY FINISHED dancing, Bill led Christina into the midst of the party where they mingled with the guests. With his arm glued to her waist, Bill expertly maneuvered her through the high class set—chatting with some, greeting others. These were his people—not Christina's—and he wanted to protect her from their catty, elitist ways. He wanted to make sure that they subconsciously understood that the Havenwood money and power were behind her now—so they had all better accept her or else.

They were talking to Mrs. Robinson, an influential art patron, when Christina spotted a smiling William walking towards them. And walking beside him were her parents—Nunzio and Gabriella Matteo! Oh God! What were they doing here? Shocked, Christina froze.

Bill felt her tense up and he instinctively pulled her closer. He turned to look in the direction she was staring and saw his father approaching with two guests.

William drew near and he had a twinkle of mischief in his eyes. "My dear, look who's here," he said, pointing to her parents.

"Mom! Pop! What are you doing here?" Christina squeaked out.

Her father, Nunzio, was wearing a tuxedo and her mom, Gabriella was wearing a beautiful floor-length blue dress. They both looked as if they fit in—except for the angry expressions on their faces.

Nunzio piped up first, "William invited us. He flew us in and we're staying at the Plaza. What's the matter? You couldn't invite us yourself? Did you think we were going to embarrass you in front of all your new friends?"

Both Christina and Bill glared at William who, still smiling, nodded in agreement with Nunzio. Yes, he had invited them—to put more pressure on Christina and make sure she did walk down that aisle in three weeks time.

William reasoned that Christina hadn't invited her parents to her engagement party because on some level, she was still thinking that she'd get out of this mess before she'd have to actually marry his son. So why bother telling her parents anything? Might as well keep them in the dark until the last possible millisecond.

So, William had taken matters into his own hands and informed them of what was going on. And they looked like a strong couple that would put considerable pressure on their daughter to marry his son—once the ball got rolling. And looking around the party tonight—that ball was definitely rolling. Nunzio and Gabriella Matteo were going to be allies for him in his scheming plot to get these two married off.

William smiled at his own cunning brilliance. No one was going to outsmart him—and his son and the girl were going to do what he wanted—which was to marry and produce grandbabies for him.

Gabriella was speaking. "Aren't you going to answer your father?" she demanded of her daughter.

"I...I..." Christina was speechless. Her parents always had this intimidating effect on her. Suddenly, she felt Bill give her a quick squeeze around her waist and then he was speaking for her.

"Mr. & Mrs. Matteo, I'm afraid the fault is all mine. Christina told me to make arrangements for your trip here but I forgot. Everything's been so rushed. I am very sorry." He threw his most charming, dazzling smile at them and although Nunzio grunted in disbelief, Gabriella melted under her soon-to-be, handsome son-in-law's gaze.

Surprised, Christina swiveled unbelieving eyes to Bill's face.

Had he just saved her butt by taking the blame? That was decent of him—and nice.

She hated it when he did anything nice!

Christina didn't realize it but she unconsciously snuggled deeper into his arm that was still protectively encircling her waist. But Bill sensed it. She was coming to him for help. There was something primal about a man protecting his woman—and he loved it.

"I'm Bill, by the way," Bill extended his hand out to Nunzio who shook it reluctantly. He then turned to Gabriella and kissing the back of her hand, he drawled, "I can see where Christina gets all of her fire and beauty, Mrs. Matteo."

Gabriella gushed under Bill's flattery before nodding her approval at her daughter. "Handsome and charming. This is good husband material, Christina." Not to mention, Gabriella thought to herself, that this boy came from one of the richest families in the country and her daughter would be living in this big house and not have to want for anything material-wise. It wasn't that Gabriella was greedy—she just wanted to see her little girl taken care of, as any mother would.

"Th… Thanks, mom." Christina stammered.

"Let me see your ring." Gabriella asked as Christina brought her left hand up. "Oh," she gushed, "It's beautiful." Then she looked up at her daughter's face and touched her cheek. She had tears in her eyes. "And you're beautiful. I can't believe it. My baby's getting married and soon, she'll be having babies of her own."

Fat chance of that, Christina thought, but for her mom's sake, she smiled like a happy bride.

"I still think you should have told us yourself about this shindig," Nunzio was still annoyed with his daughter.

Bill placed his hand on Nunzio's shoulder and steered him away. "Mr. Matteo, why don't I introduce you to some people and get you something to eat?"

Gabriella quickly stepped in. "Good idea, Bill. Take the pig away and feed him. I need to talk to my baby in private."

She wrapped her arms around her daughter. "Christina, we have to make a guest list for the wedding. And I want to see your dress, and we have to give you a bridal shower and I'm not inviting your Uncle John…"

Oh no! Christina thought, as her mom yammered away. How much more difficult was this going to be when she'd call off the wedding eventually? Which she would, of course—because she and Jenny were even more determined now to find dirt on the creep.

Throughout this whole little scene, William had been grinning like a diabolical cat. Yes—Nunzio and Gabriella would make sure their daughter definitely married his son—or else.

Suddenly, William's smile dropped at who he saw walking towards them. "What in, God Almighty blue blazes in hell, is that blasted woman doing here?" he hissed.

Bill, Christina and her parents all turned to look. It was William's ex-wife, Bill's mom—Maddie Havenwood. Dressed in a flowing, green dress that matched her glorious green eyes, Maddie Havenwood was a very beautiful, statuesque 55 year-old-woman who proudly walked across the lawn as if she owned the place—which she had, of course, up until the divorce five years ago.

Christina suddenly saw where Bill got his striking good looks.

"I invited her," Bill smirked at his father. His dad wasn't the only one good at pulling stunts.

William angrily rounded on his son. "Why, in hell, did you do that?"

"Because she's my mother and this is my engagement party and I wanted her to meet Christina," Bill smugly answered his father.

"Bloody hell!" William let out on a whoosh of air. He was not happy.

Maddie finally approached them. Many of the rich snobs had

been cattily watching her walk across the estate. They all knew her, of course, as she'd been part of their crowd up until the divorce. How would she and William act towards each other, they wondered? They knew that there was a lot of bad blood between them since Maddie had left William to go live on the commune in Arizona.

"Hello, William," Maddie said as she raised her chin, defying him to throw her out.

William straightened his spine, "Maddie. Did you fly out here in a plane or did you come on your broomstick?"

Maddie laughed, "Why William, the broomstick, of course… the one you taught me how to ride."

William pretended to laugh. He knew everyone's eyes were on them. "You look well. Obviously your hippy-dippy lifestyle suits you. Been practicing your crystal ball readings?"

"Aura readings, actually. And I can see yours has become blacker than ever. Still up to no good?"

William seethed. "I'm surprised my aura hasn't gotten lighter since I got rid of that demon that was on my back five years ago."

"Don't look now but the demon's back," Maddie giggled.

William scowled. The blasted woman was laughing at him!

Stepping between them, Bill kissed his mom's cheek. "Thanks for coming, mom," he said.

"Anything for you, my darling," she replied, as she hugged her son.

Bill reached for Christina and pulled her towards him. "I want you to meet Christina," he proudly announced. He then turned to his bride-to-be. "Christina, this is my mom, Maddie Havenwood."

Christina could tell he loved his mother very much and was fiercely proud of her, no matter what William said.

Christina shook her hand, "It's nice to meet you, Mrs. Havenwood."

Maddie smiled, "Please call me Maddie." She turned to her son, "She's very beautiful, Bill and I'm so happy that you've asked me to be a part of this." She patted her boy's cheek—and he bloomed under her loving gaze.

"I wouldn't have it any other way mom."

Off to the side, William was still frowning. "I'm not happy about this. I'm not happy at all," he proclaimed, before walking away.

"He's such an asshole!" Bill exclaimed at his father's retreating back.

Maddie patted her son's arm. "Never you mind about him. I know how to handle your father."

Bill smiled at her and then proceeded to introduce her to the Matteos. After all, they were soon to become one big, happy, dysfunctional family—if he had anything to say about it.

CHAPTER 46

AFTER FIELDING HER mother's zillion questions about her upcoming 'wedding', Christina finally managed to pawn her off on the Latimers, an older couple who were soon to embark on a holiday in Italy. Her father was busy at the buffet table and Bill's mom, Maddie was catching up with old friends by the pool. Christina scanned the party for Bill and saw him walking towards her.

"Things are going well, don't you think?" he beamed.

"Except for my parents showing up," Christina replied dryly.

"I see Satan is trying to control our lives again, but this time I've got a secret weapon."

"You mean, your mom?"

Bill nodded. "I told her to come and get the old goat off our backs. If he's fighting with her, then he's not fighting with us and maybe we can get married without his damned interference."

"Assuming I don't find the ring, of course," Christina quipped.

Bill gave her a devilish grin, "Always assuming that. Anyway, mom said to leave it to her and she'd handle the 'evil one'."

Christina was surprised. "That's exactly what my mom calls my dad."

Bill laughed. "Looks like we have more things in common than you thought. Maybe we're soulmates?"

"More like cellmates," she fired back.

"I'm not your jailer, Christina. You can walk anytime."

"Sure, I can walk… right into court where you'll sue me for the ring money."

Bill shrugged. "I need you." His words carried more meaning than Christina realized.

She rolled her eyes, "Yes, yes, I know… so you can keep your greedy fingers in your father's billion dollar cookie jar. But why do I have to be the sacrificial lamb?"

She unintentionally batted her beautiful eyes up at him and he almost caved. He almost told her that their deal was off—and that she didn't owe him anything—and that she could leave here anytime. He almost told her he'd do anything to make her happy.

Almost.

But he stopped himself. Love could be selfish like that sometimes—or was that fear?

"I wasn't the one who lost a quarter of a million dollar ring, Christina. Now I wonder why you did that?" he teased.

Christina's eyes flashed anger at him, "You're making it sound like I did it on purpose."

He winked at her, "Maybe subconsciously you do want to marry me."

Christina was taken aback, "Are you insane?"

"Maybe you want me and by losing the ring, you can have me without having to admit to yourself that you want me. It's Psychology 101."

He was laughing at her now and Christina was getting madder. "Another college course you flunked since you were so busy with your farming and drinking," she tartly replied.

Bill laughed out loud at that one. "See how well you know me? We were made for each other, babycakes. Admit that at least."

"You… you… you asshole!" Christina spluttered. He was getting too close to the truth and she unconsciously sensed it.

He continued to laugh at her, "Darling, don't be like that. All I want is some of your sweet sugar. Why don't you plant one right here…" he pointed to his lips, "…and we'll kiss and make up."

"My lips are not what I want to plant right there," Christina seethed through gritted teeth as her fist clenched.

Laughing, Bill inched closer and tingling sensations coursed up and down Christina's spine as his powerful, male chest came up against her soft, womanly curves. He looked down at her from his superior height.

"Try it… and see what happens," he whispered wickedly as his sensual gaze roamed over her face.

Seconds ticked by as they both stared at each other. But Christina backed off first. She knew he was enough of a rat to take advantage of the situation.

Several guests approached them and for their benefit, Christina lovingly smiled up at him. "Excuse me, my love. I have to go powder my nose," she sweetly announced, then softly hissed at him, "Before I break yours."

He bent down to her ear, "You know I like it rough," he whispered. He winked at her then before breaking out into another grin as he took in her livid expression.

Christina's eyes narrowed as she seethed at him for getting the better of her. What was that damn tuxedo of his made out of tonight? Teflon? No epitaph or insult she was hurtling at him seemed to be sticking.

As she turned to storm off, William approached them carrying two flutes of champagne and stopped her.

"Christina, where are you going?" He thrust a glass in each of their hands and hurriedly said, "I'm doing the toast now."

He then turned to the crowd, motioned to the orchestra to stop playing and started speaking in a loud voice. "Excuse me, everyone. I'd like to make a toast to the bride and groom."

Christina glanced over at Bill whom she saw had stopped laughing and whose eyes were now glued to the glass of bubbly he was holding in his hand. He was almost hypnotized by it and she saw his hand was suddenly shaking slightly.

She knew what he was thinking. His father was going to make a toast and everyone would drink to it—and with all of their eyes on the bride and groom, Bill would be on center stage where he would have to take a sip of the alcohol in front of everyone. He couldn't very well 'not' toast to his own engagement, now could he?

Bill's hand was shaking ever so slightly, not enough for anyone to notice—except for Christina. Good. Why should she feel sorry for him? She wasn't his babysitter and bastards didn't deserve help.

But Christina wasn't built like that. She was tough, but she wasn't ruthless—and when it came right down to it, she didn't have the killer instinct. And every nerve in her body was screaming out to her to help him. Suddenly, her thinking processes stopped and she began to operate on pure instinct.

William continued with his speech as he lifted his glass high in the air. "To Bill and Christina, long life, much love and many babies. Congratulations."

Everyone saluted them with their glasses and began to sip their drinks. Quickly, Christina put her hand on Bill's arm to prevent him from raising the glass of alcohol anywhere near his lips and brought her face up to his for a kiss instead. Bill swiftly realized what she was doing and lowered his lips, capturing hers in a strong kiss just as everyone was sipping their champagne. The crowd started to clap as they thought the engagement kiss the two were now sharing was part of the toast.

As Christina pulled away from him, she took the tempting glass of champagne out of his hands and put both hers and his on a nearby table. She smiled at him then as a silent form of communication passed between them.

Bill was floored. That had been the nicest, sweetest thing anybody had ever done for him. She had come to his rescue at a moment of crisis when he had needed help the most. And even though she was mad at him and he was forcing her into this diabolical arrangement, she had still come through for him. Maybe she cared for him a little? Could he hope?

His eyes turned serious as he let his gaze wander over her beautiful face. "Thank you for that," he whispered, looking for any clues that would indicate she had true feelings for him.

But Christina quickly lowered her eyes and retreated back into her business-like shell. "You helped me with my parents earlier. I owe you one," she abruptly stated, before walking away.

Confused and frustrated, Bill cursed under his breath as he watched her leave.

*

Christina quickly walked into the house on her way to her bedroom. Her face was hot and she needed to splash some cool water on her wrists. She couldn't deny it any longer. She loved him—bastard or not—she loved him.

The way he had looked at her just now—so sweet and sincere—it was all she could do to stop herself from wrapping her arms around him and comforting him. She knew how much his sobriety meant to him and the hell he'd been through to achieve it—and the hell he was still going through because he blamed himself for Jake's accident.

In that moment, she'd had an overwhelming urge to tell him she would help him anyway she could—that she'd be there for him—that she'd protect him—that she'd love him.

But he didn't love her.

And the bastard was blackmailing her again.

And she wouldn't give her love to a bastard. She had too much self-respect for that and too much self-preservation.

And she still owed something to that young girl she'd been all those years ago.

Christina had needed a few minutes to get away from him and from everyone in order to regain her composure. That's why she'd escaped so quickly after that kiss.

"Christina?"

As she was walking through the foyer, Christina heard a woman's voice calling out to her. Spinning around, she saw Stephie standing there, gorgeous and model-perfect as ever.

"What are you doing here?" Christina was cautious.

She'd had a taste of this viper's venom at the restaurant that day.

Stephie sneered, "I'm here to give you an update... Mrs. Havenwood."

A chill coursed through Christina's heart. "Did Bill invite you?" She asked, already knowing the answer.

Stephie maliciously grinned and ignored her question. "He may be sleeping with you now, but he's still sleeping with me. You're just a passing diversion for him. He's always had a voracious sexual appetite and I let him indulge. I know how to please my man."

That's interesting, Christina thought. Where did this bitch get the idea that she and Bill were sleeping together? Had Bill told her, and if so, why?

Christina smiled back, "He may be your man but he'll be my husband. Stay away from him or else I'll bring every Havenwood resource I can get my hands on... including his father... down on your head."

Christina had no idea what 'Havenwood resources' she could get her hands on, but judging from the way the bitch had flinched just now, the threat seemed to be a good one. Stephie believed it.

"It's not me you should be threatening. It's your husband-to-be because if he still wants me he can have me. In fact, he wants me to join the two of you on your honeymoon."

"What?" Christina spluttered.

Stephie gave Christina the 'I-have-a-secret' smile. "He's taking you to the Cayman Islands in the Caribbean for two weeks for your honeymoon... for appearance's sake. And he's invited me along too because it's me he really wants. He's bought the tickets and everything. I'm to fly down one day before the two of you and meet him there."

"You bitch!" Christina was livid—at her—at him—and she believed every word.

"So you see Mrs. Havenwood, you may be fucking him but you're not satisfying him. That's why he's still coming to me."

"Get out!"

"Another thing? Bill's told me he's marrying you for his father's sake, but he's got plans to divorce you in a couple of years when the heat's off. And then he's marrying me. He said so. So enjoy your tenure as Mrs. Havenwood because it's not going to last."

Christina gave the other woman a lethal glare. "I said—get out!" she spat.

Stephie sneered. "Congratulations on your engagement. It was a lovely party." Confident, she turned and glided out the front door.

Christina remained rooted to the spot—shocked, stunned and fuming. Had the big bitch been telling her the truth? Did Bill have plans to divorce her after a couple of years? That should have made her happy. After all, it gave her a release date on her prison sentence, but in fact, it made Christina angry—very, very angry, especially since she'd just admitted to herself that she loved him.

And were Stephie and Bill still sleeping together?

Probably, Christina thought—but was he really planning on taking that witch on their honeymoon? Bill hadn't said anything to Christina about a trip, but if she eventually had to marry the creep and they did go on one—she'd be damned if he was going to take his slut mistress along with his new wife on their honeymoon! Christina was not into threesomes—in any way, shape or form! She wasn't even interested in a twosome because she had no intentions of sleeping with him anyway. It was just the principle of the thing!

That bitch was not coming on her honeymoon. End of story!

Christina quickly ascended the majestic staircase—on the way to his bedroom.

CHAPTER 47

THE SLUT HAD said something about tickets. Christina snuck into Bill's bedroom. She needed to find those tickets if she was going to confront him. If she didn't have tangible proof to throw in his face, he would deny everything just as he'd been doing all along.

Where they here—or at the office? She'd look here first and worry about the office later. She moved to his dresser where papers were strewn on top—but they were only company reports.

She glanced around the room. Maybe they were in his bedside tables? Like a cat, she quietly moved to the first one, to the left of his bed. She opened the drawer and spotted them right away. There were three airline tickets resting on top of one of his smut magazines.

Snatching them up, Christina opened the first one. It had his name on it—and sure enough, it was for a flight to the Caymans leaving the day after their supposed wedding date and coming back two weeks later.

Her heart started to pound.

She flipped the second ticket open. It was for the same flight and dates, and the name on it was 'Christina Havenwood'. Her pounding heart skipped a beat. She'd never seen her name coupled with his before in print. She stared at it—not quite believing what she was seeing.

Then, her eyes narrowed dangerously as she glared at the third ticket. Like a jealous wife, she opened it. Inside, the name on it was Stephanie Hartwell—and all three tickets had been charged to Bill Havenwood's credit card.

Christina saw red. So—the bitch had been telling the truth! That louse was going to take that viper along on her honeymoon. How could he? How bloody could he? Okay—maybe their marriage wasn't a real one—and maybe their honeymoon was for show—but it was still a honeymoon, damn it! Oh, he was such a snake—a rattlesnake! What a perfect couple he and Stephie made—the rattlesnake and the viper!

Christina may have finally admitted to herself that she loved him, but she wasn't going to let him take her for a fool—and she certainly wasn't going to put up with this type of nonsense—not on her honeymoon! She was going to get him tomorrow and get him good. She was going to teach him a lesson, one he wouldn't forget for a long time.

She was so angry that not once did she rationally step back and think that maybe finding the tickets had been too easy? And maybe her meeting with Stephie had been too convenient? And maybe this was all a setup?

No—none of these thoughts even dared cross her jealous, furious mind.

*

It was Sunday morning, the day after the engagement party and Christina was already on her way to Jenny's apartment, needing to talk things over with her friend. She had quietly slipped out early while the rest of the house was still asleep. It had been a late night and the last of their guests, including her parents and Bill's mom had all left at 3 a.m.

Now sitting at Jenny's kitchen table, Christina had just finished telling her friend all about the party—about the high society luminaries that had shown up—about how her parents and Bill's mom had unexpectedly appeared—and about how the evening had been a huge success.

"I wish you could have been there Jenny," Christina said.

"I know Chrissy, but he could have recognized me and we

couldn't take that chance," Jenny sighed. "So tell me the best part. How did he look in his tuxedo?"

Christina smiled, "Amazing, of course. But that's not the best part. I had a little chat with his girlfriend."

Shocked, Jenny gasped. "You mean Stephie was there?"

Christina nodded. "Bill invited her. She said so."

Jenny was doubtful. "Chrissy, are you sure? To the same party where his father's at?"

Christina nodded, "Yes, and she told me he's taking me on a Caribbean honeymoon and she's coming too."

Jenny gasped even louder, "No way!"

"He's already booked everything. I found airline tickets for all three of us in his bedroom last night."

Christina reached into her purse and threw them down on the table. Jenny quickly grabbed them and flipped them open.

"What did he say when you asked him?"

"I haven't asked him yet... but I will, tonight."

Christina's eyes glinted dangerously and Jenny caught the look. "Chrissy, what are you up to?"

"I'm going to teach that jerk a lesson like he hasn't learnt in any school that's he's ever flunked out of."

"Chrissy... don't."

"I need to go shopping this afternoon to get a few supplies and then I'm putting my plan into action tonight."

Jenny looked backed at the tickets, "What if Stephie's lying?"

"Lying? No way. The proof is in your hands."

"Anybody can get tickets made up, Chrissy."

"What about his credit card? All three were charged to it."

"You told me Bill and Stephie dated for over two years. It's very possible she could know his card number and maybe she did all this to come between you two."

Christina calmly sipped her tea and raised her nose in the air. "I don't think so. She knows too many details about mine and that swine's business arrangement, details that only he could have told her. Sure, she may be telling me things in order to break us up. She believes he and I are sleeping together anyway."

"Really?"

"She told me so last night. And she's probably confronting me because she's jealous, but what she doesn't know is she's actually doing me a favor. She's telling me where things really stand between him and I; and information gives me power."

"Does he still want you?"

"Yes, but he doesn't love me."

"Chrissy, are you sure?"

"Jenny, those tickets prove it."

"Do you love him?"

Christina paused. Her answer was slow in coming. "Yes… but that doesn't mean I'm going to give up my self-respect for a few crumbs of affection from him. There are women in this world that'll do anything for love, including giving up their power to a man, but I'm not one of them."

Jenny laughed, "I know you're not, but you're playing with fire."

"But he's going to get burned, not me," Christina confidently remarked.

Jenny didn't believe her, but she knew her friend had to make her own mistakes. "Before I forget," she continued, "I called Robert and he's going to check out that 1625 Shelley Ave. warehouse."

"Great. He's the best reporter Streetwise has and he'll find something."

Jenny giggled. "So what's your plan for tonight? How are you going to get him?"

"Well… it's like this…" and for the next half hour Christina told her friend what she planned to do to Bill Havenwood to make him pay for wanting to bring his mistress along on their honeymoon.

When Christina was finished, Jenny burst out laughing, "Oh Chrissy, that's so diabolical."

Christina's eyes glinted with pride, "Isn't it?"

CHAPTER 48

BILL HADN'T SEEN Christina all day. He'd gotten up early that morning wanting to have breakfast with her, but he was surprised when he'd passed her open bedroom door and saw Tilly already making the bed. He'd asked her where Christina was and he'd been told that she'd already left the house.

That had spurred his curiosity. Where the hell had she gone at that hour of the morning? Probably into the city to see her boyfriend, that's where! Jealousy coursed through Bill. He was in love with her and he didn't want any other man touching her, but she was a free, independent woman whom he had no claims over—not yet anyway.

Bill had then gone out in the afternoon and met up with Jake at a very discreet restaurant. He had an envelope of Havenwood money to give to his friend for the GME cause.

Bill was funding the organization with his and his dad's money. Sometimes he'd give them straight cash and sometimes he'd funnel funds through several bank accounts he'd set up in the Caymans, a favorite haunt of his that he'd taken Stephie to several times when they'd been dating. He'd created a clever layer of dummy corporations through the Caribbean and Switzerland that prevented anyone from tracing the source of that money back to him. No one knew that GME was his baby and being financed by the blood money his father made on his shaky business deals. In Bill's mind, some of that blood money was now being washed clean because it was being used to do good.

Jake had been in good spirits today and had wanted to know everything about the engagement party. Bill had wanted his best friend to be there but Jake had refused. New York high-falutin' society, as he called it, wasn't his scene. Besides, all the guys at GME were preparing to throw Bill a bachelor party the likes of which he'd never seen even at the height of his wildest, partying days. Bill had laughed. That was going to be some outrageous party, he'd said.

Bill had then told Jake to call a GME meeting that week at the Shelley Ave warehouse—usual time of midnight—in order to discuss his father's counter-attack moves which were already being planned at Fido Foods. Acting as liaison between Bill and the boys, Jake agreed. Bill wasn't the only who was secretive about his involvement with the environmental group. Jake was too. Since Bill and he had been best friends since high school, and William knew Jake as Bill's friend, Jake was very careful about being seen with GME.

On the drive home, all Bill could think about was—her.

Had she been with her scumbag boyfriend today? Is that why she'd left the house so early? To see him? To be with him? To sleep with him?

And how could he get her to like him—Bill—and not that sleaze? Could she ever love him? She had helped him out last night with the champagne toast incident, so maybe...? All these thoughts raced through his brain as he pulled into the Havenwood drive.

As soon as he stepped through the front doors, Eudora came up to him. "Master Bill, Miss Christina said she needs to see you. She's in her room, I believe," she said in her Irish lilt.

Bill smiled at the elderly maid. "Thank you, Eudora." He loved her very much. She was like the grandmother he'd never had.

Quickly climbing the curving staircase, Bill reached Christina's bedroom door in seconds and knocked.

The door opened—and there she stood—wearing a partially opened black silk robe that revealed a black lace bra, panties and stay-up stockings.

"Hi there," she saucily smiled at him.

Bill's eyes practically popped out of their sockets as fierce desire shot through him at the sight of her dressed like that.

"Holy shit!" he inadvertently exclaimed. Then regaining his composure, he amended, "I mean… hi."

He was practically speechless and was suddenly having problems breathing. But for one split second, he wondered what she was up to. Why had she answered the door like that? His eyes feasted again on her almost naked body—and the thought vanished.

Christina opened the door wider, "Come in," she temptingly invited.

Bill didn't need to be asked twice. He quickly entered her bedroom and she shut the door behind him.

He turned to her then, his eyes glued to her hot, luscious body being exposed by the open robe. He couldn't help himself as his gaze roamed over every juicy curve of hers from her breasts, down to her womanly stomach and hips; and right down to her fire engine-red polished toes peeking through the black stockings. His eyes traveled back up her body and came to rest on her eyes.

She gave him another sexy smile, "Do you like what you see?"

"Ye… Yes," the one word came out in a gasp. All the blood had instantly drained from his brain and was now pooling in his privates. One look at her was all it took to make him hard.

"Good," she announced before walking to her dresser.

As she moved away from him, her black kitten-heeled slippers caused her hips to sway in an erotic rhythm and his eyes were riveted.

She reached for her perfume bottle and spritzed some on. Bill could smell the alluring fragrance from where he still stood near the door. Damn, that smell was hot! He was so hard right now that he felt he would burst at any second, like an inexperienced school boy. He began to shuffle nervously from foot to foot.

Christina watched him through the dresser mirror and smiled to herself. She could almost see his forehead getting damp with sweat. Oh yeah, she thought to herself, everything was going according to plan all right.

She turned to him then and as she did, her robe parted. His eyes grew bigger as he continued to gawk at her and he didn't know what to do. Was she inviting him to make a move or what?

"Eu...Eudora... said... you wanted to see me?" Was that really his voice that had just squeaked out those words? He cleared his throat.

She slowly walked back to him. "I couldn't sleep last night. I kept thinking about what you said."

As she reached him, he looked down at her—then quickly stuffed both hands in his pockets, otherwise, they would have touched her soft breasts of their own volition—and he still didn't know what was going on.

"I...I... said... a lot of things," he stammered.

Where was the cool, suave, confident Bill Havenwood who'd had a legion of women over the years? The one who was in control at all times, who'd experienced every kind of sexual position with every blond, brunette, redhead he'd ever wanted—and had so effortlessly gotten? What had happened to that guy? Because the one standing here was unsure of himself—and about to burst in his pants.

Suddenly, Christina ran a finger softly down his cheek. "Are you really that good at farming?" she whispered.

He gave her a lop-sided smile at that, "Honey, I can give you a ride on my tractor like you'll never forget." He paused before whispering, "Interested?"

Her finger reached his lips and slowly traced their outline. "Maybe." She seductively smiled at him then as her eyes pierced his. "Excellence in anything always interests me," she challenged before licking her lips.

Bill couldn't take anymore. Pulling his hands out of his pockets, he reached for her and with a low groan, pulled her roughly against his chest. His greedy lips swooped down and began to kiss her with a softness she never would have expected from him.

In an instant, she was responding to him and with another low groan from him—or was that more of a growl—he increased the pressure. Her lips opened to him and he thrust his searching tongue inside, probing the depths of her soul.

She matched him, movement for movement, and her hands entwined themselves in his hair. His hard hands began their slow, sensual ascent from her waist to her breasts, cupping them and kneading them through the thin lacy material of her bra.

Bill had lost control.

Christina had not.

She'd never been more in control in her life. She was still so angry at him for the Stephie/honeymoon fiasco that she knew what she was doing every hot, fiery second she was now sharing with him. Even though she too felt the passionate heat the two were now generating, the bastard wasn't getting her this time. She was getting him.

Her hands dropped from his hair, traveling down his arms and to his wrists. She pulled his hands off of her swollen breasts and abruptly broke away from him. Both were breathing heavily as they stared into each other's eyes.

Confusion flashed through Bill's eyes. Was she telling him 'no'? Did she want him to stop? But then she smiled at him—that smile that women do and he knew she wanted him—right now—as much as he desperately, achingly wanted her.

"So, Bill Havenwood, you wanna come out and play with me?" she seductively smiled, as she pulled him towards her bed.

"I'm all yours, my little wildcat," he smirked as his eyes devoured every nuance of her beautiful face—from her swollen, kiss-ravaged lips to her flushed cheeks before roaming down her lush, sexy body. She was going to be his and he could barely stand it.

They reached the edge of her king size wrought iron bed and she stopped. Her hands left his wrists and moved up his chiseled chest to his shoulders. Slowly, she removed his jacket and let it drop to the floor.

Bill stared at her—hard—mesmerized by every move she was making. He wanted her so badly that he didn't stop to think about why she had suddenly changed her mind about him or why she suddenly wanted to be with him or if she still loathed him, as she'd said last night. No—he wasn't thinking at all.

Christina giggled as she gave his muscular chest a strong push, causing him to fall backwards onto the bed.

He smiled invitingly. "Are you going to join me?" he said.

She nodded. "But first I'm going to undress you." She straddled him then, joining him on the bed. Resting on top of his hard erection, she moved her hips back and forth and he closed his eyes in ecstasy.

"Oh God," he barely choked out. "If you don't stop that, I'm going to embarrass myself in three seconds flat."

Christina stopped and lowering her torso onto his, planted a swift, hard kiss on his lips. Reaching for her, he was about to extend the kiss even longer when she pulled away and shook her head 'no'.

She giggled again, "I don't think so, Mr. Havenwood. We're going to do things my way." Slowly, she unbuttoned his shirt and ran her hands up and down his naked chest.

Bill watched with hungry eyes. "Whatever you want, Miss Christina. I'm here for your pleasure."

"That's what I like to hear." She returned his piercing stare with one of her own before reaching for his belt buckle. Expertly unbuckling it, she slowly unzipped his pants. The only sounds in the room were his heavy breathing and the metal rasp of zipper teeth coming apart. As her hand came into contact with his hard erection still concealed by the material of his pants, he winced and closed his eyes briefly.

Her hand stopped and his eyes flew open to her face.

"I have to tell you something… before we go any further," she said.

"What? Tell me." His words came out in a rush.

Suddenly shy, her eyes lowered. "I'm not like other women.

I… have special… needs." Her eyes came back up to his and she gave him a gamine smile. "Are you game?"

Bill's eyes raked boldly over her. He was so desperate for her, right now, that he would have jumped off Mount Everest if she'd asked him to. He gave her his best smile back—that perfect, movie star smile that had captured the attentions of many a female. "Sugarbear, I'll do anything you want me to."

His hands reached for her then and plastered themselves on her hips, which were still astride his clothed crotch. Sitting on top of him as she was, he gently rocked her back and forth across his fullness, making sure she understood how badly he wanted her.

Christina briefly closed her own eyes. Her thin, lace panties were no barrier against the heat emanating from his hard penis, even though it was still concealed in his pants and—damn it—she could feel herself getting wet. It would be so easy to lose control—and so much fun.

But Stephie's beautiful face popped into her mind then and that put the brakes on her desire. She was back in control. She opened her eyes and looked at him. He knew exactly what he was doing to her as he gave her a devilish grin.

"Don't be shy, my little wet flower. Tell me what you like and I'll do it for you," he offered.

Acting nervous, Christina bit her lip. "Okay," she whispered. She reached over to her bedside table drawer and pulled out a pair of men's cartoon character's underwear. She held them up and temptingly said, "I want you to strip and put these on."

Surprised, Bill did a double take, as he took in all the cartoon faces plastered all over the boxers. Hey, if that's what it took to turn her on, why not, he thought to himself.

"Give them to me. I told you, I'll do whatever you want."

He took the shorts from her hands and getting off the bed began to strip for her. She stayed on the bed and watched him intensely.

He let his open shirt slide off his chest before reaching for the waistband of his pants. With one sexy shake, the pants fell down around his ankles and Christina giggled like a schoolgirl.

And with one kick, he threw the pants across the room and he was standing there in front of her naked except for a pair of briefs.

"Do you like what you see, my little minx?"

Christina giggled and gave a small clap. "I like, I like," she laughed. "Give me more."

With his eyes still focused on her hot, flushed face, he tugged at his underwear and slipped them off in one fell swoop, freeing his hard erection. As he stood naked in front of her, Christina's eyes nearly popped out of their sockets. Oh my, she thought, Jenny was right—he was big—and perfectly shaped. In fact, everything about his body was perfect—not an ounce of fat on him. He had a beautiful face and a well-endowed manhood. How did bastards get to be so lucky?

He was talking to her again as he preened for her, "What about now? Still like what you see?

"I like, but you know what I need," she dared him.

In one graceful movement, he slipped on the cartoon boxer shorts and modeled them around the room for her. Christina giggled some more.

She stopped giggling then and turned serious. "Come here," she ordered.

"Your wish is my command," he announced and with one good lunge, he threw himself on the bed, landing on top of her.

She laughed, enjoying herself in spite of herself. But she was still in complete control.

His arms came around her and he brought his face inches away from hers. She was lying underneath him, but he expertly kept his weight off of her.

"I think it's about time I start sowing some of those wild oats, don't you think?" He laughed before letting his lips lock onto hers, giving her one of the most passionate, deep, delicious kisses she'd ever experienced in her life.

Wow—he'd been telling the truth when he'd said he was good

at—farming, Christina thought. His lips and tongue left hers and began a slow descent down her neck, onto her chest, down her belly and were on their way down to her crotch, his hands expertly parting her thighs when Christina almost lost it.

Almost.

But she regained her wits and steadied her breathing just as his fingers were clasping the elastic band of her panties, ready to pull them off. She laughed then, a sexy, throaty laugh and with one strong push managed to put him on his back and her back on top of him.

He laughed too, as he let her do it. It was all part of her game Bill thought, and however she wanted to play it was fine by him. Besides, she was full of surprises and he was having so much fun. She lowered her lips to his and gave him a strong, deep kiss which he returned, tongue for tongue. As his hands reached for her bra clasp, she pulled back up and away from him and looked into his eyes.

"There's something else I need you to wear before we can make love," Christina whispered.

Oh shit, Bill thought. He'd been so crazy insane to be with her that he'd almost forgotten the condoms. His lips stretched into a knowing smile,

"Baby, I've got some in my bathroom. I'll be right back." He made to get up but she pushed him back down on the bed.

"No, I've got those too. It's…" she paused for effect, "…something else that I need."

"Whatever it is, bring it on, sweet pea," he teased.

Christina reached into the still open bedside drawer and pulled out a pair of handcuffs. She dangled them on one perfectly manicured finger as she dared him with her smile. "Wear them for me?"

Bill didn't think he could get any hotter for her than he already was, but he was wrong. His temperature shot up 10 degrees.

Smiling, he brought his wrists together, "I'm all yours, sweetheart."

"No, like this," Christina instructed and she sensuously brought both his wrists up over his head and ever so slowly hand-cuffed him to the wrought iron posts on her headboard.

The handcuffs clicked into place—and he was her prisoner—with both hands securely locked over his head.

He smiled at her then. "Now what?" he playfully asked.

She smiled back at him as she climbed off, "Now this."

She stood beside the bed, looking down at him, handcuffed to the bed, with his hard erection forming a teepee in those damn, silly cartoon shorts.

Suddenly her smiling, sexy face disappeared and was replaced by an angry, shrewish look. She folded her arms across her chest. "How dare you want to bring your slut on our honeymoon!" Christina accused.

For a second, a look of confusion crossed Bill's features. Then his lips broke into a wide smile. "Oh I get it. This is role playing. Part of your little game. Well, you just tell me who you want me to be and I'll be it."

"How about an asshole husband-to-be? You're good at that."

Confusion crossed Bill's face again. There was something wrong here. The way she was standing—the way she was looking at him—he was getting an uncomfortable vibe, but he wanted her so badly that he pushed the thought from his mind.

He smiled at her again—that devastatingly, wicked smile that told her he was game for anything. "Okay, sweetlips," he agreed. "I can do that. If angry sex is what you need, then angry sex is what you'll get."

Christina looked down at him with disdain. "Any kind of sex from you is the last thing I need, you asshole."

Bill's smile dropped. It suddenly dawned on him that some-thing else was going on here besides a little foreplay fun.

He looked up at his hands shackled to the bedposts. This was not a good position for him to be in—not when she looked like that.

"What's going on?" he cautiously asked.

Christina put her hands on her hips. "I know all about your honeymoon plans, so don't deny it."

Bill shook his head as if shaking out the cobwebs in his brain. "What are you talking about? I haven't made any honeymoon plans."

"Really?" Christina sarcastically announced before moving to her dresser. She pulled out the tickets and fanned them out in front of him. "What are these, then?"

"I don't know? What are those?"

Christina shook her head. "Unbelievable. Deny every-thing even when I'm holding proof in my hands? You are truly amazing."

"Christina, I don't know what this is about, but please, unlock me and we'll discuss this like two rational adults." He tried to sound firm but was failing miserably.

Christina ignored his request and approached the bed. She waved the tickets at him. "Okay, if that's how you want to play, fine. These are airline tickets I found in your bedroom."

Bill was indignant. "You were snooping in my bedroom?"

"Well, how else am I going to catch you in your lies?"

"What lies?"

"The lies you've been telling me when you've been swearing that your relationship with that tramp, Stephie is over."

"I've haven't seen Stephie since before I met you."

"Still sticking to your story, huh? I kind of admire that—if it wasn't so pathetic."

"It's not a story, it's the truth." Bill was getting angry himself, especially since he was being accused of something he hadn't done. "Release me, Christina; now." He forcefully pulled at the handcuffs causing the bed to shake, but not accomplishing much else. He was securely tied and those steel bracelets weren't com-ing off.

"Not until you tell me about these." She waved the tickets in his face.

"I don't know."

Christina couldn't believe his gall. "They're the tickets for our honeymoon to the Caymans."

Bill was surprised. "How did you know I was thinking about taking you to the Caymans?"

Christina rolled her eyes up. "Let's see." She threw the first ticket onto his naked chest. "There's one for you." She took the next one and threw that too. "And one for me." She waved the last ticket in the air before launching it at him. "And one for your slut girlfriend, Stephie. What were you planning? Two separate hotels… one for screwing her and one for trying to screw me? Busy little beaver, aren't you?"

Bill yanked hard at the handcuffs but they weren't budging. He looked at her stone face. "I've never seen these tickets in my life. I did not book anything either." Suddenly, a thought popped into his mind. "You said you found these in my room. Where were they?"

"Like you don't know."

"I don't!" he shouted.

"They were in your bedside table drawer."

"How did you know to look there?"

"Your girlfriend told me all about your little plan."

Bill was shocked. "What? You talked to Stephie? When?"

"Last night at our beautiful, loving engagement party."

Bill let out a gasp. "Stephie was here?"

"You should know. You invited her."

Suddenly, things were becoming clear in Bill's befuddled brain. "I didn't invite her."

"She told me you did. And she told me all about your honeymoon plans… how you were going to bring your wife and your whore and how you had already booked everything. So I went looking for proof and guess what? I found it."

He looked hard at her then. "So this whole production… did you ever at any time during the past 20 minutes ever have any intention of having sex with me?"

Christina laughed out right at that one. "Sex with you? Please! I can do a better job of it myself."

Bill plopped his head back onto the pillow. "I'm such an idiot!"

Christina turned and walked over to a chair by the window where some clothes were thrown on it. She pulled off her black silk robe and her movements instantly riveted Bill's gaze. As she stood there in front of him with her black lace panties, bra and stay-up stockings, he could feel himself getting hard for her again. Damn it—after everything she was doing to him now, he still wanted her badly.

He watched her as she quickly threw on a pair of jeans and sweater—and Bill could feel himself getting even more turned on than he already was. This was the first time he'd ever gotten hard by watching a woman 'put on' clothes! What a total moron he was that he was so besotted with her that he was willing to take whatever she dished out—and love it.

"Christina, Stephie lied. It was all a setup. Untie me and we'll get to the bottom of this." Christina ignored him as she finished dressing. "Christina, did you hear me? Untie me. Now."

The blood was draining out of his arms and he could feel his fingers going numb. He gave the cuffs another good yank but they weren't budging. "Christina, damn it, let me go." He was trying to keep the panic out of his voice, but he could hear it anyway.

She picked up something off her dresser then. It was a key. The key. She approached the bed again, holding it in the air.

Bill breathed a sigh of relief. "Thank God," he said.

She smiled then—a wicked, diabolical smile—that sent shivers up his naked spine. "Christina?" he questioned, unsure of what she was going to do. She turned then and marched into the bathroom. Two seconds later, he heard a flushing sound.

"Nooooo…" His scream could be heard down the length of the massive upstairs hallway.

Christina came back out with a satisfied grin on her face. Yes, she had indeed flushed the key to his handcuffs down the toilet.

"What did you do?" he shouted at her.

"Exactly what you think." She shouted back. She then grabbed her purse, threw open her bedroom door and stalked out.

Bill frantically squirmed on the bed trying to get out of the handcuffs, but she had tied him to the middle iron posts of the bed and he couldn't even reach the sides of the bed with his legs to stand up. And the worst part about it all—was that he was still horny as hell for her. His bulging ridiculous cartoon shorts proved the fact.

He started yelling after her. "Christina, come back here. Don't you dare leave me like this!" He was fuming now. She had no right to do what she had done—no right at all—especially since he was innocent of all charges. "Christina!" he yelled at the top of his lungs again.

*

Christina could hear him yelling out her name as she confidently walked down the main staircase to the foyer. Looked good on the two-timing rat! But there was one last thing she had to do before she left. Christina went to William's office door and knocked.

"Come in," she heard him say in his British accent.

She opened the door and peeked in. He was sitting at his desk. "William, Bill needs to see you. He's in my room." She smiled at the old man before turning to walk out the door.

She needed to get away from this place tonight—and away from 'him'. His kisses and the intimate moments they had shared upstairs had affected her more than she cared to admit.

*

As Christina's BMW was peeling out of the Havenwood drive, William was already on his way up the stairs to Christina's bedroom. He could hear his son screaming out for her.

What the hell was going on?

William approached Christina's open bedroom door and peered in. There was his son—naked except for a pair of silly underwear, which were bulging up at a most inopportune angle—and the boy was handcuffed to the bloody bed.

Bill watched his dad slowly walk into the room. Oh no, this had to be the most embarrassing, humiliating, mortifying, moment of his life for his damned father to see him like this.

His father burst out laughing.

"Well, well, well," he said. "What did you do now?"

Bill was seething inside. "Nothing. I did nothing."

"Looks like it." William kept laughing as he came closer to the bed. "Did Christina do this to you?"

"No, I did it to myself. Of course she did it to me," Bill gritted through his teeth. "And when I get my hands on her, there's going to be hell to pay."

"I'd say that was kind of difficult to do… getting your hands on her, I mean… considering that your hands are handcuffed to the bed." William burst out laughing for another round of guffaws at his son's expense.

Bill glared at his father. "Get me out of these!" Frustrated, he tugged hard at his handcuffs. He didn't liked being laughed at, especially by his old man.

"Son, I like that girl." William almost had tears streaming down his face.

Bill felt impotent and that was something he never felt. Oh—he was so angry at her for making him feel this way, for putting him in this god awful vulnerable position, for his father finding him like this—and for her making him still want her after it all.

"I'm so glad you approve dad, but do you think you can maybe help me get out of these damned things?" Bill sarcastically replied, as he yanked at the cuffs again.

"I don't suppose you have the key?"

Bill seethed as he was forced to admit, "She flushed it down the toilet."

This brought another round of laughter from his father. "Down the loo, that's a good one. What a pistol!" He shook his head in between laughs.

"Dad? My handcuffs?" Bill jangled them, trying to bring his father's attention back to his predicament.

"Oh, right." William came over to inspect them. "I'll get Tom and ask him to bring..." William burst out laughing again. "...his tools from the potting shed."

William kept laughing as he walked out the door but Bill was fuming mad. First he'd deal with Stephie—and then he'd deal with—her!

In the end, Tom the gardener had to saw through the steel handcuffs with Bill still trapped on the bed. To Tom's credit, he didn't ask any questions or say a word about the boy's situation—but man, would the story ever make the rounds of the house tonight!

CHAPTER 49

BILL WAS ON the warpath. He entered the dark, noisy interior of Shades, one of the city's hippest and hottest nightclubs and gave himself a few seconds for his eyes to adjust to the dim lighting. A few seconds was all he needed. He knew the confines of this place like the back of both hands. It had been his home away from home many moons ago when he'd been dating Stephie.

Everyone who was anyone in their rich, cosmopolitan set was here tonight and Bill saw many familiar faces as he scanned the crowded dance floor. But he was looking for only one person and Bill knew that she was here—somewhere. She was always here, guaranteed—partying, drinking, dancing, getting high and generally wasting away her idle, privileged life.

Like he had once done—many moons ago.

He spotted her then. She was standing in the back, with drink in hand—and the center of attention of two men. Typical, Bill smirked to himself. Leopards really didn't change their spots especially dangerous, sharp-clawed felines like Stephanie Hartwell.

Bill pushed his way through some of the dancers and reached her side in five seconds flat. He grabbed her wrist and surprised, she turned around to see him by her side.

A welcoming smile stretched across her face. "Well hello, lover," she purred, obviously glad to see him.

Bill's face remained stony. "Let's talk," he ordered, then proceeded to half drag her, half pull her across the dance floor into one of the VIP private rooms off to the side.

The second they were in the room, he released her wrist as if it had burned him and he slammed the door shut. He pulled out the three airline tickets and waved them at her.

"Your handiwork, I take it?" he accused, as he threw them at her. They fluttered to the floor.

Stephie looked down at the tickets before raising her eyes back to Bill's angry face. "You can't blame a girl for trying, now can you?" she taunted him.

Bill was livid and he started shouting at her. "How dare you pull a stunt like this, coming to my house uninvited and spewing a pack of lies to cause trouble between Christina and me."

Stephie's smile dropped and her true malicious self shone through. "I can't believe you really want to tie yourself to a non-descript, little nobody like her when I gave you so much—and I still can." Stephie bridged the gap between them and wrapped her graceful arms around Bill's neck. "It can be me, you know, instead of her. I can be your wife." She sounded desperate.

Bill pulled her arms off of his body. "Stephie, no. It's over. We're over." He was adamant and he pushed her away.

"You don't love her. How can you love a little mouse like that?"

"My relationship with Christina is my business, so stay out of it."

"You can't mean that?"

"Oh, I mean it. And if I hear that you've approached her again in any way with anymore of your lies or tricks or schemes, I won't be so nice next time. I'll make sure the bank calls in every one of your loans that I helped you get."

"You wouldn't!" she gasped.

"Try me." Bill was deadly serious. It was written all over his face.

Stephie was shocked. In the back of her mind, she had always thought that she and Bill would somehow get back together, that this Miss Nobody was just a passing fancy to help him out with his father, but now she saw that he had genuine feelings for her. The little bitch had won! She'd won him and the pot of gold he came with. Stephie's jealousy soared to new heights, as did her vindictiveness.

She raised her nose up in the air. "Don't you threaten me!" she threw at him.

Bill glared at her, "Stay away from Christina or else."

With one last disgusted look at her, he turned and walked out.

Stephie's rage boiled over. Looking around the room, she spotted a tray of glasses and taking them one by one, started to throw them against the wall, smashing them into a million pieces.

She wasn't finished with those two—not by a long shot. If she couldn't have him, she'd somehow make damn sure that the little bitch wouldn't have him either.

*

Outside the nightclub, Bill strode to his parked car.

One down, one to go, he thought to himself.

CHAPTER 50

CHRISTINA ARRIVED AT the Baldora couture shop in the afternoon. She had another scheduled fitting for her wedding dress and was meeting Mindy, the wedding planner there to discuss the plans.

Even though she had spent last night in her own bed at her own apartment, she hadn't been able to sleep at all. If truth were told, she was worried about Bill's reaction when she went back to the house tonight. Would he still be mad at her for what she'd done to him? Would they have another fight and she'd have to storm out again?

Christina didn't regret what she'd done. He'd had it coming for trying to sneak that slut into their honeymoon—not that Christina had any intention of actually going on a honeymoon since she still hoped to get out of marrying the creep. It was just the idea that he was taking her for a fool by trying to pull a cheap, scumbag move on her like that.

Christina giggled to herself. He did look pretty funny dressed in those stupid shorts chained to the bed. Wonder what William thought when he'd seen his son like that? Probably got a big kick out of it, as well. And how in heaven did they get those cuffs off? And how long had that scoundrel stayed like that? Maybe, he was still handcuffed to the bedpost right now?

Christina giggled some more at the image of that.

But she, suddenly, stopped giggling when she remembered the hot, sizzling kisses they'd shared—and the way his greedy hands had run all over her body—and how she'd felt when she'd been sitting on top of his hard erection—and then those sweet kisses he'd trailed from her neck, down her stomach almost reaching her privates before she had stopped him.

She hadn't meant for things to go that far. She hadn't meant for him to give her those soul-destroying kisses or have his hot hands travel all over her body. Although her anger at him had kept her in control the entire time, her physical attraction for him had allowed her to push the envelope when it came to her little foreplay games.

It would have been so easy to give in and forget her plan and her self-respect—and spend all of last night making love to him. She had wanted to do that so very badly but she was in a big mess when it came to Bill Havenwood. This wasn't a normal, everyday relationship. There was no love here, at least not on his side—and there were too many games, deceptions and lies on all sides. No— she needed to stay focused and somehow extricate herself from this disastrous situation before she'd have to say any real 'I do's'.

Having changed into her wedding dress, Christina came out to stand on the platform where two seamstresses were waiting. As she was turning around as per their instructions, Mindy walked in followed by Christina's mom, Gabriella and Bill's mom, Maddie Havenwood.

Christina was stunned. "Mom? Mrs. Havenwood… Maddie? What are you two doing here," she asked.

"I invited them. I thought we could all sit down and discuss your wedding plans together," Mindy innocently piped up.

"What a good idea, Mindy," Christina replied as she pasted a phony smile on her lips. She was not thrilled.

"Darling, you look beautiful," Gabriella choked on her words as she lovingly gazed at her daughter in her wedding gown. She dabbed her wet eyes with a tissue.

"Mommy, please don't cry."

"I can't help it. You look like an angel."

Maddie put a comforting hand on Gabriella's arm. "She does look beautiful, Gabriella." She then turned to Christina. "My son's very lucky."

Christina smiled, "No, I'm the lucky one, Maddie. Your son

is… amazing." Yeah—an amazing creep, she silently added to herself.

Gabriella was still tearing up and Maddie grasped her hand. "Gabriella, let's wait outside and give these hard-working ladies…" meaning the seamstresses, "…some privacy, okay?"

Her mom nodded, "We'll be right outside, sweetheart," she mumbled to her daughter.

"Okay, mommy." Great, thought Christina. Now she'd have to deal with those two!

Christina spent the next twenty minutes standing still for the seamstresses, then went to change and joined her mom, Maddie and Mindy in the lounge area.

Sandwiched between her mom and Maddie on the antique couch with Mindy opposite them, Christina had to endure an hour of discussions on her stupid, damn wedding which was never going to happen anyway, if she had anything to do about it.

As the two mother hens took over the decision-making, Christina's mind kept wandering back to last night—and how his hot kisses had tasted—and how he had smelled of some exotic male cologne, or had that been his scent? Whatever it was, it had driven her wild. And then, when their bodies had been plastered on top of each other on the bed—and she'd been kissing him—and he'd been kissing her back—doing to her what she was doing to him—why, she could feel the heat again now.

"My dear," Mindy examined Christina. "You look flushed. Are you all right?"

All three women studied Christina's red face.

"Ye… yes, it's just awfully hot in here," Christina stammered.

Appeased, Mindy continued. "Anyway, my dear, you have to tell me who your bridesmaids and maid of honor will be? We need to get their dresses made and the wedding's three weeks away."

Oh no, Christina thought, who else was she going to have to involve in this debacle?

"We'll ask your cousins Angela and Connie and your maid of

honor will be Theresa. I owe her mother," Gabriella immediately piped up.

"Mom, no; I don't want any of those people involved."

"But your aunts will make my life hell if we don't ask your cousins."

"Mommy, this is my wedding." She turned to Mindy. "I only want a maid of honor and one flower girl; and that's it."

"But my dear," Mindy began, "You have to have bridesmaids."

Maddie, on the other hand, saw that Christina had already made up her mind. She turned to the other two women. "Wedding etiquette isn't set in stone. If Christina doesn't want any brides-maids, then she won't have any. After all, the Havenwoods make up their own rules." She smiled at her daughter-in-law-to-be.

Christina gave her a warm smile back. She liked this woman a lot. Too bad things had soured between her and William. She could see how the two had been initially attracted to each other. They were both no nonsense types with he, providing the brains and drive of the team; and she, providing the warmth and nurturing.

"Maddie's right. I'm going to ask my friend, Jenny and her daughter, Taylor. I'm firm on this."

Gabriella was about to argue when she took in her daughter's determined and set face. She threw her hands up in surrender, "Okay. What do I know? I'm only your mother!"

Christina gave her mom a quick kiss on the cheek, "Thanks, mommy."

Christina needed someone to pose as her maid of honor who could come in for dress fittings and be part of several wedding strategy meetings with Mindy, but be in on the scam that the wedding would never happen. The most perfect accomplice for the position was Jenny, of course.

The meeting wrapped up and as they were all about to leave, Maddie pulled Christina to the side. "Christina, why don't we have lunch tomorrow? That way we can get to know each other better."

Christina smiled, "I'd love to, Maddie. How about one in the afternoon? You just let me know where you want to meet."

Maddie smiled. "I'll give you a call tomorrow morning to confirm."

Oh great, Christina thought, how was she going to get through a lunch with Bill's mom? Maddie would probably ask all kinds of personal questions about her supposed love match with her rotten son. How many lies would she have to tell then?

The sooner Christina found something to hold over the rat's head, the better. This entire fiasco couldn't be over soon enough for her.

CHAPTER 51

CHRISTINA STUDIED HER appearance in her full-length bedroom mirror. Not bad, she thought. It was the custom at the Havenwood manor to dress for dinner and she had decided to wear a very sexy, low-cut black dress that enticingly skimmed her curvy body.

Hopefully, if Bill kept his dirty mind on her figure, he wouldn't keep it focused on his anger at what she'd done to him last night. Maybe it would take some of the sting out of the confrontation with him that Christina knew was waiting for her downstairs.

She took a deep breath. Okay, time to face the Bill Havenwood music, which in this case was going to be a full-fledged concert of screaming, accusations and fury.

*

Christina entered the salon. That's where they all usually had drinks before dinner.

But tonight no one was there yet.

There were, however, two long tables set up by the north wall with what looked liked gift-wrapped wedding gifts piled high on both. Christina walked over and began to read the gift cards. She recognized some of the names as some of the high society set she had been introduced to at her engagement party.

She sighed with frustration, as she knew all of these gifts would have to be returned eventually. Still, it might be fun to open them up and see what was inside.

Bill, dressed in his elegant dinner suit, walked in and spotted her at the gift tables. She hadn't seen him yet as her back was turned to him, and this gave him a chance to study her.

In that dress, she looked amazing. Every soft curve was on display for his enjoyment. And her hair was piled high on top of her head, exposing her long, swan-like, creamy neck and back. Yes, she was definitely delicious eye candy and he could kick himself for having had all that within his grasp and then lost it. But it hadn't really been his fault, now had it? In fact, it had never really been in his grasp at all. She'd only made him think that so that she could embarrass the hell out of him for something he hadn't even done. It had all been a plot to teach him a lesson.

Bill's anger resurfaced at what she had done to him.

Instead of asking him about the tickets—or maybe even screaming at him about the tickets, like any other normal, rational woman would have done—she'd played dirty. And he, idiot that he was, had fallen for it—hook, line and sinker, at the speed of a ship's steel anchor dropping into the sea.

Yes, she was definitely a dirty fighter.

But so was he. He was going to get her just as she had gotten him, but not tonight—maybe not even tomorrow—or the day after that. She'd be expecting a big blowout on this first meeting but he wasn't going to give her that. No—he was going to make her sweat it out, like someone who was on death row but didn't know the date of the execution. The waiting would be worse than the punishment.

He pasted a sexy smile on his lips and turned on the charm switch. "Are you going to open them?" he asked, in his most debonair, suave voice.

Christina gasped and quickly spun around. He was leaning against the wall by the double doors with his hands in his pockets—and outrageously handsome as ever. And he was watching her like a lion would watch their prey before the kill. She could see the dangerous glint in his eyes.

"How… how long have you been standing there?" She sounded nervous.

"Long enough to notice how beautiful you look in that dress," he smiled then and added, "But then again, you could wear a potato sack and still look beautiful to me."

Christina straightened her spine in self-defense. "Well, next time I go shopping, I'll buy one," she sarcastically retorted.

She thought he would be angry at her snippy reply, but instead he laughed—that irresistible laugh that all male super rats had and was so alluring to female saps like her.

He smiled at her again. "Do that and then you can model it for me."

Something was wrong here, Christina thought. He didn't seem mad at all. In fact, he was being nice—too nice. Why wasn't he mad? What was he playing at?

Bill pushed himself off the wall and strode deeper into the room towards her. Christina didn't consciously realize it but she took two involuntary steps back—away from him. But he saw it. So, the little hellion was scared of him tonight? Good, he thought to himself.

Christina raised her nose in the air. "I'm not apologizing, you know," she dared him with her voice.

He smiled at her again as he continued to approach her. "Did I ask you to?" He raised an inquiring eyebrow demanding an answer.

"N... no." Damn it! She had stammered again.

He stopped a couple of feet away from her and Christina's stomach was doing somersaults. Her fear of him and what he was going to do next, plus the intense sexual magnetism he was exuding were all playing havoc with her insides.

"May I give my lovely wife-to-be a peck on the cheek?" he gently asked.

"Why? There's only the two of us in here." Christina instinctively folded her arms in front of her chest to protect herself from his strong, sexy presence.

"Because I haven't seen you since yesterday and I missed you. Is that so bad?"

When Christina didn't answer, Bill leaned into her and gave her a sweet kiss on the cheek. As he pulled away, he looked into her eyes and gave her a sexy laugh. "Now that didn't hurt, did it?"

She stared at him with frightened eyes. She'd better get a hold of her nerves tonight, Christina thought, otherwise the creep would win whatever game he was playing at.

At that moment, William walked in and taking note of the close proximity of the two lovebirds, remarked, "Good. I'm glad to see you two have kissed and made up."

"Why wouldn't we?" Bill smiled, as he turned to his father.

He sounded so calm and so casual—as if all she'd done to him yesterday was—nothing. Christina was scared. For the first time, she was scared. And suddenly, she knew. He was going to get even with her, but not tonight. Who even knew when? Only he knew that and he wasn't telling.

He turned back to her then. "Christina, can I get you a drink?"

He sounded so nice—so fucking, damned nice—but she now knew why. She stared into his beautiful, green eyes and turned on the charm herself. "Thank you, yes, but don't put arsenic in it."

He burst out laughing. "Not before the wedding anyway. I want to get you to the altar first." He paused and gave her a devilish grin. Bending down to her ear, he whispered, "Then we'll see."

He straightened and moved to the drinks cabinet—a picture of elegant, refined, sophisticated—evil. Oh no, Christina thought, she'd guessed right about his plans. That meant she was in for a bumpy ride for who knew how long.

The louse was going to make her sweat, not knowing what was going to hit her or when. He was going to slowly torture her with uncertainty and doubt and fear. Oh—he was good. If the big guns weren't being trained on her, Christina could almost admire his cunning. It was something she would have done—if she'd thought of it first.

"Why don't we go into dinner instead?" William innocently

asked, not understanding any of the dangerous undercurrents that were swirling in the room.

"Sure, why not." Bill agreed. He walked back to where Christina was standing and offered her his arm. "May I escort my beautiful bride-to-be?"

Christina would have told him to 'stick it', but William was there and they had to keep up appearances for his sake. Besides, she was going to give him back whatever he dished out and see who broke first.

She smiled at him—a full wattage smile that almost made Bill go suddenly weak at the knees. "Of course," she replied.

And taking his arm, the two walked towards the dining room.

If Bill wasn't being controlled by his anger tonight, he would have marched her right upstairs and begged for forgiveness for something he hadn't even done—all so that he could have her in his arms again. Her nearness and the vulnerable way she was clasping his arm now as they were walking into the dining room was all it took for him to want her badly again. He ached for the fulfillment of what had been promised to him last night and never received—for what he'd been cheated out of…

But he had time.

And she had to pay for her sins first.

And this time he was the one in control.

*

Dinner turned out to be a pleasant affair.

William chatted about business and politics, and Christina was surprised to see that Bill added many intelligent comments to the conversation. He was definitely a lot smarter than he let on. He wasn't exactly the wasted, ex-partier he pretended to be.

Towards her, he was very charming and polite. He made every endeavor to include her in the discussions and asked for her opinions throughout the evening. He was gracious, sweet and nice, the perfect dinner companion and host. Yes—the rogue was definitely up to no good.

William didn't stay for dessert. Excusing himself, he left the two alone in the cavernous dining room. As soon as the door closed behind him, Christina rounded on Bill.

"I know what you're doing and it's not going to work," she threw at him.

Bill acted surprised, "Sorry? I don't understand?"

"You're being nice to me… too nice!"

"That's right, I am. What's wrong with that?"

"Don't play stupid. The longer I know you, the more I realize how smart you really are. You're being nice to me to keep me off balance until you decide it's time to exact your revenge for what I did to you last night."

"Those are your games, sweetheart, not mine," he said innocently. "In fact, about last night, I spoke to Stephie and she admitted everything. It was all a plot of hers to come between us. I had nothing to do with any of it." He reached for his glass of mineral water and took a casual sip.

"And I'm supposed to believe that?"

Bill shrugged his shoulders. "That's up to you."

He was so cool, so matter-of-fact that Christina had an overwhelming urge to walk around the table and slap his face hard. But she didn't do any such thing.

"Let's get a few facts straight," she tartly replied. "The tickets were in your room and that's proof enough for me. And you're planning something, so come on; take your best shot now." She dared him with her eyes.

He scraped his chair back and stood up and Christina flinched in her seat. She was scared.

Confident, Bill smirked at her. He knew exactly what he was doing to her and what she was feeling. "Christina, you're being paranoid. I'm not going to do anything to you. I had nothing to do with those tickets, but I understand how it must have looked. So, I forgive you for what you did."

Bill slowly came around the table to where Christina was sitting. Immediately, she was on guard. As he bent down, a frightened Christina nearly jumped out of her chair, but all he did was to give her a quick kiss on her cheek before straightening up again.

"Good night. Sleep tight," he whispered, before strolling out of the room.

As soon as he was gone, Christina let out a panicked and tense breath. She'd been right. He was planning something, but what? And when?

*

For the next couple of days, Christina was a basket case.

She was waiting for the axe to fall on her head but it hadn't yet. And she knew that this waiting game was part of her punishment. The bastard was playing it beautifully.

Throughout these past two days, he had been polite, thoughtful and caring towards her. He hadn't wavered once nor had he shown any anger or impatience. He was proving himself to be a master at these types of games—her types of games. She was being outwitted and outfoxed.

Damn him to hell!

Today, Christina was on her way to pick up Jenny and Taylor to drive them to the couture house for their first dress fitting for their matron of honor and flower girl dresses.

Later, Christina was going to meet Maddie Havenwood for an early dinner. She was going to have to act like the happy, in-love bride and today she just didn't feel up to it. The anxiety and fear she'd been feeling because of Bill's tricks had sapped all her energy lately.

As Christina pulled up to her apartment building, she spotted Jenny and Taylor waiting outside. They waved and then quickly got into the car. Jenny had left work an hour early so that they could make this appointment as soon as Taylor got out of school.

Jenny had agreed to be the 'pretend' matron of honor and go for the dress fittings as she thought it would be fun, even if she was never going to get to wear the outfit. At the very least,

Christina had told her friend, she would have an original Baldora hanging in her closet at Havenwood expense.

"Thanks for doing this for me Jenny," Christina said as she pulled out into the traffic.

"So it adds a bit of excitement to my dull life. What else have I got?" Jenny laughed. Then she turned to Taylor in the back-seat and said, "Put your seatbelt on honey." She turned back to Christina. "Oh, Robert said he was calling you tonight with some information about the Shelley Ave. warehouse."

"Great. Hopefully he's got some good news."

"How you holding up?" Jenny was concerned.

"Awful, just awful. Look…" Christina took one hand off the steering wheel and showed Jenny how it was shaking slightly. "My nerves are shot and I'm on edge all the time."

"Why are you letting him get to you like this, Chrissy?"

"I don't know, he just is."

"You're playing into his plans."

"I can't help it." With panic in her eyes, Christina turned to her friend. "I've got to somehow get out of this mess, Jenny. I can't marry him for real, I can't. And there's only two weeks left."

"Don't worry. We'll get something on him." Jenny smiled but Christina was not comforted.

In the end, Christina, Jenny and Taylor had a wonderful time trying on their dresses. It was such a fun, girlie thing to do and Christina did forget about her problems for a little while.

*

After dropping Jenny and Taylor back at their apartment build-ing, Christina went to the West Indian restaurant that Maddie had picked out for their meal. On entering the exotic establishment, Christina spotted Maddie already sitting cross-legged on the floor at one of the low tables in the corner.

Maddie waved to her and Christina came over.

"I thought you'd like a change of pace from all that Havenwood glitz," Maddie greeted.

Christina laughed, "This place is so you, Maddie." She followed Maddie's example and sat down cross-legged opposite the older woman.

"It wasn't once, you know. I used to be queen of glitz. Now look at me. I'm sitting on the floor for my dinner."

"Do you ever miss your other life?"

"Sometimes, but I think I miss my son more. And I do miss being part of a family unit, even if the head of that unit was a stubborn, old mule named William Havenwood."

Christina laughed again, "I'm sure you two have quite a history together."

"Oh yes, we go way back, but it wasn't all bad. We did have some good times together."

"Would you ever consider getting back with him?" Christina dared to ask.

Maddie laughed. "I've thought about that alot lately, but it was a bad divorce and I don't think William has ever forgiven me."

Christina's eyes narrowed suspiciously, "Interesting response, but you didn't really answer my question."

Maddie's gaze lowered. "Yes, I do love that old goat and if we could somehow work it out, I'd like to try again. Being away for five years and having had time to think about things… where we went wrong… yes…I can say I still love him. But sometimes, Christina, love is not enough, especially when you do mean things to each other and you don't have forgiveness."

Christina sighed, "Yes, William is very stubborn."

Maddie laughed, "And an asshole too. Let's not forget that! But he's not all bad. He just has very definite ideas about how people should act and be. And he's been especially hard on our son… and rightly so, I might add. Bill was a real, spoiled little shit growing up. I'm his mother, so I can say that. And I can also say that I overindulged him and his father was too busy and ignored him… and the drinking got out of control."

"I know Bill's had a problem with that… since high school."

Maddie nodded. "Oh yeah, we sent him to several rehab pro-grams when he was growing up and every time he came out, he went right back to his partying ways. I've been scared for his welfare for many years, Christina. I kept expecting the phone call where they'd tell me he'd gotten into a drunk driving accident or the one where they said he'd died of alcohol poisoning." Maddie involuntarily shivered. "Thank God he's now in recovery and stopped drinking."

Christina was shocked. "You know about his sobriety?"

"Of course, why wouldn't I? Bill tells me everything. He and I have always been open and honest with each other."

"But… he doesn't want to tell his father… he's very adamant about that."

Maddie nodded again, "It would make my son's life easier if William knew, I know that. But…" She shrugged her shoul-ders, "Men! They have their own ways of relating to each other, I guess."

"I guess." Christina was deep in thought. So Bill told his mom everything? What had he said about her—and him—and their phony marriage?

As if reading her thoughts, Maddie suddenly patted Christina's hand. "My dear, my son has told me that he loves you very much and he's going to do what he can to make you happy. He said you were the one for him and he's so grateful to fate for bringing you into his life. You know, I've never seen him like this… so full of life… so hopeful for the future…so… in love."

Christina was skeptical. "He… told you all that?"

"Of course, he did. And I'm glad he's found you too. He needs an ally in that house and I know you're strong enough to stand up to William's controlling ways." She smiled at Christina before picking up the menu. "Now let's eat. They make a delicious tan-doori chicken here."

And for the rest of the meal Maddie kept the conversation light. They talked about Christina's job as a photojournalist and Maddie's new life on the commune in Arizona. Maddie did not ask personal questions of her daughter-in-law-to-be nor did she put Christina on the spot about her relationship with Bill.

Christina was surprised about that. She'd come here tonight prepared to face an inquisition and it hadn't happened. These Havenwoods never did what you thought they were going to do!

In fact, Christina enjoyed herself so much with Maddie, that she felt a little sad and alot guilty that she was deceiving this sweet person into believing she would one day soon be her daughter-in-law.

On saying their good-byes, Maddie gave Christina a big hug and welcomed her into the family. And she said that she hoped this would be one of many wonderful meals they would share together now that Christina would be marrying her son.

Maddie was such a nice person! Too bad Bill wasn't more like her. No, he was more like his father—and just as devious, considering the hell he was putting her through this week.

But if Maddie thought her son was honest with her about everything then she was sadly mistaken. What was all that malarkey he had told her about being in love with Christina?

That wasn't being honest—that was called being a big, fat liar to your mother's face. In love with Christina, indeed! Guess he had to say that to keep the story going.

It was almost 8 p.m. at night and Christina was driving back to the mansion. Her cell phone rang and she saw it was Robert, the Streetwise reporter who was checking out the 1625 Shelley Ave warehouse for her.

"Hey, Robert," Christina answered her cell.

"Hi Christina, I've got some info for you about that warehouse."

"Great, shoot."

" First off, it's owned by some investment firm in the Cayman Islands."

"The Caymans?" That rang a bell with Christina. That's where Bill was going to take her for their honeymoon.

"Yeah, the Caymans are these small islands in the Caribbean

that are notorious for anyone who wants to hide a paper trail for anything. Their banking system is as sophisticated and secretive as Switzerland's."

"Really?"

"Yup. And from what I've been able to piece together from the other small business owners on Shelley Ave, the only people who seem to use the warehouse are some sort of environmental group who meet there occasionally at midnight."

"Midnight? What kind of time is that to meet?"

"It's a perfect time if you want to keep a low profile."

An idea popped into Christina's head as her calculator brain was starting to put two and two together. "Robert, do you think this has anything to do with the GME group?"

"Why do you say that? Where did you get the address, Christina?"

"I can't say right now… not until I've checked things out myself, but do you think it could be them?"

"Maybe. I don't know. The people I talked to didn't seem to know who they were except that they were environmental."

"Did you find out anything else?"

"No, that was it."

"Let me do some spying on my own and I'll let you know what I find out."

"Okay but be careful, Christina, it's not the best part of town."

"I will. Bye Robert."

She closed her phone and promptly made a U-turn with her car. Might as well go to her own apartment in the city and get her cameras ready—for a midnight stakeout.

As Christina drove, the thoughts raced in her head. Why did Bill have that address in his pocket? Was the environmental group that was meeting at the warehouse, GME? Was Bill having the place staked out for his father? And where did the Caymans fit into all this?

Hopefully, tonight she would find her answers.

CHAPTER 52

CHRISTINA WAS PARKED half a block away from 1625 Shelley Ave and she had her zoom lens trained on the entrance. It was almost midnight now, but so far, no one had arrived. The street was deserted and quiet, as the area was mostly industrial and didn't have a lot of street traffic.

The clock ticked on—past midnight—past 12:30 a.m.—past 1a.m. but no one came.

Empty-handed, Christina drove back to the mansion, but she was determined. She'd be back tomorrow night and the night after that—as long as it took to find out if this was a lead or a dead end. Either way she had to know.

*

He was being so nice to her that he was making her crazy. He still hadn't made any moves towards her—just that quiet, serial-killer politeness which he always showed her whenever they bumped into each other in the house. So, over the next few days, Christina spent little time at the mansion.

She'd taken on another assignment for the Magazine and during the day, she was busy photographing a new up and coming artist and at night, she was staking out the Shelley Ave. warehouse. By the time she'd get home, it would be after 2 a.m. and the house would be quiet.

And no sign of him—thank God.

*

Her wedding date was less than two weeks away and she still didn't have anything she could use to get herself out of this jam.

Part of her—the part that loved him—yearned to marry him. She wondered what it would be like to be his wife, to come home to him every day, to talk and laugh with him, to be with him, to make love to him and wake up in the mornings wrapped in his strong arms.

But the other part of her—the cool, rational part knew—that he didn't love her. And she couldn't stand to be tied to someone who only saw her as a means to an end for money.

She couldn't live like that. To always be so close to him and know that he didn't have any true feelings for her would eventually break her heart and her spirit.

And what about that little girl that she'd been all those years ago? The one who'd been so hurt and who'd had her life so drastically pulled from under her when he'd played his stupid prank on her? Christina had promised that little girl that she would make him pay somehow for what he'd done. Could she break a promise to herself?

It was true that she was a big girl now and saw things differently, but she still felt the hurt at what he'd done to her.

She'd thought that getting revenge on him could erase that hurt but could it? Or would it make it worse? Was forgiveness the way to erase that pain instead? But could she forgive him?

No, not when he was being a bastard and forcing her into something she didn't want to do for his own selfish purposes.

No—she wouldn't marry a bastard.

All these thoughts ran through Christina's mind as she staked out the Shelley Ave warehouse for the fourth straight night in a row. She checked her watch. It was 11:35 p.m. and it looked like it was going to be another wasted evening with nothing to show for it.

Suddenly, a van pulled up to the curb in front of the building. From her position inside her parked car concealed half a block away, Christina quickly raised her camera with the zoom lens and began taking pictures. She took a photo of the van's license plate number, then furiously began snapping as five men piled out of the vehicle. They looked like a scruffy bunch—hippy types.

And Christina immediately recognized them all!

They were indeed members of the GME group that had been picketing outside the Fido Foods building. She knew all of those faces since she'd taken many pictures of them when she'd been on assignment for the magazine. And she even recognized Tommy, the one whom she'd spoken to.

Christina saw Tommy reach into the van and pull out what looked like a folded wheelchair. He unfolded it on the sidewalk, then went back into the van and carried someone out in his arms—another man—and carefully deposited him in the chair.

It was Jake Monroe!

Christina gasped, "Oh, my God, it's Jake!"

She continued to snap picture after picture. This was incredible!! Jake Monroe was associated with GME, but why?

And did Bill know that his best friend was betraying him?

Suddenly, a Jaguar pulled up behind the van and she gasped, "Oh my God!"

It was him!

Christina was stunned! Jake Monroe wasn't stabbing his friend in the back. No, Bill Havenwood was part of GME and he was the one stabbing someone in the back—his father!

Christina kept taking all the pictures she could. She got pictures of Bill getting out of the Jag, of him shaking hands with the protesters and of them all high-fiving each other. It was clear that Bill was one of them. Suddenly, they all entered the warehouse and Christina lowered her camera.

"Checkmate, Bill Havenwood," she whispered to herself.

She had him!! And she wouldn't have to marry him. And she'd get her revenge for the past by showing these pictures to William.

In the span of five minutes, her whole world had tipped on its axis—as had his. But Christina didn't feel any joy or relief. She felt sad—sad that it was now finally all over.

Suddenly, she wasn't satisfied with what she had. She needed to know more. Why was he involved with them? What was this all about? And what was he thinking!!????

Christina stepped out of her car into the dark, deserted street and quickly made her way to the warehouse.

Approaching the building, she ducked into the narrow alleyway that ran along its side. A shiver went up her spine.

Crouching low, she crept to a window and carefully peered inside. The lights were on and everyone was seated on chairs—except Bill. He was standing in front of them, speaking but she couldn't hear what he was saying.

Christina's eyes roamed to the back of the warehouse and saw that a backdoor had been propped open. If she wanted to hear what was going on, she needed to get as close to that door as possible.

Crouching back down, she scooted along the wall until she reached the backyard that turned out to be a messy area filled with stacks of wooden crates piled on top of each other and a large trash bin.

Christina dashed to the trash bin and snuck behind it. From her vantage point, she was well concealed and could see into the warehouse through the open back door. And she could clearly hear what Bill was saying too.

"Everything's in place and his plan is going into effect as we speak," he was saying to the guys.

Then Christina heard Jake ask, "Do you know which detective firm he's using?"

"Websters & Lloyd," Bill responded.

"Man, they're good," Tommy added.

"Yeah, only the best for my old man," Bill smirked. "And if he's putting you guys under surveillance, then Jake and I can't come here anymore. We can't meet again until this heat dies down, and we'll have to be very careful about how we contact each other from now on. He may have your phones bugged, illegally of course."

Someone else piped up, "What about the money, Bill? How are you going to get it to us?"

"Yeah," Tommy added, "And the insider info you supply. You know we can't do without that?"

"Don't worry. I'll come up with a plan that Jake will somehow let you know about. As for the money, that'll start coming through the Caymans." Frustrated, Bill paced. "Instead of putting a stop to that damned oil spill, I should have known he'd hit us head on. So typical of him." Christina heard disappointment in his voice.

"Do you want to quit, Bill?" Jake said that.

"Hell no! I'll never quit." Everyone nodded in agreement and Bill continued, "I started this because he wouldn't listen and I'm going to keep going until he does."

Christina's mouth dropped open in shock. GME had been Bill's brainchild from the beginning? She hadn't expected that!

Tommy was now speaking, "What about his plan to plant spies inside our group? For God's sake, we can't screen people who want to join. That's not what we're about."

"I know," Bill agreed. He then expelled a frustrated breath as he exclaimed, "God—I can't have this thing blowing up in my face just before my wedding."

At the mention of the word 'wedding', Christina involuntarily brought her hand up to her mouth. As she did so, her elbow bumped one of the wooden crates and the entire stack fell over, making a loud, crashing noise. Squeaking with fright, she slinked deeper behind the trash bin as a dog in the distance started to bark. Paralyzed with fear, Christina held her breath.

She heard someone inside say in a panicky voice, "What was that?" and then she saw Bill appear at the open door, peering into the darkness. A light switch was turned on, illuminating the entire area.

Oh God, Christina thought, please don't let him find me! Please!

Bill stepped outside and approached the spot where the crates had fallen. Looking around, he waited for anything to breathe, for anything to move, but all was quiet. He tapped one of the crates with his foot and suddenly another stack fell.

Frightened, Christina shut her eyes tight and covered her mouth to prevent any sounds from coming out. She then heard him walk closer to the trash bin—and closer to her hiding spot.

Oh no, he was going to find her and then what?

The rest of the guys were watching Bill from the open door.

Christina heard Tommy say, "Forget it, Bill. It's nobody. Those crates are always falling and we're having this mess cleaned up next week."

"Yeah," another of the guys agreed. "Come back in and we'll finish up with our meeting."

With the excitement over, some of the guys disappeared back inside. Not quite convinced, Bill slowly walked back.

Reaching the open door, he glanced around one last time before shutting it with a strong thud. The light was switched off and pitch darkness once again enveloped the area.

Christina sighed with relief. Slowly standing up, she stealthily crept back along the side of the building and back to her car.

*

It was 4 a.m. and Christina was sitting at her kitchen table in her dumpy apartment, staring hard at the pictures she had taken tonight of Bill and the GME members.

Unbelievable!

Incredible!

Shocking!

GME had been started by Bill to fight William, and if William were to ever find out, it would spell the end for his son—wedding or no wedding.

To use William's own money against him—was a masterstroke of sheer genius and courage. Christina's opinion of Bill went up immeasurably as did her admiration for him. He was as good at games and deceptions as his father was, and that was saying alot.

And Bill was doing it for a good cause too—to heal the planet. That meant he had a good heart concealed somewhere in that handsome bastard's body of his and Christina admired that even more than his smarts.

After leaving the warehouse, Christina had driven to her apartment in the city to download and print up her pictures. She had then created another 'blackmail letter' but this one was addressed to William. With pasted, cutout letters from magazines, as she had done for Bill's letter previously, she created a 'letter' that stated "Every Caesar Has A Brutus – Look To The Son."

With the added pictures of Bill associating with GME, it clearly indicated that Bill was behind GME. She had then addressed a manila envelope to William at his office and stuffed the letter and pictures inside. She licked it shut and put stamps on it.

All Christina now had to do was mail it out—and all her problems would be solved. In one fell swoop, she wouldn't have to marry him—and she'd get her revenge, so why was she hesitating?

She propped the envelope against a drinking glass on the kitchen table and stared at it hard.

If she sent this to his father, Bill's world would crash down around him like hers had all those years ago. William would throw him out of the house and out of the money. It would destroy what father-son bond they had and cause a rift in their relationship that could never be healed. William was not a forgiving man, even Maddie had said so.

And it would be Christina's fault.

No—not quite. It wasn't Christina that had made Bill start GME. And it wasn't Christina that had made him lie to his father and use his father's money to fund the protests that had caused their company share prices to fall. And it wasn't Christina that had made him stab William in the back. But it would be Christina's fault if William were to find out about his son's betrayal. Could she go that far?

Yes—he was a big jerk. And yes—he didn't love her but she loved him and in the end, she couldn't do it.

She still wasn't going to marry him though because he didn't love her and she had too much self-respect to ever tie herself into a situation like that. But she wouldn't be the one to tell William about his son. If she had to, she'd use the information she found out tonight to threaten Bill with if he refused to let her go—but no—she wouldn't be the one to tell his father.

Getting up, Christina suddenly had an overwhelming urge to go back to the mansion and sleep in her own bed there.

Funny, that place was beginning to feel more like home than this place was—even though it wouldn't be home for long.

She reached for her purse and left her apartment, leaving the sealed envelope addressed to William propped up on the kitchen table—against the drinking glass.

CHAPTER 53

BY THE TIME she got back to the mansion, it was almost 5 a.m. and Christina was bone tired. This had been a long, exhausting night and all she wanted to do was crash in her bed and sleep for a few hours.

Walking into her bedroom, she shut the door behind her then threw her purse on the dresser. She unbuttoned her blouse and slipped it off, letting it fall to the floor. She was even too tired to pick that up. Unzipping her jeans, she was about to pull them down when she suddenly saw 'him' reflected in her mirror!

Gasping, she whirled around.

There he was—in her room, sitting in one of the chairs by the window—watching her like a hunter watches a deer he's about to shoot. His eyes were zeroed in on her.

"Don't stop now," he sensuously purred. "You were just getting to the good part."

Christina was stunned and scared out of her pretty little wits.

"What the hell are you doing in my bedroom?" she seethed, as she stood before him in a lacy pink bra and unzipped jeans. Her matching lacy pink underwear was peeking out of the opening in her pants and his eyes were glued to the spot.

Ignoring her question, Bill's eyes came back up to her face and Christina saw the raw, fierce desire reflected in them. He wanted her, they silently said, and she owed him—and he had come to collect. It was time to pay for her sins!

Suddenly, realizing how little she had on, Christina quickly retrieved her blouse off the floor and threw it back on, protectively wrapping it around her body. He watched all of her movements intently.

"It's five in the morning. Where have you been all night?" he softly asked.

Christina defiantly raised her nose in the air. "Out," she replied.

"With whom?"

"That's none of your business. I'm not married to you yet."

"I'm making it my business," he stated quietly. "Tell me."

Christina didn't like being ordered to do anything. "Get out," she dared him.

"Not until I've finished with you," he whispered, again in that soft, silky voice.

Christina liked that even less—but if he tried anything, she had a secret ace up her sleeve she could threaten him with—the information she'd discovered tonight.

She smirked at him then, "Oh, I think we're finished."

"Not quite." And with one lithe, graceful move, he stood up out of his chair—and Christina took one terrified step back.

Even though ten feet of space still separated them in the large suite, Christina could feel the intense sexual heat emanating from his body towards hers.

He took two steps forward. She took two steps back.

He was the hunter—and she was on the run.

Her heart was beating wildly and she was scared.

"You're not frightened of me, are you Christina?" He was laughing at her—she knew he was laughing at her.

"N…no," Christina barely recognized the hoarse voice that was coming out of her. Yes, she was frightened and too tired to think straight. The bastard was going to get the better of her and she knew it.

"Good, because there's nothing to be scared of. I'm not going to hurt you."

He took another two steps forward. She took another two steps back.

"What… what do you want?"

"To make peace," he murmured softly and then dangerously added, "… with you." Christina knew he was referring to what she'd done to him with the handcuffs—or was he?

Trying to act brave, Christina again lifted her nose in the air. "You forgave me already. You said so."

"You believe everything you hear?" he teased her.

"Are you saying you lied?"

He didn't answer her question, but instead reached into his pocket and pulled out a blue box that obviously contained some piece of jewelry.

"I've brought you a peace offering." He held the box out to her. When she didn't make any move to bridge the gap between them to take it, he smirked at her obvious distrust of him. "I promise, it won't bite." He was laughing at her again.

Christina didn't respond and stood where she was.

"Okay, I'll open it for you," he told her, breaking the deadly silence between them.

He opened the box and inside was the most exquisite diamond necklace Christina had ever seen—not that she'd seen that many except through shop window glass. The necklace had diamonds shaped into flowers dripping all around it. It must have cost a small fortune, but then these Havenwoods never did anything halfway.

Christina kept staring at it, but not because she was overly materialistic—it was just that she'd never seen anything so beautiful before. The diamonds were glistening and hypnotizing her— and she was having a difficult time tearing her gaze away. When she finally raised her eyes back to his, she saw that he had been studying her reaction very closely.

He lifted the necklace out of the box then and threw the box on the floor. He dangled the bauble in his hand—like a hunter using bait to lure their prey in.

"For you," he offered smoothly.

"No thanks. I don't want it," she defied him.

He burst out laughing at that. "I've never known a woman to refuse diamonds before."

"I'm not like other women."

"Oh yes… I can appreciate that," he softly agreed.

"Well, since you've now said what you came here to say, can you please leave my room?"

He didn't move. "Oh come on now kitten, don't be like that."

Half of Christina didn't like the way he called her 'kitten'—the other half did.

"What else is there to say? You forgive me. I forgive you. Everybody's satisfied," Christina replied.

"Not quite… satisfied," he smirked at that.

Christina's eyes angrily flashed at him. "Well, that's all you're going to get." She kept staring hard at him, making sure he understood her meaning. He did. She could tell by the way his eyes were insolently glaring back at her, but he still kept up his pretence of charm.

"It gives me pleasure to give you pretty things. And it might give you pleasure to receive them. So why deny ourselves… pleasure?" he whispered.

Christina's internal temperature soared. Her fear of him and her lust for him were fighting each other in her body—and lust, wanting, desire were suddenly winning. His hot words and his magnetic presence were wrapping themselves around her like a boa and squeezing the breath out of her. She was beginning to breathe harder—and faster—and she saw his eyes rivet to her chest as he watched her breasts underneath her blouse rising and falling to the rhythm of her increased breathing rate.

"I… I think… you should go," her voice came out in a breathy whisper.

His gaze quickly came up to rest on her beautifully flushed face. "Okay, if that's what you want."

"It is," she breathed a sigh of relief at having him finally agree.

"I'll go then, but first let me at least give you this? I bought it just for you." He held the diamond necklace out to her again. "Please?"

Christina had been prepared to tell him 'no', but the soft, gentle way he had said the word 'please' did her in. He sounded like a little boy who had spent all day at school drawing a picture for the girl he liked and then she had rejected him and his gift.

Okay—so she'd let him give her the necklace and then he'd leave. What harm was there in that? Bill took a few steps forward and Christina remained rooted to the spot. Slowly, he continued to approach her—as if she were a skittish colt who would bolt if he made any sudden moves.

He reached her then—and stopped a foot away. Leisurely, he lifted the necklace and unclasped its opening. His slow, deliberate movements were mesmerizing Christina. Whether it was her fatigue at being up all night or her strong physical attraction to him or her love for him she didn't know, but she was falling under his spell.

Christina let her hands drop from her blouse, causing it to fall open and revealing her lacy pink bra. She then lifted her hair up off her neck and turned her back to him. She didn't see him bridge the last few inches between them but she felt him.

She saw his powerful arms come around from behind her and felt the weight of the cold, heavy necklace as he placed it around her neck. He snapped the clasp and from behind, he lowered his lips to her ears.

"You look beautiful, my little spitfire," he whispered and his breath erotically fanned the delicate insides of her ear.

Christina briefly closed her eyes as she felt an intense longing for him shoot through her body. God—she wanted him so badly—and her lack of sleep had removed all her inhibitions, excuses, defenses and rationale against making love to him.

Why hadn't she wanted to make love with him before?

She couldn't remember.

With a low moan, Christina spun around and wrapped her arms around his neck. She began to kiss him with a soft, ravenous passion, like a starving man eating his first meal after a hunger strike. She couldn't help herself—and she couldn't stop.

To say that Bill was stunned was an understatement of massive proportions. He hadn't expected her to make the first move. In fact, he'd been gearing up to do that himself and had even braced himself for the slap across his face that he'd been sure he was going to get for his efforts, but this—her kissing him—and with such hot, sensuous abandon?

It took Bill all of one second to greedily take what was being offered. After all, he'd been hard for her the minute she'd walked into the room. All it ever seemed to take was just one look at her and he was a goner. Quickly, he placed his hands on her waist, letting them run all the way up to her breasts which he began to massage through the thin, lacy material of her bra as he returned each of her tongue-thrusting kisses with his own.

Christina was on fire for him—and this time there was no stopping her. No more games. No more strategies—just pure, wet pleasure. She bit his lower lip and he grunted with satisfaction. Her lips briefly left his so that she could gasp out her pleasure at what he was doing to her. His thumbs had pushed the lacy material of her bra aside and were now brushing her erect nipples roughly. She threw her head back and moaned again. What he was doing to her felt so good—and she wanted more.

Dislodging her hands from his hair, Christina yanked off her blouse and let it fall to the floor. She then reached for his shirt and started to tug it open—some buttons came undone—some popped off. She didn't care—and neither did he, as he watched her do it.

She stripped him of the shirt, then pulled him towards the bed and pushed him onto it. She gazed into his fiery eyes and they matched hers in intensity.

Bill gave her a rakish smile as he leaned back on his elbows on top of the bed. "I've told you before, Miss Christina. Whatever you like or need, I'll do it for you. You just have to ask."

Christina gave him a breathy, sexy smile back. "Now, that's an offer a girl can't refuse."

And with one fell swoop, she pushed her jeans down her legs and stepped out of them. Bill let his hungry eyes slowly roam over every square inch of her luscious body, as she stood there in front of him in her pink bra, panties and the glittering diamond necklace he had given her.

He gave her another bad boy smile. "Very nice, now come here." He patted his hard thigh still clad in his pants.

Christina giggled. "Unfair, Mr. Havenwood. Here I am in my skivvies and you're still dressed."

At the speed of lightning, Bill kicked off his shoes, tore off his socks, unzipped himself and pulled his pants off, balling them up and throwing them across the room.

"Problem solved," he announced as he lay back on the bed in his briefs. "Now I'm in my skivvies too."

Christina laughed and took several steps towards the bed. As she did, something shiny caught her attention and her head instinctively turned to see what it was, and she suddenly froze.

There, lying half in/half out of one of Bill's pant's pockets was a pair of shiny, metallic handcuffs. Christina's smile dropped and she walked to where the pants lay on the floor.

"Sugar puff, I'm waiting," she heard Bill say, as she was bending down to retrieve them.

She straightened back up and let the cuffs dangle off one finger as she turned to the rat reclining on the bed. "What are these?" she innocently inquired.

Bill stared at the handcuffs. "Oh shit!" The words rushed out of his mouth and he leapt off the bed. "Christina, I can explain." He was in big trouble and he knew it.

Christina kept dangling the steel bracelets on one finger as she approached him. "No explanations necessary, sweetie. I think I'm smart enough to figure it out," she calmly replied. "This is my day of reckoning, isn't it?" He didn't reply and she continued, "Am I warm?"

Bill studied her beautiful, suddenly cold face. He'd been caught and there was no use in denying it. "You're burning hot." He smirked at his own stupidity.

Christina was angry. In one second, she'd gone from loving him to hating his guts all over again. Jenny had told her love and hate were the flip side of the same coin. She now truly believed it.

She played it cool as she approached him, still dangling the handcuffs in her hand. He watched her with a wary expression.

"And what were you planning?" She fingered her diamond necklace. "To trap me with shiny bait, then do to me what I did to you?"

Bill didn't take his eyes off her. "Pretty much," he admitted honestly. "I've been angry with you and I wanted to teach you a lesson."

"Then why didn't you? Instead you threw your pants with the handcuffs still in them halfway across the room."

"Because I…" Bill stopped himself. He'd been about to say, 'because I love you'.

Christina slowly walked up to him and reaching out, caressed his cheek.

"Because you… what? Because you want me? Because I threw myself at you? Because why?" she purred in her sexy voice.

Bill was staring hard at her and she was casting her witch's spell all over him again. His eyes traveled from her fiery eyes to her swollen, bruised lips, down her soft body and he was remembering how her skin had tasted like heaven only a few minutes before when he'd been kissing her.

Bill's breathing increased and the blood drained from his brain back to his crotch. He wanted her so badly and he couldn't think straight anymore, but instinctively he knew enough to be careful of her. She could be a dangerous, clever, little minx when double-crossed.

"All of the above, I guess," he softly admitted, not really sure what she was up to and not really caring—not if it meant he could touch her again.

Still holding the handcuffs in her right hand, Christina gave him a warm smile as she wrapped her arms around his neck and plastered her body against his hard erection. Bill couldn't help gasping with the intense pleasure that alone gave him but he didn't put his hands on her body. With a Herculean effort, he held himself back until he could be sure of her intentions. She brought her lips within inches of his and her sexy eyes lifted to his.

"I'm glad you were honest with me, Bill Havenwood," she whispered into his mouth. "I forgive you. And you can still have me because I still want you."

Bill saw her desire for him flash in her eyes and with a low groan he broke down. Reaching for her, he began to kiss her with a fervent intensity he'd never experienced with anyone before in his life. His hands traveled down her warm, curvy body and he pulled her back to the bed, falling backwards on it and bringing her down on top of him.

Christina matched each of his hot kisses. She dropped the handcuffs on the pillow beside his head and laid both hands on his bare shoulders. Still kissing him deeply, she caressed his hard chest before moving to his nipples, then further down to his flat belly and back up again.

His hands traveled to her derriere and began to knead and squeeze her flesh in an erotic rhythm. Christina, suddenly, grabbed one of his hands and slowly brought it up over his head—while at the same time feeling, with her other hand, for the handcuffs on the pillow beside his head. Her hand locked onto them—and she knew she had one second to bring them up to his wrist and handcuff the rat to the bedpost. If she was going to pull this off—again—she needed both speed and God on her side.

She had neither.

She went for it anyway—but this time, he was ready.

As she tried to slip the manacle onto his wrist, Bill quickly grabbed both of her hands and held them away from him. Their locked lips broke apart and they were both breathing heavily.

"Not this time, you little hellcat!" he gritted, as he used all of his strength to subdue her.

Still on top of him, Christina started to squirm. "Let me go, you lowlife," she shouted.

Not yet!" he shouted back.

He was so big and so strong compared to her, that before she knew what had happened, he had effortlessly flipped her over and Christina found herself underneath his heavy, male body. She tried bringing her knee up to kick him in the groin, but he effortlessly pinned downed her legs with his own strong, muscled ones.

He gave her an evil smile then. "Dirty little fighter, aren't you?"

"Go to hell," she threw at him.

"Honey, I'm already there but this time, I'm taking you with me." His eyes glinted dangerously.

Frightened, Christina squirmed even harder, but it was no use. She was no match for his superior male strength. Then, as if she were no stronger than a feather, he easily transferred both of her wrists to his hand and held her tight. Christina stopped squirming and looked into his face, inches away. She was breathing heavily from her futile efforts to escape and from his heavy body weight pressing down on her.

"What are you going to do?" she breathlessly asked him.

He gave her a naughty grin. "Exactly what you think I'm going to do."

Suddenly, Christina's wrists were handcuffed to the bedpost in the same position she had locked him in a week before. As she yanked at her bondage, Bill slid off and stood by the bed looking down at his handiwork and was pleased.

"I knew not to trust you when you started coming onto me again after you found the handcuffs," he mumbled to himself.

Christina's eyes shot poison darts at him. "Uncuff me, you slime. Now!" she shouted.

He laughed, "Bitter tasting, isn't it?"

Christina glared at him. "What is?"

"Your own medicine."

"Why you rotten, lousy worm! Let me go!" She yanked harder at the steel bracelets but to no avail.

"Oh, I almost forgot," Bill winked at her before walking to where his pants lay on the floor. He fished into one of the pockets and found a handcuff key. He held it up for her to see.

"Is this how your little game is played?" he taunted her.

"Don't you dare!" she yelled, clearly reading his mind.

"Why not? You did." He smirked as he walked to the bathroom.

Squirming frantically, Christina screamed at the top of her lungs, "Don't you do it, you sleazeball! Don't…"

She heard the toilet flushing—and Christina let out a 'noooooooo' that was as loud as Bill's had been the week before. She glared as he smugly came back out.

"You snake!" she threw at him.

"Hey, these are your tricks honey, not mine. I simply learned from the master." He crossed his arms in front of his chest and beamed down at her.

And there, Christina was—handcuffed to the middle of the bed—wearing her lacy pink bra and panties that had been twisted from all of his rough love play—and wearing his damned, diamond necklace that branded her as his possession.

She sat up as far as the handcuffs would let her. "Feel better?" she sarcastically asked.

He nodded, "Much."

"So, now we're even?"

"Even Stephen."

She gave him a phony smile, "I'm glad. Now this is the part in my little game where you have to go get Tom, your gardener and ask him to bring his tools." Christina had heard it all from Tilly about how Tom had taken over an hour to saw through Bill's handcuffs last week.

Bill shook his head. "No, I don't think so. You look pretty hot tied to the bed in your underwear and you might give poor, old Tom a heart attack."

"What do you suggest we do then? You flushed the key down the toilet."

Bill pretended to think. "We could finish what we started?" he suggested.

"You mean, have sex with you with me tied to the bed?"

"It's an idea."

"A bad one."

"Okay, how about we make love with you untied from the bed." He held up the key that he'd been secretly palming in his hand.

Christina gasped. "You didn't flush it?"

He shook his head. "No."

Christina's anger vanished in an instant. "Why not? I did it to you," she softly asked.

He shrugged his shoulders. "Maybe you don't feel the same way about me that I do about you."

Christina's heart skipped a beat. "And how do you feel about me?"

He stared at her for a full minute and Christina thought he wasn't going to answer her. Then he moved closer to the bed.

"Like this," he said, before bending down and unlocking her handcuffs.

Christina rubbed her sore wrists as the manacles slipped off. She studied his face, looking for clues about what he meant. Part of her wanted to believe—desperately—that he had feelings for her. As he straightened and started to walk away, she put a restraining hand on his arm.

"I don't understand?" she questioned.

He looked at her for what seemed an eternity then raised his hand and let his finger trace the soft outline of her lips.

"I love you, Christina," Bill whispered. "I've loved you from the moment you threw that damned ring in my face and threatened to walk out on me."

Christina was stunned. "You… you love me?" she stammered.

Bill nodded 'yes'.

Christina's heart pounded in her chest as she came off the bed and stood in front of him. He was saying he loved her. Did he love her—for real? Was it possible? It was almost too good to be true!

Suddenly, her eyes narrowed and she defensively crossed her arms, throwing him a suspicious glare. Wait a minute! If she were in his desperate, pathetic position with his father, this is exactly what she would say to keep her hapless stooge in line. Yes, indeed—it was too good to be true!

"No, I don't think so," she defiantly announced.

Bill was dumbfounded. "What?" The word rushed out in an explosive fury.

"Of course, you're going to say that. You'll say anything to get into my pants not to mention have me marry you for your father's money."

Anger coursed through Bill. "Unbelievable! Here I am laying my heart at your feet and you're trampling all over it?" he shouted.

"Come on, you're going to have to do better than a couple of phony 'I love you's'."

Speechless, Bill glanced around the room in shock. He couldn't believe what he was hearing. "Don't you get it? I've fallen for you, damn it!" he suddenly yelled at the top of his lungs.

"Sure, you've fallen… on your head, if you expect me to believe that!"

"You know what, Christina? You really are a piece of work!" he shouted back before collecting his pants from the floor and violently throwing them on. "And you know what else?" He retrieved his shirt and stuffed his arms into the sleeves. "I love you so damned much that I'm throwing you out of here."

"What?" Now it was Christina's turn to be flabbergasted.

He came up to her and poked her in the chest. "That's right. I want you to pack your things and get the hell out. We're through!" Bill turned and stalked to the door.

Christina was stunned. "What? What are you saying?"

Still furious, he turned back to her. "I'm saying, you're free, Christina, you're free. I'm releasing you from all of your contractual obligations to me. You don't owe me a thing. You don't owe me for the car, you don't owe me for the ring and you don't have to marry me. I'll have my lawyer draw up the papers today and I'll sign them. Everything you wanted, you got. You win!"

"But… your father… if you don't marry me, he'll throw you out! You won't have any money!" Christina was astounded at what she was hearing.

"Yeah well, you know what? Maybe I fucking love you more!" He screamed the words at her and then strode out the door, slamming it so hard that it rocked on its hinges.

Christina's mouth dropped open in shock and her breathing stopped. Could it be true? Could Bill Havenwood love her—for real? If he let her walk and they didn't marry, Christina knew William would immediately cut him off. If Bill was willing to give up everything in order to set her free and make her happy—that only meant one thing…

The rat bastard was truly in love with her!

And she was in love with him.

CHAPTER 54

CHRISTINA WOKE UP with a start and bolted upright out of bed. Was it true? Did Bill really love her or had she dreamt the whole thing?

For a few seconds, she wasn't sure. Then it all came streaming back to her. He did love her! Bill Havenwood, the man she had hated most in the world, was in love with her—and what was even crazier was that she was in love with him. Smiling, she flopped backwards into her pillow and gazed dreamily up at the ceiling.

But what about her revenge plan to get back at him for what he'd done in high school? What about the promise she'd made to herself all those years ago? Well, Bill wasn't that same person anymore. He was sober now and trying to change his life for the better. In fact, she understood a little better now why he'd been that way back then.

A dysfunctional home life coupled with the disease of alcoholism had made him into a pretty messed up kid. She saw things clearly now with the eyes of an adult. She'd come to know him—and she'd come to love him. And life was about second chances, wasn't it? Everybody deserved that. He did. And so did she.

Christina glanced at her bedside clock. It read 1:15 p.m.

She was now going to shower, get dressed, go downstairs, find him and tell him that she loved him too. The time for lies was over. But would she tell him about her revenge plan and what she'd really been up to? Yes, but not today. Today was for love.

Having made her decision, Christina felt a twinge of

apprehension that she might be making a mistake by not telling him everything today but she pushed the feeling aside.

*

As Christina was crossing the foyer, she spotted Eudora, the elderly maid.

"Eudora, have you seen Bill anywhere?" Christina had checked in his bedroom and he wasn't there.

"Yes, mum. He left early this morning, for the office I assume."

So, Bill wasn't in the house. Well, she'd just wait for him to come back and then she'd tell him that she loved him—and everything would turn out fine.

CHAPTER 55

IT WAS ALMOST 6 p.m. when Christina finally saw his Jag drive up to the house. The butterflies in her stomach fluttered and her heart pounded. She was nervous. How would he react and what would he say when she told him?

Dressed for dinner—and for him—in a sexy blue halter dress, Christina moved away from the salon windows and went to sit on the couch. She knew he'd come looking for her.

He did.

Bill walked into the salon—and his face was set in stone.

He didn't smile at Christina nor greet her. Still fuming from his morning encounter with her, he marched to where she was sitting and handed her a folded document.

"Everything you wanted… madam," he coldly told her.

Slowly standing up, Christina unfolded the document and scanned the contents. It was legal and signed—and it released her from all debts she owed Bill. She was free.

He continued in that frozen voice. "My lawyer says it's all legal and above board but if you don't 'believe' me…" he emphasized the word 'believe' since Christina had called him a liar when he'd declared his love for her. "Then take it to your own lawyer and have them check it out." Still furious, Bill could barely stand to look at her.

Christina studied his set face. "No, I believe you. In fact, I…"

He cut her off. "I've already signed it. All you have to do is sign it too and our arrangement is over. You can leave anytime." He looked at her then—with chilly, frosty eyes.

Christina refolded the document and handed it back to him. "No, I don't think so. I'm not signing this," she said.

Bill was taken aback. "Is there something in there you don't like? I've told you, you can take it to your own lawyer and have it verified."

"I'm sure the document's fine. It's just… well… maybe I don't want to leave." Christina took a few steps closer and captured his eyes with hers.

Bill was still cold towards her. "You don't want to leave? I don't understand."

Christina breached the last few inches between them and wrapped her arms around his neck. She stared into his eyes. "Do you love me, Bill Havenwood?" she purred, in her sexiest voice as one finger traced his cheekbone.

"Yes, I love you." Mesmerized, his words came out in a gasp. "But you don't believe me."

"I believe you now." Her finger moved to his lips.

Bill was skeptical. "You do?"

Christina nodded her head. "Yes."

Bill kept his arms to his sides. "And what brought on this change of heart?"

"Well, you were willing to give up everything for me and that proves you love me." She paused and stared deeply into his eyes. "And I love you too." She held her breath, waiting for his reaction.

She didn't have to wait long as surprise flashed in his eyes.

"You love me?"

Christina smiled. "I love you, sweetie and I don't want to go."

"You're saying you… really love me?"

Christina nodded, "Yes."

Suddenly, Bill's hands came around her in a steel grip and he beamed with happiness. His next words came out in a rush, "This is… amazing. I can't believe it. You love me? You're saying you're in love with me?"

Christina nodded again before bringing her lips up to his and tenderly kissing him. He reciprocated in kind, as he clung to her for dear life.

Their lips broke apart and he smiled into her sweet eyes. "How… God, this is incredible… how long have you known?"

"A while."

"But… you didn't say anything? You let me believe that…"

Christina put a finger up to his lips and stopped his words, "Shhh… I know… and I'm sorry, but I was afraid you didn't feel the same way. Now I know how wrong I was."

"Does this mean you'll marry me… for real?"

"Yes, my sweetheart, I will marry you."

Christina was secretly breathing a sigh of relief. Everything was going so well that she almost wanted to pinch herself. Maybe she was dreaming and none of this was real?

She raised her lips again to his and he gave her another warm, ravenous kiss and she knew that—no, she wasn't dreaming—that kiss had been real, as was his passion—and it was all for her.

Bill tore his lips away and stared into her beautiful eyes. "Baby, you've made me the happiest man on this planet and there's something very special I need to say to you before we start our lives together."

Christina smiled at him, her love now freely shining in her eyes. "So tell me."

"No, not here. I want to say it outside by the rose garden. I want you to remember this moment and I want us to be in a special place when I tell you what I have to say."

"Then, let's go," Christina laughed, and grabbing his hand, she tugged him towards the doors that led outside onto the mansion grounds.

They half walked, half ran as Christina laughingly pulled Bill towards the beautiful rose garden by the pool. The warm breeze fanned their hair as the sun shone brightly over the green, well-manicured lawn. It looked like a magical fairyland.

They reached the roses by the pool and with her eyes and face flushed by the excitement of newly found love, Christina turned to Bill. "What is it you want to tell me, sweetie?"

Bill smiled at her—then reached down and scooped her up in his powerful arms. Happy, Christina giggled as she was lifted off the ground.

"I want to tell you this…" Bill replied.

Then, before Christina had an inkling of what he was intending, Bill—with one good swing—launched her—cocktail dress and all—into the pool!

She hit the water with a resounding splash and sunk to the bottom. One second later, she resurfaced, gasping for breath. Splashing to get her balance, she quickly pushed her wet hair out of her face and looked up at a furious Bill who was standing by the pool's edge.

Spluttering water, Christina half gasped, half shouted, "What… what the hell did you do that for?"

"That… was for fucking lying to me in there!" Fuming, Bill shouted as he pointed to the house. "How dare you tell me that you love me!"

Frustrated, Christina hit the water with her fists, "But I do love you. I wasn't lying!"

"You expect me to believe that? That you suddenly love me and want me and want to marry me when you've talked about nothing else for weeks but getting the hell out of here?" He yelled at full volume.

Christina, still splashing in the middle of the pool, started to get mad. "I do love you, damn it… you stubborn, crazy fool! Why would I say it if it wasn't true?"

"Look around you. Look where you are. It's the lifestyle, baby, and the money; and you don't want to lose it. You've had all day to think about what you'd be giving up if I released you from our deal, so you decide to bullshit me with your lies of love. Well, it's not going to work because I'm on to you, honey."

Wet to the very core of her being, Christina again hit the water with her angry fists. Sprays of water shot up in the air.

"That's not true. And even if it was, what do you care so long as I marry you anyway? You were prepared to marry me yesterday when it was all bullshit for your father's sake, so why not now?"

"Because today I told you I love you and that changed everything," Bill yelled back. He then turned and stalked back to the house.

"Come back here and help me out, you louse!" Christina shouted at his retreating back but Bill ignored her and kept walking. He disappeared into the mansion.

An angry Christina again pounded the water hard with her hands before swimming to the edge of the pool. Climbing the stairs, she hauled herself out and pushed her sopping wet hair back.

Looking down at herself, she saw that her beautiful blue halter dress was ruined and plastered to every curve of her body. And she was barefoot. Both of her shoes were now resting at the bottom of the pool.

What an idiot that man was!

She'd been telling him the truth about her love for him and he hadn't believed her. Yes—she had done the exact same thing to him this morning and maybe it did serve her right, but damn it—she was still mad as hell!

*

With her head proudly held high as if she was wearing a jeweled tiara, Christina walked through the French doors from outside into the salon.

Her wet hair was plastered to her head, her drenched cocktail dress was plastered to her body, her mascara was running, her makeup was ruined—and she was barefoot. William was sitting on one of the couches having his usual pre-dinner martini and Bill was leaning against the fireplace with a club soda in his hand.

As she walked in, Christina stopped in front of a shocked

William. "William, will you be so kind as to delay dinner until I've had a chance to change, please?" she elegantly requested.

Stunned at Christina's wet appearance, William shot up out of his seat. "My God, Christina! What happened to you?" he gasped.

"I ran into a skunk. A big one," she retorted.

"That's impossible. We don't have any skunks here."

"Oh yes, you do," she replied, then turned towards Bill and shot him a dirty look. Bill raised his glass in a silent salute to her.

Still livid, Christina turned and gracefully walked out of the room.

Bill watched her walk out—his eyes glued to her luscious, curvy ass clearly emphasized by her wet dress. In fact, every juicy curve of her sexy body was on display for him in that soaked piece of blue cloth she called a dress. And the way she was walking out—with pride and dignity—Bill had to admit the lady had class, even if she was a big liar.

William had seen the angry look that had passed between the two. He rounded on his son. "What in the hell is going on here?"

Bill stood up to his father. "That's between me and her, so stay out of it, dad. I'm warning you."

William wanted to keep prodding to find out what had happened, but he very wisely decided to keep his mouth shut and let the two of them handle it themselves. His son was showing some moxie lately—in the way he was handling Christina and in the way he was standing up to him—and William was beginning to respect him for it.

CHAPTER 56

IT TOOK CHRISTINA exactly thirty-five minutes to shower, change, blow dry her hair and apply a light makeup before she was presentable enough to go back downstairs. She'd chosen to wear a low-cut, black dress with spaghetti straps that exposed her creamy arms and chest. Even though she'd rushed to get ready, she knew she looked good.

When Christina reentered the salon, both men were still there, waiting for her. William had a curious expression on his face while Bill's was set with a stern, icy look. William smiled and gallantly led her into the dining room. A sulky Bill followed.

Dinner was a quiet affair with William doing most of the talking. He tried to draw them both out, but all he got for his efforts were one-sentence responses.

Neither Bill nor Christina addressed each other or even looked at each other. By the time coffee was served, a frustrated William had had enough.

He forcefully threw down his napkin and rose out of his seat. "I don't know what's going on, but it's going to stop tonight. The wedding is less than two weeks away and things better be patched up before then," he threatened, before stomping out of the dining room.

When the doors slammed behind him, Christina turned to Bill and glared at him. She was still fuming about the dunking in the pool that he'd given her—and the fact that he hadn't believed her love for him.

Bill glared back. He was still furious at her for pretending to love him so that she could keep her cushy, Havenwood position—and the fact that she hadn't believed his love for her.

Neither said anything to the other. It was an impasse.

As if on cue, they both rose up out of their chairs at the same time, intending to leave.

Christina shot him a dirty look. "I can't believe I'm in love with a bastard," she announced.

He returned the glare. "And I can't believe I'm in love with a bitch."

"Go to hell," she angrily retorted.

"Same to you," he seethed.

Christina's blood was boiling and she was about to burst. How dare he! How dare he—about everything!

Acting on impulse, she looked down at her half-eaten plate of food. Scooping up a handful of mashed potatoes, she turned back to him—ready to fire.

Reading her mind, he threatened, "If you do what you're thinking about doing, then let me warn you, I won't be a gentleman."

"When were you ever a gentleman?" she snapped back.

"I was a gentleman tonight by the pool. That dunking you got… let me tell you, you got off easy," he angrily replied.

Christina still had the fistful of mashed potatoes poised at his head. "It figures someone like you would think that," she shot back.

"And what the hell is that supposed to mean?"

"It means… you are an asshole, Bill Havenwood and you don't know the first thing about how to treat a lady."

"Show me a lady and I'll show you how well I can treat her."

"Are you implying I'm not a lady?"

"Hey… you're the one standing there with food aimed at my head and I don't think that definition is in the dictionary if you look up the word 'lady', do you?" he taunted her.

Christina's anger went up two more degrees, hitting the danger zone. Her hand went back—ready to fire the gooey potatoes at him.

Bill softly warned her. "Don't you…"

He never got that last word out as the mushy mess hit him squarely on his right eye and cheek. Slowly, Bill's hand came up and wiped off the food. He stared at her hard—then reached down and scooped up his own handful of mashed potatoes and aimed it at her.

"You dare throw that at me and you prove that you're a louse," Christina warned.

"Then I'm a louse," he replied, before promptly launching the food at her.

It landed on her hair and face; and specks fell on the table, on her chair and on William's wildly expensive rug on the floor.

Christina gasped in shock at his audacity. How bloody dare he! With her napkin, she wiped off as much of the mess as she could.

Fuming, she rounded on him. "You've got some nerve, buddy!"

He smirked at her then—that damned, smug Havenwood smirk that she hated so much. "Hey, you threw the first punch, lady!" he mocked her, implying she was no 'lady'.

"Why you…" She furiously looked down at the table of food trying to see what she could throw next.

She spotted the silver bowl with the thick, gummy cream of corn. Scooping up a large handful, she hauled back and threw it at him with as much force as she could muster. It caught him on the nose and mouth, and landed on his jacket.

Angry, Bill wiped it off with the back of his hand.

"So you like it rough, do you?" he gritted through set teeth. "Well, so do I!" He too looked down on the table and spotted a large bowl of chocolate pudding that no one had touched during dessert. Grabbing it, he menacingly started to walk around the table towards Christina.

Christina backed away. "Don't you dare!" she screamed at him.

At that precise moment, Geoffrey, the under butler, walked in to clear the table off. On seeing Master Bill and Madam Christina caked in food—and Bill advancing on his fiancée with the bowl of pudding, he quickly did a one-eighty out of the room—and shutting the door behind him, ran to tell the rest of the staff what was going on in the dining room.

Meanwhile, Bill was still approaching Christina with the pudding while she kept backing away.

"I warn you, Bill Havenwood, stay away from me," she threatened.

"Or else what? You'll leave? We both know you won't do that. You've got a great setup here and you don't want to lose it."

"That's crap and only a pea-brained ninny like you would come up with an idiotic idea like that."

Bill laughed, "Oh, so I'm a ninny and an idiot, am I?"

"Yes," Christina shouted, just as her back came up against the wall. She gasped in surprise.

Bill took a few more steps towards her and he had her cornered. He gave her an evil smile, "Well, it's better than being a sharp-tongued witch like you!"

And then he smoothly dumped the whole contents of the bowl of pudding onto her little black dress. Christina gasped as the creamy, slimy concoction slid down the front of her dress, onto her chest and exposed cleavage. She was breathing heavily from anger, not believing that the rat had actually had the nerve to do it. She looked back up at him and saw the twinkle of laughter in his eyes, as he brazenly looked her up and down.

"Now there's something you don't see everyday—chocolate covered breasts. Yummy." He said, laughing at her again.

"Well, eat this then…" she angrily replied as she ran both of her hands over her 'chocolate covered breasts' and scooped up as much of the pudding as she could.

And before he'd even had a chance to stop laughing, she smashed the dessert into his open laughing mouth and smeared it down his damned, expensive jacket, making sure she used enough force to grind the food mess into the fibers.

"There! I'd like to meet the dry cleaner who can get that out!" She yelled at him.

Stunned, Bill looked down at his ruined suit. "This was an Armani," he seethed at her.

"Well, now it's garbage," she retorted.

His angry eyes locked onto hers—as hers did to his. They were both furious, both shocked at what had happened—and they were both breathing heavily.

Suddenly, in an instant, the charged air in the room changed. The anger disappeared and was replaced by a sexual energy that was almost electrical in nature. Christina felt a tangible pull on her lips emanating from his lips, as if a string were attached and someone was pulling them together.

Bill felt it too.

Who kissed who first—neither of them knew. But in a flash, both of their lips had locked onto the other's and they were wildly, passionately kissing each other, tongues darting in and out, each tasting a mixture of mashed potatoes, cream of corn, dark chocolate pudding—and sex. It was dirty. It was messy. It was fun—just like their relationship together had been all along.

Christina's 'chocolate covered' breasts caked the front of Bill's jacket with pudding as she plastered her body to his and their hands slipped in the gooey mess as they tried to touch each other. They laughed in between kisses as neither could get a firm grip.

Christina's sticky hands ran up to his shoulders and pushed his jacket off of his body. It fell to the floor in a heap.

Her hands then frantically yanked his shirt out of his pants and quickly started to unbutton it. Exposing his chest, her hands greedily ran up and down his naked skin, leaving streaks of pudding everywhere. Still wildly kissing him, she moaned into his mouth at the intense pleasure it gave her to touch him.

His hands had slipped her spaghetti straps down her arms and the top part of her dress fell to her waist exposing her pudding-caked breasts to his touch. His hands massaged and kneaded, taking their fill, before finding her nipples. He began to roll them between his thumb and index finger as if he were winding a watch—and Christina began to moan again, this time like an animal in heat. What he was doing to her was making her crazy as shards of exquisite pleasure ran down from her breasts to her privates.

Here they were, making love in the dining room where anyone could walk in at anytime, where the staff might overhear their moans through the doors—and she didn't give a damn and neither did he.

Too far gone, their lips separated and Christina pulled Bill to the floor. She landed on her back and he, on top of her—and their food-streaked, half naked bodies smeared pudding and creamed corn and mashed potatoes onto William's antique Aubusson rug.

Neither cared about that either.

For a brief second their eyes locked into each other as their breathing continued to keep pace with their rapid heartbeats. His eyes were silently asking her for permission to continue and with another low moan from her, she grabbed both sides of his face and pulled him again to her lips, eating and tasting him as much as she could.

He grunted with satisfaction then and returned wild kiss for wild kiss. She tasted so good to him—and he was on fire for her.

Suddenly, he made an odd sound deep in his throat and pulled away. He stared hard into her wild eyes.

"Christina… I can't stop…" he gasped, in between his heavy breathing.

She stared back at him, her breasts rising and falling as her breathing matched his. "I don't want you to," she whispered.

Bill briefly closed his eyes and shook his head from side to side. "No… you don't understand. God help me… I don't have a rubber."

Christina grabbed both sides of his face with her hands and gazed into his hot, fevered eyes. "God help me too, because I don't care," she whispered back.

It was crazy, it was insane and it was irresponsible. They were both adults and they should have known better, but the time for 'should haves' and 'could haves' had long past—and they were both at the point of no return.

He hesitated then—and Christina looked into his face and saw he was trying to get control back for the both of them.

But she wasn't having any of that. She wanted him now and she was going to have him now—and damn the consequences.

Christina opened her legs to him, nestling his hard erection, still concealed in his pants, more deeply into her pantied crotch and she started to kiss him again with frenzied abandon. With a low moan of surrender, Bill began to kiss her back. The moment had passed as had all sensibility—and they were both lost to their passions again.

Bill's lips left hers and his tongue began to lick its way down her neck, to her chest, to her breasts. Tasting pudding and skin, he took one nipple in his mouth and stroked it back and forth with his slippery tongue before moving on to the other one. Christina began to mew like a little kitty cat, a sound she'd never heard come out of her before. She was so hot for him and she couldn't help herself.

At the same time as he was laving her breast, his hands had hiked her dress up to her waist, exposing her black panties. As he groped for them, his hand came into contact with the delicate lace covering her V and he palmed her there for a few seconds before grabbing the thin material and tugging. The fragile, black lace ripped in his fingers and he yanked them off and threw them to the side.

His fingers came back to her and he began to stroke her back and forth. She was wet and it was all for him. A thrill shot through him that turned him on even more—if that was at all possible.

Christina loved every hot thing he was doing to her as she arched her back to his hand. He was giving her so much pleasure that she could barely stand it. She wanted him inside of her—and she was going to have him.

Crazed with desire, she reached for his belt buckle and undid it. Then, her shaking hands found his zipper and unzipped him. She snaked inside his pants and freed his hard erection. Her hand wrapped itself around him and she began to stroke him firmly.

At the touch of her soft, delicate hands on his fullness, Bill groaned and his lips left her nipples and came back up to her swollen lips—sucking, and biting, and tugging, and licking, and kissing. They were like two animals mating—no reason, no logic, all instinct.

Then she felt his hand remove her hand from him and in an instant, he'd plunged into her—deep and swift and hard. She cried out at the exquisite delicious sensations that shot up into her body as she felt the walls of her body wrap themselves around him.

He began to move inside her and she closed her legs around him and arched her back again. She rode him as hard as he was riding her, matching each of his strong strokes with her own— their breathing harsh, their bodies damp with sweat.

It was fast.

It was furious.

And it was all on the dining room rug.

Christina came first. She cried out as she felt her release and the walls of her innermost place began to contract and milk him. He felt her spasms and with one last thrust, he buried himself deep within her, as deep as he could get before climaxing himself. It was primal, it was possessive—but he just desperately needed to be as deep within her as he could be before he came. She was his—and he was branding her.

With a low moan of satisfaction, he released and experienced a wave of intense pleasure as he emptied himself into her.

As each of their climaxes subsided, their breathing began to slow down and their bodies now satiated with sex, began to calm down too. His eyes focused on her face—as hers were on his—and he watched her reaction intently as he slowly eased himself out of her. She almost winced with the pain of having him leave her.

Suddenly, Bill buried his face down into the hollow between

her shoulder and jaw, and muffled words into her hair that she could barely make out—but she did.

"God, Christina… I'm sorry," he whispered hoarsely.

Christina was taken aback. "Sorry? Sorry for what?"

Suddenly, she was worried. Did he regret having made love to her? Was he disappointed with her? Did he not love her after all? Her arms instinctively wrapped themselves around his back and held him tight. She didn't want to let go.

His face came up then and he lovingly gazed into her eyes. His eyes were tortured with regret—but not the regret she thought.

"I'm sorry for this. For taking you like this… here… on the floor… dirty with all this food on us. This was our first time… and you deserve better."

Relief washed over Christina. So that's what was bothering him. She smiled at him then. "You let me be the judge of that. You don't hear me complaining, do you?"

He gave her a half laugh at that. "No, but I'm not an inexperienced teenager and that's exactly how I acted."

"Well, it takes two to tango and I did my fair share of dancing tonight too."

He laughed at her wise quip, then his eyes turned serious again. "And… I'm sorry… that I didn't use a rubber." He let out a gasp. "God… am I ever sorry about that." He shook his head at his own unbelievable stupidity. "That's never happened to me before."

Christina smirked. "I'm glad to hear it," she smartly announced and he smiled at that. She then turned serious herself. "It was stupid on both of our parts but it's done now… and we'll just move forward from here."

She grabbed his face then with both hands, making sure she had his full attention and stared deeply into his eyes.

"You do know that I love you, don't you? And it's not your money, or this damned monstrosity of a house or your posh Havenwood name. I… love… you… for you… and only for you. Tell me you believe me?"

He paused for a second, as he returned her gaze. "I believe you."

Christina breathed a sigh of relief. Then her lips broke into a wide smile as she took in their appearance. He was still on top of her, unzipped and exposed; and she was half naked with her little black dress twisted around her waist, with her breasts and lower half also exposed.

"Do you think William will be coming back in here for his tea anytime soon?" she cracked.

He burst out laughing at the thought of that. "Oh Christina, no woman has ever made me laugh like you do."

"Are you saying I'm your woman?"

He stopped laughing then and grew serious. "No; I'm saying you're my wife." He then added with a smile, "Or you very soon will be."

A surge of happiness shot through Christina at the thought of being his wife. Never in a million, billion, trillion years would she ever have imagined herself married to the man she had hated most in the world only a few months back—not to mention have imagined what they'd just done together. Life could be funny like that. You think you have it all figured out and then just the opposite happens—and you love it!

"What do you say we get up, slink out of here before somebody catches us, go upstairs and take a shower together?" she slyly offered, then added. "Are you…up… for it?"

Bill caught on to her double meaning. "Not yet, but gimme a little time to recuperate; you're a handful, you know." He wickedly winked at her and Christina laughed.

CHAPTER 57

AFTER THEY HAD straightened their clothing while in the dining room, Bill and Christina, hand-in-hand, had carefully crept up the stairs to avoid being spotted. When they'd reached the upstairs landing and saw that the coast was clear, they had run down the long hallway into Bill's bedroom. Laughing like a couple of kids that had gotten away with doing something naughty, they quickly shut the door behind them. They had made it and no one had seen their disheveled, food-caked, debauched appearance.

Safe, in their own private cocoon, Bill pulled Christina into his arms and began to kiss her again with abandon. Entwining her arms around his neck, Christina responded in kind, brushing her own soft lips over his hungry, greedy ones, slipping away into that mindless pleasure that only he seemed to be able to give her. She just couldn't get enough of him.

Bill's hands traveled from her luscious breasts, down to her waist, to her back and down to her derriere. Cupping both cheeks, he squeezed them and tightly pressed her pliant body against his crotch. He could feel himself getting hard again, and if he didn't put a stop to this now, he was going to repeat his schoolboy, sex-starved performance from downstairs only this time it would be on his bedroom floor.

Breathing heavily, Bill reluctantly dragged his lips off of hers. "God, Christina…" he rasped, "I want you again and again and again."

"And you can have me, again and again and again," she purred before reaching for him, ready to pull him back to her lips.

He stopped her. "No, I want to do it right this time."

Confusion registered in Christina's eyes. What was he talking about? She saw him glance over her head to the bed. Suddenly, she realized that he was still regretting their amateurish performance in the dining room earlier.

She smiled, "Honey, I can assure you, the job was done right last time."

He laughed at that, "Thank you for that; but I think it's about time I start putting into practice some of those… farming credits… I earned back in college, don't you? After all, I have a reputation to live up to."

Bluntly put, he wanted to give her the best lay she'd ever had and he knew he could do it if he could just control his lust a little more where she was concerned and take things a bit slower—but he was finding that almost impossible to do.

Christina studied his pinched expression. She, suddenly, realized he was desperately trying to rein in his ardor, wanting to prove himself to her. That was so sweet of him!

But he didn't have to do that. She wanted him so badly again that the bedroom floor was just fine by her. But, it seemed to be important to him and he was asking for her help in a roundabout way—so she'd help him.

She gave him a wicked smile, "Okay, Farmer Bill, let's play a little game." She put a foot of space between them as she pulled away. "And these are the rules. Why don't we go take that shower together? You'll wash my body. I'll wash yours. But no kissing and no touching any private parts. We'll save all that for later. How does that sound?"

Bill gave her a half smile. "I like your little games."

"Good because I have lots of them."

Pleased with her clever idea, Christina took him by the hand and led him to the bathroom.

*

The hot shower spray water was deliciously cascading over both of their bodies washing away the remains of their food fight earlier. With a soapy sponge in hand, Bill began to slowly go over every angle and curve of Christina's body except for her breasts and privates. He studied every twist and turn as if he was a sculptor lovingly crafting a piece of marble that he was working on. Christina felt every sensuous stroke and she'd never felt more alive in her life.

Leisurely, he turned her around and began to soap her back, squeezing the water-filled sponge and letting the droplets trickle down the sexy curve of her derriere. Christina briefly closed her eyes, her heart was racing, her breathing was faster and she desperately wanted him again—now. But she'd told him they were going to take things slow. It was what he wanted—and she'd give him what he wanted.

With her back to him, she felt his lips lightly kiss her shoulder. His hand holding the sponge came around her from behind.

"Your turn," he whispered in her ear.

Christina took the sponge from his hand and slowly turned around. They were facing each other now and it was her turn to study every angle and curve of his naked male body.

Her eyes roamed his form up and down. Yes, he was definitely magnificent. His shoulders were strong, his belly was flat and his legs were muscled. His form was so perfect he could have been a male model—he was that gorgeous.

And he was hard for her again. In fact, he'd been hard for her since they'd started their little shower game together but he was trying to take things slow for her sake. She knew he wanted to please her—and she loved him even more for that.

Christina looked up into his fevered eyes and gave him a wicked smile. "You missed a spot," she brazenly told him as she held the soapy, plastic foam over her body.

He stared at her hard. "Where?"

Without saying a word, she let the sponge gradually travel over both of her breasts before moving down to her crotch. His hot, passion-filled eyes grew even bigger as he watched her hand use the sponge to rub languorously back and forth between her legs. Bill couldn't tear his eyes away. What she was doing to herself was so hot that Bill was on the verge of losing it again.

"No fair, Christina," Bill gasped. "That's not part of the rules."

"I only said you couldn't touch me. I never said I couldn't touch myself," she teased him in a saucy manner.

"God…I'll never last if you keep this up. You're torturing me, you know that?" he pleaded.

"Maybe that's the whole point?" she returned with a vixen's smile.

He gave her a lopsided smile back, "You are a wicked, wicked woman, Mrs. Havenwood."

"Baby, you ain't seen nothing yet," she tartly replied.

Christina removed the sponge from between her legs and taking the bar of soap, soaped it up even more. She then dropped to her knees in front of him and began to leisurely lather up his powerful legs, making sure her soft, pouty lips were mere inches away from the head of his erect penis. Her eyes looked up at him then and gave him a taunting smile.

Teasing him even more, her tongue darted out. It was so close to him—so close, only an inch away—yet she didn't touch him. Bill groaned out loud and his breathing became raspy.

"Christina… I can't take much more," he choked out.

"You will," she confidently announced.

She rose slowly from her kneeling position and let the sponge travel from his leg, around his rigid arousal, up his flat stomach and to his strong chest. Bill's burning eyes were glued to every sensuous move she was making—and he was on the point of losing his control.

Christina then wrapped both her arms around him without touching him. Carefully keeping space between their chests and making sure the front of her body was almost touching his hard erection but not quite, she squeezed the sponge onto his back, letting the soap drizzle down his hard, muscled cheeks.

"Does that feel good?" she innocently asked him, as she watched his aroused reaction flicker across his taut face.

She was driving him crazy with her teasing and taunting—and he couldn't take anymore. Within a millisecond, he had lost it completely and groaned in capitulation.

"To hell with your game," he whispered hoarsely.

Bill swiftly bridged the space between them and pulled her into his arms. He began to kiss her with a deliberate softness and tenderness that surprised Christina. She opened her mouth to him as she dropped the sponge behind his back and wrapped her hands onto his heated skin.

In response, he let his tongue plunge into her mouth and began to dart it in and out, silently telling her that his body was ready to do the same thing to hers. Christina moaned with pleasure.

His hands moved over her wet, slippery curves; and hers tangled themselves into his damp hair. The shower spray was still falling on their overheated bodies and it had been running so long that suddenly, it began to turn cold. Christina and Bill's lips yanked apart as they gasped with the change in temperature on their skin. They laughed and Bill reached over and turned the faucets off.

"Wait until my father goes and takes his shower. All the bedrooms are on the same water tank," Bill cracked.

Christina burst out laughing at the thought of William having to take an unexpected cold shower. "Hope he checks the temperature before he jumps in," she replied.

"Hope he doesn't," Bill retorted with an evil gleam in his eyes and Christina laughed again.

Bill kissed her quickly then pulled away. He gazed in her face. "You are so beautiful." His words came out in a rush. "And I'm the luckiest son-of-a-bitch to have you in my life."

Christina reached up and planted a soft kiss back on his lips before pulling away herself. "I love you, Bill Havenwood and I'm so proud of you," she announced.

Bill was taken aback. "Proud of me? For what?"

It was time to get serious and Christina wanted him to believe every word she was about to say. She lovingly reached up and caressed his cheek.

"I'm proud how you've handled your sobriety. And I'm proud how you've been trying to turn your life around. And I'm proud how you've been standing up to your father. And I'm proud for the good man that you are... deep down in your heart..." she traced his heart with her finger on his chest. She looked back up at his intent eyes. "And I'm proud to be your wife in two weeks time. It'll be an honor."

"Nobody's ever been proud of me before, Christina," he admitted sheepishly, still surprised at her words.

"That's because they don't see what I see and they don't know what I know."

"And what do you know?"

A little voice inside Christina urged her to tell him everything—tell him now. Tell him who you really are—the girl from high school. Tell him what you did, how you spied on him, what you had planned for him, tell him that you know about his involvement with GME—tell him everything now. He'll forgive you, if you confess now. Just tell him.

But Christina lost her nerve and she didn't tell him. Maybe, she'd tell him tomorrow, she reasoned—maybe. She looked up and he was still waiting for her answer.

"I know that I love you very much, and I desperately need you in my life."

He wrapped his arms tightly around her naked body and crushed her to him. "My god, Christina, don't ever leave me!" he exclaimed. "I love you so much too."

"I won't leave you; ever!" she muffled into his shoulder. "I promise." She hugged him back just as tightly.

Christina could feel her lashes getting damp with her tears. She could feel his soul in torment and she wanted to cry for him. She wanted to cry—for the man she had once hated!

She had been so wrong to have judged him and his past actions so harshly. Now that she understood him better, she had come to love him—and she would love him forever, no matter what.

He felt her shiver and mistakenly thought she was getting cold. He planted a swift kiss on the top of her head and reached out past the shower door to grab a fluffy towel.

"Let's get you dried off. I don't want you catching a cold before the wedding," he said as he started to rub her down.

"No, I don't suppose I'd look too attractive in our wedding pictures with a red nose and sniffles."

Bill carefully wrapped the big towel around her. "You'd look attractive to me, red nose and all, no matter what."

Christina beamed. It was what every woman wanted to hear. "You're not so bad yourself. In fact, you have the best shoulders of any man I've ever seen."

"Really?" he replied. "Even better than your boyfriend's?" Bill just had to know. Was it over between her and the lout? Has she given him his walking papers?

Christina reasoned that she'd better come clean about that at least. She could see the jealousy beginning to pool on Bill's face as she turned innocent eyes up at him.

"Which boyfriend are you talking about?"

"How the hell many are there?" He angrily retorted, still unsure of her love for him.

"I don't have a boyfriend."

"So you've broken it off?"

"No."

Bill was confused. "Then what are you saying?"

"You said that you haven't been seeing Stephie from even before we met."

"That's right."

"Well, I haven't been seeing anyone either the whole time I've known you."

"What?" The word came out in an unbelievable gasp. "But... you said you had a boyfriend."

"No... you said I had a boyfriend. I just didn't tell you I

didn't," Christina coyly added then waited for the explosion she knew was coming.

She didn't have to wait long.

"Why, you little hellcat! You let me believe you were sleeping with someone else? Do you know what it did to me to imagine you in the arms of some other man? Of you being with him, kissing him, making love to him? I was going out-of-my-mind with jealousy."

"I know exactly what that feels like, only I knew her name and her face," Christina launched back.

Bill wanted to say more but he held his tongue. "Everything I told you about her was the truth."

"I know that… now. And I believe you."

Looking down at her, enveloped in that big fluffy towel with her wet hair slicked back she looked like a sweet, innocent, little girl. And he couldn't stay mad at her. He hadn't exactly been a choirboy himself during their relationship. After all, he had forced her to participate in his scheme to fool his father, hadn't he?

With a wicked glint in his eyes, he suddenly scooped her up in his strong arms and stepped out of the shower stall.

"Oh no, you're not going to throw me in the pool again?" Christina shot out.

He walked with her in his arms, into his bedroom. "No. I have a different kind of punishment in mind for bad girls like you," he replied, before dropping her unceremoniously on his bed.

Christina saw he was half smiling and he wasn't angry with her anymore. Her mood instantly lightened. "It's not the handcuffs, is it?" she giggled.

"Good idea but no," he said before heading back to the bathroom. "I'll be right back."

He disappeared from view for a couple of seconds before reappearing. He had with him a box of condoms and he slapped them down on the bedside table. "This time, I'm prepared."

Christina looked at the box and quirked an eyebrow at him, "That's ambitious; a whole box?"

"With you, I think I'm going to need them all," he announced as he proudly stood naked at the foot of the bed, looking down on her, still wrapped in that oversized towel.

"So, what's my punishment going to be?" she prodded him with her foot, giving him a challenging look.

"This," he said, then grabbed each of her ankles and suddenly dragged her to the foot of the bed where he was standing. Christina screamed with laughter as her towel twisted off.

He had such a wicked gleam in his eyes and Christina was already hot for whatever he was planning. She tried squirming out of his grip but he was holding on tight. She could feel the heat and strength emanating from his steely fingers.

"You're not getting away so easily, Miss Christina," he threatened. "You're going to take your licks… and like it."

"What do you mean… my licks?" she questioned.

"I mean that I'm hungry and I'm going to eat you up," he announced, as he yanked her forward even more so that her derriere was resting on the edge of the bed. Christina squealed again and he parted her legs.

"If this is a punishment, then what's a reward?" Christina saucily threw at him, still giggling.

"You'll have to wait to find that one out. In the meantime, I've been fantasizing about doing this to you for weeks."

He went down on bended knee in front of her and parting her thighs even more, lowered his head between her legs. At the instant his hot mouth touched her delicate parts, Christina let out a gasp and threw her head back. What he was doing to her felt so good and her mind could focus on nothing else but the exquisite pleasure he was giving her.

And he was doing it all ever so slowly and expertly.

Every lick and flick was tattooing itself on her brain, and when she felt his hot, wet tongue dip inside her, she lost it.

Christina began to moan and she couldn't stop. Wow, he really was good at—farming! Those college credits had been well earned.

Christina arched her back against him and she could feel herself on the verge of exploding. Her breathing quickened and she suddenly felt herself reach the point of no return.

She came in his mouth and she spasmed against him.

Returning back to reality, she looked down at him. He had lifted his head and was studying her with a smoldering expression. He came up to her face then and she saw his mouth was wet with her juices.

"Kiss me and taste yourself," he ordered.

And with another low moan, Christina did just that. She just couldn't get enough of him—and he couldn't get enough of her.

For the rest of the night, they made love and when they were finished, he wrapped his arms around her and they spooned together, falling asleep in that position. His body was telling her that now that he had found her, he wasn't letting her go.

And he held her tight to him even in his deepest sleep.

CHAPTER 58

THE NEXT MORNING, Christina awoke first. She was still being held tightly in his arms and she had her back to him. She turned her head to get a good look at his sleeping face. He looked so rested and peaceful—and happy.

Christina bit her lip nervously and turned her head away. Her little voice was nagging her again to tell him everything now. Confess it all—this morning—in this bed—with his strong arms wrapped around her. Tell him who you are and what you did. He'll forgive you and you can move forward, and you can marry him with total honesty between the two of you. No more lies. No more games. No more deceptions. Clean the slate. He'll understand—but you have to tell him now.

Christina was so scared.

Last night had been amazing and wonderful and perfect. They had loved each other in body and soul, and she didn't want the memory of that to be marred in any way. This had been their first night together—and maybe—this morning was not a good time to spill secrets. They should get to know each other first, spend more time together as a couple, make love more—and then the right moment would present itself and she would tell him everything then. She'd definitely tell him everything before the wedding—or maybe after the wedding. He might be mad but he'd forgive her, wouldn't he?

But the little voice kept droning on in Christina's mind. The moment is now, it said. Tell him now and he'll forgive you.

A deep frown crossed Christina's brow and she bit her lip even more at her undecided thoughts.

Bill had been intently studying her worried face for the past minute. He had awoken a few minutes before and for a split second, before he'd opened his eyes, he'd thought that last night had all been a dream—that they hadn't made love, or told each other how they felt—that she still hated him.

But then he'd felt her warm, soft, naked body wrapped in his arms and knew it had been real. He'd opened his eyes then, ready to tell her how much he loved her when he'd seen the sour, worried expression on her beautiful face. She was staring up at the ceiling, biting her lip and clearly distressed about something.

Bill felt as if someone had punched him in the stomach. Was she regretting last night? Did it seem a mistake in the morning when everything came back down to reality? Did she maybe not love him after all? Had she changed her mind about that— about him? Maybe she wanted her freedom and didn't want to marry him? Maybe—? The 'maybes' swirled in his brain until he couldn't stand it anymore.

"What are you thinking about?" he whispered, desperate to know her thoughts.

He felt her flinch in his arms, obviously surprised at having been caught out; and Bill didn't like that response one bit. It boded ill for him.

She turned to him and smiled—that beautiful, sweet smile of hers that melted his heart every time he saw it.

"I was thinking about that large food stain we made on the rug last night. Do you think it's going to come out?" she laughed.

It wasn't what she had been thinking about—and Bill knew it. "Are you sure that's all you were thinking about?" Bill asked, now scared out of his wits to know the answer; and his arms tightened around her even more.

Christina anxiously looked at him. 'Tell him' her little voice was now screaming in her head, 'tell him everything—he'll understand and he'll forgive you.'

"I was thinking about… how much I love you… and what I'd do if I ever lost you."

Christina had chickened out. She couldn't tell him today, she just couldn't. Maybe she'd tell him tomorrow. The right moment would present itself and she would know. She'd tell him everything then but not today, not right now.

What Christina didn't know was that today—right now—had been the right moment and she had let it slip away forever. There would never be another right moment again.

At her words of love, Bill breathed a huge sigh of relief. "You're not going to lose me, Christina. I love you and nothing's going to change that. What I said to you last night, and what we did together, that was the truth…and in a couple of week's, we're going to be married and nothing and no one is going to come between us, I promise you."

Christina turned around in his arms then so that she was facing him and smiled, relieved at not having had to tell him about her duplicity.

"Got time for a quickie?" she winked at him.

Bill laughed, relieved that she still loved him. "You are insatiable," he exclaimed.

Christina grabbed a lock of his hair and started to play with it. "But you're so good at it, babe, that you're addictive."

"Well, I do have to get to the office early this morning since I've got an appointment with my old man… actually it's more of a summons really… but…" He let the word linger… "I think I could squeeze you in."

"Squeeze all you like," Christina giggled, as he reached for her again.

*

It was still early morning and Christina had gone back to her own bedroom after Bill had left for the office. The morning had been wonderful. They had made mad, passionate love again and then Christina had helped Bill pick out his suit and get ready for the office even to the point of knotting his tie for him.

He'd given her a deep kiss before he'd left—wanting to make

sure she remembered how much he loved her and he'd told her again how much 'in love' he was with her. Nothing—and no one was going to come between them—ever—she could bank on that, he'd said.

After he'd left, Christina went back to her own bedroom and telephoned Jenny. Her friend was still at home and hadn't left for work yet.

On hearing Christina's voice at that time of morning, Jenny was immediately worried. "Chrissy, is something wrong?" Jenny instantly asked.

"No, Jenny; everything's right for a change," Christina dreamily announced. "He told me he loves me and wants to marry me for real."

"Really? And did you tell him how you feel?"

"Yes. I told him I love him too and we spent all night making love," Christina sighed. She still couldn't believe how well things had turned out for her.

"And is he hot in bed?" Jenny squeaked out.

"Raging inferno hot! Remember all those stories we used to hear in school about how good he was?"

"Yeah…"

"He's even better."

Jenny giggled. "Oh Chrissy, I'm so happy for you. You do really love him, don't you? Truly?"

"Yes, I do, with all my heart. He's not the same person he was back then and I've come to know him better and I'm crazy about him. And he loves me too."

"This is fantastic! I had a feeling you two would end up together. Too much karma between you and all. And I suspected you always had a crush on him in high school even though you'd never admitted it to me."

Christina laughed. "You know me better than I know myself! I always did think he was kind of cute back then, even if he was a big, drunken rat."

Jenny laughed too. "And what did he say when you told him

about what happened back then between you two? And about your little plan to get even with him?" There was silence on the other end of the phone, as Christina kept quiet. "Chrissy…?"

"What?"

"What did he say?"

Christina remained silent again.

"Chrissy… I'm getting a bad vibe here."

"What vibe?" Christina was evasive.

"Christina Matteo, you didn't tell him, did you?"

Christina's response was slow in coming out. "Nooooo… not exactly."

"Oh, Chrissy!" Jenny let out an exasperated sigh.

"I'll tell him everything, I will."

"When?"

"Soon. Before the wedding. I will. I just couldn't tell him today. He was so happy… and this was our first night together and I want him to get to know me better first."

"Chrissy, tell him now. Today. Don't wait. Please."

"I will tell him… soon. I promise. I know what I'm doing, Jenny. Trust me."

Jenny let out another sigh. "Okay, it's your life. But make sure you tell him. Don't wait!"

"I will, I promise." Christina quickly changed the subject. "Jenny, could you do me a favor? Could you just go in and make sure everything's okay at my apartment? I don't think I'll be coming back there for a while. Just keep an eye on things?"

"Sure, no problem; and Chrissy, I really am happy for you! But tell him soon. I want to meet the rat bastard again and be a real maid of honor at your wedding and I can't do that until he knows the truth."

Christina laughed again. "I promise you, Jenny. I'll take care of everything before the wedding."

After she hung up, Jenny shook her head. She had a bad feeling about this and her 'feelings' seemed to be right lately.

Chrissy should have told him everything right away. The

longer she waited, the angrier he might be when he did eventually find out what she had really been up to. Jenny had learnt from her own ill-fated marriage that mistrust and lies could kill love faster than even another woman.

Before heading off to work, Jenny let herself into Christina's apartment. She took a quick look around.

Everything seemed to be in order. As she made her way to the kitchen, Jenny spotted the manila envelope addressed to William that Christina had unintentionally left propped up against a drinking glass on the table.

It was the 'blackmail' envelope that Christina had prepared for William with the pictures of Bill associating with the GME group. It also contained her pasted note with the message, 'Every Caesar has a Brutus – Look to the Son', clearly spelling out Bill's betrayal of his father.

Thinking it was just outgoing mail that Christina had left for her to post, Jenny grabbed it and dropped it into a mailbox on her way to work.

*

Bill walked into his father's office. William was already sitting behind his desk, controlling his business empire. He looked up when he heard his son walk in.

"You're on time for a change," he quipped, in his British accent.

"You barked, I crawled," Bill smirked.

"Still the wise ass? Something you got from your mother, no doubt."

"Oh, I don't know, dad. You can be quite the wise ass yourself."

William shot him a dirty look but didn't respond to the crack. Instead, he reached for a legal document in front of him and handed it to his son. "Here."

Taking it, Bill looked at the paper. "What's this?"

"Your pre-nuptial agreement, for Christina to sign."

"What?" Astounded, Bill gasped.

"It's very generous, I assure you. In case of a divorce, she'll get a lump sum of two million dollars plus one million for every year you two are married."

Bill's blood pressure shot up. "How dare you draw up this piece of crap!"

"Of course, I dare. It's my money and one day it'll all be yours, and your children's. We have to protect ourselves."

"You can keep your damn money. I never asked for it."

"No but you've got it anyway; and I want you and I protected. You never know how these things work out. We have to be sensible."

"I will not ask Christina to sign a pre-nup. Whatever's mine is hers and that's final." Bill was adamant and he wasn't budging.

"Oh, don't be daft. Everybody in our circle does this. She'll understand."

"My answer is no," Bill forcefully shouted, as he ripped the pre-nup in half. "I love her and she loves me. I'm going to share everything with her. That's what love means. And you can take this damn agreement and shove it up your rich, billionaire ass." Bill threw the torn pieces down on his dad's desk.

"Watch how you bloody hell speak to me. I'm still your father!" Angry, William shot out of his chair.

"Well, start acting like it then," Bill shouted back, before stalking out.

As the door slammed behind him, a stunned William plopped down in his chair.

"My god, he really loves her! The boy really loves her!" he mumbled to himself.

He suddenly broke out into a wide smile. Not only had his plan to get those two married off worked but his son was truly in love with the girl. And maybe she felt the same way about him? And if that was the case, he, William, had a shot at getting those grandbabies he desperately wanted. Well, well, well, his schemes had worked once again. What a clever genius he was!

And as for the pre-nup? Well, he, William, controlled all the purse strings anyway and he could get around all that in his will, so that really wasn't a problem. So, his son was in love with the girl for real? It was about bloody time. He wickedly smiled to himself, proud of the part he'd played in forcing those two stubborn kids together.

CHAPTER 59

LATER THAT DAY, William was in his office going over some figures when Charlotte, his secretary, buzzed him on the speakerphone.

"Excuse me, sir? Mrs. Havenwood is here to see you," she announced.

Maddie was here? What the bloody hell did she want, William thought?

"Tell the bitch to wait," he decreed.

In the outer office, Charlotte sheepishly looked at Maddie who had clearly heard everything. "I'm sorry, Mrs. Havenwood," Charlotte was very embarrassed.

"Don't apologize for his rude behavior, Charlotte. You deserve a medal of honor for having had to put up with that man all these years; and I deserve two for having had to sleep with him," Maddie tartly replied.

Charlotte giggled.

Inside the office, William was donning his jacket, straightening his tie and making sure every strand of his hair was neatly slicked back into his ponytail. He instinctively wanted to look good for the blasted, damn woman.

He pressed the button on his speakerphone and commanded, "Charlotte, please tell Mrs. Havenwood she can fly in on her broomstick now."

Outside, Maddie made a face at the disembodied voice coming out of the phone on Charlotte's desk. Ooooo… that man was so insufferable!

Holding her head high, Maddie proudly walked into William's

office. He was standing behind his emperor's desk, with hands clasped behind his back, Napoleon-style.

Maddie gave him a dirty look. "Where shall I park my broom, William? Up your ass?"

William had to laugh at that. Maddie Havenwood was the only woman on the entire planet who could dish it out to him and that he would take it from.

"Maddie, Maddie, Maddie, let's not be mean to each other. It'll only prolong the agony of having to be in each other's presence. Just tell me why you're here and then get the hell out."

"Now there's the Havenwood charm I fell in love with. Just hearing your wonderful witty remarks makes me want to stick a fork in your eye."

"But my beloved, don't you remember? You already tried that in our fifth year of marriage? You really should get some new material."

"Well, how about this, you start treating our boy right or else I'll put a voodoo curse on you that'll make your head spin exorcist-style." Maddie smiled but her eyes were deadly serious.

"That's a new one. Something you picked up on your hippy dippy, freak-parade commune?" William threw back.

Inwardly, Maddie was livid. The man was just impossible! She walked deeper into the office and approached him. "Listen to me, you old goat! I've come here today to give you a few home truths about our son that you're too obtuse to figure out on your own."

"There's nothing that you know that I don't already know so you can get back on your broom and fly out of here."

Maddie ignored him. "Home truth number one, that boy loves you. I don't know why but he does. Home truth number two, he also happens to love Christina very much. He can't wait to marry her and start a life together."

"Is that all? I already knew that, so you see, your visit here has been a colossal waste of my time."

"Home truth number three. Our son has been in Alcoholics Anonymous for over a year. He's clean and sober, and recovering."

William was shocked. "What? That's impossible!"

"It's the truth. When did you last see him have a drink?"

"Why... I saw him..." William racked his brain. When had he seen Bill drink alcohol? "The toast... at his engagement party."

"I was there, William and I didn't see him drink. I saw him kiss Christina while everyone else was drinking but he didn't drink the champagne."

William was stunned. That was right. Bill hadn't had a sip.

He, suddenly, snapped his fingers at his ex-wife. "He had some the night he and Christina announced their engagement to me... at dinner back at the house."

"Did you see him actually drink it, William, actually see him with your own two eyes?" William's fevered brain went over that night's events. No, he hadn't. He stared at Maddie and remained silent. "Exactly," Maddie declared. "He's been sober for over a year and he's been trying to change his ways."

For the first time, William was speechless. "But...but... why didn't he tell me?"

Maddie's eyes narrowed. "Because he's got this crazy idea that a father should maybe care enough to notice these things about a son without having to be told. But I know differently where you're concerned. I don't have that kind of faith in you that he seems to have. So, that's why I'm here today to tell you to your face."

William was angry that his ex-wife knew something that he hadn't known. "He should have told me himself," he shouted.

"He's your son and his thick skull can be just as hard-headed as yours."

"He's... sober?" He unbelievably shook his head.

William was still so amazed at this revelation that the fire suddenly seemed to go out of him. He plopped down in his chair. His son had given up drinking and he had been sober for over a year? It was almost too incredible to believe. After all, how many times had he and Maddie put him in one rehab clinic or another when he was growing up, praying that each time would be the time he would finally give up his addictions?

Maddie could see how shocked her ex-husband was and she was satisfied. It was good to see the great William Havenwood come down a peg. A little humility was good for the soul.

"And another thing, William. Don't even think about telling Bill that I told you this. He's told me many times that I wasn't to tell you and I don't want him finding out from you or anyone that I broke my word. Sometimes a mother has to do these things for the good of her children but that doesn't mean I want him to know."

William was still in a state of shock. "No… I won't tell him."

"Good. Now I'll just remove my broomstick from your ass and I'll fly out of your hair."

Maddie turned and was about to leave when William called her back. "Maddie?" She turned to him again. "I want to give a dinner next week, a few days before the wedding for the family, including Christina's parents. Will you come?"

Maddie didn't respond as she was slightly taken aback at having William invite her to anything. He continued, "I mean, I'm only asking you for Bill and Christina's sake, of course."

"Of course," Maddie agreed. "I'll be there."

"I'll have Charlotte call you with the details."

"See you then, William." Maddie walked out.

Still deep in thought, William didn't notice his ex-wife leaving. He was thinking about his son and the fact that he was now sober! He broke out in a big grin. How fantastic was that!

*

William barged into Bill's office.

"Dad?" Surprised, Bill rose from his desk chair. What did his father want? He never came to Bill's office.

"Son, I just want to say that you're getting married now and starting a new chapter of your life… and… you've picked a wonderful girl to be your wife. I adore Christina and you'll be starting a family soon and…" William stopped his awkward speech.

Bill prodded him, "And…?"

William stared at his son. "And… I'm proud of you." Suddenly, William approached his son and hugged him. Releasing him quickly, he added, "That's all I came to say."

He then, promptly, left the office.

Bill was floored. What had that been all about? And his father had said he was proud of him? He'd never said that before! In fact, that was the second time in Bill's entire life someone had ever said those words to him, the first being Christina last night. Amazed, Bill shook his head. Was there something in the drinking water?

CHAPTER 60

THE NEXT WEEK was the happiest week Christina had ever experienced in her life.

She and Bill spent a lot of time together, laughing and talking, and making love like rabbits. They went out. They stayed in. They were inseparable. During the day they couldn't keep their hands off of each other and the nights were steamy as well.

They were in love and they wanted everyone to know it.

The whole house noticed the change in their relationship, and the love they generated was contagious among the staff.

Everyone was in a good mood and excited about the upcoming nuptials. A cleansing breath of fresh air had swept through the huge, stale Havenwood house and it signaled new beginnings.

The only wrinkle in Christina's week of happiness was her nagging little voice that told her she should have told Bill about her revenge plan days ago.

Each day, she would decide that today was the day she would tell him. But then something always happened to thwart her plan—and he seemed so happy—and the right moment never came—and she would lose her courage.

She'd tell him before the wedding, though.

Maybe…

*

During Christina and Bill's week of bliss, another person also experienced her own brand of joy. Stephanie Hartwell was called into her detective agency for a meeting.

"Miss Hartwell, this is for you," Drummond Sinclair said, as he handed her a black writing journal.

Stephanie took the book and flipped it open. It was indeed a journaling book written in longhand. As she turned several of the pages, her eyes, instantly, zeroed in on Bill's name written in some of the paragraphs.

She looked up at Drummond's smug face. "What is this?"

"It's Christina Matteo's personal journal written in her own handwriting, with her thoughts, feelings, ideas… and plans for your ex-boyfriend, all clearly spelled out."

Stephanie was shocked. "My God, where did you get this?"

Drummond laughed, "If I tell you, I'll have to kill you."

Stone-faced, Stephanie didn't laugh at his pathetic joke.

Embarrassed, he cleared his throat and turned serious. "Let's just say, we liberated it from her apartment."

"You broke into her place and stole it?"

"If you really want to know the details, then you could be an accessory to the fact."

Stephanie quirked a snooty eyebrow at him. "I don't care how you got it, Mr. Sinclair and I'm not really interested in the details either. I've paid you enough."

"In that case…" he handed her an invoice from his desk, "… the rest of your bill."

She gave him an evil smile as she snatched it, and then triumphantly flipped through the book again.

CHAPTER 61

THE WEDDING WAS five days away—and tonight was the night of the in-law dinner at the Havenwood mansion. The dinner menu had been prepared and the dining room had been elegantly set with the best china and silver serving pieces. The house staff had worked long and hard to make this night special for the happy couple.

Christina's parents, Gabriella and Nunzio, had been invited as had Maddie. They were to be joined by Christina, Bill and William. It was to be a private dinner, for family only—a chance for everyone to get know each other better before the wedding.

Christina had dressed in an elegant, cream-colored sleeveless long gown that emphasized her sexy, curvy body. Her hair was up and her makeup was perfect, and she looked every inch the happy, beautiful bride-to-be.

She was wearing the diamond necklace Bill had given her along with her diamond engagement ring and one karat diamond stud earrings, which her sweetie had surprised her with earlier in the week.

Christina looked old money chic, perfectly suited to her new position as lady of the manor and wife to one of the richest men in the country.

It was almost 7 p.m. and dinner was to be served at 8 p.m. sharp. Oddly, both William and Bill had still not arrived home from the office, and Christina was left to greet her parents and Maddie by herself.

Gabriella, Nunzio, Maddie and Christina were all sitting in

the salon having pre-dinner drinks. Christina was slightly embarrassed by William and Bill's absence.

"They should be here soon. They're probably delayed at the office. I left messages for both of them," she explained, as she sipped her drink.

Maddie patted her hand. "Don't worry, dear. William probably got tied up in some silly meeting and Bill is probably stuck in traffic. Those two are never on time for anything, believe me, I know."

Christina smiled. Maddie was such a nice person and Christina felt very lucky to have her as a mother-in-law.

Gabriella came to sit beside her daughter on the couch and put a comforting arm around her. "My darling, you're learning the hard way that husbands are undependable and unreliable." She turned to Nunzio who was sitting across the room and gave him a dirty look.

"Hey!" Nunzio retorted. "What are you looking at me for? I was here on time."

Christina chuckled to herself. Her parents had always been like this and they were never going to change.

Suddenly, she frowned. But where were Bill and William? Bill had promised her that he would be here when her parents and his mom arrived—and William should have shown up on time if only not to give Maddie any new ammunition to use against him.

Oh, where were they?

*

Earlier that afternoon, Bill had been in his office when his secretary, Julie came in carrying a gift-wrapped box with a big bow on it.

"This just came for you, sir. It looks like a wedding present," she announced as she placed it on his desk.

"Thanks, Julie," Bill replied and she left.

The box had a gift card on top with his name written on the envelope. He opened it. The only words on the card were

'You're welcome.' That was odd. What did that mean? And who had sent this gift? There was no name anywhere on the card or the box. Bill tore the wrapping off and opened it.

Underneath layers and layers of tissue paper, was a black, hardcover book. Curious, he started flipping its pages. It was a handwritten journal of some kind that—wait! He, suddenly, recognized the handwriting. That was Christina's scrawl. She had written this—but what was this all about? Was this some sort of secret wedding surprise that his sweetie had sent him?

Smiling to himself, Bill sat down at his desk and began to read. But his smile quickly faded as he began to learn the truth—about who Christina Matteo really was—and what she had planned for him. His heart sank as every word he read speared another arrow into his soul. He forced himself to read every single word—and he felt such pain—pain like he'd never felt before.

Everything had been a lie.

Everything!

She had been a lie and her love for him had been a lie.

She had gotten her revenge because she had indeed destroyed him.

And in that moment, after he had turned the last page, Bill felt his whole world collapse around him.

*

William was at his desk engrossed in financial reports when he glanced at his watch. Damn! He was going to be late for the dinner party and that blasted ex-wife of his would definitely lord it over him. Well, a few more minutes wouldn't make much difference.

It was then that he spotted the large manila envelope marked 'Private & Personal' near his telephone. Reaching for it, he ripped it open. Inside, were 8-1/2" x 11" colored photographs, along with a note. The note had cut-out and pasted magazine letters on it and it spelled the words, 'Every Caesar Has His Brutus – Look To The Son.'

Annoyed, William made a face. What the hell was this?

He checked the envelope but there was no return address on it. His intuition went into overdrive. This didn't look right. He scanned the photographs.

Suddenly, he recognized his son who was shaking hands and socializing with a bunch of people whom William didn't know. And then he recognized Bill's friend, Jake but he was in a wheel-chair? What the hell had happened to him? He hadn't seen Jake in over a year and a half since he never came to the house anymore. William placed the pictures under his table lamp and took a closer look.

Suddenly, he gasped. He knew these people. They were those damn GME hippies that had been protesting outside his offices for almost two months now! This slimy, rotten bunch had been responsible for his company's share prices falling but what were Bill and Jake doing fraternizing with them?

William studied the pasted note again.

'Every Caesar Has A Brutus – Look To The Son.'

And, suddenly, he knew! His son—his own flesh and blood—had betrayed him! Bill had stabbed his own father in the back. And not only was he a member of GME but in all probability was financing their operation!

Just look at this rowdy, dirty bunch. They wouldn't have enough money between them to buy a packet of gum let alone finance a clever, well-oiled machine like the Guardians of Mother Earth.

No, his son was behind them and was giving them his, William's hard-earned money—and was also probably giving them insider secrets on the machinations of Fido Foods and Samco Oil. That's how they'd managed to keep one step ahead of William at all times! That's how they'd done it!

It was the first time in William's life he felt like truly crying. But he didn't. His rage put a stop to that.

CHAPTER 62

CHRISTINA, MADDIE, GABRIELLA and Nunzio were all still sitting in the salon having drinks when Bill arrived at half past 7. He walked in and he had Christina's journal tucked under his arm. He smiled for the benefit of his guests but refused to look at Christina.

"Sorry I'm late; the traffic was brutal," he explained, as he walked towards Maddie.

"See, I told you," Maddie directed the comment at Christina before accepting the peck on the cheek from her son.

"Hey, mom," he said. Then he turned to Christina's parents and kissed Gabriella on the cheek and shook Nunzio's hands. "I hope you've been making yourselves at home, Mr. & Mrs. Matteo. Has Christina been taking good care of you?"

He turned to her then and she was smiling at him. His heart skipped a beat. God—she looked beautiful tonight—every inch the Havenwood princess—but she didn't love him. She hated him. Those had been her very written words.

And she was no princess. She was a she-devil bent on revenge and retribution. She had used every tool in her arsenal—her smiles, her words of love, her luscious body, sex—everything she had, to pull off her plan. And he, idiot that he was, had fallen for it—and fallen hard.

And now he was in torment.

Was it only a few hours ago that he had been the happiest he'd ever been in his life? And now, he was devastated. It had all been a lie—an illusion, a sham, a plan to destroy him—and it had destroyed him. This was his lowest point, even lower than when he'd hit rock bottom with his drinking.

He pasted a phony smile for the benefit of his guests as he came towards Christina and gave her a quick kiss on the cheek.

"Sweetheart, you look lovely tonight," he said, before quickly stepping away from her.

"Thank you," Christina replied but her smile, suddenly, slipped as she felt him emotionally pull away. There was something wrong with him tonight. Why hadn't he kissed her on the lips? And why were his eyes looking at her like that, with that frosty glare? Christina was so focused on Bill's face that she didn't even notice the book he was carrying under his arm.

"May I speak to you privately, Christina?" Bill asked, staring at her as if her presence disgusted him.

Worried, Christina put her drink down. "Yes, of course," she replied before turning to her guests and excusing herself.

Bill put his hand under her elbow and steered her out of the room and into William's office.

"Okay, tell me what's wrong," Christina asked, as Bill closed the door. He turned to her then and she almost gasped at the hate she saw reflected in his eyes.

"I read a good book today, a real page turner," Bill sarcastically replied.

He threw the book at her and she quickly caught it. She looked down at the black hardcover in her hands and knew before even opening the pages what it was. It was her journal, the one detailing her revenge plan for Bill Havenwood—and her loathing for him. She was stunned—and scared. Her breathing became shallow as fear coursed through her body.

She looked up at him again and he was looking at her with cold eyes. "Where... where did you get this?" she whispered, barely getting the words out.

"It came to my office today... anonymously; a wedding present."

"But… this… it was in my apartment?" Confused, Christina shook her head.

Bill left out a sarcastic half laugh. "So it is yours? You're admitting it?"

Christina breached the gulf between them and put her hands on his arms. "Bill, just let me explain… this isn't…"

He violently threw her hands off his body. "Don't touch me. You save all that for your next victim."

"Please… you don't know everything…"

"I know enough and what I know disgusts me. It makes me sick to my stomach at what you've done, the lengths you went to, to get your revenge on me. And you make me sick."

"Bill, please, you don't mean that…" Christina pleaded.

"I mean it." Anguish shone in his eyes as he glared at her. "My God, Christina, you had sex with me… for revenge? Why? So that I would feel the pain of losing you when you finally left me, is that it? You prostituted yourself because you hated me that much? What kind of a person are you?"

"No… it's not like that. I love you…"

"Stop it. Just stop the lying," he rasped. "You got what you wanted and it's over. Mission accomplished. The knife is in my gut and you've twisted it beautifully. I'm bleeding and I'm in pain; and I hope you're happy. I hope it was all worth it." The last words sounded shaky as Bill was at the point of losing it but his anger kept him in check.

Christina looked at him. She saw he was hurting—and she saw that he hated her. She looked down at the book still in her hands and her hands started to shake. What could she say to him? It was all true. Everything in the damn book was true—or at least had been true a month ago. Now she loved him but she saw that he wasn't going to believe her. Her spine straightened and she resolved to act with dignity as she looked back up at him.

"All I can say is, I'm sorry; but I do love you and I went to bed with you because I loved you and for no other reason."

He laughed at that. "You're an accomplished liar, Christina. How can I believe anything you ever say to me again?"

"It's the truth."

"The truth? Come on… every word out of your mouth is a lie, not the truth." He laughed again then brazenly looked her up and down. "So you're the girl under the bleachers from high school? You turned out very well, I have to give you that."

"So, you do remember me?"

"Now I do. But I was so drunk back then that I never associated you with her."

Christina stood her ground. "Why did you do what you did to me back then? Why me?"

"Because I was a stupid, drunken, immature kid and I'd caught you staring at me a few times, so we picked you out to pull the prank on." Bill shook his head in disbelief. "Jake and I used to think we were the best at pulling pranks but you Christina… you're the master."

"I'm sorry."

"Save it!" he yelled back.

Bill's anger started to hit the danger zone as he took a few involuntary steps towards her. God, she was so damn beautiful and he still wanted her—and that made him madder.

He grabbed her arm and yanked her to him. "You're so beautiful… and ruthless," he gritted. "It's too bad it's over between us because you would have made a perfect Havenwood." His other hand began to caress her cheek. "No wonder my father liked you so much. He saw himself in you." He then savagely thrust her away from him and Christina stumbled back. "You disgust me."

Christina was breathing rapidly now. "I love you."

"Stop it. Just stop it," Bill shouted. "Just answer me one thing. The day of the car accident… were you really following me?"

Christina lifted her head up. She wasn't going to cower in front of him and she was going to take her punishment proudly. Maybe somehow, she could make him believe that she truly loved him but it all had to start with the truth—and the time was now.

"Yes," she admitted. "I recognized you when I was shooting the GME protesters outside your father's building and I wanted to get back at you for what you did to me in high school. I hated you and so I followed you."

"Was hitting me with your car part of your plan too?"

"No, that was an accident, and the rest, dragging me into your life to help you with your father, that was all you but I used it to my advantage."

"I know you did and how! Clever girl! And were you really going to marry me? Maybe get your hands on some Havenwood cash before destroying me completely?"

"I never wanted your damn money, only…" Christina stopped herself from saying the word.

"Revenge. The word is revenge, Christina and you played it like a maestro." Suddenly, the cool façade evaporated and he put his hands in his hair in anguish. "My God… I loved you… I… loved… you… and now it's all gone."

"Don't say that, please don't say that…" Suddenly, Christina's cool façade also dropped and tears started falling down her cheeks. "I'm sorry. I'm so… sorry. I didn't know who you really were deep down when I started all this. I thought I hated you but… I… I fell in love with you instead and I was wrong… so wrong… to have ever tried to get revenge on you. Please believe that… please…" She went to him then and tried putting her arms around him but he stepped back.

He looked at her and his torment was clearly etched in his eyes. "It's over, Christina. We're over and I never want to see you again in my life."

"Don't say that!" The tears fell faster down Christina's cheeks. "I… love you…"

"And I don't love you. That's finished… and gone… and we're through," Bill choked out the words. They were the most difficult words he'd ever said in his life and they were a lie. He still loved her—madly, crazy, and hopelessly in love with her—but he was so angry with her that he refused to acknowledge those feelings.

"No," Christina didn't want to believe it and she shook her head.

"My love for you is dead… and you're dead to me!"

"No, give me a chance. We can work this out…" Christina made a grab for his arm but he shrugged her off and started to walk to the door.

Suddenly, they both heard William shouting in the foyer. "Where in hell is that traitor!" he yelled at the top of his lungs.

The door of the office was thrown open and William came stalking in.

"You!" he shouted at Bill. "It was all you!" He pointed an accusatory finger at his son.

"What are you talking about?" Bill responded.

"This!" William seethed as he threw Christina's manila envelope with the photos at Bill—as Bill had done earlier with the journal book to Christina.

Bill caught the envelope and Christina, seeing what it was, audibly gasped. Bill turned to her and suddenly knew this was something that had to do with her. He slowly looked down at what was in his hands. It was a brown envelope addressed to William. Bill pulled out the photos and the pasted note. And he knew—he knew this was Christina's handiwork and that it was she that had sent it to his father.

William rounded on his son. "You… my own flesh and blood betrayed me. How could you do this to me? How?" he shouted at the top of his lungs.

Bill looked at the photos and at the note with the pasted letters, and uttered a self-derisive laugh. He turned to Christina then and saw the shock etched on her face.

"Brilliant move, Christina. I'm in awe of you. You've not only twisted the knife in my gut and in my heart, but one last stab and you've finished me off. You've destroyed me completely in every possible way that you could. Bravo."

"Bill… please… that was never supposed to have been mailed

out. Please, you've got to believe me…" Christina was now desperate. How had that gotten into William's hands?

William was shouting at his son again. "What the hell has Christina got to do with your duplicity? You're the one who's betrayed me. You! My own son! Why, damn it, why?"

Bill shouted back. "Because dad, you were destroying the environment and you didn't give a damn about any of it. You'll do anything for profit and that's not right. And somebody had to do something about it. Somebody had to teach you a lesson."

"And that was you?"

"Yes, that was me. What you were doing was wrong and I couldn't stand by and do nothing, not anymore."

"I'm your father. You don't stand against me. Ever!"

"You were never any kind of father to me. And I was always your property, not your son."

"How dare you say that to me, after everything I did for you… everything I gave you… and this is how you repay me?"

Christina came between the two, trying to put a stop to this.

"William, please listen to me, Bill loves you…"

Bill turned to her and yelled, "Christina, stay out this. You've done enough for one night, don't you think?"

"I'm sorry. I'm so sorry… for everything," she whispered at him.

The tears were falling down Christina's cheeks again and Bill felt his heart break for her but he held back. It was over between them and he couldn't ever forgive her—or trust her again.

William was shouting again. "Leave Christina out of this. This is between you and me."

"Yes, dad, you and me…"

"My own son tried to destroy me. How could you? And you did it with my money."

Bill laughed. "I was just washing the blood off of it, dad. Trying to clean up your tricks and lies and deceptions and every other evil you've pulled to make your fucking, damn billions."

"Well, you've lived quite handsomely off of my fucking, damn billions but that's going to stop tonight. I want you gone, out of this house, by the first light of dawn."

Christina interrupted again, "William, please… no…"

"Fine by me," Bill shouted back at his father.

"You're not my son anymore and I never want to see you again," William announced.

Even though Bill knew that was coming, he flinched—but he still stood his ground. "Goodbye, dad," he smirked, as he let Christina's envelope and photos flutter to the floor before stalking out of the room—and out of the house.

"Bill… wait…" Christina called after him but he didn't stop. She frantically turned to William. "William, please listen to me… he loves you… and… and… those pictures… they were a mistake…. and…"

"Christina, no. I don't want to talk about this anymore," William decreed as he, too, left the room.

Christina stared at the journal book in her hands, and then slowly picked up the envelope and photos off the floor. Bill was never going to forgive her and she had successfully gotten her revenge on him. His life was destroyed. He had lost his belief in her love for him, had lost his father, the money, his position as a Havenwood—he had lost it all! He was ruined.

And she? The love of her life was gone and he didn't want to have anything to do with her ever again. She had successfully destroyed that too. Devastated, Christina ran sobbing from the room and up the massive staircase on the way to her bedroom.

"Christina, what's going on?" Maddie shouted up at her, as she and Gabriella and Nunzio came running out of the salon at all of the commotion they'd heard.

Crying, Christina just kept running.

CHAPTER 63

SOBBING HER HEART out, Christina flung her bedroom door open, launched her journal and the photos in a corner of the room, and threw herself on the bed. She was inconsolable and it was all her fault. Her hunger for revenge against a fellow human being had destroyed him—and had destroyed her.

Gabriella and Maddie quickly came rushing in.

"Christina, my God, what's happening?" Gabriella said, as she ran to the bed and put a comforting arm on her daughter's shoulders.

Christina turned around and hugged her mother, burying her wet face into Gabriella's shoulder. She was still crying uncontrollably.

"Oh, mommy…" she wailed. "I… I did something… bad… and Bill… will never forgive me. He…he… said it's over… and… and… it's my fault, it's all my fault." She could barely get the words out between her sobs.

"Shhhhh…." Her mom hugged her tight and tried to calm her down as she gently rocked her back and forth. "Don't worry, sweetheart, he doesn't mean it. All couples go through things like this."

Christina shook her head back and forth as the tears continued to stream down her red cheeks. "No… you don't understand. I… I… did something… and it's over between us. It's over."

"What did you do?"

"No, mommy… I… I… can't tell you. I… just can't… Don't make me… please." She choked out the last word as a desperate plea.

A worried look passed between Gabriella and Maddie.

Maddie then silently shook her head as if to say 'I have no idea what this is about.'

She spoke up as she came to sit beside them on the bed. "Christina, darling, Bill will cool down and then you'll be able to work this out. He loves you; you've got to believe that."

Christina shook her head again as she raised herself away from her mom's shoulder to look at Maddie. Her eyes were red and her face was swollen, and tears were still falling.

"No, Maddie… you said it yourself… love is not enough when people do mean things to each other and forgiveness is not an option."

"Forgiveness is always an option, especially where there's love."

"No, not when love is dead." She paused and took in a steadying breath. "It's over. We're over. Bill can't forgive me and I don't blame him because I can't forgive myself."

Christina took a quick look around her large opulent bedroom. "And this isn't my home anymore." She turned her red swollen eyes to her mom. "Mommy, please. I… want to go home… to my home… tonight. I want to leave here tonight."

Maddie piped in. "Christina, no! This is your home. Bill will come back and you'll see. Things will look better in the morning but you've got to stay. You've got to be here for him."

Christina shook her head again. "No, Maddie; you don't understand… and I'm sorry I can't explain it to you. Please don't make me."

"Of course not, darling." Maddie put a comforting arm around Christina. "You don't have to tell us anything, if you don't want to. But please, reconsider your decision to leave. Please."

"I can't." Christina's tears stopped falling as she now had a mission to accomplish—to get the hell out of here before she really fell apart. She turned back to her mom, and then noticed her dad, Nunzio, impotently standing in the open doorway. "Please, help me leave here. Take me away tonight. Please, I'm begging you."

Gabriella hugged her daughter again. "Of course, sweetheart. Whatever you want, we'll help you."

Another very worried look passed between the two mothers over the top of Christina's head.

"If that's what you want, Christina, I'll help you too," Maddie added, as she stroked Christina's back.

Christina pulled away from her mother's arms and wiped the tears off of her face with the back of her hand. "It is. It's what I want. Thank you."

And for the next hour, Gabriella and Maddie helped Christina pack her things. It had been decided that her parents were going to drive her back to her own apartment in the city.

When she was ready to go, Christina approached Maddie with all of the diamond jewelry that Bill had given her.

"Maddie, I need you to do me a favor." She handed the luxurious boxes to Bill's mom. "I need you to give all of this back to Bill. It's a diamond necklace he gave me and a pin and earrings and both my engagement ring and my wedding ring."

"Christina, no! You keep this. This is yours. He bought it for you," Maddie countered.

Christina was adamant as she shook her head. "No, it's not right. He bought it for the woman he loved and I'm not that woman anymore. Please… just do this for me, I'm begging you."

Maddie reluctantly took the items. "Of course, I will."

Christina smiled, "Thank you." She hugged Maddie tightly. "I'm so sorry we're not going to be family anymore. I would have loved having you as a mother-in-law."

"Oh Christina…" Maddie was on the verge of tears herself. "Don't give up on him… please, please don't. He'll come around. He loves you so much."

But Christina knew better—she knew what she'd done—and she knew there was no hope for her and Bill ever again.

"I'm sorry, Maddie; I'm sorry for everything." She kissed the other woman on the cheek and hugged her tightly one more time.

And with one last look around the bedroom where she'd

spent so many happy, delirious, loving moments with Bill—where they'd laughed and talked and sparred and made love for hours—Christina walked out.

It was indeed over—and she had no one to blame but herself.

*

That night, Christina's parents drove her into the city and helped her get settled back into her own apartment. After her things had been put away, Christina put on a brave face and convinced her parents that she was going to be all right. She told them to go back to their hotel because she needed some time to be alone and get some sleep.

Gabriella and Nunzio were not happy about her decision to be alone that night but their daughter was a grown woman with a stubborn mind of her own and there was little they could do to dissuade her of the idea. Reluctantly, they both agreed but Gabriella said that they would be back bright and early the following morning and they would brook no opposition to that plan. Christina smiled for their benefit and insisted that all she needed was a goodnight's sleep and she'd feel better in the morning.

As her apartment door closed when her parents left, Christina's brave façade dropped and the tears started falling again. And she sobbed her heart out all night long—for what she'd done to him—and for what she'd done to herself.

CHAPTER 64

THE NEXT MORNING, her parents did indeed arrive at the crack of dawn and stayed with her all day. She put up another brave front for them and managed to convince them that she was fine.

By 6 p.m. that night, they had left due to her insistence that she wanted some quiet time again. Christina then called the only person in the world that could truly understand what had happened. She telephoned her friend, Jenny who had just come home from work—and told her everything.

When Jenny heard about the manila envelope to William, she gasped and apologized profusely to her friend. She explained that it had been she who had mailed it out but she had thought Christina had left it for her to do just that.

Christina instantly told Jenny not to worry over that. It had been Christina's mistake and what was done, was done.

Worried about her friend, Jenny insisted that Christina come to her apartment and she'd fix something for all of them to eat.

When the door was opened to Christina, Jenny flung her arms around her friend and hugged her tight.

"Chrissy, I'm so sorry," she said, as she pulled her friend inside.

"You were right, Jenny. I should have told him everything right away. Maybe he could have forgiven me then." The tears had stopped now and they had been replaced by a deep, dark depression. Christina had never felt so hopeless in all her life.

Jenny steered her friend to the living room couch and made her sit down.

"But are you sure it's really over? I mean, he loved you, Chrissy and that type of love just doesn't go away like that."

"No," Christina shook her head. "He said I was dead to him and that I'd killed his love for me… and that he never wanted to see me again in his life."

"But, we all say things in the heat of the moment that we don't mean. Have you tried talking to him again? Maybe… now that he's had a chance to calm down, he feels differently about everything."

"I don't even know where he is. His father threw him out and I can't ask William."

"Did you try his cell phone?"

Christina nodded 'yes'. "Several times but it's off."

"So call the house. Maybe he and his father have patched things up?"

"I… don't know," Christina was confused and didn't know what to do anymore.

"Well, think about it. Don't just give up on him," Jenny insisted.

Christina gave her friend a long look. "I was wrong to go after him like I did, Jenny. You told me not to but I wouldn't listen and now, I'm paying for it." She paused as she gave her friend another long, speaking look. "I loved him. I really and truly loved him."

Suddenly, the tears started falling down her cheeks again.

"Oh, honey, I know you did." Jenny hugged Christina and let her friend cry on her shoulder.

*

Christina spent the rest of the week, crying and moping around her apartment. At Jenny's insistence, she plucked up her courage and decided to call the Havenwood house to try to find out where Bill was. Maybe—just maybe—he would see her—and she'd apologize again—and maybe he could somehow forgive her—and…

With shaking fingers, Christina dialed the house and asked

for Eudora. If anyone would know where he was, she would. The elderly maid came on the line.

"Eudora… it's Christina," she breathlessly said.

There was a pause. "Hello, miss," Eudora answered frostily. Obviously, she knew something of what had happened.

Christina's next words came out in a rush. "I…I'm calling because… I need to contact Bill. Is he there?"

"No, miss."

"Have you… seen him at all this week?"

There was another pause as if Eudora was deciding whether to get involved between the two ex-lovebirds. "He came once, miss, a few days ago, to pick up his things and then he left again."

"Oh, I see." Christina paused.

"Do… you know where I can reach him, maybe?"

"He said he was going to be at some office called GME and he gave me the number."

Of course, Christina should have thought of that on her own but her mind had been in such a fuddle all week that she wasn't thinking clearly.

"Can I… have that number please?" Christina was almost afraid to ask.

Another pause, then… "One moment, miss."

After a few minutes, Eudora came back on the line and gave Christina the number.

"Thank you, Eudora. Thank you so much."

Another pause. "I'm sorry, mum but my Billy is a good boy and whatever happened between the two of you, he didn't deserve. I just had to say that."

Christina's tears were about to fall again as she squeaked out, "I'm sorry too, Eudora."

After their goodbyes, Christina hung up. Quickly, she dialed the GME phone number before she lost her nerve. A reception-ist answered and when she asked for Bill, she was put on hold. Christina waited as her heart beat frantically against her rib cage.

He came on the line then and she recognized his "Hello."

"Bill, it's me. Please don't hang up..." Christina's words gushed out.

But he did just that, as his phone was forcefully slammed shut in her ear. And Christina knew then that it was really over between them. He would never forgive her and he would never forget—and his love for her was gone.

Slowly, she replaced her own telephone receiver and suddenly, she realized that today would have been her wedding day—hers and Bill's. They would have been married today and they would have started their lives together today and they would have been happy and in love today and...

Feeling her stomach heave, Christina barely made it to the washroom before she threw up what little food she had eaten.

CHAPTER 65

FOR THE NEXT month and a half, Christina went through life as if in a fog. After convincing her parents that she was going to be fine, they'd finally gone back to Florida.

Needing money to live on, Christina had reluctantly picked up the pieces of her life and started to take some out-of-town assignments for the magazine. Her work was the only thing keeping her sane. It allowed her to focus on something else besides her sadness, otherwise she was certain she'd just curl up in a ball on her bed and die. She'd not gotten over her feelings for Bill—or her guilt at what she'd done.

Jenny had helped her immensely throughout this time.

She'd listened to Christina pour out her heart and had been there for her when she'd needed a shoulder to cry on. But Jenny was worried for her friend. She hated to see her like this—depressed and heartbroken—and didn't know what to do.

Christina also hadn't been eating very much and she'd started losing weight. She didn't have much of an appetite anymore and whatever she seemed to put in her mouth, came out just as fast. She was throwing up—repeatedly. Every morning, she'd open her eyes and remember that she'd never see Bill again—and she'd feel sick to her stomach. It was all she could do to run to the bathroom in time before she threw up again.

One morning, Jenny stopped by Christina's apartment before leaving for work. A pale, green-to-the-gills Christina answered the door. When Jenny asked her what was wrong, Christina was about to answer when another wave of nausea hit her. Leaving her friend standing at the open doorway, Christina ran to her bathroom again… and threw up.

Concerned, Jenny rushed in after her and helped her through it. When it was over, Jenny helped Christina back to her bed and put a wet washcloth on her forehead.

"Chrissy, you're making yourself sick over this mess," Jenny admonished.

"It's nothing. Just something I ate," Christina squeaked, as she shut her eyes trying to stop the next wave of nausea.

Jenny frowned as a thought popped into her head. "Is this the first time you've been sick like this?"

Christina shook her head slowly, "No, I have these dreams… and then I wake up… and I don't feel so good."

"So, this has been happening in the mornings?" Christina weakly nodded 'yes' and Jenny shook her head. "Chrissy, are you pregnant?"

Christina's eyes popped open. "What?" she gasped.

"You heard me. This could be morning sickness. I went through it myself when I was pregnant with Taylor."

"No, you're wrong. It's just a flu bug."

"Chrissy, I think you should take a pregnancy test."

"Jenny, I can't be pregnant, that's not possible…" She stopped in mid-sentence and gasped in shock, "Oh my God." She turned worried eyes to her friend. "The first time Bill and I made love… we… didn't use anything. Oh my God… could I be…?" Her eyes turned downward to her stomach. Could she be pregnant with Bill's baby?

"When did you have your last period?" Jenny quizzed.

Christina closed her eyes and tried to remember. She was usually good at keeping track of these things but lately she'd been such a walking zombie and hadn't thought about it at all.

"Oh no, Jenny, it was back at the Havenwood house! I haven't had one since."

Jenny nodded. "I thought so. Okay, I'm calling in sick today at work and you are resting in bed while I go to the pharmacy to pick up a pregnancy kit and then we're finding out for sure."

Determined, Jenny left the apartment. Taking a deep breath, Christina felt the lines of her stomach. Could she be pregnant with his baby? Was his child forming inside of her right this second? A thrill shot through her. And should she tell Bill? Or should she keep the information to herself? She didn't want him coming back to her just because of the baby…

All these thoughts swirled in Christina's brain.

*

When Jenny returned, Christina took the pregnancy test and it came up positive. She was indeed pregnant—and she was elated. She was carrying Bill's baby!

Jenny insisted on taking Christina to the doctor to make sure. The doctor confirmed what both women already knew. Christina was indeed pregnant—seven weeks along. When they got back to the apartment, Christina took her friend aside.

"Jenny, you have to promise me that you won't tell Bill," Christina implored.

"Of course, but Chrissy, he's the baby's father. He has a right to know. You have to tell him."

"I haven't decided yet. I don't want him back in my life out of pity or some sense of duty."

"Chrissy, you have to think about the baby first, now. And a child needs their father in their life. Look at Taylor. My ex-husband is a creep but he is a good father and she needs him. We make it work for her sake."

"Jenny, I'm so confused and I don't know what to do," Christina wailed.

"Okay, don't get excited. You don't have to make any decisions today, do you? Just go over all the pros and cons. The baby does have a right to have their father in their life and you're going to need child support."

"No way do I want his money. No!" Christina burst out.

"Think about it before you make a final decision. A child is very expensive and you want the best for your baby, don't you? And you can barely afford to live off of your salary, let alone you and a baby."

"Jenny, no!"

"All I'm saying is, think about everything first and then decide."

*

In the end, Christina decided to tell Bill about the baby after all. But she couldn't face him, person-to-person, and tell him.

What if he told her he didn't care? What if he accused her of planning the pregnancy to trap him? What if he didn't believe it was even his baby? He could hurl a thousand accusations at her and she didn't think she was strong enough to handle it.

No—what she would do was write him a letter, telling him about the pregnancy and send it to the GME office. He would certainly get it there.

It took a whole day for Christina to compose the letter. She wanted it to be just right. In it, she was brief and to the point, telling him point blank about her pregnancy. She stated she'd leave it up to him to contact her if he wanted to be part of this baby's life— or not. Whatever decision he made, she told him, she would abide. She then mailed it out and waited for his reply.

She didn't have to wait long. By the end of the week, the letter had been returned—unopened. She recognized his writing on the front of the envelope where he'd written 'Return To Sender'.

There—that was her answer.

Even though he hadn't opened the letter and obviously didn't know about the baby, he'd made it perfectly clear he still hated her and didn't want anything to do with her. And Christina had too much pride to try a second time. No—now she knew what she had to do. She'd have this baby on her own and she'd never tell him.

It was truly and irrevocably over between them. The love they had shared was gone—and she was on her own.

CHAPTER 66

OVER THE NEXT few weeks, Christina's spirits picked up and she started taking better care of herself. After all, she had a little person to think about now. She still hadn't told her parents or anyone else about her pregnancy. Only Jenny knew. She'd tell everyone when she'd start to show more.

During this time, Jenny was still very worried about her friend. And she couldn't let go of the idea that things really weren't over yet between Christina and Bill, especially now with a baby on the way. If only those two could talk, if they could see each other again—maybe, just maybe—there was hope? Love like that didn't just die and go away.

The idea kept rambling on in Jenny's brain and she did something she shouldn't have. She made a cold call to Bill's friend, Jake Monroe at the GME office, without Christina's knowledge.

"Jake Monroe here," the voice on the other end said.

Jenny took a deep breath and rushed on. "Hi… Jake. My name's Jenny Lewis… well, actually it used to be Jenny Street back at Cloverdale High. You probably don't remember me but we went out once and…"

"I remember you. We went out and then you moved away right after that. Was it something I said?" he joked.

Jenny nervously laughed. "No… I… my father got transferred. I… ummm… the reason I'm calling is… I'd like to meet with you and discuss my good friend, Christina Matteo."

There was a long pause before Jake replied. "I don't know what you'd have to talk to me about her for."

"Please, I just want to talk to you. Can we meet somewhere… maybe for coffee or something?"

There was another long pause. "Sorry, Jenny but I don't know Christina. I only ever met her in high school."

"Please, just a cup of coffee and if you think I'm out of line, then you can leave." There was another pause. "Please?"

Jake sighed. His best friend had been hurt terribly by that woman but the way Jenny was asking him and the fact that he was curious to see her again after all these years, he reluctantly agreed to meet her.

*

Jake Monroe was already waiting for Jenny at the coffee shop when she arrived. He had parked himself and his wheelchair at one of the tables in the back and Jenny thought he was even more handsome than he'd been in high school.

"You'll excuse me if I don't stand up when a lady arrives," he joked.

"Thanks for meeting me, Jake," Jenny laughed, as she sat down opposite him.

"So, what do you think of my new wheels? Not as cool as the ones I used to have in high school," he joked again. Jake was nervous. He didn't know whether Jenny had known he was in a wheelchair or not, and he was trying to ease the awkwardness if she hadn't.

"Oh, I don't know; they look pretty cool to me," she smiled at him.

Jake was taken aback at her beauty. "Wow, you're even prettier than you were in high school!" he quipped.

"Thank you." Jenny was slightly embarrassed. She was such a mom these days, focusing all her energy on Taylor that she'd forgotten what it was like to get a compliment from a man—especially one as gorgeous as Jake Monroe.

They ordered their coffees next and then Jenny got down to business.

"Jake, I'm a very good friend of Christina's and I know everything that happened between her and Bill."

Jake's eyes narrowed. "Bill's my good friend so I know it all too, and Christina is not one of my favorite topics of conversation right now. In fact, you could say, I don't really like the woman at all."

"She's a good person, really. She's not like what you imagine at all. She's…"

Jake interrupted her. "Jenny, all I know about her is what she's done to my friend and I'm not impressed."

"Maybe, since you're Bill's friend, maybe you could ask him to see her again… to talk to her, maybe give her a chance to explain?"

"That's not a good idea."

"But if they just saw each other one last time, maybe…"

"Did she put you up to this? To come here and ask me?"

"No! She doesn't even know I'm talking to you. She'll have my head if she finds out."

"Then maybe it's best if the two of us stay out of it. She's not good for Bill and he doesn't want to see her ever again."

"Look, I just know that if they talked, maybe they could work things out and then…"

"No, Jenny!" Jake was so forceful that Jenny was taken aback. He looked at her then and said, "I'm sorry. I didn't mean to shout but you don't understand." He paused as if deciding whether to tell her something or not. "Bill's in rehab."

"What?" Jenny gasped out her surprise.

"He started drinking and partying hard again. He's been on a booze binge 24/7 since the split with Christina, a really bad one. Some of us… his friends… we had to do an intervention this week and we got him into rehab a few days ago."

Jenny was shocked. "He's drinking again?"

Jake nodded. "Your friend really did a number on him. I've never seen him this devastated. He didn't even give a crap about his father throwing him out of the Havenwood money. It was all her. He went back to drinking because of her. So you see why it's imperative that she stay away from him, especially now?"

Still flabbergasted, Jenny nodded. "How long is he in rehab for?"

"At least twenty-eight days, more if necessary. And when he comes out, he's going to have to pick up the pieces of his life and move on... without the alcohol. He'll still be destroyed over her but he's got to deal with it sober and that's going to be hard to do. I don't even know if he'll make it. He was that hurt. So tell your friend, if she really cares for him to please leave him alone. That's the best thing she could do for him."

Jenny was still so shocked she could only nod her head again. "I'm sorry. I had no idea."

Jake suddenly felt bad for being so harsh with her. "Hey, I'm sorry too. I didn't mean to come down hard on you."

"It's okay. I understand." She stood up then. "Thanks anyway for meeting me."

"Hey? Where are you going? We still have to drink our coffees."

"Well... I..."

"Please, Jenny, sit back down. Let's at least do that."

Slowly, Jenny sat down. "So tell me all about what you've been up to since our big date in high school." He smiled at her, clearly interested.

*

The next day after work, Jenny went to see Christina at her apartment. She was going to come clean about what she'd done in meeting Jake Monroe.

They were sitting on Christina's couch and Christina had just walked in with the coffee. Jenny put a restraining hand on her friend's arm as she sat down.

"Chrissy, I have to confess something and I think you're going to be mad at me but I only had your best interests at heart and..."

"Oh God, Jenny! You didn't tell Bill about the baby, did you?" Christina gushed out.

"No! I promised you I wouldn't and I meant it. No, what I did was... I called Jake Monroe and asked him to meet with me."

"Oh no, Jenny, why'd you do that?" an exasperated Christina sighed.

"Because you're so unhappy and I hate to see you like this and I thought maybe he could talk to Bill and..." Jenny paused.

"He refused?"

Jenny nodded. "Yes. He also told me some things that I don't want to tell you but I think you should know."

Suddenly, Christina was very worried. "Is it Bill? Has something happened to him? Jenny, you have to tell me what you know."

Jenny paused again. "Chrissy, Jake said that Bill's in a rehab center. He started drinking again after your split."

"Oh my God!" Christina's hands started to shake and her face paled.

Jenny continued. "He apparently was so hurt by what happened between the two of you that Jake said Bill has been drunk for the past couple of months and they only got him help this week. He said..." She paused again, reluctant to go on.

"He said what, Jenny? You have to tell me, please!"

"Jake said that if you really care about Bill, you'll leave him alone. He needs to get on with his life, sober, when he gets out and you're too dangerous for him to deal with. I'm sorry."

Christina's heart sank. Deep, deep down, she'd harbored a fantasy that somehow, in the not too distant future, this baby would somehow bring them back together, and he would forgive her, and they could be a real family.

But it was all a pipe dream. It wasn't going to happen for her—ever. She was bad news for him. He would always remember what she'd done to him and she couldn't ever take the chance that somehow it would be her fault that he would go back to drinking again—as it had been her fault this time.

No—she and Bill were never meant to be and it was best for his sobriety if she stayed away from him—forever.

A thought popped into Christina's mind. "Jenny, you didn't say anything to Jake about the baby, did you?"

"No! Never!"

Christina breathed a sigh of relief. "Thank you for that."

Jenny was nervously biting her lip. "Chrissy, you're not mad at me for going to see Jake, are you? Please say you're not."

Christina smiled at her friend. "No, I'm not mad. If you hadn't gone, we would never have found out about this."

Jenny kept biting her lip. "There's something else. Jake… well, he kind of asked me out… but I won't go out with him if it's awkward for you. Our friendship means more."

Christina smiled for her friend's sake. "Oh Jenny, you're such a good friend. No, you go out with him and have fun. Just because I screwed up my chance with one of the rat bastards from high school doesn't mean you can't have your chance with the other one." She was trying to lighten up the situation and not show Jenny how worried she really was about Bill.

Jenny hugged Christina. "Thank you. And I promise, I won't say anything about the baby."

*

Christina didn't have to worry about Jenny mentioning the baby because of what happened later that week. She was so worried and stressed about Bill drinking again that a few days later she started spotting. Jenny quickly took her to the hospital emergency and Christina lost the baby. She miscarried just short of her third month.

And she was devastated all over again.

The baby had been her last link to Bill and now she didn't even have that anymore. The doctor at the hospital told her it was perfectly normal for a woman to miscarry her first pregnancy especially during her first three months—that it wasn't anything that she'd done wrong or should blame herself for. But Christina knew differently. This was all karma coming back at her for what she'd done to him.

And the tears came down again…

CHAPTER 67

IT WAS THE beginning of December and Christmas was in the air in New York City. Lights were up, stores were decorated, snow was falling and the mood was joyful. A year and a half had passed since that fateful night when Bill had thrown Christina out of his life. It had felt more like a lifetime to Christina.

But Christina was made of stronger stuff than even she would have believed. After she had lost the baby and knew there was no hope for reconciliation with Bill, she had picked herself up and moved on. Her survival instincts had kicked in as she had faced herself in the mirror and realized that she had to put this chapter of her life behind her and forge ahead.

So, she had buried all of her feelings for him, put the past behind her and started her life over again. What else could she do? She had cried enough tears to fill a swimming pool.

She'd spent too many days moping around her apartment; and too many sleepless nights thinking about him and what might have been.

No more.

The baby was gone.

He was gone.

And if she didn't start her life over again, she would spiral downwards into a hopeless pit of depression that she'd never be able to climb out of. And she wouldn't do that to herself.

What was done… was done.

It was over.

No more pity, no more regrets, no more sorrow. It was time to get on with the business of life.

Christina decided to focus on her career instead. That had always made her happy in the past. Photojournalism had been her passion and she would rekindle that passion and it would help her out of her sadness.

And it had.

Over the past year and a half, Christina had begun to take more and more assignments for Streetwise Magazine and had even begun to freelance for other magazines as well. Her job started to take her around the country as she'd begun to concentrate on the political scene in different states. Several of her photos had even been published in some of the more respected political magazines and she'd begun to make some decent money for a change. Her career was definitely on the upswing.

Because she'd been traveling so much for her job, she'd not been able to see Jenny as often as she would have liked.

But they still lived in the same apartment building and they still were the best of friends. If they couldn't see each other as often as they had before, they still constantly telephoned each other and were always up on the latest gossip in each other's lives.

Jenny still worked as the receptionist at Streetwise, and she and Jake Monroe had been dating for the entire year and a half. She'd fallen in love with him and he was in love with her. Little Taylor adored Jake and all three were now considering becoming a family and making it official.

The subject of Christina was still a bone of contention between Jenny and Jake, though. Even though Jenny had explained things to Jake about her friends' motives for her revenge plan against Bill and how she had been deeply scarred by their high school prank, Jake was still mad at Christina. He had seen the devastation she had caused in his friend's life and he couldn't forgive her.

Jake had met Christina a couple of times now—accidentally—when she'd dropped by Jenny's apartment and he'd been there too. Jenny had introduced them to each other and Jake had been very cool towards her.

After Christina had left, Jenny and Jake had had a huge fight.

Chrissy was her best friend, she had told Jake and he'd better learn to accept that because she would never give up that friendship for a man. She had put her foot down and Jake had begrudgingly agreed to, at least, be civil to Christina from now on whenever they met.

Jenny had then privately apologized to Christina for Jake's rude behavior but Christina had told her not to worry. She understood the situation perfectly and didn't blame Jake at all. He was simply being a good friend to Bill and she, Christina, deserved his censure for what she'd done to his friend.

Still—Jenny had insisted that Jake's behavior was unacceptable and that he'd better learn to accept Christina if he wanted to continue to be in Jenny's life. Jenny could be just as tough as Christina when it came to what she expected from a man.

Christina encouraged Jenny to give Jake some time and after this first meeting between them, maybe the animosity would lessen? And it had—a little. The other times they'd met, Jake was more civil to Christina and that was fine by her. At least they managed to have a conversation together, even if it was only about the weather.

During this time, Jake had also introduced Jenny to Bill. They'd even all gone out to dinner a few times. When Jenny had told Christina that Jake wanted her to meet Bill for the first time, Christina had begged Jenny not to mention Christina's name during the dinner. Jenny hadn't wanted to promise because she still harbored hope that somehow those two belonged together.

But Christina had begged and pleaded, and Jenny had reluctantly agreed. She gave Christina her word that she would not bring up her friend's name but if Bill did it first, that was another matter. Then it would be open season and Jenny would sing Christina's praises to him.

Christina agreed to that. Jenny was her best friend and she trusted her with her life—and with her secrets. Jenny had never even told Jake about the baby Christina had lost, and never would, if that's how her friend wanted it. Some things were just meant to be between friends.

When Jenny had met Bill Havenwood again, she'd been impressed with him. She could see why Christina had fallen so hard for him. He was charming, smart and absolutely gorgeous—even more so than he'd been in high school. Brains and male beauty in a hot body was a lethal combination, and Bill Havenwood had it all.

Bill, too, had been impressed with Jenny and had remembered her from high school. And he was thrilled for his friend. Bill had never seen Jake this bewitched over a woman before and he could tell his buddy was in love. He was happy for him and wished him the best.

During that first dinner together, Jenny had been on pins and needles waiting for Bill to mention Christina's name and ask about her but he never did. And the other times they'd all met up together, he was equally silent.

Jake had later explained to Jenny that after Bill had come out of rehab, he'd never mentioned Christina's name again. It was a taboo subject and Jake had never pushed. If his friend wanted to talk to him about her, he would listen but if he didn't, that was fine by him too.

Jake didn't even know how Bill felt about Christina anymore. Her name was just never brought up again. The only time Christina's name was mentioned was when Jake had first told Bill about his relationship with Jenny, and that Jenny was Christina's best friend. All Bill had said to him was that wasn't a problem for him and if Jake was happy, then he was happy too.

And Christina's name was never mentioned again between the two of them.

Over the past year and a half, Jenny had provided Christina with some information about Bill that she'd learned by dating Jake. She had told her friend that after Bill had gotten out of rehab, he had not gone back to drinking again, as everyone had feared but had remained clean and sober, and had turned his life around.

He'd resumed his position at the helm of the GME environmental group and had begun to run it with brains and boldness.

When the press had realized that William Havenwood's son had been the one causing problems for the billionaire and that he'd been thrown out of the Havenwood fold, a mini-scandal had erupted and Bill's picture had appeared in the media. That had garnered a lot of good publicity for GME and their name had become better known.

Not only were they now still taking on Williams' many companies for environmental infractions but the group began to go after other corporate polluters as well. As they garnered more positive press, donations began flowing in and their membership increased. And they actually began to make a difference as some of the companies they went after began to change their policies for the better.

Everyone was impressed with what a success the GME group had become and a lot of that was owed to Bill's smarts and initiatives. He had really come into his own as a leader and as a man. He wasn't his father's whipping boy any longer. He had taken charge of his own life and now had pride in himself and he'd begun to get the respect of others. As his and GME's good works began to be appreciated more and more by the public, Bill's name was even being bandied about as a possible candidate for Congress.

Christina had heard these rumors herself. As she'd become more involved with the political scene through her job, her connections had kept her informed about Bill's very good chances at winning a congressional seat, if he decided to run.

She was proud of him. He had moved on without her and he was succeeding. He was his own man now and she longed for him to be happy.

Yes—she was still in love with him—but it wasn't meant to be. She'd faced that months ago. Now, all she wanted was the best for him, even if that didn't include her. She loved him that much.

And now she was facing another Christmas without him.

Last Christmas had been a blur as she still had been upset over their breakup and losing the baby. But her life was back on track now—the sadness had lifted, she was moving on and it was time to celebrate the holidays.

CHAPTER 68

AND WHAT BETTER way to celebrate the Christmas holidays than with shopping.

Christina had spent all afternoon at Bloomingdale's and had been able to cross off many names on her gift-giving list. She'd spent a month's salary but she'd managed to buy for her parents, some business associates, for Jenny and Jake, and of course, little Taylor.

Laden with packages and shopping bags, Christina was maneuvering herself through the Bloomingdale's doors on her way outside. As she stepped onto the slippery sidewalk, her head was turned to the left as she was trying to look for a taxi and wasn't watching where she was going. Suddenly, she ran smack into someone that she hadn't seen coming from her right—a man.

Christina let out a gasp. As she careened into his large chest, her foot stepped onto a patch of ice, and because her arms were filled with packages, she lost her balance. She slipped, her purchases scattered and she fell flat on her back in a snow bank by the curb.

"Ohhh…" Christina moaned, as pain shot through her back.

"Oh, God I'm sorry," a male voice penetrated her senses.

As she opened her eyes, the male stranger was bending down over her—and she stared into his face. It was Bill Havenwood—her Bill.

"Bill!" she gasped.

"Christina!" he expelled, as he recognized her and froze.

The moment hung suspended in time as they continued to stare at each other, both dumbstruck by this incredible coincidence. How had fate arranged it so that they would meet like this—at the exact moment she was coming out of the store, he would be going in?

And what was even more ironic was that this was how they'd told William they'd met—that they'd crashed into each other as she came out of Bloomingdale's with packages in her hand. Stunned, they continued to stare at each other.

He broke the silence first.

"Oh my God, Christina, are you all right?" Bill came down on his haunches beside her and put his hands on her arms. Concern was etched in his face.

Christina was speechless. She hadn't seen him in person since that fateful night and she had to admit he still looked great—still handsome, healthy and hot.

"I… I… I…" Christina stammered, as she continued to stare into those gorgeous green eyes of his that had haunted her in many of her dreams. And that face—that perfectly proportioned face and that incredibly strong jaw—and those delicious lips of his. Yes, he was still movie star handsome. She hadn't imagined any of that—and the memories of them together came flooding back to her at breakneck speed.

"You… what? Are you in pain?" Worry crossed Bill's face as his eyes frantically roamed her body looking for clues if she was hurt.

"I…" Christina was still so shocked at seeing him that she couldn't get her mouth to form any words.

"Are you hurt? Do you feel pain anywhere?"

Bill was getting very worried as his hands began to roam over her arms and down her legs looking for breaks or swelling. And his heart was beating a mile a minute. Was it worry or shock at seeing her again? Both.

As Christina felt his hot hands on her body, her senses came back. "I… I'm okay. I'm fine." She tried to sit up.

"Don't sit up!" he shouted at her. "You could have injured your back. Stay still." He was more forceful than he should have been—but it was her! It was Christina! He still couldn't believe his eyes—and his heart was about to burst out of his chest.

Christina looked up at him again. "I'm fine. Now help me up," she commanded.

"No. And we're a calling an ambulance." Yes, he was going overboard and yes, he was making a big deal out of everything—but it was her! It was Christina!

She glared at him in response to his imperial tone. "Don't be ridiculous. I'm fine except for the frostbite on my backside from you forcing me to lie in this dirty snow bank for so long." Still stubborn as ever, was he, Christina inwardly fumed.

Bill paused. Still stubborn as ever, was she? Undecided about what he should do, he continued to stare into her beautiful, and getting-angrier-by-the-minute, face.

Christina's patience evaporated. "Oh, for crying out loud…" she mumbled and started to get up herself.

People were beginning to walk around them and were even stepping on her packages that were strewn all over the sidewalk.

"My packages…" she wailed, as she saw her shopping bag with her mom's crystal bowl kicked out into the curb. As she lunged for it, Christina felt a sharp pain in her back. "Oahu…" she grimaced, as her hand instinctively went to her sore tailbone.

"I knew it! You're hurt!" Bill was suddenly so worried by the look of pain that had crossed her face that he shouted the words at her more forcefully than he should have. He grabbed her arm and prevented her from getting up further. "And I told you not to move. If you have a back injury, you can make it worse." His face looked furious.

"I'll do whatever I damn well please! I don't need your bloody two-bit medical opinions, thank you very much," Christina shouted back, as she went to stand up, leaning heavily on his arm.

"Hard-headed as ever, I see," Bill gritted through his teeth, as he helped her up.

"And you're still a jerk!" she retaliated.

Christina was mad because he was mad. She had pictured an

accidental meeting with him a thousand times in her mind—and it was nothing like this. In her imagination, he would say 'hi' and she would say 'hi'. Then he would tell her she looked good and she would say he did too. And maybe he would smile at her—and she would smile at him—and maybe he would ask her out for coffee and—maybe…

No, she'd never pictured this.

As Christina finally stood up, with his help of course, she tried to straighten her back. Suddenly another sharp, excruciating pain, radiating from her tailbone, shot through her body.

"Ohhhh…" She gasped out as her hand went to her tailbone again and she immediately hunched over at a 45-degree angle.

Bill grabbed her arms in the nick of time as she almost lost her balance again on the slippery sidewalk. God—was he ever worried now. His fear made him shout at her again.

"We're going to the hospital and that's final," he decreed.

Still hunched over, Christina turned her head to look up at him. He looked so angry with her—probably for having to meet her again—and she was so angry with him—because he was so angry with her.

"No, I'm going home and you're going to hell," she shouted back at him. "And maybe if you had watched where you were going, this would never have happened."

"Me! This wasn't my fault. You crashed into me. You should have watched where you were going but you didn't because you were foolishly carrying too many damn packages that were blocking your vision."

If they both hadn't been so angry at each other, they would have noticed that this was almost a replay of their first meeting when Christina had smashed her car into his. And they would have noticed how ironic this all was—and how funny—and how silly…

But they didn't.

He was so worried about her that it manifested itself as anger, and she was equally angry at him, because this wasn't how it was supposed to have been when they'd have finally met again.

"Yeah, yeah, yeah, whatever," Christina yelled back. "Why don't you do something useful and help pick up my stuff. Oh no…" she suddenly wailed, as she saw a passerby step on one of her bags, smashing it deeper into the snow. "That's Taylor's dress."

She went to reach for it and another sharp pain shot through her. She instinctively grabbed Bill's arm for support.

"That's it. I'm taking you to the hospital if I have to carry you there kicking and screaming the entire way."

Christina was in serious pain and she knew she'd have to go to the hospital—but she wasn't going with him.

"I'm not going anywhere with you. Just call me a cab," she demanded, still hunched over at an awkward angle.

"No, I'm not getting you a damn cab. You're coming with me," he shouted back as he steered her hands onto a mailbox for support before bending down to pick up her parcels.

Christina watched him as he brushed snow off of her bags and piled them neatly at her feet. If truth were told, she wanted him to be the one to take her to the hospital because she was suddenly scared. The pain in her back was getting worse and she couldn't straighten herself up—and she desperately needed his strong support, literally and figuratively. But she wasn't going to give him the satisfaction of telling him he was right.

So she stood there, hunched over, holding onto the mailbox for dear life, watching him retrieve her parcels with an irritated look on her face. And she kept her mouth shut for a change.

When he finished, he came back to her.

"Don't move and I'll be right back with my car," he ordered, then gently began to brush snow off of her coat from where she'd fallen.

"I don't think I can move even if I wanted to, thanks to you," Christina threw back at him, as his gentle hands kept stroking the snow off her body.

He was so close to her now and she could smell his heavenly cologne, and she could feel the electrical heat that they'd always generated together, start to fire up. After all this time, and everything that had happened, it was still there.

And he felt it too, as his hands continued to touch her.

But Christina had to put a stop to her traitorous thoughts. What good was there in traveling down that road if nothing would ever happen between them ever again?

She looked up at him then, defiant. "I could sue you, you know, for bodily injury."

He stopped his ministrations to her coat and looked back at her. God—the way she'd looked up at him just now, with those spunky eyes of hers and that sweet, luscious mouth spouting off some dare—it was like they'd never been apart.

"You could," he quipped back. "But I have to warn you, I have no money now and you won't get much out of me. No more Havenwood billions."

Christina lowered her eyes. She still felt guilt about that since she'd been responsible for his father throwing him out. Her eyes came back up to his face and she saw he was watching her closely.

"Well, go get your damn car then and drive me to the hospital. It's the least you can do," she challenged back.

"Golly gee, now why didn't I think of that?" he sarcastically retorted.

He was still mad at her—because she was still so beautiful—and still so exciting—and he could still feel the sparks flying between them—and he still wanted her—and he still loved her—damn it all to hell!

Hanging onto the mailbox, Christina lifted her nose in the air. "So, what are you waiting for? A memo? Go get your damn car. I'm freezing out here."

Frustrated, he expelled an exasperated breath. "You are an impossible woman, you know that!" he shouted at her before stalking off down the street and around the corner to where he had parked his car. The woman was just so maddening—and he loved every minute of it.

Christina watched him go. This meeting him again and not having him, was sheer torture. Oh, why did this have to happen to her?

But now, that he'd gone to get his car was her chance for escape. She hobbled as best she could to the curb and tried to hail a cab. But it had started to snow and the cabs that were whizzing by her were already occupied. Damn! Why didn't things work out the way you wanted sometimes? A few minutes later, she saw him pull up to the curb in one of those hybrid environment-friendly cars. That was a far cry from his Jag or Ferrari.

He got out and smirked at her. "No luck getting a cab?" he cracked.

Christina shot him a dirty look. "I don't know what you're talking about? I've been waiting here for you the whole time." Oh why, did he have to know her so well? Was she that obvious?

"Really?" he murmured, as he came to her side. He obviously didn't believe her.

Bill put his arm around her and slowly helped Christina into the passenger side of the car. To be this close to him—to have his arms around her and know that this was all temporary—was sheer agony for her. Oh why, did she have to meet him again?

She had been doing so well.

Bill drove Christina to the nearest hospital. Not much was said in the car between them on the way except for a few grimaces from her when he ran over some potholes and a couple of 'sorrys' from him when he heard her wince in pain.

At the emergency, Christina got lucky as one of the doctors saw her right away. She was taken down for x-rays and finally put in one of the cubicles to wait for the diagnosis. As she was sitting gingerly on the edge of a chair in order to get some relief from the back pain, she saw Bill walk in.

"I don't think you're supposed to be in here," Christina said.

"So, let them try throwing me out," Bill was still very worried about her and he'd spent the past hour pacing the waiting room until he couldn't stand the suspense any longer. "How's your back?"

"Sore."

"Did they give you anything for it?"

"Not yet. They wanted to wait for the x-rays first. So how come you're still here?"

"Why wouldn't I be?"

"Well, you did your duty. You brought me to the hospital. And I'm not exactly one of your favorite people, so I thought you'd left."

"Christina, I…" he paused as he stared at her—wanting to say more but not quite sure what.

"It's okay. I know I'm not on your Christmas list. You don't have to say anything," she returned, trying to sound tough but failing miserably. He still hadn't forgiven her. She could read it in his eyes.

At that moment the doctor walked in with her chart.

"Mrs. Matteo, you've bruised your tailbone. Luckily, there were no breaks. So I'm sending you home with some painkillers and you should be fine in a week. Try to get some rest but walk around too. Don't just stay in bed. Walking is very good for back injuries like yours but stay close to home for the week." He then turned to Bill and smiled. "And tell your wife no more shopping until this has healed, okay?"

The doctor was obviously assuming they were married and another type of pain shot through Christina, one that came from her broken heart. What she didn't know was that Bill had felt the same pain too from his own heartbreak.

Bill smiled at the doctor then, "Thanks, doc. And I'm sure the credit card thanks you too." He tried to cover the awkwardness of the moment with a joke.

The doctor left and Bill reached for her arm. She pulled it out of his grasp.

"What are you doing?" she said indignantly.

"I'm taking you home. What does it look like?"

"I can make my own way, thank you. You can leave now. You heard the doctor. Some rest and some pills and I'll be fine."

Suddenly, Christina wanted him gone. Every second she was in his presence was one more second she was being reminded of what she'd lost and could never have again.

"I'm driving you home."

"And I said no."

"Then, how are you getting home? You're not going in a cab, that's for damn sure."

"I'll call Jenny. She'll pick me up. So you see, your services are no longer required, Mr. Havenwood." Christina lifted her chin and stared him down.

"No. I brought you here, I'll take you home." Bill was being equally defiant.

Christina paused and gazed deeply into his eyes. "Tell me something, Bill? Have you forgiven me for what I did to you?" There she'd said it. She'd mentioned the 800-pound gorilla in the room.

He turned his green eyes onto her beautiful face and stared hard at her. But he didn't respond. He just kept looking at her.

Christina answered her own question, as she nodded to herself. "I thought so. I think you'd better go."

They both continued to stare at each other as a few more seconds ticked away. Suddenly, he lowered his eyes and half turned away from her.

"I'll leave your parcels at the nurse's station," he said, then turned and walked out.

And he was gone—just like that.

Christina let out the breath she'd been holding and sank deeper into the chair she was sitting in. So, now she knew where things stood between them. But she wouldn't cry. No—she was too tired and too numb and too sore to do that. And she had cried enough tears over him. No more.

A very worried Jenny showed up at the hospital to pick

Christina up and drive her home. On the way, Christina told her friend about her accidental meeting with Bill and what had happened.

Jenny was shocked but not surprised. She still felt those two belonged together and if they were both too stubborn to see it, well then, fate would intervene and force them together to deal with their issues.

Back at Christina's apartment, Jenny helped Christina undress and get into bed. She made her friend some tea and made sure she'd taken her pills. She told Christina to call her at any hour if she needed anything at all and she, Jenny, would come right down. She also insisted on taking Christina's spare apartment key in case Christina couldn't get up to open the door and Jenny had to get in for some reason.

Jenny was a true friend—and even better than Christina knew because a devious plan was starting to form in Jenny's mind. Those two, Christina and Bill, belonged together and it was about time that bull-headed Bill Havenwood realized that.

Maybe, all he needed was a little shove? And maybe, she, Jenny Lewis, was just the person to do the shoving.

*

After leaving the hospital, Bill couldn't stop thinking about her—not that he'd ever stopped really. He didn't think there was a day that had gone by since their split that her beautiful face hadn't popped into his mind at one point or other.

And that one night, a few months back when Jenny had invited him over to her apartment for dinner with Jake and her daughter, Bill had spent the entire evening thinking about Christina, knowing she was only a couple of floors below in her own apartment—so close and yet so far.

Every instinct in his body had been urging him to go down there, pound on the door and push his way back into her life but his anger had kept him at bay. That entire evening had been torture for him, although he'd put on a happy face for the sake of his hosts.

And now—today—this had happened? Meeting her again? Like this? And she'd asked him if he'd forgiven her, and he hadn't answered. What could he say? That he still hadn't, not completely? That he was still angry with her?

He had dealt with some of those feelings for her in rehab. But when he'd got out, his feelings for her were still there and they were too painful to look at. So he'd buried them and had resolved in his mind not to look at them and not to deal with them and not to think about her. But he had thought about her—almost everyday. He knew he still loved her but he was still mad at her and he just couldn't get past that.

God—he needed a drink. But he knew he would never go down that road again. It had nearly destroyed him again last year and it hadn't solved anything.

CHAPTER 69

IT WAS TIME to put her plan into action, Jenny thought to herself. She had learned from Jake that Bill had started dating again. He'd gone out a couple of times with a woman named Linda who worked at the GME offices.

According to Jake—after Jenny had prodded and pried him for specific details—Linda had practically thrown herself at Bill during the previous months. The whole office knew how she felt about him. She had flirted and smiled and complimented him, all the while wearing short skirts and low tops—anything she could do to attract his interest. And it had worked. He had asked her out—well actually, she'd asked him out—and she'd caught him in a lonely moment and he'd agreed.

They'd only had a few dates together—and it was about time the guy started getting on with his life again, wasn't it, Jake had told Jenny. Jenny had smiled and told Jake he was right. There was nothing wrong in going out with someone new. Bill needed that.

But deep down, Jenny knew the time was now to do something about this situation between Christina and Bill before he really did find someone new and truly moved on.

And she, Jenny, was the one to do it. But she didn't say any of this to Jake. She just smiled and humored her sweetheart, all the while pumping him for more information about Bill.

And she didn't mention any of this to Christina who would have had a fit if she knew what her friend was planning behind the scenes.

*

Jenny was sitting behind her receptionist's desk at work.

A week had passed and Christina's back had healed nicely. It was no longer sore and her friend was back to normal.

According to Christina, Bill Havenwood had not called her once all week to ask how she was feeling but Jenny had told her friend that he had called Jenny instead—calling every single day asking about Christina. And in fact, those first few days right after Christina's fall, he had called Jenny twice a day for updates.

He had sounded worried about her condition and he'd given Jenny all of his office, home and cell phone numbers in case Christina's back got suddenly worse. He had instructed Jenny to call him immediately, day or night, if anything happened or if Christina needed anything at all.

Jenny knew he was still in love with Christina and she knew her friend was still in love with him. So what was the harm in putting a little secret plan together to bring those two together?

Sitting at her desk, Jenny saw Stanley Moore walk in. He was the thirty-something lawyer Streetwise Magazine had retained for any legal issues or questions that cropped up and today he was here for a meeting with Giselle, the editor.

And Jenny also knew that Stanley Moore had a major crush on Christina.

"Hi Stanley, how are you?" Jenny asked.

"Busy. It seems everyone has legal problems that always come up at Christmas time." Stanley shrugged the snow from his coat as he took it off.

Jenny watched him with a cagey look on her face. "Giselle will be with you in ten minutes, if you want to take a seat," she told him.

"Thanks but I think I'd rather come and talk to the prettiest girl in the room," he joked, as he approached her desk.

Jenny laughed. "Since I am the only girl in the room right now, I'm not sure that's exactly a compliment."

Stanley was suddenly, flustered. "Oh, I'm sorry, I didn't mean it that way." Stanley was sweet, conventional and not a player—which were points definitely in his favor.

"Oh Stanley, I was just teasing you. Don't worry about it,"

Jenny laughed again. "You know, someone was asking me about you the other day. Christina." She crossed her fingers, which were hiding, under her desk and prayed for forgiveness for all of the lies she was about to tell.

Stanley was immediately interested. "Really? Christina? She was asking about me?"

Jenny nodded. "Yes, she was. She said she hadn't seen you in awhile and wanted to know how you were."

Stanley was clearly taken aback. "Christina Matteo? She was asking… about me?"

Jenny motioned him to come closer and he complied. "Stanley, I'm assuming you know all about her broken engagement from last year?"

Stanley nodded. "I know that she was supposed to get married to Bill Havenwood and then didn't."

"That's right. Christina's my good friend and I have to tell you she's had it rough this past year and a half. She's finally getting on with her life though but she needs to… go out more… with different people, know what I mean?"

Stanley didn't really but he nodded anyway. He was clearly interested in anything to do with Christina Matteo.

"Anyway…" Jenny continued, all the while keeping her fingers crossed underneath her desk, "She's been hinting lately that she wants to go see the opera Parsifal… Christina loves the opera but I don't and none of her other friends do, so she has no one to take her and…" Jenny let the word hang in the air.

"And…?" Stanley prodded, not knowing what Jenny meant.

Oh brother! Jenny wanted to roll her eyes up to the heavens but didn't. For a smart lawyer, Stanley really was obtuse when it came to matters of the heart. She would just have to spell things out for him.

"And… I was thinking if you got tickets to Parsifal for this

Saturday night and you called her up and asked her to go with you, I know she would." Jenny gave him a wink to seal the deal.

"Me? She'd go out with me? You think?" Stanley was so unsure of himself. In the courtroom, he could be a tiger but not in the bedroom.

Jenny nodded. "Yes. If you ask her, she'll say yes. I can almost guarantee it. She's been asking about you, you know and you'd be doing me a big favor because she'd stop pestering me about going with her to this stupid opera. Think about it."

Stanley clearly was thinking about it. "Oh well… maybe… I guess… but I… have to see what my schedule is like first."

"Oh of course, I understand. I'll leave it with you. But in case you are free, I'll give you Christina's home number and you can give her a call," Jenny quickly wrote the number on a piece of paper and handed it to Stanley. "But please Stanley, do me a favor. Don't say anything to Christina that we had this conversation. If she finds out how I tried to pawn her off on you because of how much I hate going to the opera, she'll be really mad at me. So please, don't say anything."

"Jenny, of course; you can count on my discretion. I won't say a word," Stanley quickly promised.

Of course, he wouldn't say anything to Christina, Jenny thought to herself. He'd want to make it appear that asking her friend out was all his idea, not Jenny's. She knew she was safe there. Satisfied, she sat back in her chair as Stanley went into the offices for his meeting.

One down, one to go, she mused.

*

After work that night, Jenny stopped off at Christina's apartment before heading home herself. They were sitting at the kitchen table and Jenny had just finished asking Christina about her back, which was now completely healed. Now was the perfect moment to drop the bomb, Jenny thought to herself.

"Someone was asking after you today down at the office,"

Jenny cagily threw out.

"Who?" Christina was curious.

"Stanley Moore. He came by today for a meeting with Giselle and he was asking how you were doing. You know he has the hots for you, don't you?"

Christina laughed. "You've told me often enough."

"Well, he told me today that he's got tickets for this Saturday night to go see some opera… Parsifal, I think he said, and he's going to ask you to go with him."

"Jenny, no! I'm not ready to start dating again. I hope you told him that," Christina adamantly decreed.

"I told him no such thing! Christina Matteo, it's been over eighteen months since your breakup with Bill Havenwood. You've got to start going out with other men now. It's time. Now, I'm not saying you have to get serious with Stanley Moore. Or even keep going out with him. But you should go out with him this once. Think of it as a practice run, to get back into the swing of things. You don't even have to kiss him goodnight after your date if you don't want to. Just go out somewhere with a man on your arm and have fun. You need this."

"Jenny, I don't feel up to it."

"Well, force yourself then. Stanley is sweet. He won't try to take advantage of you and he'll treat you like a lady. Just this one time, go out with him. You'll definitely make his week."

"Jenny, I don't think it's a good idea… I don't know."

Jenny sighed. Time to bring out the big guns. "Chrissy, I didn't want to tell you this but Bill has started dating again."

"What?" Christina was stunned as a jolt of anger shot through her. Even though she had suspected as much—after all he was a man and he definitely wasn't a eunuch—it was still surprising to hear your fears confirmed.

Jenny nodded. "Jake told me it's some chippy that works down at the office. So if he's moving on, you've got to move on too. And Stanley's the perfect guy to test the waters with again. He's safe and sweet and a gentleman."

So, Bill was seeing another woman was he? Well, maybe Jenny was right and it was time for her to start seeing other men too.

Christina nodded. "Maybe you're right, Jenny."

"Of course, I'm right. Now, Stanley's going to be calling you to ask you out for this Saturday night. And you're going to say yes. You're going to get dressed up like a lady, you're going to get your hair done and you're going to enjoy yourself at the opera. It's time, Chrissy."

"Yes… it's time," Christina agreed.

Jenny was secretly thrilled. Who knew she was so good at scheming!

And why was Jenny so adamant about having Stanley take Christina to the opera this Saturday night? Because Jake had told her that Bill had box seats to the event and was taking that little harlot, Linda from the office. And guess who else was going to be there—Christina and the new man in her life, handsome lawyer Stanley Moore.

Take that, Bill Havenwood!

CHAPTER 70

BILL HAD SPOTTED 'her' the minute she walked into the auditorium.

He and Linda were sitting in box seats high above the main seating area of the theatre where they had a first class bird's eye view of all the patrons walking in to get to their seats. Bill had gotten these tickets from one of his friends. Just because he wasn't rich anymore didn't mean he still didn't have rich friends who could afford to give him great tickets. And he had promised Linda to take her to this opera last week before he had met 'her' again.

And now—sitting there, bored—his eyes had roamed the theatre waiting for the curtain call, when suddenly he had seen 'her' walk in. His senses had instantly come alive and he had sat up straighter in his chair.

It was 'her'.

It was Christina.

His Christina.

She was dressed in a formal black gown that molded itself to those sexy curves of hers, her hair was pinned up in an elegant style and her smile was breathtaking. Bill could see all that from his perch high up at the side of the theatre.

And he could also see that her arm was linked through that of some man dressed in a tuxedo, as they made their way to their seats in the center section.

Jealousy surged through Bill's system. Who the hell was that? Who was that man with Christina? And why was her hand linked with his? And why was she smiling at him like that?

His expression turned sour as he watched them take their seats. And then he saw the creep—whoever he was—lean towards her and say something in her ear. Bill's eyes shot beams of fire down at them as he saw Christina laugh in response. Then he glared even more as he watched her look in her purse and pull out a tissue and then—damn it—she wiped something off of his clad thigh with it! What the hell was she doing that for? And why was she touching him in that way? And why was he looking at her like that—staring at her—leering at her—lusting after her?

Was she sleeping with him?

Bill wanted to march down there and break every single bone in that asshole's body, whoever the hell he was!

Suddenly, he felt Linda's hand intertwine itself through his. He turned to her then; and she smiled but he didn't smile back. His mind was fully occupied with 'her'—Christina and her fucking, damn date.

Linda's smile dropped. "Is something wrong, baby?"

Bill pasted a fake smile on his face for her sake. "No; just waiting for the show to begin."

Linda seemed appeased as she turned her eyes back to the stage. Bill's phony smile vanished quickly as he turned his own angry eyes back to the more interesting show down below where 'his' Christina was obviously enjoying herself with some other man.

Damn it all to hell!

The opera began but Bill didn't watch any of it as wave after wave of hot jealously coursed through his entire system and his glare remained glued to the happy couple down below.

At intermission, he saw them get up and walk up the aisle towards the back of the theatre. They were probably going for a drink, Bill surmised. He grabbed Linda's hand and pulled her up.

"Let's get a drink," he stated bluntly, as he half dragged her out of the box.

Linda looked at him oddly. Something was definitely wrong with Bill tonight. He was not in a very good mood.

Well, when he took her home tonight, she knew exactly what she'd have to do to put him in a good mood. After all, men were her area of 'sexpertise' and Bill Havenwood was top-of-the-line, prime, male beefcake.

*

Christina and Stanley were standing near the bar enjoying their drinks and chatting about nothing in particular. Jenny had been right, Christina thought. This evening was turning out to be very pleasant and she was having fun. Stanley was a gentleman and had treated her like fine china.

He was nice and comfortable and handsome, and she was having a great time. It was obvious to Christina that Stanley found her attractive and would have been interested in more than a casual date with her. That he admired and wanted her made Christina feel good. It was nice to feel wanted by a man for a change. She had wasted over a year and a half of her life pining over someone who didn't want her anymore that she'd forgotten that there was a whole world out there with different people waiting to be explored and savored.

Jenny had been right. It was time for her to move on—with new people and new relationships and new men. Life was too short to waste away. Look at how quickly a year and a half had gone by already?

Christina smiled back at Stanley as he continued to regale her with another tale of courtroom drama. He wasn't the best conversationalist and he did tend to say the wrong thing at the wrong time but he was sweet, he had a good heart and he was trying—and Christina was charmed by that.

"Hello, Christina," a male voice said from behind her.

Christina swung her head around and knew who it was even before she saw him. There, standing a few feet away was Bill and he had his hand clasped in some other woman's hand—probably the new girlfriend that Jenny had told her about.

In a millisecond, Christina had studied the 'chippy' and made her catty conclusion. She was young and pretty and very amply endowed and a little too simple for his tastes. She wasn't up to his speed but then again maybe conversation and mental challenge weren't what he was looking for now.

Maybe all he wanted now was some good ole' fashioned plowing down on the farm? After all, how many times had he told her, and proved to her, that 'farming' was indeed his specialty? And Christina could see that this new girl in his life was built for exactly that.

Christina instinctively moved a couple of inches closer to Stanley for protection and the handsome lawyer instantly wrapped his arm around her waist. Bill witnessed the subtle move and it only added to the jealous fury he was feeling. He hated to see another man touching 'her' and in such a sweet, intimate, protective way. It infuriated him and made him feel primal!

Christina suddenly gave Bill a bright smile. "Bill! Fancy meeting you here," she said.

Bill did not smile back. In fact, he looked—mad—very mad. "Yeah, fancy that," he sarcastically replied.

So, Christina thought, he was probably upset at his bad luck at having to run into her again. It was obvious from his livid expression and his rigid body stance that he still hated her, wanted nothing to do with her and couldn't wait to get out of her sight. Well, she wasn't going to allow him to spoil her wonderful evening.

Christina kept her beautiful smile trained on him. "Are you enjoying the show?"

Bill's cold eyes traveled to Stanley's face before returning to hers. "It's been... very interesting." No one realized that he wasn't talking about the opera but the 'show' he'd been watching between Christina and Stanley.

Bill was so jealous and angry right now that his mind had to exert extreme force on his body to prevent him from punching this asshole in the face.

"Oh, I'm sorry, where are my manners," Christina quipped. "Bill, this is Stanley Moore." She turned to Stanley. "Stanley, this is Bill Havenwood. He runs the GME environmental group."

Stanley knew exactly who Bill Havenwood was—that he wasn't just some business acquaintance but Christina's ex-fiancé—but he smiled anyway and politely extended his hand out to Bill for a handshake.

"It's nice to meet you, Bill," he smiled.

Bill glared at him and didn't shake Stanley's hand. He just stood there, like a stone statue, shooting daggers of hate at Stanley.

Stanley's arm remained suspended in mid-air in front of Bill for several seconds more before he finally realized that Bill wasn't going to take it. His smile slowly dropped, as did his pre-offered hand.

How bloody rude, Christina thought to herself! Just because Bill hated her didn't mean he had to be such an ass towards other people who had nothing to do with what she had done to him. Ignoring him, she turned to the woman beside him and politely extended her own hand out to her.

"Hi, I'm Christina Matteo," she said. Yes, Christina was jealous of this new woman in his life but she wasn't going to show it and give him the satisfaction.

The woman smiled, oblivious to all of the undercurrents flowing between them and she shook Christina's hand. "I'm Linda, nice to meet you," she replied.

"Nice to meet you too," Christina smiled.

"How's your back?" Bill barked out, still angry and jealous at seeing Christina with another man.

Christina's eyes turned to his stony face and gave him a small laugh. "My backside's healed very nicely, thank you for asking," she joked with a twinkle in her eye. She then turned her face up to Stanley's. "Don't you agree, Stanley?" She gave a little wiggle with her well-shaped bum.

Stanley was confused as he continued to feel the waves of intense dislike emanating from Bill.

"Oh…" he gave Christina's derriere a quick look before replying, "Very nice… yes… it's… very nice," he awkwardly stammered and he laughed to cover up that awkwardness.

The comment had sounded sexual but it wasn't how Stanley had meant it. It was just that Bill's furious stance was making him flustered and you could always count on Stanley Moore to say the wrong thing at the wrong time when he was flustered. This wasn't his area of expertise. The courtroom was. No, this was real life and he wasn't very good at real life—especially when he had such a hot woman as Christina Matteo on his arm.

Bill's glare grew even chillier at Stanley's lewd remark and the way the creep had looked at Christina's ass. If they weren't in such a public place, Bill thought he would have pulled his fist back and landed a right hook to the bastard's jaw right then and there.

At that moment, the first chime sounded, signaling that intermission was over and the opera was about to begin again.

Christina raised her chin up. "Nice to see you again, Bill," she spouted as she placed her hand through Stanley's arm and turned to walk away.

Christina was fuming inside. That man obviously hated her guts. He had never forgiven her for what she'd done and never would. He'd been so rude, so nasty to them that Christina knew that chapter of her life was finally over. And she had no one to blame but herself and her own stupidity.

She had killed his love for her with her lies and revenge plans, and it was all now truly over.

Bill watched the couple walk away and he gritted his teeth in anger. He loved her—and he wanted her—but he just still couldn't forgive her. What was he to do?

*

Christina had strict instructions to immediately come to Jenny's apartment after her date with Stanley Moore, no matter what time it was. Jenny wanted details.

It was 2:30 in the morning when Christina finally rang Jenny's doorbell. Jenny opened the door and pulled Christina into her kitchen.

"I want details and start from the beginning," Jenny ordered.

"Did I wake Taylor?" Christina hadn't wanted to wake the little girl up by coming at this late hour but Jenny had insisted.

"Nah, the door to her room is closed. She didn't hear a thing. So, how was Stanley?"

"A perfect gentleman and a sweetheart."

"Did you kiss him?"

"He saw me to my door just now and I kissed him on the cheek."

"So how was the opera? Did you have fun?" What Jenny really wanted to know was—did you see Bill Havenwood there?

"I had lots of fun, Jenny. Thanks so much for pushing me to go. It was the best thing I could have done for myself and it was the perfect evening except for one small thing that happened."

"What?"

"Bill was there and we met up at intermission."

Jenny pretended to be shocked. "What? He was there?"

Christina nodded. "With the chippy."

"Really? And what was she like?"

Christina shrugged her shoulders. "Big boobs, little brain but she seemed nice, if a little too obvious."

"And what about Bill? What did he say?"

Christina turned indignant. "Bill Havenwood is an ass! He was extremely rude to Stanley, refusing to even shake his hand and he was really abrupt with me. He's still mad at me, Jenny for what I did to him, I know it. It was all over his face."

Jenny pretended to think. "Maybe he was jealous at seeing you with another man? Did you think of that?"

Christina shook her head. "No, he hates me and he was angry for having the bad luck of running into me again."

Jenny rolled her eyes upwards. "Chrissy, for such a smart girl, you can be really dumb sometimes. Bill Havenwood is probably still in love with you and what he hated was seeing you with another man. That's why he was so upset."

"Jenny, you're wrong. You weren't there. You didn't see the dirty looks he was giving me and poor Stanley. No, he hates me. And seeing him like this again has made me come to a decision. I'm putting him out of my life completely."

"Chrissy, no! He still loves you. You still love him. Love like that is rare and hard to find. Don't give up on it, please!" Jenny wailed.

Christina was adamant as she shook her head again. "No, Jenny. He hasn't forgiven me and never will. But before I move on with my life, there's something I have to do. Something I owe him."

"What?"

"I need to try to smooth things over between him and his father. It's the least I can do after the part I played breaking them up." Christina paused. "So you said that William and Bill haven't spoken to each other since the night he got thrown out of the house?"

Jenny nodded. "That's what Jake said. William is still furious at being betrayed by his son and refuses to even acknowledge him."

Christina made up her mind. "Jenny, I'm going to see William. I'm going to try to patch things up between the two of them and then I'm breaking all ties with Bill Havenwood... mentally and emotionally, and I'm moving on." Christina gave her friend a saucy smile. "Who knows, maybe I'll go out with Stanley again? He asked me out again tonight, you know."

Jenny pouted. "Oh no, Chrissy..."

Jenny was extremely upset at the way things had worked out. In her imagined scenario, Bill Havenwood was supposed to have been so incensed with jealousy at seeing Christina with another man that he was supposed to have come to his senses, punched out poor old Stanley, told Christina he was still madly in love with her and begged to be a part of her life again.

Instead, Christina was about to write Bill out of her life for good and she was even thinking about accepting another date with that nerd!

Jenny was mad. Maybe she wasn't so good at scheming after all!

CHAPTER 71

CITY LIGHTS MINGLED with twinkling Christmas lights, lighting up the December evening skies as Christina entered the Fido Foods office building. It was 6 p.m. and she was positive William would probably still be in his office. But would he agree to see her? That she didn't know.

But she shouldn't have worried. The moment her name had been called in to the upstairs offices from the security desk in the lobby, she was immediately ushered through into the private elevator. When the elevator doors opened, she was greeted with a hug by Charlotte, William's secretary and told to go straight into William's office because he was waiting for her.

As Christina opened the door to the office, William came out from around his desk and hugged her tightly.

"My God, Christina, it's so good to see you," he enthused and he gave her a big kiss on the cheek.

Christina was a bit taken aback by the warm welcome. "William… I… wasn't sure I'd be welcome."

"Nonsense; you are always welcome here." William steered her to the couch and he sat down beside her.

Christina took a good look at him and smiled. "William, you haven't changed at all. Still handsome and debonair as ever I see."

William drank in the compliments. "And you are as beautiful and stunning as the last time I saw you. So tell me, what can I do for you?"

"Well, it's not what you can do for me but what I can do for you," Christina cryptically replied. She paused as she saw she had his undivided attention. "It's Christmas and I'm here to give you a present."

"A present!" William laughed. "How wonderful! Nobody ever gives me a present. They all assume I have everything and never get me anything."

Christina laughed and pretended to feel sorry for him. "Oh, poor you! But the present I'm here to give you is something I know you don't have." She paused again for effect. "The truth."

William's smile dropped. He had an inkling of where this was going. "About my son?"

"Yes... and about me."

Suddenly agitated, William stood up and began pacing the room. "I already know all there is to know about him, thank you; and I don't want to hear anymore about it. So you see you've wasted a trip."

"You still haven't forgiven him?"

"What he did to me was unforgivable."

Christina let out an exasperated sigh. "You are as mule-headed as he is. No wonder you two were always butting heads. You're both the same!"

"Christina, I don't want to hear anymore," William raised his voice.

Angry, Christina also stood up. She wasn't giving up so easily. "He's your child, the only child you have. What he did to you might have been wrong but he felt it was the only way to get through to you. He was standing up for his convictions and he was trying to make you a better man. He loves you, William."

"Well, he had a bloody hell of a way of showing it!" William was getting angry all over again, remembering how Bill had betrayed him.

Christina went up to him and put her hand on his arm. "William, look around you. You have everything a man could possibly want in life except for a family. You have no one who truly cares about you that's not on your payroll... and you're not getting any younger."

"Thank you, Christina for making me feel so good. And Merry Christmas to you too," he sarcastically cracked.

Christina smiled. "I'm sorry, William but I promised myself I would come here and give you the truth, and that's what I'm going to do." She tugged on his arm and pulled him back to the couch. "Please, please just listen to what I have to say. Let me say it all and then I'll leave. Please?"

William looked into her pleading eyes. He had loved this girl like a daughter for the short time she'd been in his life and he couldn't deny her anything.

"My son is an idiot to ever have let you go, you know that?" William angrily spit out the words.

Christina lowered her guilty eyes and she shook her head, "No, he wasn't. I was the idiot… for what I did to him." She raised her eyes back up to William's, "You don't really know what happened between Bill and I, do you?"

"No, not really. Maddie told me that you said you'd done something to him that he couldn't forgive. I thought maybe there was another man involved, which isn't surprising since my scheming son was forcing you to marry him so he could keep his fingers in my money till."

Christina gasped in shock. "You knew about that? That we were lying to you about being in love… and getting married?"

"Of course, I knew! I knew it from the very beginning, from that first night we all had dinner together and you announced your so-called engagement. I'm not stupid, Christina."

"But… but… why? Why didn't you say something?"

William cracked a smile. "Because it was fun to watch my son squirm. But then, I got to know you and I liked you, and I liked how my son seemed to be changing his debauched ways for you… so I started pushing for a real marriage. I wanted you to be a part of my family, Christina. That was all real."

Christina had tears in her eyes. "Thank you for that, William." She gave him a hug. She then pulled back. "But what you didn't know… and what Bill didn't know or remember… was that the car accident with the Ferrari… wasn't the first time Bill and I had met." She saw she had William's complete interest again as his eyes bore into hers. "We… met in high school and when we had the car accident, I'd been following him because I hated him and wanted to get revenge on him." There she'd said it.

"What!" William was clearly shocked.

Christina nodded. "Bill and his friend Jake pulled a very nasty, humiliating prank on me in my freshman year in high school and I was sent away to boarding school because of it. I hated him for it and when I met up with him again last year, I came up with a plan to get even with him. So you see, William, I'm not as innocent in all this as you think."

"I… had no idea."

"No, neither did Bill. My plan was to somehow follow him and get some sort of damaging information on him so I could ruin his life like he ruined mine. And when he forced me to pretend to be his fiancée so you wouldn't throw him out, I thought it would be a perfect opportunity to spy on him and learn his secrets from the inside."

William was impressed. "That was very clever of you."

Christina closed her eyes briefly, regretting her past actions. "Yes, that's me… clever. So while I was living in your house, I spied on him, I searched his room for clues, I followed him with my car, I listened in on private conversations, I sent him an anonymous blackmail letter to frighten the hell out of him, I found out about his GME connections… and I created the blackmail package you received with the incriminating evidence on him. Yes, you could say I was clever. But I was also stupid… stupid enough to actually fall in love with him for real. And I think he fell in love with me too."

"My God, Christina! I had no idea." William was almost speechless.

"So you see, William, when Bill was lying to you, I was lying to him. And I never told him the truth of what I had done and when he found out, he broke it off with me. I hurt him very badly,

I know that. And he hurt you very badly. Now I know its over between us… between Bill and me… but he's your son and there's hope for the both of you if you'll just forgive him and ask him back into your life."

"Christina…" William was about to refuse and she stopped him.

"William, just think about it; that's all I ask." She paused as she bit her lip nervously. "There's more… and Bill doesn't know any of what I'm about to tell you. You have to promise me… to swear on all your billions… that you'll never say a word to him; ever."

William was suddenly very curious. "I swear I won't say anything."

"You promise?"

"Yes, I promise you."

"A month after I left your house… I found out I was pregnant with Bill's baby."

William was stunned. "Oh my God, Christina, a baby!" His eyes lit up with excitement.

"No, you don't understand. I…" Christina looked down at her shaking hands in her lap. This was still very painful for her to relive. "I… miscarried short of my third month."

William's hope deflated. "Oh my dear, I'm so sorry." He wrapped his arms around Christina and hugged her tightly.

"The doctors said it was normal… for a first pregnancy. There was nothing I could have done."

"No, I'm sure you did everything right. But my son… he doesn't know about this?" Christina shook her head 'no'. "But why?" William continued.

"When I found out, I wrote him a letter telling him about it but it came back to me unopened." Christina smiled as she tried to put on a brave face. "It's just as well. I lost the baby after that and there really was no point for him to know then. I mean, he hates me for what I did and I can't blame him. It's too late for us…

but not for you and him. Just promise me you'll think about giving him another chance? Just think about it? Please?"

William couldn't say no to her pleading eyes. "All right, my dear. I'll think about it. But I still say my son's an ass for letting you slip away."

Christina smiled, "Thank you, William." She kissed him on the cheek. "And I have something else to tell you."

"More surprises?"

"When I was still living at your house, Maddie and I had dinner together one night."

"And what did she eat? Eye of Newt and fried bat wings?"

Christina laughed at William's dry wit and then continued. "I asked her how she felt about you and after she finished calling you an old goat and a mule and an asshole…"

William's eyebrows lowered at his wife's caustic tongue. "My dear, that's not news. She's called me all those things to my face."

"Well, what she didn't tell you, to your face, is that she still loves you and would come back to you in a new age minute if you were willing to forgive her and start fresh."

"What?" William was shocked for the third time that evening. "That's impossible! She said all that?"

Christina nodded. "Yes, she told me exactly that. So if you have any feelings for her left, William, don't let anymore time drift away. Do something about it… now."

Having said her piece, Christina stood up and looked him straight in the eye. "Put your family back together again, William. You're the one holding all the cards." She leaned into him then and gave him another kiss on the cheek. "And Merry Christmas. I hope you liked your present."

William was too shocked about everything he'd just learnt to say anything in reply, as he watched Christina walk out.

CHAPTER 72

IT WAS A snowy, blustering day and Jake and Bill were lunching on hot dogs beside the street vendor's cart, watching the busy mid-day, New York City traffic whiz by.

Sitting in his wheelchair, Jake suddenly put his hot dog down and gave his friend a long pensive look. Bill saw it right away.

"Whatever it is, I don't want to talk about it," Bill decreed.

"Well, I want to talk about it. It's about Christina," Jake was equally determined.

"No, Jake!" Bill had figured it was about 'her' by the way Jake had been looking at him.

"Yes, and I've been thinking about this for a long time now. I feel bad, Bill, for what we did to her in high school. It was cruel and mean and she didn't deserve any of it."

"Are those your feelings or Jenny's?"

Jake raised his voice. "They're mine. Jenny's not my conscience, Bill."

Suddenly, a flash of anguish and guilt flashed through Bill's eyes. "Don't you think I feel the same way? I'm ashamed, deeply ashamed of what we did to her."

"Good! I'm glad to hear it."

"But what she did… how she lied to me and hated me…"

"So, she got back at you. So what? The girl has spunk. Maybe you deserved it. We all do, for all of the drunken shit we've pulled over the years. We weren't saints, you know."

"I never said we were."

"No, but you sure as hell are acting like it. We were all sinners,

Bill. But it's time to heal. Forgive and forget. Why don't you give her a call and see what she has to say, huh?" Jake pleaded.

Undecided, Bill gave his friend a hard look. Jake could see that he was almost on the point of capitulating. He knew his friend still loved Christina and wanted her back—it was just that he was too pig-headed and proud to do something about it.

Jake continued in a forceful tone, "Maybe it's you that should be begging her for forgiveness and not the other way around? Did you ever think about that?"

Bill gave Jake another wavering glare before he turned, tossed his half eaten hotdog in the trash bin and walked away.

Jake shook his head at his friend's stubbornness.

*

William casually walked into the low-rent offices of the GME environmental organization. There were about ten people bustling around, sitting at desks, working and answering phones. The place was a beehive of activity for such a small, under-financed operation. He immediately recognized Jake in his wheelchair off to the left; and then looking further about the room, spotted Bill sitting at a desk working at a computer in the back.

Suddenly, everyone stopped what they were doing and the room went deathly quiet as they all realized who had just walked in. It was William Havenwood, ruthless businessman, top polluter, archenemy—and Bill's father.

On hearing silence, Bill looked up from the screen and saw his father. Shock registered on his face, as he slowly stood up out of his chair. Father and son stared at each other from across the room. They hadn't seen or spoken to each other for a year and a half, since that night when William had thrown Bill out of his life.

William gave his son a smirk as he came towards him. People parted out of his way, like Moses parting the Red Sea, but he kept his gaze focused on his son.

"I still know how to make an entrance," he jokingly quipped.

All eyes in the room were on the pair. Even the phones stopped ringing as if on cue. Bill stood up straighter as his father came nearer.

"Are you going to stop pumping that oil through that decrepit pipeline?" he fired off to William.

"No hello, dad? No... how are you... how's your health? No greeting of any sort for your father?"

"You stopped being my father a long time ago," Bill's face was very serious. What was his old man doing here? What was he up to? He didn't trust him at all.

William took a good look at his son. He had to admit the boy looked good. He looked healthy and well and motivated. He then looked at all of the curious faces staring at him and let his gaze wander around the office.

"So this is your brainchild?"

"Yes, so what?" Bill cautiously replied

"Organization and initiative coupled with deviousness and lying. I'm impressed. You may have inherited my genes after all," he half-laughed to himself.

Bill's face remained frozen. "Why are you here? I doubt it's to critique my business plan," he demanded.

"I'm here to tell you a few home truths. Is there somewhere more private where we can speak?" William gave another glance around the bare bones office.

"I have nothing to say to you."

"No; but I have a lot to say to you. And I don't think you'd appreciate your private life discussed out here. Or maybe you do?" William raised a challenging eyebrow at his son.

A few seconds ticked by as Bill deliberated whether he should throw his father out on his wealthy ass—or hear what he had to say first and then throw him out on his wealthy ass.

William sensed his son's indecision. "Christina came to see me yesterday and she told me some things that you don't even know about."

Instantly, Bill perked up at the mention of his ex, and William, seeing his son's interest, cagily continued, "Christina told me that…"

"Wait! Not here." Bill interrupted his father as he quickly took in all of the curious faces staring at the pair of them from around the room. "We can go in the back." He motioned to his father to follow him into a back room.

After his father had entered what looked like a large stockroom, Bill closed the door behind them and turned to William with a sarcastic smirk on his lips. "Let me guess. She made you promise not to tell me?"

"Yes. She begged me not to."

"And you're breaking that promise?"

"Of course; why wouldn't I? You, of all people, know what I'm capable of when it's in my best interests. Christina doesn't."

Bill knowingly laughed. "That's so typical of the great William Havenwood. So, tell me what lies was she spewing out yesterday?"

"No lies; just the truth," William said, as he studied his son's countenance. Bill was trying to act casual and tough and not interested but William knew differently. The boy was very interested and it was obvious to him that Bill was still deeply in love with the girl.

"Or her version of the truth, which is the same as a lie," Bill retorted.

Bill was being deliberately obstinate and William reasoned it was time to use some shock therapy on him.

"Christina was pregnant last year and you were the father. Did you know that?"

"What!" Bill was stunned as he gawked at his father in complete shock.

There—William thought to himself—that had got the boy's attention and shut him the hell up.

"After you threw her out of your life, she found out she was going to have your baby but she miscarried a few months into it. She was devastated and you weren't even there to help pick up the pieces," William accused.

"I… I… didn't know," Bill nervously ran his fingers through his hair as he tried to get his bearings. This was incredible news! His baby? Christina had been pregnant with his baby? "Why… why… didn't she tell me?" He turned amazed eyes back onto his father.

"She did. She wrote you a letter but you sent it back to her unopened."

"Oh my God!" Bill put his head in his hands. Yes—he remembered that he'd done just that. "I… I had… no idea… I didn't even think…"

"No, you didn't think, did you? You were drunk out of your mind at the time." Bill turned surprised eyes back onto his father and William nodded his head, "Oh yes, I know all about you falling off the wagon and your stint in rehab last year."

"Who told you about that?" Bill was defensive.

"My detectives, who do you think?"

"Of course, you had me under surveillance."

"Not just you, this whole place. You knew I'd do that."

"Yes, I knew. I just didn't care."

"No and you didn't care about Christina either otherwise you would have found out about the baby," he accused.

"I cared about Christina!" Bill shouted at William.

"Of course, you did. That's why she had to go through all that on her own," William sarcastically responded.

"I would have been there if I had known." Bill was angry, mostly with himself.

"But the point, dear boy, is that you didn't know. And why was that? Because of your stupid, stubborn pride that kept you away from her, that's why."

"You don't know everything that happened between me and her, dad, so keep your half-assed opinions to yourself."

"That's where you're wrong. I know it all. Christina told me everything yesterday. Did you know she was sent away to boarding school because of your moronic prank in high school?"

Guilt coursed through Bill's system, as he was stunned again for the second time that day. Suddenly, he shook his head feebly, "No… I… didn't know that."

"No, I assumed as much. And I'll bet my last nickel that you were too drunk back then to even notice or care that the girl was no longer there. Am I right?"

Bill smirked to himself, "Never bet William Havenwood when he's down to his last nickel."

"And you're indignant because Christina hated you and wanted revenge? The girl has bite, my boy. I would have expected nothing less from her."

Bill was feeling too much guilt to respond to his father's comments. And he was still in shock about almost having been a father. "How… how… did she lose the baby?" he suddenly, quietly asked.

"She told me she just miscarried. The doctors said there was nothing anyone could have done."

Bill's eyes lowered to the floor as feelings of grief washed over him for what he'd almost had and lost. A baby—Christina's and his baby—a baby they'd made together. If only things had been different—if only…

William watched his son closely. He saw the anguish and the sadness flicker across Bill's face. Good. Maybe the boy would come to his senses now and get back together with the girl.

William broke the silence. "Yesterday, Christina also told me what she'd done to you… about her revenge plan. I must say I was very impressed at her craftiness. She's quite a woman."

Bill's distressed eyes came back up to his father's face. "You would think that, dad, wouldn't you?"

"She reminds me of your mother actually… tough, strong and goes after what she wants. I admire those qualities, even when they're being trained on me, as your mother constantly has done over the years. In fact, I've been thinking that maybe I should… make peace with Maddie."

Bill gave an incredulous laugh, "You're joking, right?"

"No. I've never been more serious in my life."

"But… you hate mom… for leaving you… and you'll never forgive her. You say that all the time!"

"Well… maybe it's time to bury the hatchet… but not in each other's backs anymore," William laughed at his own joke. He turned pensive then. "Time is too precious to waste and if there's something out there you want… or someone… grab them and don't let go."

William opened the stockroom door to leave and turned back to Bill. "Son?" He hadn't called Bill 'son' in a long time. "If I can make peace with your mother, then you can make peace with Christina. If you're half the man you appear to be, you'll stop this stubborn foolishness and beg that girl to be a part of your life again."

Bill remained silent as his father walked out. Suddenly, William stopped and turned back to his son who was watching him from the open doorway.

"And I'll expect you for dinner at the house this Saturday night to discuss this dreadful pipeline situation," he imperially decreed in his British accent before walking outside to his waiting limousine.

All of the GME employees had heard that last statement and they turned incredulous eyes to Bill.

"Does this mean he'll listen to our complaints and maybe do something about it?" Jake asked Bill from across the room.

"Yes, that's what it means," Bill confirmed.

A whoop of joy went up in the office. Bill knew his father very well. What William had said was an olive branch—a sort of 'come back into the fold and all is forgiven' type of announcement. Bill had won where his father was concerned. And it sounded like he was back in the Havenwood money too. He should have been elated.

But he wasn't—because he had lost 'her'—and their baby.

CHAPTER 73

CHRISTINA'S DOORBELL RANG. Who could it be at this hour, Christina thought? It was almost 10 p.m. The doorbell rang again and whoever it was, impatiently kept their finger on it, causing it to ring incessantly.

Looking through her peephole, Christina saw Bill standing there. She was shocked. What the hell was he doing here? She yanked the door open and silently stared at him— and him at her. He wore a murderous expression on his face.

Suddenly, he muscled his way past her into the apartment. "Is he here?" he demanded, as he went into the kitchen and took a good look around before stalking into the living room and doing the same.

"Who?" Christina was still confused about what he was doing here. She followed him on his search.

"Your new lover, Stanley Moore," he rasped.

"How dare you?" she indignantly replied.

"Oh, I dare," he savagely countered as he threw her bedroom door open and went in, looking around to his satisfaction. The asshole wasn't here after all.

"I could have a hundred men in here and that's my business. It has nothing to do with you," Christina shouted back.

Bill came out and faced her. "Oh I agree. You can sleep with a thousand men and that's your right except for one little thing. You… love… me."

Christina could only glare at him. Yes, she loved him! But she wasn't going to admit it just so that he could throw her love back in her face. Livid, her chin came up. "Get out of my apartment!"

Bill took a few predatory steps towards her and she took a few frightened steps back.

She shouted at him again, "Did you hear me? I said, get out!"

Without saying a word, Bill grabbed her upper arms and yanked her roughly towards him. Before Christina knew what he was planning, he had planted his lips on hers and began to kiss her with passionate abandon. As her soft mouth opened in protest, he took the opportunity to plunder it with his teasing tongue.

In a split second, Christina was on fire for him and it was like they'd never been apart. She kissed him back as her hands wrapped themselves around his neck and his were plastered on her back, molding her to his strong, aroused male body.

Breathing heavily, he pulled away first and rested his forehead on hers. He closed his eyes briefly. "Oh God… it's been so long… and I needed to taste you again," he groaned. It was still there! The electricity and the sparks were still there between them. He hadn't imagined any of it.

Christina suddenly pulled away from him and took a step back. "Is that why you're here? For sex?"

"No. I'm here about the baby; our baby."

Christina gasped. "How did you find out?"

"My father told me. You should know by now, Christina, that he always breaks his promises."

She straightened her spine with courage and determination. "I'm not apologizing, you know. I wrote you."

Bill shook his head at his own stupidity. "I know." He paused. "And I'm here… to apologize to you. I'm sorry I wasn't there for you… for the baby… for what happened. I guess I let you down. I'm sorry for that." He spoke the words softly.

He nervously ran his fingers through his hair, messing it up in a boyish fashion. Wow, Christina thought, he's just as gorgeous and hot as ever. But she wasn't going to let her guard down with him. She still needed to be on the defensive where he was concerned.

"Well, it's done and over with. Me losing the baby… it wasn't my fault," she challenged.

"I know." He paused for a few seconds as he searched her face, looking for clues about how she'd really felt about having his baby. "I… guess it was a relief to you. You wouldn't have wanted to be saddled with my child."

"How can you say that to me?" Christina angrily answered back. "I desperately wanted to have that baby and it killed me when it was gone. And if you think that it was a 'relief' to me, then you don't know me at all." She took another step away from him and there were unshed tears in her eyes. "Maybe you'd better go."

He came to her then and wrapping his arms around her, hugged her tight to him. "Oh Christina, I'm sorry. I didn't mean it like that. I don't know what I'm saying anymore. Please forgive me."

She broke out of his arms. "You've said your piece. Just go."

Bill took a deep steadying breath as he looked at the hurt expression on her face. "I would have been here for you… if I'd known. Please believe that. I would have wanted my baby, Christina; don't ever doubt that."

She turned away from him. "There's nothing more to discuss. The baby's gone."

Bill felt her pull away from him emotionally. If he didn't do something, say something now, tonight, he knew he'd never get another chance with her.

"There's another reason I'm here tonight. And that's to say I'm sorry for what I did to you in high school."

She quickly spun around to him at hearing those words. "You've never said that to me before."

"No, but it's time that I did. I was a drunk and a jerk and what Jake and I did to you was mean and cruel. Jake feels the same way. I had no idea you'd been sent away to boarding school. My father told me today. I just thought you decided to go to another school but I was so drunk and spaced out back then that you might as well have been on another planet for all I knew." He took a long look at her and shook his head in amazement. "You're the girl under the bleachers. Do you know you're the first girl ever who told me to go fuck myself? Figures." Bill laughed. "I couldn't believe anyone had the balls to say that to me, let alone a girl. You certainly got my attention back then."

Christina had been listening very closely to his speech and she smiled at that. "You deserved it."

"Oh, I know I did. I even knew it back then. It's just that no one ever had the guts to put me in my place but you did." He stopped for a few seconds as if gathering up his courage. "I got away with a lot. And I never realized the damage it had caused you. So, on behalf of that stupid, immature, drunken kid I was, I want to say that I'm sorry. You had every right to hate me and I can understand now why you wanted to get revenge on me. It was payback and I had it coming... not just for what I did to you but for all of the other drunken, stupid things I've done over the years. Life kicked me in the teeth, with your help of course; and it's taken me these eighteen months to realize that I deserved it all. I'm sorry, Christina."

Christina was stunned at Bill's admission of guilt. He was actually taking responsibility for his past actions and he was apologizing to her, not waiting for an apology 'from' her—which is what she'd thought when she'd first opened the door to him tonight.

She slowly smiled at him. "You know, I hated your guts for the longest time and when I found you again, the only thing I could think of was revenge. I wanted to hurt you as much as you had hurt me. So, I set my plan into motion. And it was a damn good plan if I say so myself except for one little catch..."

"Which was?" Bill warily looked at her. He still didn't know where he stood with her—if he still had a chance to patch things up.

"Like an idiot, I fell in love with you and I didn't hate you anymore. And I was ashamed of what I had been doing to you.

And I guess... I'm apologizing too. I want to say that I'm sorry for the hurt I caused you and I hope you can forgive me." Christina smiled at him then and put out her hand towards him for a handshake. "No hard feelings between you and me?"

A feeling of triumph coursed through Bill's system. This was going so well and maybe he did have a shot with her again after all. He suddenly gave her one of his megawatt, dazzling movie star smiles and he clasped her hand in his. "No hard feelings," he agreed.

And they shook on it.

For some strange reason, the atmosphere in the room felt cleansed and lighter as their hands released. For a few seconds, they just stared at each other and smiled. They both instinctively knew that they had passed a test of some kind that life had thrown their way.

"I have something for you," Bill said.

He suddenly, reached into his jacket pocket and pulled out a long box. Opening it, he presented it to Christina and she gasped. Inside were all of the diamond jewelry pieces that Bill had given her during their brief engagement—the necklace, earrings, pin, engagement ring and wedding band.

She was shocked. "It's my jewelry," she whispered as Christina took the box and began to lift out the pieces. She turned incredulous eyes back up at him, "I... I thought you'd have returned all this?"

Bill was studying her closely, hoping. "I couldn't. They all belong to you; they're yours."

"I can't accept these."

"You can... if you're my wife."

Christina held her breath as her heart pounded against her ribs. "What are you saying?" She could barely get the words out.

Bill reached into the jewelry box clutched in her hands and pulled out the engagement ring. He held it up.

"I'm saying that I'm crazy in love with you. There hasn't been one damn day that's gone by since I left you, that I haven't thought about you, wondered what you were doing, what you were thinking, how you were feeling? You get to me, Christina. And I'm so hopelessly, desperately in love with you… and I want a life with you. Please say you'll marry me; please say yes."

There—he'd said it—and now it was his turn to anxiously hold his breath, waiting for her answer.

She stared at him and a smile slowly started to form on her lips. "Yes," she breathlessly whispered back.

A triumphant smile beamed across Bill's lips as he slowly took Christina's left hand and gently placed the engagement ring back on her third finger—where it belonged. The diamonds twinkled in the living room light as she raised her hand and stared at it.

Suddenly, she launched herself into his arms and he grabbed her, holding her tight to him.

"I love you so much, too," she cried as she held him.

"God, I've missed you," Bill rasped as he kissed her temple and buried his head in her hair. "And I was such an ass for sending you away like that." He pulled back and suddenly cupped her face with his hands. "I've been a fool… a stubborn, mule-headed fool to have stayed away from you for so long."

Christina gave him a sexy smile. "I agree there," she teased as she clung to him.

He smiled at that. "I promise you, Christina, that I'll never leave you again and I promise that I'll love you and cherish you… and…"

"And… what?" she prompted.

"And… that I'll stay sober." He lowered his eyes from hers in shame. "I don't know if you know this but I went back to drinking after we broke up."

"I know," she softly whispered as she caressed his cheek. "And it's all right. We all make mistakes and do stupid things. But you came out of it and you're not drinking anymore and from now on we'll work on it together."

"Together; I like that word," he teased her.

"Get used to it because we're going to have a lot of 'together', you and I, starting right now," Christina claimed his lips with a sweet, breathy kiss and he responded with a promise kiss of his own that seemed to go on forever.

He pulled back from her and gazed into her eyes.

"Christina, there's something you should know... before you marry me."

Oh no, Christina thought, now what? "You can tell me anything," she softy encouraged him.

"I... I'm not rich anymore. In fact, I don't have any money. As the head of the GME group, I get paid the least of all the employees there and a portion of what I do make is plowed back into the cause." Bill paused as he kept his worried eyes focused on her. "I... live in a one-room apartment and my furniture is Goodwill secondhand cast-offs," he laughed as he continued, "In fact, your apartment is a palace compared to mine... so..." he turned serious again, "I... I won't be able to buy you any more diamonds for quite awhile. You probably make more money than me anyway. I don't have very much now and nothing to offer you..."

Christina became angry. "Bill Havenwood, how dare you think I care about that stuff. I love you, not your money and not your Havenwood position and together we'll do just fine." She smiled at him as she snuggled deeper in his arms. "Besides, I happen to like Goodwill castoffs. Where do you think I got my couch?"

Bill laughed as he started to feel better.

Christina gave him a swift kiss and coyly added, "And if I make more money than you, then maybe I should be making you sign a pre-nup rather than the other way around?"

He laughed again as he returned her kiss. "I'll sign anything you want me to sign, Miss Matteo so long as you promise to be by my side for as long as I live."

"I promise, so long as you promise to make an honest woman out of me and marry me."

"That's one promise you can count on, so long as there aren't anymore Stanley Moore creeps mooning over you."

"Well, they can moon over me all they want but I'm only interested in you, Mr. Havenwood."

"I hated seeing you with him at the opera. I was so jealous that he was there with you… touching you and who knew what else… that I almost hit him."

Christina was shocked, as she gasped, "You didn't?"

Bill nodded. "Yes, I did. I came this close…" he brought his index finger and thumb up with an inch of space between them, "… to sucker punching him at the bar at intermission."

Christina giggled, "So that's why you were so angry that night. Jenny was right. I promise, no more Stanley Moore's." She pulled him then onto the couch and positioned herself on his lap. "I think it's time we sealed this deal with more than a kiss, don't you?"

"What did you have in mind?"

Christina wrapped her arms around his neck and wiggled her sexy derriere into his hard lap. Her eyes twinkled with mischief and desire shot through Bill.

"Well, I still have your handcuffs in the other room. We never really did get to use them properly," she giggled again as Bill lowered his mouth to hers.

They came together then…

And they knew they would never come apart again.

EPILOGUE

THE FOLLOWING SATURDAY night, Bill brought an uninvited guest to the Havenwood mansion for dinner with William.

Christina.

And they announced their engagement—and William was thrilled.

The dinner went well.

Christina acted like a referee between the two—and it was the first step in repairing the bond between father and son.

*

A month later, Christina and Bill were married on a beach in the Cayman Islands in the Caribbean. Jenny was the maid of honor, Jake was the best man and little Taylor was the flower girl.

The only other invited guests were Christina's parents, Gabriella and Nunzio; William and Maddie; and Eudora, of course, the Havenwood maid whom Bill adored and was like a grandmother to him.

The ceremony was simple. The bride and groom were both barefoot in the hot sand—and Maddie caught the bridal bouquet.

William had been upset at first when he'd heard about the wedding plans. He had wanted a big, high society New York splashy shindig where he could invite all of his rich friends.

But Christina and Bill had stood firm. No way. No Havenwood billionaire wedding for them. They had wanted it to be simple, a special day just for the two of them and their loved ones.

In the end, they caved a little and agreed to have William and Maddie host a large post-wedding reception party on the

Havenwood grounds to introduce the couple to their rich, snobby crowd. After all, William argued, Bill could use the high society connections if he truly had plans to run for Congress, couldn't he?

THE END

ALSO BY ANNA MARA...

WHY ROMEO HATES JULIET
(a romantic comedy)

&

SIN & SAVAGE
(a romantic thriller)

Visit her website at: http://www.annamara.com
Email her at: annamara@annamara.com

45209842R00268

Made in the USA
Middletown, DE
27 June 2017